ARTIFICIAL SELECTION

A BIO GRIMDARK ROMANTASY

THE DAEMON PROGENY
BOOK ONE

DANIELLE KAHEAKU

ARTIFICIAL SELECTION

Book One of the *Daemon Progeny*

Cover Design: Christian Bentulan

ISBN (Paperback): 979-8-9934992-1-5

ISBN (eBook): 979-8-9934992-0-8

ISBN (Hardcover): 979-8-9934992-2-2

Library of Congress Control Number: 2025924972

Kaheaku, Danielle.

Artificial Selection / Danielle Kaheaku.

— First edition.

— (Daemon Progeny; book 1)

Summary: A romantasy novel blending grimdark elements, ancient tech, and a deadly love triangle as a young woman fights for her kingdom, her freedom, and herself.

Subjects:

1. Fantasy fiction.
2. Romance fiction.
3. Dark fantasy.
4. Love triangles—Fiction.
5. Apocalyptic fiction.

Classification:

LCC PS3621.A345 A78 2025

DDC 813/.6—dc23

First Edition: **2025**

Paradoxical Frog Press

Pasco, WA.

For information, visit: **kaheaku.com**

Printed in the United States of America.

ARTIFICIAL SELECTION

A BIO GRIMDARK ROMANTASY

THE DAEMON PROGENY
BOOK ONE

DANIELLE KAHEAKU

*For every woman who realized
she was never meant to be tamed.
We chose ourselves with teeth and fire,
stepped out of the smoke,
and claimed lives far bigger than the cages
we escaped.*

CONTENT WARNINGS

Before you dive in, here's your fair warning: this story isn't soft. It doesn't apologize. And it absolutely doesn't stay in the shallow end.

If you need to know what you're walking into, here's the list. If you don't... well, proceed at your own risk.

This book contains:

- Violence, blood, gore, and the occasional body coming apart in ways it really shouldn't
- Death, including on-page deaths of major and minor characters
- Torture, captivity, and medical experimentation
- Alcohol abuse and withdrawal
- Sex (consensual, emotional, complicated, sometimes unwise)
- Coercive dynamics tied to power, rank, and desperation
- Emotional manipulation and psychological trauma
- Suicide attempt on-page
- War violence, battlefield trauma, and moral collapse

- Body horror, mutations, monstrous forms
- Betrayal, heartbreak, grief, and the kind of choices that ruin people

If any of these hit too hard, protect yourself first. Take breaks. Come back when you're ready.

If you're good to go... then welcome to the chaos.

PROLOGUE

"How was it that time?"

The patient closed his eyes and let his breath out in a quick, heavy sigh. If his lips hadn't been numb from the drugs pumping through his veins, he might have made one of his typical smart-ass remarks. If they'd given him the use of his arms, he'd have flipped the bird. He closed his eyes tighter.

Nope. Can't even move my fingers today.

The doctor in the starched white coat leaned over the patient and frowned, chewing on his lip and making his white, neatly trimmed beard tremble.

It used to be long—the beard—reaching his navel, the patient remembered. His eyes opened, blinked, stayed open. He wasn't sure, though. His mind didn't seem to want to remember.

"Did it hurt?" the doctor asked.

The patient struggled against the nylon straps that bound his wrists, ankles, and neck against the bed. No, it wasn't soft enough to be a bed. A table with sheets. That was it.

Damn, the drugs really make it hard to concentrate.

He didn't know where he was, but by the musty smell lingering

1

in the stagnant air, he knew they were underground. The constant whirring of the single, outdated air conditioner mounted on the right wall just under the low, rocky ceiling meant they were probably *far* underground.

Probably in hiding.

From whom or what, he didn't care. His eyes flicked to the left and right, trying to find something interesting to look at today.

The table he lay on sat in the middle of a large room, surrounded by monitoring equipment and side tables with steel pans full of sterilized scalpels and drills. The bright, fluorescent lights hanging from thick, slightly rusted brackets flickered occasionally, the tubes buzzing as they fought to stay alive. Three men in white coats with clipboards wandered around the large, concrete room. Their soft-soled shoes squeaked on the recently mopped floor as they jotted down notes and glanced at anatomy charts hanging in clusters around the room. Two armed guards stood outside the steel-enforced airlock. The tops of their heads were visible through the small, rectangular Plexiglas window in the door as they paced back and forth on their hourly rounds. Surveillance cameras mounted in each corner of the low ceiling silently rotated to track every movement within the room, their little red lights blinking in a maddening, steady rhythm.

The patient sighed again and squeezed his eyes tighter. He knew it was no use to try and fight; not when he could barely resist the pull on his swollen eyelids.

Screaming didn't help either. He'd tried. God knows he'd tried, nonstop for the first three days until they tied him down and shoved an IV in his right forearm, pumping in a steady supply of sedatives. It didn't really matter what he did. No amount of yelling, biting, or crying had made any progress in getting him out of this concrete hellhole. He doubted anyone within a five-mile radius of the lab gave a damn that one of the experiments didn't care for their treatment. Beyond that...

Well, beyond the lab, there was nothing else but miles of open desert and high-powered solar fields.

He was alone.

"Here," the doctor said. "See if this helps."

The doctor smiled as if speaking to a child. "There now. You'll be yourself again soon."

Hardly.

Tiny ants crawled their way up the patient's cheeks toward his nose and mouth, scrambling over each other in their desperate rush to invade his already non-existent personal space. His tongue twitched, thick in his mouth, rubbing against the back of his teeth, teeth that hadn't been used for... for how long he wasn't sure.

Weeks, at least.

The patient's eyes widened, and his neck jerked to the side as his jaw muscles spasmed. He swallowed down warm bile and glared at the old man above him.

"Good," the doctor said softly. "That's it. Use your words."

"F-fuc... y-you."

"Now, that isn't polite," the doctor said calmly as he hung the new IV drip bag on an empty hook. He held up a long, thin finger. "I just gave you your mouth back. If you don't agree to behave, I might have to put you on another time-out."

If it weren't for the drugs, I'd bend this fucking table in half and level this godforsaken structure into the ground.

God, how I love the drugs.

The drugs kept the beast quiet and let him think. Gave him the best dreams, and as far as he could remember, he hadn't had a single nightmare since he'd enlisted.

Though that couldn't be right either; he couldn't remember ever signing up for this shit.

The patient did a long, slow blink, then willed his dry tongue to lick across his even drier lips. He needed something to drink. Though he doubted he'd get anything besides the feeding tube shoved through a slit in his side or the multiple IVs jabbed in his arms. His eyes searched the heavy lines on the doctor's face for any hint of sympathy or regret.

The doctor's eyes flicked away from his clipboard to peer down at him, twiddled his pen once, twice, and then went back to his notes.

Nope. No help there.

Help... Someone had helped me. I'd been in trouble...

The skin on the patient's arms started tingling. The ants made their way down his neck and shoulders, the little bastards biting and nipping as they traveled to the tips of his fingers. His right index finger twitched involuntarily, and he glanced up again at the doctor to see if he had noticed.

His back is to me, so I'm good.

Sharp, stinging pain in the skin behind his left ear ripped a gasp from his parched throat. His eyes burned and threatened to leak, and he tightened his jaw and focused on the rocky seams in the ceiling.

"Sorry about that," the doctor said. "I just wanted to check the connection to your brain activity monitor. Make sure we're getting everything."

The patient relaxed against the table, at least as much as he could considering the leather buckled restraints. He tested the straps at his wrists, slowly flexing his arms and balling his hands into fists. At least he could move them again.

He started when he realized the man was speaking to him.

The doctor was leaning over him again, his eyes and mouth tight in annoyance. "...I said, how was it this time?"

This time?

Oh, right. He's asking about the changes.

The experiments the team of scientists had been inflicting upon his uselessly limp body for God knew how long. Experiments to test the limits of the human body, changing elements here and there to try and create the ultimate... the ultimate *what?* He wasn't ordinarily awake during any of their experiments, which was probably a good thing. In fact, most of what he remembered was patchy, only pieces here and there.

I do remember that it hurts like a motherfucker.

The patient's eyes flicked up to the doctor's face. He didn't think the man looked much like the mad-scientist type, with his large eyes set deep in a wrinkled face that appeared better suited for reading his grandchildren bedtime stories. Still, he guessed most serial killers didn't wear badges promoting their work either.

His mouth moved twice before anything came out. "How...hell you think?" It almost embarrassed him with how weak he sounded, rasping like a ninety-year-old man on his deathbed. He closed his eyes. "Hurt."

"I thought soldiers were immune to pain?"

The patient's eyes snapped open.

Soldier?

That wasn't right. His breathing quickened. He wasn't a soldier. He was...he wasn't sure. In fact, he wasn't sure about a lot of things. First and foremost, what the hell was *he* doing on the operating table?

"Why am I here?" he said, his voice noticeably stronger.

The doctor looked up from his notes, actually stopping this time, to stare. His eyes narrowed, the skin tightened at the corners of his mouth, and his nostrils flared. He spun on his heel and strode to the single airlock. He cocked his arm back and slammed his clipboard against the metal pane, the wooden board splintering with a sharp crack.

"Why isn't the reconstructive memory in place?" he screamed to no one in particular. "I thought we already had this cleared up?"

"It *was*, sir," came a female voice over the crackling hiss of the intercom. "And we've all but stopped the depressants. It must be his subconscious blocking it."

Reconstructive... The patient's heartbeat picked up, giving the lucid screen monitors a field day. *What the hell did* that *mean?*

The red-faced doctor spun back to the table. He ran a hand

through his thinning hair and pulled on his beard as he slowly approached the table. The skin on his face pulled tight against his bones, thinning out his lips.

"What is your name?"

That made the patient jump, despite the drugs. "You mean you've been doing shit to me, and you don't even know who I am?"

"Answer the damn question!"

"Can I have some water?" His throat felt tight. Pressure built behind his eyes, bearing down on the bridge of his nose and making it hard to breathe.

"What is your goddamn name!"

"I..." the patient hesitated. Licked his lips. "I..."

Hell, I really don't know.

The doctor spun and kicked the nearest side table against the wall, sending steel pans clattering to the floor and papers of nervous system diagrams fluttering across the room.

"Fuck!"

The airlock in the corner of the room hissed and swung open, hard enough for the knob to leave a mark on the concrete wall. Three more men came into the room wheeling a new machine and two monitors. The patient's eyes locked onto the newcomers; each of them wore a yellow hazmat suit with matching gloves, boots, and glass-faced helmets until not an inch was left uncovered. Air swished from the flexible tubes sprouting from the air tanks strapped to their backs.

The sounds of the men's breathing sent a wave of tingling over the patient's skin, as if it would peel off and walk away. He closed his eyes and swallowed down more bile, ignoring the sharp pricks as new needles were added to his neck and legs.

One of the strangers loosened the straps on the patient's left arm and rubbed the bend in his elbow with a white alcohol-soaked cotton ball as another doctor in a lab coat entered the room. The new doctor, clean cut and carrying an air of authority, glanced at the papers littered across the floor and then stepped closer and bent over the patient.

"I'm Doctor Reichard," cooed the soothing voice. He glared at the yellow-suited man to his right until the man obediently deserted his cotton ball duties and stepped away from the table. "I've been working on you along with Doctor Kiudruam from the beginning."

Names, the patient thought. *What is my name?*

"His memory should have been in place before he woke," Maurd hissed, spittle flying as he spun on the newcomer. "You were supposed—"

"I told you the reconstructive memory process takes several days to complete," Reichard said, shaking his head. "You were in such a rush to see the physical results."

"With those damned crusades going on around the country, we don't have the luxury of time to spare! You know that I wanted to finish one last trial before the lab is shut down."

The patient's eyes flicked to his left arm. The cotton ball still perched on his skin, the evaporating alcohol cold and distracting. He tensed his arm. The restraint felt loose. The doctors had turned their backs on him as they argued, and it appeared that the men in yellow suits had stepped out. He took a deep breath and slowly moved his left arm across his bare chest until his hand found the buckle holding his right arm down. His fingers fumbled awkwardly with the cold metal as he undid the hinged pin and managed to shake his hand free.

He glanced at the backs of the arguing scientists, grunted, and after three tries managed to push himself up into a sitting position. He doubled over as a sudden wave of dizziness nearly sent him tumbling to the floor. He groaned and pressed his knuckles to the sides of his head, trying to keep his screaming brain from leaking out of his ringing ears. He whimpered and clawed at the edge of the bed, then opened his eyes as the spasm of pain passed. His eyes dropped to his body.

He froze.

He sat nude; his tanned skin was a stark contrast to the white sheets on the table, covered in a thick, clear slime. His vision blurred so that his skin danced in front of his eyes. He blinked and shook his head, the breath catching in his throat.

It's not my imagination.

Worm-like shudders slipped along his legs and chest, rippling his skin as if some living creature rolled beneath, struggling to get out. His left leg started to shake, and then his right hand followed suit. The dizziness came again, and he screamed when it suddenly felt as if his skin would burst.

The doctors jumped at his cry and turned. They rushed to the table side, yelling at the intercom for backup. The machines beeped rapidly as the patient's heart raced.

Too fast.

"Help me!" the patient screamed. "Help me!"

He ripped at the wires that connected him to those damned beeping machines. Blood sprayed patterns across the pale room as the needles came loose, sending the monitors into high alert and the displays flatlining.

Yellow suits rushed into the room. Several arms reached out and jerked the patient backward, his bare skin slapping against the table's surface. He fought against them, screaming and kicking his heels against the metal. Still, his drugged limbs made movements slow and awkward, and he only managed to bundle up the white sheet and tip a side table over to clatter the floor. Straps pulled and tightened across his arms and legs, the buckles clinking as they bound him tightly down. The doctors stepped back as the patient writhed beneath the restraints. They shared a pleased nod and shook hands.

"We did it," Maurd said, a proud gleam in his eye. "It's working."

Sobs racked the patient's body as he struggled, making it hard to breathe. He felt as if they'd lit his feet on fire, the warmth spreading from his toes and racing toward his heart. He glanced down at his slime-covered body and, to his horror, watched dark brown hair sprout up through his skin and across his torso. More clear slime oozed from open pores as the hairs spread until he lay in a pool of cool sludge. Something popped deep in his chest, and his ribs seemed to crack and collapse before expanding to nearly twice their normal size.

"What have you done to me?" he gasped, jerking his head to the side. "*What have...*"

He screamed as his face stretched and grew, the bridge of his nose elongating into a long muzzle. The words died on his velvet lips pulled back in horror, and a high-pitched, terrified roar ripped from his throat.

Maurd smacked a button on the display. "Stop him before he shifts completely!"

The ceiling above the table slid open like a giant, grotesque eye. Several metal arms tipped with spinning drill bits slid down through the opening and whirred in the patient's face. The patient howled as one arm bored itself deep into his stomach, ripping open the healing star-shaped scar. The metal twisted and burned as it moved, scorching everything it touched.

"At exactly thirteen hundred hours," Reichard said calmly into his pocket recorder as he stood next to the table. "Kelpie 107 has proven successful."

Maurd smiled and shook hands with the other men in the room, wiped his hands on his lab coat, and walked out of the door, ignoring the patient's screams.

The patient had only one thought before he blacked out upon the table.

I still don't know my name.

CHAPTER

ONE

Blood tastes like a mouthful of hand-warmed pennies.

I rolled my tongue, savoring the all-too-familiar taste. I gingerly touched my bruised lip and chin in a quick attempt to assess the damage the last fall had cost me. Blood came away on my fingertips.

Damn. I spat on the ground. *Enough games.*

The woods sat quiet, the rhythmic pounding of a woodpecker in the distance the only break in the thick, peaceful silence that comes in that twilight period between the death of summer and the emergence of fall. Colorful leaves drifted in the slight breeze, lazily dancing on unseen whirlwinds as they spun to the damp earth. The breeze stirred up loose leaves, wafting up with the scent of mold and pine needles.

Rustling in the bushes several feet away brought my attention to the left. I crouched and turned, holding my breath, gripping the pommel of my short sword until my knuckles glowed white. My hands were sweaty, and I toyed with the idea of wiping them on my tunic. I frowned and shook my head, not wanting to release my hold on my weapon.

Better not, if that demon rushes me again, I want to be ready.

Something large and heavy dragged itself through the brush. My ears strained, listening intently to the sound of wet, ragged breathing off in the trees. I sunk lower into my hiding spot behind a clump of tall raspberry bushes. The twisted vines threatened to caress my face and neck as I fidgeted, wishing for a better view of my surroundings. I slowly lifted a hand and pushed aside a vine to peer farther through the shadows of the tall pines, trying to differentiate between the shadows of the dying light.

Where did it go?

I shrugged the chills away as I carefully inched forward, making sure the raspberry thorns didn't catch on my clothing. A thorn poked through and stabbed me in the wrist. I hissed and jerked my arm away, unable to ignore the sharp sting and the tiny pinpoint of red that stained the cloth.

I half stood out of my crouch, suddenly realizing that the heavy breathing had gone off somewhere down the road, away from the castle. I glanced over my shoulder, then up to the tree canopy. I squinted against the orange light, attempting to locate the sun through the thinning boughs. It was getting late. I needed to get home soon before anyone noticed I was gone.

I sighed and rocked back on my heels in the quilt of red and brown leaves blanketing the forest floor, enjoying the moment of respite.

Serene. That's the word.

I gazed at the tall trees standing silently around me. I held my breath as a yellow butterfly with purple markings on the bottom of each wing fluttered by my head. I held still, hoping for a moment that it would land on me. Then I jerked away, terrified because the butterfly was such a beautiful and fragile thing, and I was afraid that somehow, I'd accidentally find a way to break it.

It seemed I had a knack for ruining things. Or at least, that's what my two younger sisters always said. I still couldn't balance teacups on my head for over ten seconds without first breaking a place-setting for eight, and I just never seemed to be able to keep doves because I always forgot to feed them. My father said that I had busted the princess mold when I was born. Whether he meant that as a good thing, I haven't figured it out yet.

My nose wrinkled as a sudden breeze dragged the stench of rancid meat across my upper lip. The strong smell clung to the back of my throat like thick bile, and I had to fight to swallow it down. My heart skipped a beat.

It's right on top of me.

I spun at the sound of snapping branches, swinging my blade around as the bushes violently parted and the demon leaped toward me. The tip of my blade caught flesh beneath the matted mess of fur, and the creature shrieked as red blood spewed in a wide arc. I jumped back and tripped over an exposed tree root.

"Shit!"

I stumbled and righted myself just as the wolf-sized creature slammed its weight into me, knocking the wind out of my lungs. I lost my sword and fell to the wet earth. I had only a moment to catch my breath as a blur of green and brown fur came at me. Dew soaked through the knees of my pants, and I rolled away just as serrated claws slashed down to sink deep into the earth where my arm had been only a moment ago. I wasn't quite fast enough, and a claw sliced through the sleeve of my tunic, nicking my arm.

The demon screamed, and the red, reptilian face seemed to dislocate as the jaws spread open into five separate sections like a blooming flower. The lips curled back from each section to reveal endless rows of yellow, four-inch-long teeth that disappeared down the wide gullet. The stench of sulfur billowed out of its mouth, coming at me in almost visible clouds. I coughed and had to breathe through my mouth, fighting the urge to retch.

The creature raised the front two of its six gnarled, crooked limbs, each one tipped with black claws longer than my hand, and crouched, ready to pounce. Green, matted hair covered the stocky body in sticky clumps and stood on end between patches of lizard-like scales. Bulging muscles trembled in anticipation. Long rabbit ears twitched forward and back sporadically as the six yellow eyes zeroed in on me. The damn thing seemed to smile.

I didn't like being stared at like a dinnertime delicacy. I reached for my fallen sword.

Oh, gods! It wasn't there!

I didn't dare take my eyes off the demon as I slowly inched my right hand across the wet leaves, groping blindly for the sword through fern droppings. The impatient bastard didn't wait for me and lunged before I was ready. My hand wrapped around something solid, and I quickly brought it up in front of me.

A stick. *I picked up a damn stick?*

The demon's shadow passed over me, and I felt its acidic breath envelop my face as it closed in.

"Oh fuck..."

The demon screamed and jerked away, the gnarled body convulsing as it rolled to the side. I yipped and scrambled back out of reach. The demon writhed on the ground shrieking; my blade jammed to the hilt in the demon's back. I covered my ears against the sound of a thousand swords scraping against dry stone. Dark-red and black-spotted blood pooled around the furred body, and pink foam dribbled from the open mouth as it jerked in the final throes of death. I waited to lower my hands until after the screaming had stopped.

A dark figure stepped out of the shadows beside me.

Wearing only a pair of green trousers, Vestro stood at nearly six feet and three inches and was built entirely of coiled muscle and tendons, with broad shoulders and long legs. The sunlight filtering through the trees played across his naturally tanned skin as he stepped over the dead carcass of the demon. He walked with a grace that was unnatural for a man his size, smooth as a cat yet emanating a barely concealed sense of danger.

I gave Vestro a quick once-over as he stood in the dappled sunlight. I could not deny that he was handsome; with his dark complexion and untamable mane, he had the body of a natural athlete and a personality that was charming and boyish at once. His toothy grin always seemed to get me, no matter how foul of a mood I was festering in. And those eyes—solid black, ringed with faint laugh lines at the corners—should have unnerved me. Instead, I found myself drawn to them more often than I cared to admit. Except for a large, star-shaped scar in the middle of his abdomen, he was pretty much perfect.

If you ignored the part where he was a demon.

Vestro shook his head and crossed his thick arms as he stood over me. I frowned up at him so that I stared at the underside of his jaw rather than his broad chest. At five-foot-two, I really had to crane my neck back.

"I had that under control, Vestro," I said, giving him a stern look.

"Sure, you did, Nadia." Vestro rolled his eyes and squatted beside me. He gingerly touched my arm and looked me over. "Are you hurt?"

I shook my head and let the tension seep from my shoulders. "My pride."

Vestro caught my arm. "You're bleeding."

I almost pulled away, almost told him it was nothing, but I knew it would be no use. Vestro's strong hands lifted the sleeve of my tunic, and he hissed at the sight of the cut. He bent to sniff at the blood, then pressed his mouth to my skin. His tongue swept once, deliberate, and the sensation sent a shiver up my arm that had nothing to do with pain. I went still, suddenly too aware of the warmth of his breath, the careful pressure of his hands. He looked up at me through his lashes as he worked, black eyes holding mine in a way that made my pulse stumble.

For a heartbeat too long, neither of us moved. Then he pulled away, clearing his throat as he glanced back at the wound and nodded.

"It's not deep," he said, releasing me.

"I could have told you that," I replied—too quickly, too defensive. I rubbed my arm, pretending the gooseflesh was from the cool air.

His fingers absently played with my arm, feeling me beneath the tunic. "Are we done? I'm getting hungry."

"You're always hungry," I said. "And you always want to cut my fun short. I should loan you to Cook and then you'll be pulling carts of potatoes like a normal horse."

"At least I'll get to eat on a set schedule. Besides, normal horses don't have to go around babysitting bored princesses."

"You're not a normal horse."

"You're not a normal princess."

That made me smile. He was right. I had never been the type to stitch hems or sit quietly through lessons on courtly manners; I climbed trees, broke curfew, swung practice swords until my hands bled. And Vestro, despite grumbling the whole time, always stayed by my side. As I grew older, the mischief became risk: slipping past guards to explore ruins, shadowing demon hunters, testing Damewood's borders. He complained, as usual, but he still covered my tracks and carried me to places where no princess was meant to go.

Vestro was a kelpie, a water demon said to lure riders onto his back and drown them in rivers to feed on their flesh. Or so the histories claimed. I had never seen him eat anyone, but he never denied it either. When we met eleven years ago, I was nine and too fascinated to be afraid. He needed a place to hide from the hunters who prowled Damewood, and I—bastard daughter of a king with too much freedom—needed a friend. So, I hid him in plain sight, pampered as my prized steed.

Harboring a demon was punishable by death, but I was never very good at following rules. And Vestro never minded—not when it meant evenings at the hearth with me, keeping watch while I read or talked myself hoarse, steadying me when I slipped on wet stones, or raced too fast through the dark corridors. Sometimes he slept curled near the fire in my chambers once the castle slept, a silent sentinel between me and the world. Those quiet hours where I could simply exist—not as a princess, not as anyone's duty, but only myself.

I blinked, realizing I still had a death grip on the useless stick. I reached behind Vestro and playfully poked at his ass. He quickly and gracefully jumped out of the way.

"What was that for?" he grumbled, furrowing his brow.

"If you're going to be a man," I said, "then put your shirt back on before I gag." I stood up and brushed myself off as best I could.

"Please." Vestro threw back his head and laughed, flashing a mouthful of wide, white teeth. "You know you enjoy this way too much."

He posed and flexed, ridiculous as ever, and I looked away before he saw my smile. He already spent half his life naked as he shifted between his horse and man forms, but I was used to treating it like nothing. I did not need to encourage him.

"Let's go. As soon as we get back, I'll make sure you're fed."

"Yes, Princess." Vestro bowed, and then paused. He rolled his tongue on the inside of his cheek and raised one eyebrow. "Did you see that?"

"See what?"

He pointed to my stomach. I looked down, and my heart sank. The demon blood had soaked through my tunic, looking like someone had taken a wet paintbrush and flicked it across my tunic. A spattering of red and black streaks started between my breasts and fanned out down to my navel.

"Shit," I muttered under my breath.

Warm breath brushed my ear, close enough to raise gooseflesh.

"You know," Vestro whispered. "You should really work on that mouth of yours. Cursing is not very becoming of a lady."

I snorted and twisted my head to frown at him.

Vestro shrugged and turned away. "Oh, I forgot, you're not a lady."

I bent and picked up another stick and swung at him. Vestro chuckled and easily hopped out of my reach. I growled and threw the stick as far as I could into the darkening tree line.

"This was supposed to be a quick ride before the ball tonight," I groaned. "There's no way I can sneak through the halls looking like this."

"You're the one who decided to go demon hunting."

"Well, what else was I supposed to do for fun with the free time before the ball?"

Vestro smirked. "I could think of a few things."

He turned before I could respond and jogged past me to where we'd left our gear. I smiled and jerked my sword out of the demon's corpse and started walking, hefting the blade in one hand. I followed Vestro a little slower, admiring the view of his retreating backside. Off limits or not, he was impossible not to look at.

I stopped at the edge of the clearing at the rumbling sounds of bones cracking and Vestro's pained cry, rubbing the sticky blood from my fingers against the rough bark of a dead pine. When Vestro went silent, I counted to ten before moving again.

He was already waiting, saddlebags packed, nibbling half-heartedly at a patch of browning grass. Slime from his shift clung to his coat, slowly drying into a dull sheen that caught the late sun. He flicked at flies with his long tail, ears twitching when he heard me approach. A soft nicker escaped him, and I grinned despite myself.

As striking as Vestro was in his human form, he was breathtaking as a horse. His coat was the dark brown of fresh coffee, sleek enough to look wet even hours after a change. The light caught red in it now, fire smoldering across his flanks. He looked every bit a stallion of legend—until you noticed the parts that were wrong. His legs, a little too long. The curve of his ears, sharp enough to mimic horns. And worst of all, those eyes. Pale and pupil-less, like boiled flesh, blank and unblinking.

It had taken months before I stopped shivering when he looked at me that way. And longer still before I learned to pretend I didn't notice how, in his human form, those black eyes could drain to that same sickly white whenever agitation thinned his control. Anyone else who asked, I shrugged off with excuses: blindness, mutation, bad luck in the bloodline. The stable master nearly barred me from riding at all, swearing he would not have a princess's broken neck on his conscience. But in the end, I won.

Vestro bowed his head and knelt as I settled the blanket and saddle across his broad back. The girth was slick with leftover slime, and I tried twice to cinch the saddle properly without getting any of the mess on my arm, then finally sighed and just leaned up against him to pull it tight. I shrugged the odorless slime off my shoulder as I slid my sword into its sheath on the side of the saddle.

"You know," I said, wiping my hands on the grass. "If you were really good, Ves, you'd learn to shift with your saddle on."

He flicked his ears and whinnied, then gently bumped his velvet muzzle against my cheek. A playful kiss. I scratched his forehead and kissed the top of his nose before slipping on his halter. I never used a bit with him. It felt degrading, and it was not needed. Vestro always followed my lead, with or without reins. I mounted and gathered them anyway.

"Come on, let's go home."

CHAPTER
TWO

I tried just about everything on the way home to get the blood out, even though I knew it wouldn't come completely clean. Lately, I had been solid at practicing self-control. In fact, it had been almost a week since I'd killed anything while in formal wear. Though I hadn't been able to resist sneaking out after afternoon tea when I heard of the demon hunting at the edge of the Sheepland Acres.

We topped over the rise at the edge of the wood, and I sighed as home came into view. The castle loomed above us, the largest of its kind in all the Southern Lands. The massive black walls towered over the surrounding forest, making even the most majestic redwoods look like saplings. Colorful banners flapped in the evening wind, and torch fires burned in large, metal grates at the top of each corner tower, illuminating the grounds beneath. From where we stood, I could hear the dying sounds of the evening markets and the beginnings of music drifting from the many taverns that came to life each night.

Damewood Castle was known as the absolute greatest architectural achievement in any of the kingdoms. It was the only castle throughout its history to have never had an enemy pass through the first of three outer walls surrounding its low-lying townhomes and inns. Though it was hard for me to agree, since other than visiting our western neighbors at Riverwind, I'd never been past our kingdom's boundaries to compare. I hoped that I'd soon get my big chance to change that.

We approached the outer, east castle gate, and the demon wards mounted onto the stone columns pulsed bright red as we neared. The wards whirred softly, a gentle hum emitting from the tiny black boxes and blinking red dots, as if tracking our movements. Vestro hesitated only a second before passing through, his withers twitching and ears flat back.

It always amazed me how he could just walk right into the castle past the wards—wards Maurdruik had convinced Dad to spend a year's worth of taxes to fortify the city to keep demons, like Vestro, out. Either Vestro was stronger than the wards themselves, or the wizards that had sold Maurdruik the wards were full of shit. Myself, I felt that Maurdruik had been ripped off by a bunch of con artists. Maybe he'd been too excited to try some of the new crap that had started circulating around the city streets; things like new versions of magical wards, tomes, and artifacts that were supposedly stronger, faster, and more advanced than the ones the kingdom had been using for several decades. I didn't think the small boxes did anything to keep the city safe.

We had our King's Guard to thank for that.

Vestro quickly trotted through the emptying streets reserved for merchants and traders, the air still thick with the scent of sugared rolls and fish, and then on through the second gate into the residential sector. We slowed our pace as we passed the darkened houses, doing our best not to disturb anyone as we circled around to the north entrance of the inner wall that led to the castle. Vestro's hard hooves clattered against the smooth cobblestone streets, and I grimaced each time we passed by a guard station tucked into one of the wall alcoves, not wanting to bring too much attention to our arrival. I flashed a smile at Donovan, the blond guard at the gated entrance to the castle as I passed, and he waved me through with a smile; he was used to my oddly timed outings and no longer bothered to ask what I'd been up to.

We veered to the left past the main stables toward the smaller building in the back—my own two-stalled stable and tack room. We trotted inside, and I jumped down from the saddle, hands idly brushing at the bloodstained dress. I sighed. It was a waste of energy. The dress was ruined. I didn't mind, though, because at least none of the blood was mine. It really was too bad that my dad didn't share my point of view.

I clapped Vestro on the neck as I handed his reins to the redheaded Shayn, my personal stable boy. His freckled face frowned in the light of the lamp he held in his left hand, and he shook his head at me, his curly hair bouncing on top of his squarish head. Shayn was the only stable hand that would willingly work with the pale-eyed horse without asking questions and put up with my finicky instructions. Sometimes I thought I took Shayn for granted, but I was a princess, and he wasn't. At least, that was how I justified it to myself whenever I felt a smidge of guilt.

"The king is going to be mighty upset, Highness," Shayn said, unbuckling the saddle. He slapped Vestro's muscled rump and slipped off the saddle as Vestro whinnied and flipped his tail. "You're late again—"

"I know, I know," I said. "I tried my best to get back on time."

"Eventually, the king is going to stop believing that all this blood is from helping the cook kill whatever's for dinner, and you're going to get caught." He frowned and shook his head. "And then I'm going to get flogged for saddling your horse and sending you off on your mischief."

"Would it make you feel better if I said I was sorry?"

"Not if it means I still get flogged."

I clapped Shayn on the shoulder, quickly wrapped my dirty sword in an oilcloth without bothering to take the time to clean it, and spun on my heel to run out of the stable and into the dark outside. One thing I knew, I could count on Shayn not to snitch. I chewed on my lip as I rounded the corner wall of the stable yard toward the ballroom. I knew I really needed to do something for him. Buy him a gift, perhaps. I knew that it took a lot to put up with me, and I didn't even think I could do it.

I frowned and picked up the pace. The sun was down, and the moon was visible through the thin layering of clouds. Shayn was right—I really *was* late. The ball had been scheduled to start at sunset.

Maybe I can pass through quickly and change before anyone notices.

I stumbled and almost dropped my sword.

Maybe.

I ran through the dark courtyard of planters and gardens, my soft boots flying silently over the mossy cobblestones. I dodged around the hedges and leaped over the small fishpond at the corner of the main ballroom, doing my best to stay inconspicuous. Music drifted through the air as I ducked under the eaves of the rose greenhouse, squeezing between the row of hedges and the fence. Laughter leaked from the lighted ballroom; the large open windows cast stretched boxes of light across the yards of grass as the exaggerated silhouettes of guests moved and danced around awkwardly like the clowns from a children's puppet show. The air lay thick with the stench of smoke and alcohol over the lingering sweetness of barbequed pork and peppers. I wrinkled my nose at the lingering stench of cigarettes.

The ballroom struck like daylight as rounded the corner. Candle chandeliers blazed from the open-beamed ceiling, torches flaring along the walls, the polished floor a spinning lake of silk and brocade. Couples drifted in courtly orbits near the edges as the air thrummed with violins and low talk. I crossed my arms to pin the oilcloth tight and kept my head down, threading through perfume and heat.

Faces turned toward me. I angled my body, keeping my front in shadow, and hugged the oilcloth hard to my ribs. My bundled sword became slick where blood had seeped through the seam, so I hitched it higher under my elbow like a folded wrap.

Keep moving. Smile later.

A few of the younger men paused in their conversations to glance at me, eyes widening in recognition and others smiling and shoulders squaring, chests lifting as if air alone could make them taller. I rolled my eyes and brushed past them, unamused with their boyish attempts at courtship. One took a breath like he might speak. I skewered him with a cold glare—*fuck off, I'm not interested*—before turning away to continue my hurried plight through the twirling throng.

Blue eyes caught me across the room, a smile freezing on painted lips.

Uciel.

My sister's blonde hair was piled in a miniature tower, tendrils placed just so like a portrait's signature, and—of course—she was close enough to see. Her gaze flicked to the wet stain on my front; her mouth thinned, then she surged, dragging a fan of suitors in her wake.

"No," I breathed, and veered.

"Nadia."

I froze. The deep voice behind me rolled out neutrally, but it stopped me dead in my tracks. I bit my lip and glanced right to the large double doors of the main hallway only steps away.

Of course, I had wandered straight into the open and right in front of the royal platform.

Think, Nadia.

A servant brushed past with a tray of goblets. I snatched one without thinking, tipped it hard, and let the red cascade down my tunic. It ran quickly over the wool, seeping into the darker stains

24

beneath. Sweetness flooded the air, sharp and cloying enough to smother the iron scent clinging to me. I hissed as it soaked my wrist and brushed at the mess, half show, half necessity.

Then I turned.

My father sat heavy in his throne, crown gleaming steady under the chandeliers. His eyes pinned me, sharp despite the weariness clouding his face. Old Red, the captain of the guard, stood like a wall at his right, hands clasped over the pommel of his sword. His weathered face stayed neutral except for the faintest twitch at the corner of his mouth—his closest thing to a wink. Maurdruik, the council wizard, loomed at my father's left, a heap of bright robes and bristling white beard, eyes narrowed beneath his heavy brows.

"Your Majesty," I said, "just trying my hand at drinking like the courtiers."

I furrowed my brow and gave him my saddest eyes, hoping that if I made light of the situation, he'd let it go. I wasn't ready to be locked in my room for another week with only needlepoint as entertainment.

Old Red coughed to cover a laugh. The king glared at him, then sighed and leaned back in his throne.

Then his gaze dropped to the stain spreading across my front. His brow arched, not in surprise, but in tired reproach. "Saints above, Nadia. Always determined to look anything but the princess you are." He pressed two fingers to the bridge of his nose, nudging his crown forward until its rim shadowed his eyes. "Go and change before the entire hall stares."

Relief tugged at my chest, but I only had time to dip my head before silk swept in on either side. Manicured fingers clamped my shoulders, pushing down hard. I bent with the weight before it could become a scene, dropping to one knee on the polished floor.

Uciel and Uriel leaned in like a pair of vipers, blonde curls gleaming, matching smiles sharp enough to cut.

"Daddy," Uciel trilled, voice pitched to carry. "Look what she's wearing. Trousers. At a ball." Her eyes flicked to the wine-dark stain. "And already ruined."

"You said she'd be punished if she embarrassed us again," Uriel added, her grip tightening, nails pricking through my sleeve.

I clenched my jaw. I could have shrugged them off, but that would've been another spectacle, and the court already stared. I forced a smile—small, tight, and very unamused.

My father tipped his head further into his hand so his crown slid low until it shadowed half his face. He always did that when he didn't want to decide, as if hiding behind the gold made the rest of us vanish.

"Uciel. Uriel." His sigh dragged over the polished stone. "Not tonight."

"But Daddy—"

"Go." He didn't raise his voice. He didn't need to. The flick of his hand dismissed them like gnats. "Entertain the guests. Nadia can manage her own clumsiness."

Their perfect mouths pinched, but they obeyed. Nails scraped across my shoulders as they released me, a parting scratch meant to sting. Their skirts swished close, carrying perfume thick enough to choke. Heads bent together, they stalked away, already whispering.

I uncurled slowly to my feet, shoulders tight. Ten, I told myself. Count to ten. It was safer than swinging.

When I looked back, my father had lowered his hand, his eyes clearer now, gentler. "You're dismissed, Nadia."

This time, I didn't hesitate.

"Nadia!"

I turned toward the voice as Claire trotted around the outskirts of the dance floor and entwined her elbow in mine. She glanced at the red stain on the front of my tunic and shook her head, inching away to avoid getting any of the blood on her. As my second-best friend, she knew me well enough not to say anything until I brought it up. Though she didn't have to wait long. I told her about it as soon as we'd made it into the hallway. She smiled, her green eyes sparkling.

"What I wouldn't have given to see the look on your sisters' faces!" she giggled.

Claire hugged my arm and quickened her pace toward my room. I grinned as I watched her thick body totter past the granite pillars and colorful tapestries that lined the hallway to the guest quarters, then sped up to pass her. She glanced back, then sucked in her breath at seeing me closing in and shuffled her feet into a clumsy trot up the wide marble staircase. I lengthened my stride into an exaggerated lope, only landing on every other of the large steps as I quickly gained on her.

By the time we reached the end of the east wing—the royal family's quarters—we were running full out, gaining the amused glances of several servants. We barreled through the double-door into my bedchamber and nearly collapsed to the floor to lie in a gasping, laughing pile.

My bedchamber was a simple space, especially for what could be expected for a princess. The fifteen-foot ceiling topped pale-yellow walls covered by tacked-up sheets of canvas displaying sketches of various creatures sighted around the castle, hand-drawn maps of the merchant cart locations, and lists of point marks for every demon I'd slaughtered. A massive four-post bed layered in green silk sheets and softly brushed bearskins sat against the middle of the back wall directly across from the double doors, bordered on each side by heavy oak side tables laden with rolled-up scrolls, pieces of a bridle I'd tried tooling for Vestro and then abandoned, and drippy candles amidst pools of colorful, dried wax. A small, dusty basket leaned against the table on the right, filled with even dustier rolls of faded thread and needlepoint cloth.

Heavy green, velvet curtains along the right wall were pulled back to let in the moonlight through the barred, floor-to-ceiling windows overlooking the soldiers' training yard. My father had had the iron bars added to the outside of the windows after I'd been caught climbing out and down the side of the castle to join the soldiers in the combat ring when I was twelve, and they'd been on ever since. It was too bad because they'd been a very convenient way to escape my studies.

At least he hasn't discovered the secret passage behind my fireplace.

I turned onto my back and smiled at Claire, admiring her waves of ruby-colored hair and the sprinkling of freckles across the bridge of her fine nose as she panted for breath.

"Nadia," she screeched suddenly. "Get off the rug before you get wine on it!"

I rolled back on my shoulders and pushed off the floor with my hands, kicked my legs out, and arched my back to land on my feet. I swept the tunic up and over my head in one fluid motion. Then I kicked off my boots and stripped off my leggings and tossed them across the room. I stood wearing nothing but a thin silver necklace as I bundled the clothes into a tight ball.

Claire was slower at standing, her body not quite having the agility mine did. She held out her hands, and I tossed her the ruined tunic. She shook her head as she added it to the hamper.

"It's already dry," I said. "The wine isn't coming out. Just burn the damn thing."

"I don't care if you say it won't come out," she sniffed as she turned away and proceeded to search through my closets. "*I*, at least, must try. Poor has her work cut out for her. You ruin clothes as fast as she makes them!"

I wrinkled my nose and sighed, then looked down and scratched at a speck of dried blood just above my left breast before she could notice. I sauntered over to the silver washbasin near the doors. I wet one of the newly bleached washcloths and quickly scrubbed at my face and neck, then washed my hands and replaced the now-pink towel. I hadn't realized that so much of the demon's blood had soaked through. I sighed, thinking for a moment of the poor wash-women who had to clean up after my messes.

I stood dutifully as Claire trotted up to me and pulled a pink satin gown over my head and laced up the open back. I glared at her. I hated pink. It was the color of sick fish, and it nearly made me gag just to see it, let alone wear it. Of course, she knew how I felt, but she ignored me as she fussed over my hair. I watched her in the mirror for a moment before gazing at myself.

Where my sisters took after Father with their thin faces, pale complexions, and blonde curls that fell to their waists, I followed my mother off the beaten path of royalty.

I stood several inches shorter and more compact than Uriel and Uciel and had wider shoulders than the two twigs combined. My eyes were darker, too. Not brown, but more the dirty color of murky pond water. My nose was a little too straight, and my lips a little too small in my heart-shaped face framed by brunette locks that fell just past my shoulders.

Not exactly princess material by the kingdom's standards, but it worked for me.

Though I was not surprised I failed to resemble my family at all. I was the bastard child of the young king, one out of who knew how many he might have sired, and technically, I had no right to the kingdom or anything in it. I had often wondered how bringing a bastard child into the castle must have gone over initially with his newly wedded queen, but as far back as I could remember, she had always been kind to me, and up until her death on the day of the twins' birth, she was as much my mother as theirs.

But of course, the twins had to take that single happiness away as well.

Claire finished her fussing and took a step back, proud at her handiwork. "Do you need a moment before I escort you back?"

I nodded and waved her off, and she bowed and left. The latch clicked shut behind her, and the room stilled.

For a moment, I just stood there, staring at my reflection in the mirror, drowning in silk the color of dead salmon.

Saints, I really hate pink.

I tugged at the ribbons of my gown, my fingers slipping against the silk, as the hidden hearth panel clicked open. Hands wrapped around my waist, pulling me into a quick, warm hug.

"You'll be the death of me," I hissed as Vestro's hands fell away and he stepped around the room. I motioned toward the door. "Claire's waiting in the hall! You're supposed to wait until later. One day someone will catch you."

"Not tonight," he said smoothly, already lifting the sword I'd leaned against the wall. He pulled a rag from his belt and wiped the blade clean with practiced hands, then slid it back into its sheath and propped it neatly in the corner. "Everyone's too drunk to pay attention to much."

"And the tunic," I added, nodding to the hamper.

"Already saw it." He scooped up the balled fabric and moved to tuck it into his satchel. He paused and took a sniff, then gave me an odd look. "Is that wine? Were you drinking?"

I rolled my eyes. "It was an escape plan."

Vestro snorted. "More messes. You really like to make my job difficult, don't you?"

"You're supposed to be my guard, not my maid," I muttered.

His eyes softened as he neared. "I keep you whole. In whatever way I must." He caught the silk tie at my shoulder before it slipped, finishing the knot with a neat tug. "You fidget when you're nervous. What's wrong?"

The words were so familiar that I nearly laughed. "You sound like Claire."

"Claire would faint if she knew the half of it," he murmured. He took a step back and let his eyes roam over my form, his brow dimpling. "They're determined to drown you in dead fish scales, aren't they?"

I snorted. "Tell me something I don't know. Everyone loves this awful pink, but I think it makes me look sick."

"It does," he agreed, with a rare flicker of mischief. "But Andrew will be too dazzled by his own reflection in all that glitter to notice."

I turned on him, half-indignant, half-amused. "You shouldn't talk about him that way."

"Why not? He'll be talking about himself all night. I can't join in?"

Vestro nudged my boots under the bed with the side of his foot, then glanced up at me with that crooked half-smile. "Doesn't matter what you wear. You'll be too busy glowering at the prince while he dogs your heels from one end of the hall to the other."

I narrowed my eyes. "You think you're funny."

"Funny? No." He tilted his head innocently, though his eyes glinted. "Right? Always."

I stiffened. "Don't start."

The corners of his mouth quirked as he sauntered up behind me. "What? I've watched him nearly trip over his crown trying to get to you. You'll glare; he'll grin. Your usual courtly dance. It's nothing new with you two."

Heat crept up my neck. Without thinking, I smoothed the gown over my hip, then reached to tuck back a loose strand of hair.

Vestro's gaze flicked to the motion, and for a beat, he went quiet. The dimple between his brows deepened before he played with the ribbon at my shoulder, his fingers just brushing my skin. "You should have two plates sent up." He gave me a knowing look. "One for me, one for you."

"Why me?"

"You'll be too busy glowering at him to eat."

I touched his hand on my shoulder. "Always the practical one."

He kissed my fingers and then turned away to continue tidying the room. "Hardly."

I smirked. "At least Andrew tries to be charming."

Vestro turned back and his mouth twitched. "Charming?" He dipped into a mocking half-bow, one arm sweeping low with exaggerated flourish. Straightening, he flicked invisible dust from his shoulder. "They've been polishing that boy's feathers since birth. A peacock doesn't know it's ridiculous; it thinks it's divine."

A laugh escaped before I could stop it. "You're impossible."

"And you," he said dryly, already stepping toward the hearth panel, "are very late."

He gave a quick wink as he stepped back into the passageway. I blew him a mock kiss, earning a smile and shake of his head before the shadows swallowed him whole.

THREE

I took a moment in the hall with Claire to regain my composure, listening to the throbbing music that beckoned us to join in the festivities. Together, we passed through the tall, mahogany double doors into the massive ballroom and were blasted by warm, smoky air and hearty laughter. The bards strummed passionately to the beat of the drums, and the flames from the high wall-torches pulsed to the rhythm of the dance. Faces turned as we entered, and several nodded before turning back to their conversations.

Stepping as one amid the promenading couples, we twirled each other around as we made our way to the center of the room, our slippers silent against the polished wood floors. The music changed, the flutes dying and drums taking center stage, and we quickened our pace to match the step. I caught sight of my sisters dancing in a far corner with their courtiers, their faces blurred behind a veil of smoke and flickering candlelight. When we spun around again, they were both hanging onto new courtiers.

Our twirling brought us toward the expansive buffet tables at the far-right wall of the room. The long tables were draped in crisp linen and laden with bowls of fruits, breads, cheeses, and platters of meats and fish fillets surrounded by tall, dripping candelabras. Large vats of warm ale stood at the ends of each table, with stacks of heavy mugs that were quickly replaced by servants as soon as they disappeared. Water cascaded softly down the wall behind the tables from a slit in the ceiling, catching in a thin, rectangular pool on the floor against the wall, then flowing through a small hole in the stone bottom.

Maurdruik called it a water fountain and had it installed for the harvest festival two years ago. Though I still wasn't sure how it managed to work, I figured the fountain was like the newly introduced running water faucets and showers I'd come to love.

My gaze wandered to the nearest table where a group of young men stood around a colorful display of crackers and cheeses. A flash of gold brought my attention to the center of the group, only to see the most sought-after bachelor in all the West Lands; Prince Andrew of the neighboring kingdom of Riverwind. The sandy-blond prince stood tall, with strong arms and broad shoulders. His belted tunic and tailored pants fit perfectly at his slim hips, and the richly embroidered gold clothes exaggerated his confident stance. The ideal image of a prince for any princess.

I guess I was an exception to the rule.

Andrew and I were close childhood friends, spending whole seasons side by side because our kingdoms traded often and stayed close. He'd been fun back then, easy to laugh with, and we played almost like siblings. In truth, I was closer to him than to my own half-sisters.

But then we grew up. While I found solace on Vestro's back and the freedom from the constraints of court, royal arrogance became Andrew's second nature; entitlement baked into him from years as the only heir to the richest kingdom in the West Lands and a long line of noble women willing to throw themselves in front of his horse if it meant capturing his attention.

So hubristic in fact, that he went behind my back and bartered with my father for my hand in marriage in exchange for a very, very handsome dowry. I knew the union offer was strategic, ignited by his father's desire to expand their borders beyond the coastline and control a main trade route. Though Andrew should have known me well enough to approach me first to see what I wanted instead of acting like he was buying one of my father's horses.

That was three years ago. I responded to his proposal by refusing his company and threatening my father with hanging myself if anyone tried to force my hand into marriage.

Yet Andrew still hasn't given up.

The truth was that I rather liked the freedom of being a bastard; I didn't have to put up a façade each time I left my room, be present for nonsensical town hearings, or calculate my every move to make sure it benefited the kingdom best. I would never be the queen of Damewood, and being a woman, I would never have more say in the kingdom's issues beyond what color napkins to use for that week's ball. So, considering the independence I had now, marriage to an arrogant prince in a masculine, self-congratulatory society was not for me.

Not now, probably not ever.

I looked over as Andrew chatted—no, *discussed*, as men forcibly point out that they don't chat—with the Dukes of Rothshire and Remley, both men under my father's rule. I paused in my step as I strained to listen.

"...It was unbelievable," Duke Remley said beneath his bouncing mustache. His fat jowls trembled as he chewed on a handful of crackers. "That trempkin had been terrorizing the hillside for weeks now, and this morning my men found it slain in the forest outside of my pastures."

"I have heard tales of Damewood's mystery knight," Andrew said, shaking his head. His blue eyes narrowed beneath what were obviously hand-sculpted eyebrows. "But Henry, you cannot believe that these killings have all been done by one man."

"I'm telling you, Prince," Remley said, "that I saw the carcass with my own eyes. There were only markings from one blade. And a single blow at that! All I have to say is that Damewood is blessed to have a guardian such as this to watch over the castle gates."

Yes!

I fought to hide a proud smile. It was always nice to hear that my work was being appreciated.

My right foot slipped on a slick part of the polished floor, and I nearly went down but managed to claw at Claire's arms to keep my footing. She leaned back at the last minute and pulled me upright. I hurriedly glanced over at the three men, hoping they had not noticed. They stared over at us with wide eyes and blank faces. Remley had even stopped chewing for a moment.

Damn, they had.

I blushed and lowered my gaze when Andrew grinned.

"Nadia," Claire said, "what was that all about?" She fanned herself with a pudgy hand.

I winked at her but kept an ear open as the men's conversation resumed in the corner. I tried to keep us close to the men as we danced, listening to them over the laughing crowd and music, though Claire grew annoyed, and with Andrew's quick glances in our direction each time we twirled by, he probably thought I was flirting.

Flirting happened to be the last thing I wanted to do with him, but I wanted to hear more. I grabbed Claire's wrists and pulled her a little closer toward the men as I strained to listen.

"Another attack, you say?" Remley asked.

"Last night at Farwind Castle," Rothshire said, nodding. He stood a little farther back from the other two men, giving him room to nervously tap the toe of his knee-high boots against the floor. He ran a hand over the top of his thinning hair. "An assassin managed to get into the king's chambers. The guards stopped him in time, but the villain got away before he was apprehended."

He paused and looked around. He bent forward just a bit, his thin shoulders hunching under his plain, gray tunic. "Word has it," he said, his voice dropping, "that they got a good look at its face. The guards said that the assassin..."

"Nadia." Claire pointed. "Your father has beckoned you."

I turned with her and returned to the throne. I bowed at the bottom of the two steps, waited for his nod, and then approached. I leaned close and kissed his cheek. I breathed in the spicy aroma of his cologne and the musky mink fur bordering his cloak and immediately forgot the men in the corner. My father had been so busy lately that I hadn't seen much of him, so when he decided to take the time out from being king to dote on me, I was more than happy to oblige.

He leaned back to eye me up and down and nodded.

"Much better," he said. He smiled. "You know I love that color on you."

I felt my happy face wilt. I nodded and smiled up at him, willing my eyes to shine. He knew I hated pink, too. But my place was to make him happy, not contradict him.

A male voice cleared its throat behind me. "Your Majesty."

Our heads turned as Andrew strolled to the bottom of the dais, his shoulders rolling in a confident, casual stride. He held a cigarette in his left hand, the smoke from the burning end curled up his arm in a familiar caress. Two servants trailed him, hands clasped together, and necks stretched forward, ready to jump at the slightest command.

He bowed low to my father, all formalities, and then let a sideways smile crease his face as he stared up at me expectantly.

I looked over to my father for help, but the approving tilt of his head toward Andrew told me I'd receive none.

Behave, his stare demanded.

Damn you, Andrew.

I sighed, descended the steps, and held out my hand.

Andrew took my hand and gently laid a kiss across my knuckles. He held the kiss longer than I thought necessary for a simple greeting and much longer than I liked. I tried to subtly pull my hand away, but Andrew's fingers tightened over mine. Just enough so that I'd have to make a scene to escape. I looked over to my father for help, but from the approving tilt of his head directed at Andrew knew that I'd receive none.

Andrew dropped his cigarette into the waiting palm of one of his servants, then stepped closer and looped his free hand around my waist. I glared at him and tried to step back, but his hand pressed against the small of my back and held me firm. He raised an eyebrow and flashed a dazzling white smile.

I rolled my eyes.

Andrew gave a little snort. "Are you still upholding your vow of silence toward me?"

He winked as he grasped my wrist and spun me out onto the dance floor.

I fought to keep silent but failed. "That was a cheap shot to make a scene in front of my father," I said. "You know he likes you, and you're only leading him on—"

"Right now, I just want to lead you onto the dance floor." He gave me a look. "It is just a dance, Nadia."

"Go dance with one of the twenty girls drooling over your ass," I said. "I'm not in the mood."

"It is uncanny how I have perfected poor timing with you," he said with a sigh. "And I do not wish to dance with those other girls. I want to dance with you."

Nearby couples bowed their heads and moved aside as we approached, giving us space. I glanced toward the throne and sighed when I caught my father watching. Andrew stepped to the side, and we glided across the floor to the music. Young women glared at me from over the shoulders of their dance partners, their pointy faces pinched in resentment. I fought a small smile as I leaned in closer to Andrew, for a moment enjoying being the center of their jealousy.

Andrew's arms tensed in surprise, then pulled me tighter against his body as if he had misread my intentions. I moved to create space between us, but his arm held me in place. Gentle, but firm. The music slowed. I let out a frustrated breath and closed my eyes, listening to the cry of the violin over the harp trio. Andrew twirled me under one arm, then used his left hand to cup the small of my back and lower me in a long dip. His arms were strong, yet careful.

He leaned close and, in a low voice, said, "I have missed you."

I sighed and relaxed against his warm grip, breathing past the stench of cigarettes to the clean lingering scent of sage soap and powder on his exposed neck. I let his strong hands direct me to the music, leading me from one arm to the next. I caught myself grinning at how natural our movements came; my limbs acting on memories of years spent together spinning across ballrooms under our respective kingdom's skies. I met his eyes, and a ghost of the young man from my past flitted across his features.

I didn't want to hate Andrew. I had so many wonderful memories with him. Yet the thought of being more than friends felt wrong. Marriage meant responsibilities, both to the kingdom and other... marital *duties*. I could not imagine trying to force an intimate relationship with my ex-best friend. I did not see myself as the wife of a prince, whose purpose would be to bear his heirs. That was not the life I wanted.

For a moment, though, as Andrew's familiar hands led me across a ballroom floor we'd danced countless times together, I wondered if being held by a prince was something I could get used to. Despite Vestro being near me almost constantly throughout the day, this was different. This was... real. I leaned closer to him, enjoying his natural clean scent below the layer of alcohol and cigarettes. His smell brought back memories from childhood, of times when things were simpler and happier than courtship and demons.

I caught myself before I laid my head on his shoulder. That would most definitely send Andrew off the deep end with wrong signals. I couldn't let myself get too close if I wanted to maintain my steadfast choice to remain single.

Even though it feels good to just be held sometimes and to not...

Andrew's hand inched lower down my waist, snapping me back to the present.

No, I still hate him.

"Don't you ever give up?" I asked as he twirled me again under his arm.

He snuck in a quick kiss on my knuckles. A practiced, perfected move I assumed he had used on many women before me.

"I have never given up on a hunt," he said.

"So, that's all this is. A challenge." I leaned away. "You stink of smoke."

"Why do you have to be so damn difficult?" He furrowed his brow, the skin under his eyes tightening with frustration.

"*I'm* difficult because I refuse to play the part you've written for me?"

I could tell I'd derailed his confident plan to win me over. His gorgeous blue eyes studied me, a hint of confusion in their depths. As if he could not fathom why I would not want to be an ornament on his arm.

What a chauvinistic ass.

He gave a minute shake of his head. "This is the first time you have spoken to me in three years. You could at least attempt civility."

"This *is* me being polite."

"You could marry worse, you know." Andrew paused. "At least you know what to expect with me."

"Whoever decided I needed to marry at all?"

I jerked free and strode off the dance floor, leaving the prince speechless and standing alone. I spun away through a crowd of gawking women, trying to quickly lose myself before Andrew decided to follow.

I bumped into someone and nearly tripped. Strong hands caught my shoulders, the leathery roughness noticeable through the cloth of my dress, and jerked me upright.

"For reasons beyond me," the voice said, "you still manage to look beautiful in that ridiculous dress."

I spun around. Old Red stood with arms crossed. His leathery face wrinkled and cracked as he smiled, his eyes shining. I returned the smile with a laugh. I knew the old soldier could relate to how inelegant I felt at these silly gatherings.

He winked and motioned for me to follow. "Come on, I think we can sneak away for another lesson."

CHAPTER
FOUR

"One...down...two across, and three."

I sucked in air. Sweat trickled down my spine, and I rubbed furiously at a damp patch in the center of my chest. I shook my head and hefted the short sword with both hands. Usually, I could wield the lightweight blade with one arm, but after an hour of training and the energy spent on my adventure this afternoon, it took effort just to keep standing upright. I swung with all my might, balancing my feet with each swing and focusing on my breathing as Old Red chanted.

"One down...two across..." he grunted. "When you came to me and asked me to help you train, I never asked any questions. But I did tell you it wasn't going to be easy. So, get it done."

The sword tip lodged itself deep into the wooden dummy with a resounding *thunk*. I jerked back on the grip but only succeeded in nearly tearing my own arm off. I steadied myself, placed a foot on the wooden body near the blade, and pulled. I fell backward as the sword came loose. I landed hard on my backside, smacking my wrist painfully against the cold stone floor as I fought to hold onto my sword.

Old Red held out a hand, helping me to my feet. "Damn, girl. Why are you having such a hard time with the drills tonight?"

I grimaced and hurried to pat down my dress, glancing around the room as I caught my breath.

We trained in the west wing of Maurdruik's underground study, located below the kitchens and only a stone's throw away from the gate leading to the stables. He called it his *lab*, though I never quite understood why because I had not heard the word before. I assumed there was a personal significance—something Maurdruik always took into consideration with everything he did. The wizard had allowed Old Red to set up our training studio after my father had shut down our sessions in the yard with the rest of the troops.

Because, of course, it wasn't proper for a princess to know how to defend herself.

Though Old Red's training took our session much further than self-defense; he'd made it a point to teach me how to act on the offense and how to aim for killing blows.

The large, rectangular room had yellow walls and mounted oil lanterns that brightened the area into a suitable study. The irregular, rocky ceiling came low enough to give the room a cavern-like feel but high enough that I was never in danger of scraping against it, even when Old Red worked with me on using the spear.

Deeper into the room stood rows of tall bookcases meticulously filled with old manuscripts and scrolls. A long table lined the far back wall, laden with liquid-filled jars housing the remains of captured demonlings and square, metal cages holding various small animals. Mostly white mice.

The wizard sat at the giant L-shaped desk in the corner of the room. He liked watching me practice, as it seemed to entertain him, while he worked on whatever it was that wizards did. Besides blowing something up every so often while working on what he called *chemistry* or managing to breed a new line of hunting dogs, the only real magic I'd seen Maurdruik concoct was to get running water up to the top floors of the castle. Vestro proved the wizard's wards on the gates obviously didn't work, and Maurdruik left all entertainment to the court jesters. Despite my father's steadfast belief in Maurdruik's usefulness, I really wasn't quite sure of his purpose.

I determined long ago that having a wizard on the king's advisory board was just an unspoken requirement to owning a castle.

Maurdruik had stacks of yellow-paged books out open before him on the giant desk, and he leaned studiously over an extremely old scroll. Blaze, a feather-covered lizard the size of a small pony with bright orange wings and black talons, squatted behind the wizard's chair, his sinewy neck arched as he read over Maurdruik's shoulder. One of Maurdruik's earliest breeding experiments, the lizard had lived in Maurdruik's study for as long as I could remember. He seemed content like the wizard to stay cooped up underground amidst all the crinkled scrolls. He normally just ignored me when I came to visit.

Blaze glanced up at me as I walked closer to them, ruffled his feathers, and then went back to reading. Maurdruik pulled the scroll closer to himself so that I couldn't see what was on the parchment. He didn't spare me a glance as he trailed his finger down the page.

"Perhaps...the young lady has something else on her mind," he mused.

Old Red fingered the most recent nick in the wooden dummy. "That true, girl?"

I sighed as I walked over to scratch Blaze under his chin, my fingers brushing against the warmth of the firm layer of feathers. The creature clicked his tongue and tilted his head farther into my hand, the heat spreading from my fingertips up into my palm. I nodded, surprised at the unusual amount of attention Blaze allowed.

The old captain shook his head and lifted his left leg high to kick at the dummy, sending the wooden arms flailing in a wide circle. He frowned over at me, waiting.

I shrugged. "Why does my father insist on pushing Andrew onto me?" I said. "He knows I don't want to marry him."

"You know that you ought to be thinking of your future," Old Red said as he bent to gather up the large wood chips off the floor below the dummy. He bounced them in his hand as he approached us. "A stronger alliance with Riverwind is something that Damewood has been working toward for the past five years."

"I'm not just a pawn."

Maurdruik waved me away. "Don't accuse your father of such a thing."

"Your sisters have their eyes on Andrew," Old Red said. "Just like the rest of the damn western lands. He's good-looking, smart, and going to be king. You used to be friends. Do you really want to see one of your sisters with him?"

"It's *because* we were friends that I don't want to marry him!" I yelled. "Doesn't anyone understand that?"

"Marriage is not what we should be worrying about," Maurdruik said. "There's a more pressing matter that needs to be addressed."

The ominous tone in the magician's voice brought both of us about. His eyes flicked back and forth between us, the deep lines bordering them suddenly appearing heavier, older.

"With all the assassination attacks that have been occurring throughout the kingdoms," Maurdruik said, "I think that you, as captain, should put up an extra watch around the walls."

Old Red looked confused. "What does that have to do with Nadia?"

"You remember the tale of Cipher, don't you?"

"Tell me what that old relic has to do with the attacks," Old Red said, crossing his arms. "And why should we worry? It's been so long that I'm not even sure if the legends were true, or just a story to—"

The magician shook his head, his brow furrowed, and his nostrils flared. "They're not just stories, Captain."

"What is Cipher?" I asked, breaking in.

Maurdruik looked at me over his spectacles. His bushy eyebrows danced. He gave me a long, measuring stare before looking back down at his page. He turned the scroll far enough so that I could see.

The drawing showed a small, smooth device. A rectangle shape, a few inches long, and perhaps the width of my thumb. One end was flat and black, like glass: the rest gleamed steel gray. The body was seamless, its edges too precise to have been forged by hammer or spell. Fine lines ran along its surface, meeting in a circle at the center.

The image felt wrong. Cold and unnatural.

"It doesn't look very magical," I said.

Maurdruik's mouth twitched. "A gift from the faeries," he said carefully. "They forged it with knowledge beyond our age."

I blinked and leaned back, waiting for him to elaborate.

The wizard cleared his throat. "I suppose a short history lesson wouldn't hurt. Nearly three centuries ago, men reached into knowledge better left untouched. In their hunger, they loosed demons of smoke and steel. They attempted to play God and created... atrocities. Cities fell. People were chained. Desperate, King Theliem journeyed to Ferrington Pass and begged the faerie mists for aid."

He cleared his throat and adjusted his slipping spectacles.

His gaze flickered down, voice lowering. "And the faeries... answered. They gave him the Cipher. With it, he split the mountain and bound the demons away. Theliem burned the remnants from the land and swore an oath: every ninety-two years, the Cipher must return to the Pass to renew the seals. If not—" He paused, his tongue catching on the word before he corrected himself. "—the containment fails. And what was locked away...wakes."

"Are you talking about those metal beasts?" I asked, scrambling for the word. "*Machines.* But those aren't real. They're just old legends."

Maurdruik and Old Red exchanged glances, Old Red looking almost as curious as I felt. It seemed he wanted to know the answer as well.

Maurdruik hesitated, as if searching for the right words, something that I'd never seen him do. He wet his lips, thinking. "Demons," he said carefully. "Call them demons, Nadia. Monsters worse than anything you've fought."

I frowned at him. As far as prophecies went, the ninety-two years seemed a bit odd, and overall, the story a little weak. It didn't roll off the tongue as easily as some of the other children's tales I'd been taught growing up.

Maurdruik shook his head and glanced down at his book. His white beard bounced as he chewed on his upper lip, paying close attention to the little ball of skin where his lip dipped down in the center. Then he looked up and fixed me with a piercing stare.

Old Red scoffed. "And you're saying this Cipher is behind the attacks on the castles?"

"That is exactly what I'm saying." Maurdruik folded his hands, but the gesture trembled faintly. "The cycle has come again. Nineteen days from now, the stars align. If the oath is not renewed..." He trailed off, his eyes on the sketch as though it might come alive beneath his hand. "...everything they sealed away will return. I never paid much attention to it myself until now as I had lost track of time, not until these attacks on noble lines started popping up around the kingdom."

He paused dramatically. "Someone, or some*thing*, is trying to kill off the line before the magic can be replenished."

"So why now, after all of this time?" Old Red said, shaking his head. "Why would The Holy stir up trouble..."

The Holy was a quickly growing cult that had surfaced nearly a decade ago, beginning in Krill and quickly spreading throughout the five kingdoms. Apparently had been operating underground for years too far back for anyone to count. Their main purpose seemed to be to bring about change throughout the kingdoms through a "re-enlightenment of society" and reintroducing the "achievements of past times."

Whatever the hell that meant.

"The Holy are not the problem," Maurdruik snapped quickly, almost annoyed, as he turned the page, the crisp sound resonating through the otherwise silent chamber. "There's turmoil throughout the lands. Conspiracies against the rulers of the southern kingdoms, proving a danger to all within our borders. Krill has been building an army for the past four years, their forces now greater than the size of ours and Riverwind combined."

He paused and glanced at me. "It also happens that the pickings are slim for male heirs in the West Lands. Riverwind has only one son; Nadia's charming Prince Andrew."

"He's not my prince," I said quickly.

Maurdruik smiled but otherwise ignored me. "Farwind's prince died last year in a hunting accident. The young King Eldwild of Elk Plains is a little behind in reproducing as of right now, and his only son, Peter, is not quite fourteen."

"What about Calvin, of the eastern kingdom of Krill?" Old Red asked.

"He is still missing after eleven months," Maurdruik said. He closed his eyes and sighed, leaning back in his chair and rubbing his temple with a wrinkled hand. "And with no sign or word of his ship, we can only assume the worst. Which leaves us with our beautiful kingdom of Damewood, that has graciously given us three daughters."

"So, it could be any one of them."

"I don't know," the wizard said, irritated. "As the years passed, the seriousness of Cipher faded, and record keeping became... abysmal. And while it is still casually passed from kingdom to kingdom for the sake of tradition, there's no definite answer as to which of the four kingdoms ties directly to Theliem's line."

"Where is Cipher now?" I asked, unwilling to let him get off track.

Maurdruik went still. So still, it even seemed he'd stopped breathing. He looked up at me slowly through eyes that were suddenly guarded. He looked torn on whether he would answer.

"At Riverwind."

Andrew. Could he be the heir to Theliem? Did that mean that he was on the list of nobility to be attacked?

"Cipher needs to be taken back to the pass," Maurdruik said, tapping his fingers repeatedly on the desk. "I've already spoken with Riverwind's council to prepare."

"But the journey is long and difficult," Old Red countered. "Especially with your proposed timeline and under duress. You're taking quite a gamble with the prince's life."

"Well, someone has to do it," Maurdruik said, pushing his heavy robes up his arms to his elbows as he stood up. "It's a journey that…."

I slipped my right hand to the front of my sash belt. My fingers closed about the thin hilt of a small, steel dagger. The blade always worked wonders when fighting demons—and in my hand, it always seemed to make me feel better. I'd never seen Maurdruik agitated like this, and it upset me on a deep level. I jerked the dagger free of its binding and slammed the blade deep into the desk.

"I'll do it."

Both men jumped.

Maurdruik scowled and twisted his fingers through his rough beard. "You do realize this desk is over two hundred years old?"

"Where the hell did you pull that from?" Old Red asked. He glanced up and down at my dress with an approving grin. "Never mind. I don't think I want to know."

Maurdruik rolled up the scroll and pushed away from the table quickly, making his chair screech across the stone floor. "We are not discussing some childish adventure, Nadia."

"This is the chance that I've been waiting for to prove my worth to my kingdom. What all my training has been for!"

Maurdruik raised an eyebrow, leaning back slightly on his heels. "You are not to get involved."

I ground my teeth and stormed over to the locked wardrobe closet in the far corner of the room at the end of Maurdruik's bookcases.

They teach and equip me to fight demons, but when the time comes for me to help, they don't want me to.

I snatched the silver chain around my neck and lifted the charm up to the lock. It beeped and unlocked, and I jerked open the doors.

The suit of armor sat patiently, exactly as I had last left it. The flawless metal was polished so fine that I could see my reflection in the mirror-like surface. The unique suit appeared a little odd compared to most of the armor the other knights wore; the hinges and pleats moved smoothly and silently, without any of the screeching and clanking that surrounded the soldiers practicing in the yard. Metal clips and twistable knobs secured the armor to the front breastplate and arm brackets, allowing me to open the chest area and simply step into the armor and slide my arms and legs into position, rather than having to buckle individual pieces on and off.

The armor itself was light, lighter than any full suit of armor should have been, and built so that, even being a girl of my small size so I could easily walk and move around. Maurdruik said that it was the control harness that did it—the harness kept me somewhat suspended inside of the armor casing, so the armor itself did not rest on my shoulders. It allowed what he called "force-feedback" to respond to even the tiniest movements of my skin or muscles so that I didn't have to struggle under the weight. This somehow amplified my strength, endurance, and even my speed, making me into what I could only describe as a sort of super knight. Being short all my life, I really enjoyed the extra eight inches the suit gave me, even despite the constant, faint whirring noises that whispered in the joints each time I moved. It helped with the disguise, for no one would ever guess that a girl could be under all that armor.

I smiled and brushed my fingers across the helm. The front was shaped like that of a horse's head. The heavy bridge of a nose sloped down across the front where the vision slits were designed to look like a blaze down the animal's muzzle. Two metal spikes on the top near the front gave the appearance of ears. A row of thin, fan-like barbs ran from between the two ears and down the back, acting as a metallic mane. Maurdruik had made me the helmet after I'd announced that I'd found myself a new horse. In fact, Maurdruik hadn't asked many questions after I'd introduced him to Vestro and had redesigned the helmet less than a week later.

Almost instantly, the tightness in my chest lessened as the warmth from the suit spread through my arm and across my shoulders. I closed my eyes and breathed. I almost smelled the dust from Vestro's sweaty saddle and tasted rain at the back of my throat. I opened my eyes and snatched up the helmet. I pulled it over my head and spun back toward the two men.

"I can do it!" I said. "So, I can do my part to keep my kingdom safe."

My words came low and throaty; a male's voice, not mine. It sounded a little too deep for my liking and vibrated slightly inside the metal helm, but it worked well to fully round out my disguise as a knight.

I glared at Maurdruik through the grill as he shook his head. His reserved posture and failed opportunities to answer my questions made me think there was more to his story.

"Why not?" I said.

"That's the King's Guard's job." Maurdruik sighed. "Sometimes, I almost regret putting the voice device into that damn suit."

"Yeah," Old Red added. "It was nice when she was stuck inside the castle walls chasing chickens. Now she thinks that, because she can disguise herself, she can wander around the kingdom slaying dragons."

"I've proved my worth by slaying demons around the kingdom," I said through clenched teeth. "I can—"

"No." Maurdruik held up a hand. "Your courage and heart are heroic, yes, but you're not a knight, Princess. That armor Old Red and I crafted for you was designed as an outlet for your adventurous—"

"And destructive," the captain cut in.

"—Your *adventurous* attitude." Maurdruik shot Old Red a narrow-eyed look and continued. "While wearing that protective guise, you've slain minor demons and managed to save the lives of a few sheep. You do not know what it is we're up against. I can't allow you to endanger yourself trying to play the heroine."

The dismissive attitude stung. I'm sure I looked ridiculous

wearing the helmet with my pink dress, but now, I was too pissed to care. Too many times, I had been pushed to the side because I was a girl. A princess. While Old Red and Maurdruik were mostly supportive of my training, any discussion of altering codes to allow me to do anything with my honed skills was immediately shut down.

This conversation seemed to be going down the same dead-end road.

"You will stay inside, where it is safe."

"I just want to help," I said, hating the defeat and frustration cracking my voice.

"By the way," Old Red said suddenly. "Why weren't you wearing the armor today when you went outside the walls?"

I pursed my lips and shrugged. "My tutor had his eyes on me all afternoon. I ran out at the first chance I had and didn't have time to change."

"Hells, Nadia." He shook his head. "You don't realize the danger that waits outside these walls! If your cover is blown, Maurdruik and I will be—"

What did they think I was going to *do*? Go parading around, telling everyone what a good knight I was? They should have known I wouldn't risk it. I enjoyed my freedom much more than fame.

"I've kept it a secret for two years now!" I shouted.

Maurdruik slammed a fist on the desk, rattling the candlesticks and knocking over his quill and ink. I watched the black ink pool around the small glass bottle, then spread out across the beautifully carved wood like a demon shadow threatening to consume everything that came within its reach. I swallowed as the black ink moved about on the table, little appendages spreading through the different cracks in the wood.

"You start popping up around the castle more often in that damn suit to hunt the walls," Maurdruik snapped, "and sooner or later, you're going to get caught. What I did to that suit of yours has been a banned practice from the kingdoms for centuries. If someone found out..."

"There are bigger things going on than just you right now, Nadia," Old Red said quietly, turning his back on me and walking over to the bookcases. "Your armor is just one less thing we need to deal with right now. Keep it and yourself inside for now, or I'm going to have to change the lock on that closet."

I sighed and lifted the helmet off and set it down on Maurdruik's desk. There'd be no arguing with the two of them. No matter what I said, they wouldn't listen, and I didn't want to lose access to my armor. Maurdruik studied me carefully. Old Red yawned and leaned against the open linen closet. They were both as stubborn as brick walls.

"Fine." I slumped and crossed my arms. "I won't get involved."

I left them to it, exhaustion dragging at my bones as I made my way down the corridor.

A page hurried into my path, bowing low. "Your Highness. Prince Andrew requests a private audience before he departs for Riverwind. He asked that I fetch you at once."

My steps faltered. Of course. Another attempt. I could picture him waiting below, crown tipped just so, words rehearsed and burning on his tongue.

I rolled my eyes. "Tell His Highness the hour is ill-chosen. I will pay my respects the next time he visits."

The boy bowed again, relief plain in his eyes, and fled back the way he'd come. I lingered a moment, my pulse quick at the idea of what he might have been planning, before shaking my head. I was in no mood to suffer more courtly posturing tonight. Not from him, not from anyone.

When I slipped into my chambers, I didn't bother with the latch. The gown fell where I stepped free of it, and I slid beneath the coverlets with a sigh.

The hearth panel clicked. Vestro crossed the room in silence, with just the soft rustle of cloth betraying his presence. I heard the door latch fall into place, firm and certain, before his steps returned to the bedside.

The mattress dipped under his weight. I shifted toward him, pressing my forehead to his shoulder. His arm came around me, steady and familiar, drawing me closer until the tightness in my chest began to ease.

"Relax now," he murmured, low and sure. "The court's behind you."

A laugh, small and weary, slipped out of me. "Gods, I hate them all."

"I know," he said simply.

I breathed in, unclenching by degrees as the warmth of him steadied me. Here, in the quiet of his arms, I could finally let go.

CHAPTER
FIVE

The bells pulled me from sleep before dawn, their clangor rolling through the stone like thunder.

I sat up with a start. The alarm was never sounded except in emergencies. My hand reached instinctively to the bed beside me and found only cool sheets. Vestro had been gone for some time. Yet the faint smell of leather and wildflowers clung to the linens, an echo of him that made the emptiness sharper. Without his steady weight at my back, the chamber felt suddenly exposed.

Another toll split the silence, louder this time, and dread coiled low in my gut.

I threw off the coverlets, pulled on my robe, and was out of my room before my eyes had time to adjust to the candlelight in the hall. Soldiers ran full speed through the corridor, the clink of their chain mail vibrating across the marble tiles in the pauses between the deep, resonating booms of the massive warning bells. Frantic voices and snatches of rushed conversations echoed down the turns of the hall. Screams outside filtered in through the arrow slits high in the walls. The smell of smoke and burning oil seeped through the cracks in the stones. I realized the hall was unusually warm for this time of the morning. The smoke meant a fire nearby. My heart raced.

What was going on?

"Nadia!"

Old Red appeared out of the darkness, torch in one hand and a naked sword in the other. His mass of red hair disheveled and reflected the torchlight like a blazing sun in a starless sky. A wild look filled his eyes; frantic, frenzied. He sheathed his sword and grabbed my left arm.

I tried to hold my ground. "Red, what—"

"Get dressed," he hissed through his teeth, shoving me back into my room.

I stumbled backward and stared at him, my arm still smarting from where his fingers had dug in. The captain had never handled me in such a way.

"Now!" he yelled over the sounding bells as he stepped into the room and shut the door behind him, bolting it, muffling the cries in the hall outside.

I skipped any idea of modesty and quickly shucked out of my robe and pulled on a black tunic and gray pants. I added a vest and jacket and buttoned on my black cloak. I stepped into my boots when Old Red tossed a travel bag onto my bed beside my sword, and the smell of freshly oiled leather filled the room.

I froze. My blood rushed in my ears in rapid, deafening waves.

"What's going on?" My voice sounded tiny, like a scared little girl. I hated it, but that's exactly what I was.

Scared.

"The castle is under attack," he said. "Half the Guard is dead. They were caught sleeping in their bunks. They followed the messenger inside, hidden in the shadows as we opened the gates...."

"Red," I said, "what...what are you talking about? What messenger?"

"Demons," he said as ripped through my wardrobe closet and yanked out tunics and leggings, tossing them onto the bed. "They chased a messenger from Riverwind and slipped in as we opened the gates. Cipher..."

My breath came faster until I thought my chest would fail because I could not seem to get enough air. My skin stung as if a thousand hornets stabbed me again and again until there was nothing but numbness. I pursed my lips.

"Why was a messenger—"

Old Red spun on me, his eyes haunted.

"The King of Riverwind has been murdered."

I must have blanked out, the shock rendering me useless, because I came to and found myself sitting on the edge of my bed as Old Red tied my boots. His hands shook as he worked. I laid my hands on his shoulders, shoulders that suddenly seemed thin beneath his heavy tunic. For a moment, Old Red aged before my eyes, looking not like my strong weapons tutor but a man who had seen too much.

He forced an encouraging smile. "The magic in your armor will shield you from the demon's attacks," he said. "Short of drowning, it will protect you, so never take it off."

He reached up to wipe at the tears on my cheeks; his rough hand shook as he gently brushed my skin. I hadn't even realized I was crying.

"I love you like a daughter, Nadia." He turned away and swallowed, his throat tight. "I can't bear the thought of harm coming to you. I won't have you here when..." He stopped himself and looked away.

"Where's Father? Is he all right? What about Uriel and Uciel?"

"There's no time now, Nadia," he said. "You need to escape the castle. Cipher has been stolen. Prince—I mean, *King*—Andrew is leading a party to go after his father's killers and retrieve Cipher. He has sent an army to aid us. The support will be here before next sundown...." He trailed off, squaring his jaw.

My heart skipped a beat. Next sundown. Which meant nearly a full day before help arrived.

Nothing scared the seasoned captain. Yet the look in his eyes terrified me. I grabbed his face with both hands. His wrinkled skin felt feverishly hot.

"Sundown," I said. "Red, do you think...."

I couldn't finish my sentence; *would help arrive in time?*

Old Red hesitated and then shook his head. I leaned back from him, my body shaking. I covered my face with my hands and screamed as I slipped at the edge of the crevice waiting to swallow me whole. I felt my world shift, the security of the walls around me crumble and threaten to crush me beneath their massive weight.

He wrapped his arms around my shoulders and cradled me to his chest. I screamed into his tunic until I was sure my lungs would slide up and out of my mouth, and my chest would cave inward.

We could hold on for Andrew's help. Just a few hours more...

A few hours more, and everyone would be dead.

"Nadia," Old Red said softly, "you must leave, now. Quickly, use the passage to the kitchen and gather enough food for the journey and a few days more. I'm going to go harness the horses."

"Horses? Red, are you coming with me?"

He shook his head, regret clear on his face. "I need to stay here and protect your father. I'm sending two guards to accompany you to your cousins in Semptor." He paused. "Maurdruik left to meet Andrew at Farmer's Reach to explain how to use Cipher. Andrew must retrieve Cipher before the stars align. If not...then, God help us all."

He left. I almost tripped on the rug as I dove for my bags and hefted them over my shoulder. I wiped at my eyes and gripped my sword in my right hand as I pushed aside the wall tapestry beside the hearth. I ran my fingers against the warm stone, found the lever, and pressed. A small section of the wall swung back on a hinge, and I stared into darkness.

The screaming outside intensified, and the stones of the castle walls groaned under an invisible weight above, as if the whole structure would collapse at any moment. Ash drifted down through the arrow slots, thickening the air and blotting out whatever moonlight might have tried to peek through.

I ran.

I MADE it to the kitchen in record time. I had snuck out of my room with Vestro countless times over the years, so much that I quickly navigated the stone tunnel without hesitation even in pitch darkness. I emerged in the storage pantries behind barrels of flour and salted meat. I hurriedly stuffed a bag full of bread, cheese, and jerky, and two water skins before rushing out to the main hall. I made it outside to the covered walkway without issue and started toward the stables.

I passed a low window open to Maurdruik's lab and stopped. My heart beat so loud I could hear it clearly over the screams coming from outside. I turned back and forth on my heel, unsure.

I didn't want to go to the country. This was my home. I wanted to see my sisters…I wanted to hug my father, make sure he was all right. I was about to run away from the fight when my family was left with little protection, the promised help still miles away, and there was a good chance I'd never see any of them again. I shook my head to stop myself from crying again.

I didn't want to leave. I didn't want to run and leave everything I loved left to burn behind my back.

Andrew is leading a party to retrieve Cipher.

King Andrew.

I set my jaw. I was done being forced into a life I didn't want. Done being reactive to the forces pushing and pulling me on the waves of an ocean I never agreed to sail in the first place.

It was time for me to act.

Footsteps in the dark neared, and I turned left and ducked behind a wooden crate as a guard sprinted past me on his way toward the main gate. I unshouldered my travel bags and hid them behind the crate. I waited until his retreating footsteps had gone before pushing open the glass window to Maurdruik's lab and slipping through. A large, heavy oak table full of glass concoctions and sinister-looking vials waited below the window, and I carefully stepped down, the glasses trembling slightly as I shifted the table, and then jumped to the floor. I stood listening, ears straining, but the only sounds were the soft wisp of air blowing through the cracks in the stones and the constant drip from the ceiling in the far corner.

I stood up straight and looked around.

I had never been in this part of the wizard's lab before. The massive room seemed to stretch forever. The orange light of the fire glinted off ancient swords and shields mounted around the stone hearth, bearing the marks of rulers past, dating back centuries ago. Several long tables were situated in front of the fireplace, and the light touched along the left wall where there were rows of tall, metal cages and heavy wooden crates. I took a step back away from the cages as several pairs of yellow eyes turned toward me and reflected the meager light, staring silently.

"There must be something here of use," I whispered aloud.

The sound of my voice helped fill the uncanny void, though it did nothing to quell the uneasy feeling growing in my stomach as I started my search.

Oddities and trinkets covered the tables. Volumes of ancient books were stacked haphazardly across one edge, and loose pages torn and yellowed from age littered the floor. Dozens of half-used candle stubs burned between the many glass bottles of unknown colored liquids and powders.

The creature at the end of the table made me jump, until I realized the form was just a skeleton. The polished, white bones sparkled in the firelight, and it took me a moment to see what it was. A baby dragon. The bird-like bones seemed poised to strike, wings outstretched and neck coiled in anticipation. Tiny dagger-like teeth sat in double rows along the thin muzzle, and the hollow eye sockets seemed to stare back at me, sucking me in. I reached out a hand, wanting to touch the smooth surface of the skull.

Something smooth and wet brushed against my leg. I spun around, bumping into the table and knocking over a few bottles. Liquid spilled out of one bottle, and smoke hissed as it rose, and it ate its way through the metal tabletop, dripping to the floor. I searched the room frantically for any sign of movement. Something dragged itself across the floor. Sharp nails scratched against the stone.

My pulse raced. I backpedaled from the tables and ended up too close to the cages. A low growl made me spin on my heel and head toward the closest light. Three bounds brought me into the blue glow and froze me on the spot.

The wall of the lab turned into a sunken corner and with walls no longer stone but instead sheets of metal held in place by strange-looking nails. The blue light emanated from between the seams in the metal, casting everything in the small nook in pale cerulean. Air hummed through a strange square box mounted high on the wall just below the ceiling, sending down a cool draft that circulated the stuffiness characteristic of an underground lair. Large hooks embedded in the steel sheets held lengths of what looked like transparent vines. Small, square stands made of the same strange metal as the banquet tables outside were covered in tiny, colorful circles that blinked like stars, and several flat, round objects with numbers and rotating lines that ticked every second. Glass bottles and jars filled with bright liquids were situated over small, elevated flames and were connected to each other by miniature versions of the see-through vines on the walls.

I took a deep breath as I steadied myself, listening to the boiling liquids and faint beeps and clicks that permeated the air.

A rusted contraption leaned against the doorframe, built with what looked like two cart wheels—one in front of the other—and a small, padded stool on top. I touched the curved surface of the metal frame, surprised that the front wheel turned in tune with the upper handles. Pale ribbons dangled listlessly from the pink ends of the bars, a decomposing basket strapped to the front.

I looked away and took a step closer to a table holding ten box-like objects with glass fronts, each connected by black ropes to a large black rectangle with lots of knobs and tiny glowing red dots. Black and white paintings illuminated the faces of each box, and it took me a moment to realize that the images were different angles around the castle.

"Those are views of the gates..."

Are those...moving paintings coming from the wards?

I jumped as one of the views changed. I watched a guard run from one side of the image to stand in front of the gate, stop, yell something inaudible to some unseen person, then turn to run as an arrow lodged itself deep into his windpipe. The guard fell, and then a cloaked figure came into view. The figure shifted position as it neared the viewpoint of the small box—always keeping its face in shadow— then aimed its bow. The picture jumped and went black as the arrow collided with the ward. But not before I caught a glimpse of the attacker's bright, yellow eyes.

A demon.

I slowly backed out of the room.

A scream came from somewhere outside the window, and a loud crash on the floor above me brought me back to my senses.

Fuck this place.

Every inch of my body rose with goose flesh as I ran back to the open window. I held my breath as I bunched my legs and jumped up on the table, knocking over several of the small glasses.

I clawed at the window ledge as the table tipped over and managed to pull myself up and over the wall. My legs scraped against the rough wooden ledge as I fell through and landed on the stone walkway in a heap, my neck twisted against a crate and my legs over my head.

I startled as a member of the King's Guard came running around the corner from the direction of the kitchen. His gray attire wrapped him mostly in shadow. Only his face and naked sword stood out against the darkness. His face looked smooth and young; he was probably one of the new recruits who had joined the Guard a few months ago. He looked at me in surprise, his eyes blinking rapidly as he skidded to a halt. He shook his head and stepped forward.

"Princess," he said, "what are you doing out here?"

"I'm fine." I picked myself up and hefted my bags.

"You shouldn't be out here, Princess," he said, eyeing my bags and sword. "I'll escort you back inside—"

I turned and ran. The man yelled after me, and I heard him start to follow just as the glass window shattered and clattered across the stones. I pumped my legs faster to disappear around the corner. Something snarled in the darkness to my right; a rippling growl that cut through the dark and made the blood flow from scrapes on my legs. Yellow eyes flashed and grew as a large shadow leaped past me while I sprinted across the courtyard. The guard screamed behind me, but I didn't turn to see what had followed me out of the darkness.

It was time to leave.

CHAPTER
SIX

"Nadia!"

Old Red stepped out of the shadows just as I peeled into the main stable, holding a lantern and beckoning me to follow. Horses whinnied and kicked at their stall doors, and the stench of soiled hay hung thick in the smoky air. I followed Red's lantern through the stables to the back entrance. Black soot marred the outside of the small stable, and several falling embers licked at the ground near the bales of hay.

A saddled horse stood just visible in the dark to our right, and I rushed past Old Red toward the shadow.

Please be Vestro. Please.

A familiar snort sent a wave of relief rushing over me. I stumbled to a stop in front of Vestro, dropped my bags, and flung my arms around his thick neck. He bent his head down and nibbled at my hair with his lips. I cupped his velvet muzzle and kissed it. Vestro flattened his ears and danced to the side at the sound of approaching footsteps. I turned as Old Red came up behind me, set the lantern on the ground, and lifted a canvas tarp draped behind the bales of hay. My armor reflected the light of the lantern, waiting patiently for me.

I didn't speak as Red propped the armor up and helped me step inside. I fastened myself into the harness mounted inside the suit.

"Mount up," Old Red said, breaking my concentration.

I lifted a foot to the stirrup, slipped at the sound of a scream cutting through the darkness from the direction of the yard, and finally boosted up into the saddle with Old Red's help. Vestro stood strong as I landed onto his back, gripping his sides with my knees. He whinnied and turned his head to look at me, his pale eyes nearly glowing. I noticed that Old Red had put a real double-bit bridle on him. Vestro's tongue worked at the metal as he flapped his lips and flattened his ears.

Vestro seemed to want to leave almost as much as I didn't. His head bobbed, and his sharp hooves pawed at the earth. I had to pull on the reins to keep him from bolting as Old Red walked around us, checking the bags he had already loaded and tying on the two I'd brought. He pulled out a heavy pouch from beneath his cloak and stuffed it into my nearest saddlebag.

"Gold," he said. "Enough to help you on your way."

He reached into his tunic pocket and pulled out two flat, black squares the size of my thumb. He motioned for me to lean down. I bent as best I could as he stood on his toes to reach up around the neck of the breastplate. He fumbled with the edge for a moment, then slipped the small square into a thin slit in the metal lip of the armor, centered above the middle of my chest. I heard a small beeping sound as a tiny dot of red light flashed once, twice, and then remained lit. Then he grabbed hold of Vestro's bridle and slipped the second square into a slit on the side of one buckle. He pulled another black box out of his tunic, twisted a knob, and a red light flicked on as my suit beeped again. I looked down at the old captain and caught him staring. His face changed into a look of slight surprise as if he was seeing me for the first time. He nodded, satisfied.

"Hurry up and put your helmet on," he said as he started walking toward the gate, leading Vestro beside him.

I slipped the helm over my head and clicked the chinstrap into place. My vision blurred, and I lifted the faceplate to let in the fresh air. I blinked as everything turned fuzzy, jumped, and then cleared. I rushed to take the helmet off, but Old Red slapped my thigh.

"Leave it. Your vision will clear in a moment. The image takes a moment to settle."

"What?"

"It's part of your disguise. You'll need to show your face at some point while traveling; this is just a precaution, so no one recognizes you. Don't worry. It works with or without your helmet on, as long as you're wearing the suit, and for Vestro when he's wearing his bridle."

"His bridle..."

Vestro twisted his head around on cue so that I could see one side of his face. His eyes were dark brown, just like any other normal horse's eyes, not his regular pale, fleshy orbs. The image flickered once, twice, like a candle's flame in a breeze, giving me a quick glimpse of his demon eyes, then settled back to the soft brown. He blinked and tousled his mane.

Old Red glanced back at me as he hurried us faster, his eyebrows knotted. "Don't reveal your true name to anyone until you're safe at your cousins' manor."

A horse screamed to our left, and two guards rode around the back of the main stable, towing a third horse laden with camp supplies and bedrolls. They nodded at me and then at Old Red. My heart jumped as the reality of the situation sank in. Panic welled in my throat.

"Red...where's my father?" I asked.

Old Red lowered his eyes and turned away, busying himself with my bags. "Nadia...if the attackers found out that you'd escaped, they'd follow you—"

"But what is he going to think when he finds me missing?" I shrieked. "I can't go yet, not without saying goodbye...."

I moved to get down from the saddle, leaning back to throw a leg over the saddle. Old Red roughly jerked Vestro's bridle around so that I had to hold onto the saddle as the kelpie spun. The captain shook his head sternly, though in the lamplight, I saw tears in his eyes.

"Why do I have to go?" I screamed. "Maurdruik said they were looking for the heir to Theliem...."

Old Red rounded on me. "He didn't tell you the whole story, Nadia. I never thought he...." He shook his head. "It doesn't matter. You're not safe here. No one is."

Something whistled above our heads as it raced through the black night, and we looked up to see a flaming shooting star. Vestro reared and screamed as the star-like object fell from the sky and hit the edge of the stables. Wood and dirt exploded in all directions in a blaze of fire, arcing thirty feet into the sky. The ground shook with the impact, and Old Red struggled to keep his footing. He ran toward the sally port, the small secret escape gate hidden behind the stacked bales of hay, pulling Vestro along with him. A second star fell, smashing into the parapet and blowing a hole five times larger than any damage I've ever seen a trebuchet make. Rock and timber showered down on us as we reached the gate.

"What was that?" I screamed, my heart pounding. "What is happening?"

Old Red ignored me, grabbed Vestro's bridle, and brought the kelpie's face close to his own. "I know you love her as I do," he said, staring intently. "But I swear, if you let anything happen to her, Vestro, I will hunt you down until the day I die."

I hiccupped. *How long had he known? How long had he just sat back and watched, knowing...*

Old Red glanced at me and winked. "I raised you from just a pea shoot. Did you honestly think you could keep a secret like him from me?"

Vestro whinnied and tossed his head, his long mane moving in rippling waves down his neck in the darkness. He stared straight at the soldier and bowed his muzzle toward the ground. Old Red nodded and clapped him across the jaw, rubbing the sleek hair on his cheek.

I thought it would be a good time to try to escape. I started to slide my leg over the saddle when Old Red jerked again on the reins, and I scrambled to keep from falling as Vestro stepped sideways. The soldiers' horses behind us danced nervously. Old Red nodded to them before looking back at me.

"Don't trust anyone along the way, Nadia," he said. "Understand? *No one.* Not even—"

Another falling star cut across the black sky, illuminating the ground around us as it flew overhead toward the castle. It crashed into the guard tower above the kitchen, exploding stone and mortar with a thunderous boom that rocked the ground. A billow of fire rose into the sky, and several smaller explosions took out large chunks of the walls of the kitchen. I realized that the fires must have dropped down into Maurdruik's lab, reaching his vats of strange oils and powders. Stones as tall as myself tumbled down, crumbling and knocking against each other as they landed in a growing pile of clutter with sharp, crackling thumps.

Old Red slapped Vestro across the rump and yelled. "Don't let her off your back!"

Vestro reared on his hind legs with a scream and leaped forward. I looked back to see the light from the fires reflected off something glistening between the craggy lines of Old Red's face, and I barely heard his words as we galloped away.

"God speed, my princess."

I screamed as Vestro sped out through the gate. The soldiers rode on each side of me; their swords drawn and shields up. The clattering of the hooves became lost in the succession of booms emanating from the castle and the hundreds of terrified screams that followed. I howled with frustration as I jerked on the reins, but Vestro had taken the bit between his teeth and charged faster down the road toward the city below.

"Vestro, please," I cried. "I want to go back. I'll make sure Old Red doesn't do anything to you. Vestro!"

The screams coming from around the city only seemed to quicken his pace, so that his hooves only skimmed the cobblestones as he flew across the ground, and we steadily pulled ahead of my guardians. We sped through the market streets, passing figures in hooded, gold cloaks holding torches and setting fire to the guard shacks outside the gates, the bodies of guards lying in crumpled heaps at their feet.

Were these The Holy members?

The cloaked figures looked up as we neared, and several pulled out crossbows strapped across their backs. Vestro veered to the right and leaped over a rock wall at the twang of bowstrings. I glanced back over my shoulder as the guard on my left slumped and fell from the saddle, two arrows protruding from his side. The other guard yelled and spurred his horse on, screaming for me to get farther ahead.

The figures shouted behind us, pointing in our direction. Several pony-sized wolf demons appeared in the shadows beside the road, their yellow eyes glowing in the firelight, and they fell in pursuit of us. Their black, shaggy fur rippled with each bound they took, their wide jaws open, and dark tongues lolling between rows of crooked teeth longer than my hand. The demons growled low as they closed in and lashed out with curved claws, one creature going for my legs. My shiny armor glinted in the red firelight and screeched as it deflected their teeth. Behind me, the remaining soldier yelled as two demons leaped high and latched their claws onto his back, their long jaws ripping away the chain mail at his shoulders and tearing into his neck as they pulled him down from his screaming horse. I turned in the saddle, and watched his body disappear behind the bristling demons.

"No!" I screamed.

Was I supposed to do this alone?

Vestro snorted and galloped at an unnatural speed, losing the snarling demons in a cloud of dust as we tore southwest along the merchant road. I closed my eyes and bent over Vestro's back and held on as we ran. I lost track of time as he ran, his rhythmic gallop slowly calming my rapid heart. The cool wind dried my tears and cleared my head.

The demons had to be stopped. They couldn't be left to spread across the land. I gripped my knees against Vestro's back and leaned forward over his neck, urging him forward.

Besides, Andrew's timing always seemed to screw things up. He'd probably need a little help finding that damn key token, or whatever Cipher was.

"Go north," I yelled into Vestro's ear over the pounding of his hooves. I slapped his neck when he flipped his head and gave a quick buck. "You can keep running, but go north, please. Trust me, Ves."

Vestro slowed his pace, his ears flicking. He twisted his head around to look at me. I stared back at his eyes through my visor, still amazed at their change of color. Vestro whinnied and danced to the side before taking off again. He covered the ground with amazing speed as we headed away from the distant cacophony of screams.

VESTRO FINALLY STOPPED RUNNING two hours later. He'd managed to ignore my screams and pleas for him to stop or turn back, even when I'd tried slapping on his neck or jerking the reins to pull him about. He hadn't cared, but now, looking down at his poor bruised mouth, a pang of guilt poked at my side. I let the reins fall across his neck and let him have his head.

He slowed at the edge of a small apple orchard bordering the left side of the dusty road. The thick trees seemed especially black and crooked in the early dawn light, and the sounds of the night had hushed to give way to the silent stretch that came just before dawn. It was still dark enough so that there were a few demonlings scavenging about. I kept my sword in hand, though with Vestro by my side, they didn't dare come near.

I dismounted and unsaddled Vestro as quickly as I could, pulling off the blanket and bridle as well. His pale eyes returned as soon as the bridle was off, the magic fading. White lather speckled his sides, and his chest heaved as he coughed and immediately started to shift.

I usually didn't watch, and Vestro would normally hide behind a tree or at least give me some space before shifting. The sight of his changing reminded me that he wasn't human. Most times, I tried to ignore that fact, and usually, I was successful. But when I saw things like this...it brought the fear of childhood stories back in a rush that threatened to send me bolting.

Vestro's chest collapsed as if his lungs were sucking everything into nothing from the inside out. Bones popped as they shrunk and shifted position with wet, sucking sounds that sent chills up my spine each time they snapped. His sinewy neck thinned and short-ened, and his pointed ears rounded and slid to the sides of his head. He whinnied and reared up on his hind legs as his black hooves split apart with sickening snapping sounds into tanned, outstretched hands. His brown coat slid away under a layer of clear, slimy liquid that oozed from his pores, seeping in patches at first and then in a gurgling rush.

I cringed at his cry and quickly looked away, the sounds of his change crawling across my skin. Within moments, he had finished, and the orchard went silent once more. I pulled out a washcloth and, using my waterskin, wet it for him as he limped back toward me.

"Are you all right?" he asked, his voice thick and scratchy.

I stiffened. Then I nodded.

He stared at me a moment longer, then nodded when I did not offer more. "I just need to catch my breath."

He wiped at the clear slime on his face with a shaking hand and limped to the nearest apple tree. He collapsed into a half-sitting, half-reclining position with his back against the trunk, his eyes closed, and his chest heaving. I looked away from his naked form long enough to half-heartedly swing my sword at a tiny green-winged demon that fluttered a little too close to my exposed head. It shrieked and flew away, searching for darkness in the brightening sky.

I reached up, plucked a low-hanging apple, and tossed it to Vestro. He caught it without looking, half of it disappearing within seconds. He wiped juices from his chin and looked at me, his black eyes two dark pits in the dim light.

"So, why north?" he said.

"I'm going to join Andrew's hunting party."

Even in the darkness, I saw the color fade from Vestro's stoic face. The apple fell unnoticed from his limp hand, hit the ground with a muted thump, and rolled across the soft dirt. He shook his head.

"No," he said. "No way in hell."

"Vestro—"

"I'm taking you to your cousins, and we're to wait there until we get the word to move."

"They're not even my real cousins."

"Like it matters to me. We are going south to keep you safe. End of discussion."

"I am the princess here, and it's my life on the line!" I shouted at him. "I'm tired of people telling me what to do with my life! If you won't take me then I'll find another horse and go myself."

Vestro stared evenly, his face blank and guarded. His eyes swirled pale for a moment, then darkened back to black.

"As you wish, *Princess*," he hissed through his teeth, making that word sound as if he were spitting out a mouthful of poison.

I swallowed. My tongue felt thick in my mouth. I had sounded just like my commanding sisters, and I hated that. I didn't like throwing my title around—especially at Vestro. I felt a twinge of guilt and softened my tone.

"There is a key token that needs to be returned—"

"That dongle should have been destroyed!" he shouted at me,

folding his arms and crossing his ankles. "Then we wouldn't be having this problem!"

Dongle? I stood still, staring at him. I hadn't told him anything Maurdruik had said that night in his study.

"What do you know about Cipher?" I asked quietly, staring intently at his face. I could usually tell when Vestro was lying—his left eyelid twitched when he was concentrating on his words. For a demon, he wasn't very deceiving.

Vestro scratched at his neck and shrugged. "All demons know about Cipher. It's something that makes up our past. We...." He looked away. "Something we fear."

He shook his head, stood, and turned away. The muscles in his shoulders twitched as I squinted at his back.

"Please, Vestro. I need to do this. Who knows, maybe we can get to it before Andrew."

Vestro's head jerked in my direction. His face grew serious, a dark intensity in his eyes that I'd never seen before. "What did you say?"

"I said..." I paused as I stared at him, the fine hairs on the back of my neck rising to attention.

I peered at his twitching eyelid. I understood why it would only be natural for him to hate and fear something that had the potential of locking his kind away. Though I'd known Vestro long enough to realize he didn't care much for the rest of demonkind—even regularly helping me kill them on our hunts. So, I knew he would not do anything to jeopardize Andrew's mission in retrieving the key.

Right?

"I said that we need to do this," I finished slowly, my eyes never leaving him.

He stared at me for a long moment, as if weighing something. Then he sighed. "I know it's the adventure you've been dreaming about for years. Besides, it's not like I really have the option of letting you go off on your own. But the moment things get dangerous, I'm getting you out of there."

The knot in my chest loosened just a tad. I brushed aside the ill feeling I had at his sudden change in mood. Vestro was just like that sometimes—peevish, I mean, but I was usually able to talk him out of his bad moods. I pulled my helmet off as I reached for my water skin. An indecisive smirk fluttered across Vestro's face.

I froze. "What?"

Vestro reached out to touch my face, hesitated, then brushed his fingers across my cheek.

I jerked back and stared at him. "What?" I yelled. "Do I have something on my face?"

"No," Vestro chuckled. "You just have a new one."

"A new *what*?"

"A new face," he said, shrugging. "I just didn't know Maurdruik was going to use…"

I jerked away from him and dropped my helmet to the ground as I frantically pulled off my gauntlets and touched my face. My fingers rubbed against every inch of my skin, feeling my nose, lips, eyes, and cheeks. Everything felt the same. I glared up at Vestro.

"Don't worry," he said. "It's only a visual trick. Part of the disguise."

He bent and picked up my helmet to carefully inspect it. Then he turned his attention to my suit, his fingers carefully smoothing against my entire breastplate. His eyes blinked when he found the small slit in the collar. He cocked his head to the side and frowned, a little dimple forming between his eyebrows, and his lips scrunching together.

"What did Maurdruik do to your armor?"

"Old Red stuck a little black square in it while he was helping us out of the gate, and then he pushed something on this little black box." I held out my hands for the helmet, and Vestro gave it to me. "What does it do?"

"The little square in your suit projects…magic so that the image of a new face will overlay yours. The image copies your movements, your expressions, and your mouth as you talk. It only lasts while you're wearing the armor."

"Why do I need that?"

"Nobody trusts a man who won't show his face," Vestro said as he crossed over to where the saddle sat and searched through the bags. "If you're planning on trying to pass as a man, you're going to have to show your face sometime."

I covered my eyes with my hands and took a shuddering breath. I really wanted to help Andrew and Damewood, but I had not signed up to have my facial features disfigured. I heard Vestro sigh, then felt his warm hands over my wrists as he pulled my hands away.

"It's not permanent, Nadia," he said. He hesitated and then gave me a quick, chaste kiss on the lips. He grinned at my surprise. "Don't worry, you're still beautiful to me."

He handed me my helmet before heading behind the line of trees to shift. I took a breath and then looked into the mirror-like surface. My heart leaped into my throat at the black eyes that stared back at me.

It wasn't just any face that disguised mine.

It was Vestro's.

Vestro's wavy mane framed his sturdy jaw and brushed the collar of my armor. Solid black demon eyes blinked back at me from under furrowed eyebrows, and his wide mouth pulled back, revealing large, straight teeth as I readied myself for a scream.

I paused and held my breath. *Why would Maurdruik make me look like...*

Then it dawned on me: since the only two people besides me who knew of Vestro were Old Red and Maurdruik, it sort of made sense. Vestro would be able to double for me if anyone were to catch onto us while on our journey. It just seemed odd that Maurdruik hadn't given it to me earlier.

I touched a piece of my hair that fluttered outside of what seemed to be the reach of the disguise, breaking the magic. I reached down to the armor's belt and pulled out my dagger. If I were going to make this disguise work, I might as well go all the way. I squatted and propped my helmet so that I could see my reflection better. I grabbed a handful of hair, breathed deep, and cut. I watched as the fistful of brown locks fluttered silently to the earth. I wiped angrily at my stinging eyes and grabbed another handful. Then another.

Vestro trotted up to me, his coat still wet from the shift. He nuzzled my head and then snorted in surprise and nibbled at my short hair. I sighed and scratched under his chin and then slipped my helmet on.

I tried not to touch the goop on Vestro's coat as I settled first the blanket then the saddle across his back. I grimaced as a glob of slime dripped onto my gauntlet when I tightened the cinch. I wiped it on the grass as he bowed low for me to mount. He snorted, annoyed.

"Yeah, yeah," I said as I mounted. "You wouldn't like it either, if I dripped fluids all over you."

Vestro twisted his neck around just enough to give me a long, sideways stare from one fleshy eye behind heavy lids. His heavy lashes blinked slowly, as if in silent disagreement.

It was an odd look coming from a horse, and I sat straight in the saddle and gently kicked my heels in his sides. "Come on. Let's go find the new king."

CHAPTER
SEVEN

"I think that's them."

We stood in the concealment of the tall pines overlooking the dirt road, at a vantage point allowing us to see the approaching cloud of dust close to a mile away. The air hung still and hot, and a line of sweat trickled down my back below the layers of armor padding. I lifted my helmet's visor and wiped my face with a handkerchief, and the white cloth came away streaked in brown.

A faint sound of hooves rumbled toward us from the west. Moving fast.

I groaned and shifted position in the saddle. "How are you doing, Ves?"

Vestro dipped his head, and the muscles in his withers quivered. His horse equivalent to a shrug.

A large green fly with glowing red eyes hovered near Vestro's ear. He shook his head, whipping his mane in my face. I slid my visor back down in place.

"Come on," I said. "Let's go."

I steered Vestro out into the middle of the road to wait. The last thing I wanted to do was surprise a group of armed men as I came out of the trees.

Vestro swished his tail at the fly. The annoying thing was larger than any fly I'd seen before, with four round wings that rotated in a circular motion. I swatted at the bug as it flew past me. My gauntlet connected with a tiny ping.

"What the hell?" I mumbled, twisting around in the saddle, trying to locate the fly.

It sounded like I'd hit a pebble or a tiny ball of steel, not a fly. That swat should have killed it. My eyes searched the soft powder of the road; it was untouched save for Vestro's prints. It should have been on the ground somewhere. Yet the fly was nowhere to be found.

Strange...

"Ho, there!" someone called.

I jerked up straight in the saddle, trying to make myself as tall as possible. The men had come upon me as I was busy looking for the damn fly.

Stupid, Nadia. Stupid.

I drew a steadying breath and tightened my grip on the reins. Vestro lifted his head, ears pricked, chest swelling as if he, too, knew the moment demanded pride. Together we stood firm as the riders closed in, their hands drifting to their hilts.

I barely saw them. My eyes were fixed on the man at their head.

My breath caught.

I had half expected the polished prince in silks and gold trim, the Andrew I'd left behind at the castle. Instead, before me rode a king clad for war. Blackened steel encased his frame, each plate master-fully wrought and edged with gilt lines that flickered in the fading light. Broad pauldrons swept from his shoulders like a mantle of command, and the wide breastplate rose high to guard his chest and throat. Dust dulled the surface, but not the authority that radiated from him.

Andrew sat tall in the saddle, his hands steady on the reins as he pulled his black gelding to a halt, his men stopping in unison behind him. Blond hair clung to his temples beneath the slender crown, sweat carving pale rivulets through the dust of the road. His sharp and unyielding eyes swept past me, assessing the road, before finally settling on mine.

A frown tugged beneath my helmet. Dark circles hollowed his gaze, and weariness haunted his face in a way I had never seen. My chest ached, and it took every shred of will to not throw myself from Vestro and wrap my arms around him. Seeing Andrew made my flight from the castle shatteringly real: he might be one of the last familiar faces I would ever know.

The sight of him nearly broke me. For all I knew, my kingdom was gone, my family scattered, and here he was—close enough to touch, yet utterly beyond my reach. He didn't know me. Couldn't. To him, I was only another traveler in the dust, a stranger hidden behind steel.

Because he can't see me. Not really.

My vision blurred as I stared at his worn face, looking past the armor of authority. What I didn't need right now was a king. What I needed was a friend. Another solid piece of my life to hold onto before I fell apart.

I need you right now, Andrew.

I forced my breath even, clung to the reins until my knuckles ached, and kept my voice steady.

"Well met, King Andrew of Riverwind," I said, nodding with stiff composure, though my throat burned. "I am Sir Aidan, of Damewood. The princess sent me to aid you on your quest."

The word slipped out before I could catch it. Too late to pull it back.

The princess? My brain screamed. *I was supposed to say the king!*

Andrew's posture shifted, cautious. His eyes narrowed as they flicked to Vestro, recognition fluttering across his face. Of course, he'd seen me ride Vestro before; how many times had we gone on long afternoon rides together? Would the magic masking his eyes be enough?

"Show your face, Knight," Andrew said.

I sucked in my breath. I trusted Vestro's opinion that the masquerade would work, but I couldn't help my rapid heartbeat as I reached up and lifted my visor.

Andrew sat taller in his saddle and studied me a moment longer, then glanced again at Vestro before turning back. My pulse spiked, but when he nodded, I realized he had accepted my disguise.

"I thought I recognized your horse." His tone softened. "After the last few days, caution is a necessity. Allow me to make introductions."

He gestured to the rider at his right. "This is Captain Trea Redcrane of the Elk Plains, commander of the Home Guard."

I inclined my head. Everyone knew the name. Trea was a legend. For forty years he had patrolled the borders of the Elk Plains and not a single demon had breached their walls under his watch. His steady nod in return carried the weight of that reputation.

Andrew motioned next to his left.

"Prince Peter of the Elk Plains."

The young boy straightened in the saddle, his sandy hair catching the light, freckles scattered across a face far too young for war. He grinned at me with eager blue eyes, and I forced a polite nod.

He's only fourteen. Gods, he doesn't belong here.

I glanced at the others. Abernathy Groshi lingered behind, his pale features pinched and nervous. I remembered him from the ball, his sharp tongue in council chambers. I assumed the two men in woodland garb were trackers. And I recognized one of the three soldiers in Riverwind's black armor; Benjamin regularly accompanied Andrew during his visits to Damewood.

Andrew hesitated, his jaw tightening before he motioned behind him.

"...And Damien Bloodworth."

The name of the famous demon hunter was enough. The cloaked figure urged his stallion forward, silent until the hood fell back to reveal sharp features framed by silver hair. Vestro snorted and sidestepped, ears flat, and I fought to keep him steady. Damien's dark eyes—irises nearly as black as Vestro's—lingered on me with disquieting calm, as though weighing my worth.

Vestro whinnied and danced to the side, flattening his ears and turning his head away. I jerked the reins to force him still.

I shuddered. Damien didn't look like a man I'd want upset with me, or more especially with Vestro, and I decided that it would probably be best if I tried to stay clear. Demon hunters were known for their questionable methods of carrying out assignments, and there were more than a few stories of the man plowing his way through human bystanders to complete a kill.

What was Andrew doing traveling with such a shady character, anyway?

I forced myself still in the saddle as their gazes drifted over me, lingering on the horse-helmed armor. My face heated beneath the visor, but I locked my grip on the reins and willed my composure to hold.

"I...pleased to meet all of you," I said. I hesitated at the quizzical looks on their faces. *Shit, must have been the wrong thing to say...* "My lord, I'm ready to lend my services."

"How fares Damewood?" Andrew's expression sobered. "I sent assistance, but we have no way of receiving word."

The question hit like a blade to the ribs. I hesitated, then looked away as I forced the lie past my lips. "I left before the attack to intercept you. I do not know how they fare now."

"And Na—" he cleared his throat. "—the royal family?"

My eyes shot back to Andrew as his formal facade slipped. I searched his features for sincerity. He stared at me as if he could find his answer somehow in my face. I tried not to stare as he leaned forward in the saddle and seemed to hang onto my every word.

He doesn't know of the smoke, the screams... or the way the sky itself fell...

"Damewood is strong. It would not fall easily."

Andrew's eyes lingered on me a moment longer. "I am sorry for what you have had to leave behind. Damewood has always stood strong—I trust it still does." Then his shoulders squared, and his features closed over, the cold armor of command restored.

I kept my expression composed, though inside his words twisted the knife. His confidence in Damewood, in my father and their men, almost made me believe it myself. Almost.

Andrew brushed his hair back from his face and repositioned his crown; a nervous gesture, out of place on his otherwise commanding frame. He looked over his shoulder at his men, then gave a sharp wave. "We cannot waste the day. Let us be off."

Andrew dug his heels into the horse's side, and the animal reared up with a scream and lunged forward into a gallop. The other men followed quickly on his heels, the pounding of hooves sending billowy clouds of dust high into the afternoon sun.

I sat in the haze, Vestro quivering beneath me. Damien had not moved; his eyes fixed on my armor. Only when the others were gone did he tug his hood back up and direct his horse away without a word.

"You ready for this?" I whispered, patting Vestro's neck.

He shook his head, ears pinned flat.

I sighed. "Me either."

I nudged him into a gallop, following the fading thunder of hooves into the dust.

CHAPTER
EIGHT

We made good time on our first day.

At least I thought we did, considering we'd traveled non-stop since I joined the group and had passed the farmlands that marked the edge of my kingdom and on toward the dividing line between the kingdoms of southern Farwind and northern Elk Plains.

The edge of the Western Lands.

When I was little, I used to go on weekend trips with my dad to the western borderlands of Damewood toward Riverwind to meet with the outlying towns' council members. It would take our caravan nearly a day and a half to reach the farthest ranch. Today, we'd made the same distance in about a third of that time.

Yet as we pulled into the wooden gates of Farmer's Reach for the evening, a quiet little town of farmers and local merchants, half-hidden by groves of oak and cherry trees, Andrew's first words were not of relief but impatience.

"Tomorrow, we ride at dawn," he said. The words came out clipped, precise, sharper than they needed to be.

Not the easygoing Andrew I knew, but the one who liked to sound like a king.

His jaw worked as his gaze swept the road, the villagers, even the shadows clinging to the gateposts. He tugged his reins once, too tight, then lifted a hand toward the crown gleaming on his head. His fingers lingered at the rim, tightening before he finally slid it free. For a moment, he just held it, thumb brushing the metal, as though he hated the idea of tucking it away. Then he slipped it into his saddlebag. His shoulders stayed stiff, but the restless flicker in him eased once it was hidden.

I bit the inside of my cheek to keep from smirking. He acted like hiding the thing was the greatest tragedy of the evening, when really it was the most sensible thing he had done all day. We didn't need the extra attention.

"We have already lost more time than I care to admit. Mauve will not wait on us. If we delay, others may move faster."

I nudged Vestro forward until I rode abreast of him. "How much do you know about Cipher?" I asked quietly. "What—"

"Not here." His tone snapped back to the familiar Andrew, rougher and surer of itself. His gaze flicked to the watchtowers above the gate. "Wait until we are inside."

I nodded and held back as Andrew took the lead. We followed him to the Dragon Slayer, which, he explained, was the nicest—and of course most expensive—inn in town. I had to agree. At least, considering the overall rustic feel of the rest of the old farming town. Most of the other buildings were simple: stained timber and wood shutters, dark roofs aged from sun exposure, and water damage. The Dragon Slayer looked like it had been remodeled and recently repainted with bright yellow and blue trim. Large, orange flower pots sat near the front doors. Crimson drapes showed from every window, and music and laughter poured out of the massive double doors. An awful color combination, but a welcome sight after a full day of traveling in clouds of brown dust.

I frowned as we went into the stables and dismounted. Even the stalls were painted to match the festive exterior of the inn. As if it really made a difference to the horses. I felt my coin purse and shook my head. The bag of gold Old Red had given me was large, but it wouldn't last long if Andrew kept indulging his rich tastes.

"Settle yourselves, gentlemen," Andrew said as we led our horses into their assigned stalls. "I'll go in and make arrangements for the night."

I sighed, relieved, and stuffed my coin purse back into my bag. I slipped my saddle off Vestro, leaving the bridle on, and wiped him down with a wet cloth, followed by the currycomb. I took my time, trying to keep an eye on the other men as they left one by one.

"You haven't traveled with a squire?"

I turned my head quickly. Peter's freckled face peered over the stall door at me, his left arm leaning on the wood, helping him stay balanced on what I assumed was tiptoe. I'd only met Peter a few times before, the last being a year and a half ago at the annual Gathering of the Western Kingdoms, and he hadn't changed much since. It had been hard to tell with him on horseback, but it seemed he was still about my height, which was very short for a boy his age. Hopefully, for him, he'd hit a growth spurt soon.

I set the comb down and straightened. I patted Vestro's jaw when he nudged me; he wanted the bridle off, but he would just have to wait. He snorted when I ignored him.

"I like to take care of my horse myself," I said. I wasn't sure what else to say when he didn't move. "Don't you have anything you need to tend to?"

"I do things on my own schedule," he said. "I'm a prince, remember? I'll eventually get around to it."

"Well, I don't have all night," I said, getting a little annoyed. I didn't want to be mean, but I wanted out of the armor.

"Your horse looks familiar."

"Does he?"

"Yes. I'm sure I've seen him before."

"I'd like to finish up here."

"I'm not stopping you," he said, staring at Vestro. He frowned, his face scrunched up as if he was trying to remember something. "I've never seen a knight tend to his horse while still in full armor."

"Mind your business!" I snapped. The horse-helmed cuirass clicked at its hidden pivots as I rounded to face him.

I hadn't meant to shout, but his line of questioning worried me, and I didn't like how he stared at Vestro.

He jumped, startled, and then nodded. "Knight," he said quickly, turning away.

I watched over the stall door as he followed Trea out to make sure he was gone. Vestro bumped me from behind with his nose.

I elbowed him back. "Don't start."

I turned and unbuckled his bridle and slipped it over his ears and off his nose. Vestro worked his sore mouth as the disguise faded over his eyes. He blinked his pale, fleshy eyes at me and nickered happily.

I put the comb away and hefted my saddlebags. "I'm going inside. I need to listen in on Andrew as he explains our plans. Your clothes are here by your saddle. I'll leave my window open for you, all right?"

Vestro snorted and bobbed his head. I smiled and patted his neck on my way out. I tried to latch the stall door behind me, though it took me several tries with my gauntlet on before it finally clicked into place. Vestro whinnied and flipped his mane, clearly amused.

I glared at him over my shoulder, then realized I had my helmet on. I halted mid-step and turned, raising my visor. I furrowed my brow again, scrunched up my nose, and stuck out my tongue before continuing.

Vestro's whinnies followed me out across the straw-covered entrance and onto the cobblestone pathway.

～

I FOUND the others waiting at the inn's entrance. Andrew looked up as he finished off an almost depleted cigarette, the glowing tip reflecting in his obsidian armor. I hung back at the edge of the circle, not wanting to give the men a chance to closely inspect my armor. I stood, feet braced and as strong as possible, despite my thighs and lower back aching from the long day's ride. I must have swayed at some point because Andrew paused and stared at me, the cigarette at his lips, and his brow furrowed with something between curiosity and disdain.

An old innkeeper in a tailored serving suit finally arrived and led us upstairs into a private, candle-lit meeting room. I caught myself squirming as the aroma of roasted chicken and herb-seasoned potatoes wafted up through the floorboards. The muffled laughter downstairs seemed out of place as we stood waiting while Andrew paid the man and bolted the door.

In the shadowy light, it seemed as if Andrew had gained new lines around his bright eyes, aging his face by what could have been a handful of hard-lived years. Andrew dropped his gauntlets on the table and raked a hand through his hair and then removed the dust-caked crown from his pack. He glanced down at the thin circle of gold in his hands, frowned, and placed it back on his head. It tilted a bit to the right, his father's circlet just a tad too large.

Something stirred in the shadows at the far end of the room. I jumped with the others, hand flying to my sword—everyone except Andrew, who only nodded. A cloaked figure stepped forward, his layered robes catching the candlelight. My heart leaped.

Maurdruik.

Relief flooded me. For one dizzy second, I almost blurted his name, thrilled to see another piece of home. *Yes! I forgot he was meeting Andrew here!*

Then Maurdruik pushed back his hood, and I saw his glowering face as it stared right at me.

He was pissed.

...Shit. I forgot he was meeting Andrew here.

Our eyes locked. His jaw clenched, beard bristling as his eyes pinned me with a hard, unblinking glare.

Of course. I'd survive demons and assassins just to get killed by a lecture.

"This is Maurdruik," Andrew said. "The high wizard of Damewood." He turned to me. "I am sure the two of you know of each other?"

I shrank inside my armor, feeling small and exposed.

"Indeed," the wizard said after a moment. "Knight."

I let out a slow, long sigh, doing my best to stay inconspicuous.

Andrew continued, his voice low and steady, "Maurdruik is here to lend insight into the task ahead." He scanned the circle of men, lips pressed thin. "It is unfortunate circumstances that bring us together, but we stand here because we must."

Silence. Shifting feet.

"We are here to save what is left of our kingdoms," Andrew went on. "Riverwind, Elk Plains, and Damewood. Attacks on royalty have spread like plague. Damewood is under siege. My own kingdom buries a king as we speak..." he hesitated, jaw tight. "Without me." His glance slid to Maurdruik, almost inviting him to take over.

Corbin, Andrew's squire, appeared at his elbow and offered him a cup of wine. Andrew took it quickly, spilling several drops on the table before lifting the cup to his lips.

The wizard cleared his throat. "A key token was stolen from Riverwind's treasure room last night. This is no trinket. It's a talisman of power."

My mind drifted to the drawing from Maurdruik's desk. The hard lines, the tiny slits and knobs.

"...Cipher must be brought to the Pass to reactivate the seal," Maurdruik continued, "If we fail, the demons consume us all."

"Do you know who's behind it?" I asked.

Andrew exhaled hard. "The Key hasn't been spoken of in years, but The Holy has always wanted it. Reports from my walls tie them to the assassinations."

"It's not The Holy," Maurdruik cut in. "Not this time."

"How do you know?" I pressed.

Maurdruik's glare told me to shut my mouth. My stomach tightened.

Andrew's hand twitched toward his crown before he forced it down to his side, shoulders squaring as if nothing had slipped. "Those zealots have been parading in gold cloaks, shouting that a 'new way of life' is coming for the past six months. Are you saying the timing is not suspicious?" His jaw tightened, the muscle flicking once before settling.

I knew that twitch—his temper pressing to get out. He was fighting it. *Barely.*

Trea stepped in. "We've heard the same in the south. Strange talk of something called a *reboot*. Still..." He shook his head. "If not The Holy, then who?"

"Demons," Maurdruik said flatly.

Andrew scoffed. "Demons? You are saying the beasts are organized enough to take down trained guards?"

"That's exactly what I'm saying," Maurdruik shot back. "They're not all mindless livestock-slaughtering beasts. Some are clever. Dangerous."

Andrew shook his head. "Then they have help. We saw men in cloaks outside the castle—"

"Those weren't men."

All heads turned to the demon hunter, leaning casually against the wall nearest the door. Damien reached into one of the pockets and pulled out a thin red object about four inches long. He placed his thumb over a round bump on its handle and pressed. A blade flicked open and locked in place with a tiny click. He began to clean under his fingernails.

I stared at Damien's hands as he worked with the strange knife, noticing for the first time the many crisscrossed scars across his fingers and knuckles, slightly visible in the dim light.

"They were demons," Damien's soft voice almost sounded bored. "The Holy gave them their brains. That's on them."

Maurdruik bristled. "Nonsense. The Holy has nothing to do with this!"

Andrew's hand flexed against the table, knuckles whitening before he forced it flat again. Corbin refilled his cup.

Damien didn't bother to look up. "Without The Holy's meddling, the demons would still be dumb beasts. They made them smarter, meaner. And now here we are." He clicked the blade shut. "Not that I mind. Pays my bills."

Andrew slammed his hand on the table. "Enough! Which is it? Holy plots or demon hordes? Somebody give me a straight fucking answer!"

Damien's eyes slid to Maurdruik, who glared right back. The hunter smirked, reopening his knife.

Abernathy cleared his throat, voice thin but eager to redirect. "If the Holy aren't guilty, then we're left with one clear enemy. Better to stop wringing our hands and choose."

Andrew's teeth clicked together, jaw working as though he bit back words.

Maurdruik's gaze hardened. "He's right about one thing; the demons will not stop. The more that live, the more kingdoms burn. Leaving them be is no choice at all."

Andrew slammed his palm on the table, the crack echoing through the room. His other hand drifted to the crown, fingertips pressing it as though to hold the weight in place. "Do not talk to me about choosing evils. My father was just murdered in his own bedchamber. The kingdoms ignored the growing threat, and now demons walk our streets. That ends now."

Silence gripped the circle. Peter had gone pale, shoulders hunched as if he wished himself smaller. Trea stood solid, jaw locked, but his eyes flicked once toward Andrew in quiet measure. Maurdruik gave no sign at all, though the faint glimmer in his eye told me he'd steered the conversation exactly where he wanted.

And Damien only smirked, as if watching a fire he'd seen burn before.

I pressed my lips together in a tight line. For a moment, I almost believed Andrew's fury was enough to carry us all forward. Until I remembered how easily Maurdruik and Abernathy had led him to it. Andrew's anger filled the silence, but the satisfied look in Maurdruik's eyes unsettled me most.

What in the seven hells is going on?

Trea's voice sounded weary. "Then what do you propose?"

Andrew's jaw was still tight when he spoke. "We're after a group of demons that have Cipher. Why stop with just those few? We could reinstate the bounties and set every hand with a pitchfork in the kingdom against them."

The words punched through me, sharp and cold. If he meant every demon, then he meant Vestro, too. I clenched my jaw and kept still, though my stomach turned.

Trea's voice cut in, calm but weighted. "With respect, Sire, bounties breed recklessness. Farmers with pitchforks are no match for demons. You'd be sending those men to their deaths."

For a moment, Andrew's eyes flicked to the captain, the hard line of his mouth wavering as if reason had found a crack. I held my breath, willing Andrew to hear it—only to feel the hope slip when his gaze hardened again.

Maurdruik's voice rumbled in, just a shade too quick. "Enough. Save your schemes for another day. Cipher is all that matters now. When you recover it, you must take it to Ferrington Pass. There's a spire at the center. The Token must be inserted and turned to activate." He hesitated, eyes looking to the ceiling as if trying to recall a memory. "Clockwise—yes, clockwise."

I stared at him, baffled. Judging by the faces around me, I wasn't the only one. Only Damien seemed unmoved, as if he'd heard it all before.

Maurdruik cleared his throat. "That will reactivate the seal. Without it, the demons spread unchecked."

Andrew nodded. "Then we push hard. We know where they are headed, so we ride that way and intercept them."

Damien finally stirred. "That's hardly a plan."

Andrew drew a sharp breath through his nose, jaw tight as if he'd swallowed something bitter. For a heartbeat, he seemed at a loss. "We do not have much of one," he admitted, his voice rough. "But we know where they are headed, and we will ride to cut them off. We kept our number small to stay fast and unseen. That also means fewer swords when the time comes."

Silence. No one moved.

I let my gaze travel the circle. Peter's boyish face was sober. Trea's jaw was locked in resolve. Abernathy's expression pinched, hiding something behind a polite mask. Damien leaned against the wall, unreadable as ever. Maurdruik's eyes burned into me, promising a private reckoning later.

"It has been a long day," Andrew said. "Here are your room keys." He passed them around, handing me an iron key with an engraved number seven. "We ride at first light."

Chairs scraped as the men rose. One by one, they filed out until only Damien, Maurdruik, and I remained. Andrew lingered near the table, fingers tapping once against the wood before he caught himself and straightened, forcing a solid stance.

Damien gave a grunt, pulled his hood up, and stalked out without a word. Maurdruik's robes brushed past as he walked toward the door, but Andrew halted him.

"Maurdruik. The royal family...are they safe?"

"You mean the princess?"

Andrew's throat bobbed. "Yes."

Maurdruik's eyes flicked my way, then back to Andrew. "She was sent out with an escort when the fighting broke out. To family in the countryside."

Andrew's shoulders eased, just slightly. The harsh lines of his face softened, and for the first time all evening, he looked young. Tired. Alone. His hand lifted, brushing the edge of his crown as if to steady it—though it sat straight. His lips parted as if to say more, but he shut them again, jaw working. He gave Maurdruik a brief nod and turned toward the door.

Our eyes met as he passed me. He held them for a breath, long enough that I felt the weight of something he wouldn't say—then the king mask slipped back into place. His crown gleamed as he squared his shoulders and strode away.

Maurdruik shut the door behind Andrew and rounded on me, his colorful robes flaring.

"What in the hell do you think you're doing here?" he snapped, his voice sharp enough to cut. "Do you realize the danger you've put yourself in?"

"I just want to help!"

"Where are the guards Old Red sent with you?"

I pulled off my helmet, heat pressing against my temples. "They're dead," I whispered. "The demons took them when we tried to escape. They never even made it past the city gates." My voice cracked more than I wanted.

Maurdruik's scowl faltered. He stared hard, his jaw working. Then softer, "Nadia..."

"How's Father? My sisters?" The words rushed out before I could stop them. "Are they—are they alive?"

For a long moment, he only stared at me, beard twitching as he tugged at it. Finally, he exhaled, and the fire in his eyes dimmed. He opened his arms, and even in full armor I nearly collapsed against him.

"I don't know," he murmured into my hair. His hand brushed my cheek, thumb catching a tear I hadn't noticed. "I left before... Gods, I'm just glad you're safe. I was so worried."

I pressed my face against his chest, breathing in the familiar smell of herbs and old parchment. For a moment I was a child again, clutching to him for safety. I realized absently what an odd sight we would have been had someone barged back into the room.

But for a moment, I really didn't care.

Then Maurdruik pushed me back at arm's length and felt the top and sides of my head. He raised a bushy eyebrow. "What did you do to your hair?"

"I cut it. I thought it would help with the disguise."

"It does. Keeps the hologram from being disturbed..." He gave me an approving look, then the leathery skin of his angular face tightened as he sucked in his breath. "Though it doesn't matter," he said. "You're coming with me in the morning."

"What?" My voice cracked again. "But Andrew—"

"It will be simple enough. The road is no place for an old wizard to travel alone, and I'll need an escort. No one will challenge it."

"You're going back to the castle?"

"No. But I'll take you somewhere safe. Away from here."

"I'm not leaving," I snapped.

Maurdruik's hand came up, silencing me. His gaze bore into mine, stern and immovable. "I could expose you here and now if that's what it takes."

Tears burned at the back of my throat.

He saw it, and his expression softened a fraction. "I only want to keep you safe, child. Please. Understand that." He paused and gently touched my face. "Go get some sleep. Stay in your room until I come for you. We'll leave after the others so there's no questions."

I nodded, slowly turned, and sauntered out of the room. I didn't have an argument ready, so I didn't say anything at all. Maurdruik shut the door behind us and then went left toward the opposite end of the hall. I watched him over my shoulder—through a wet blur— as he disappeared around the corner.

I stuck my key in the brass lock and fumbled with the knob, my gauntlet screeching across the metal. I winced and finally managed to open the door. I looked down. I'd left a few long scratches across the painted handle. I stepped into the room and shut the door behind me, locked it and flipped the dead bolt in place.

The room felt small. The full-sized bed in the center took up most of the floor, the little bit of remaining space filled with a tall wardrobe cabinet and a single chair shoved in the corner. A lit candle flickered atop the bedside table, reflecting off the hanging mirror. A small, open window trimmed in light-blue paint to the side of the mirror was bordered by heavy crimson drapes that moved occasionally, rustled by the slight breeze. I assumed the second door on the far back wall led to a private bath.

I leaned against the door, trying to build up the strength to strip off the armor.

I'd been so close—so close to being part of this quest. Now Maurdruik is going to tear it from my fingers.

A trickle of sweat down my lower back settled it. I leaned against the door a long moment, then began unfastening the clasps. Piece by piece the steel dropped to the floor with sharp clanks, each one loosening my body but tightening the knot in my chest. Sweat clung to my skin, the stink of Vestro's horse and dust wrapping me like a shroud.

I hobbled past the bed over to the second door and opened it and immediately knew why this inn was rated best in town.

The separate bath area with detached garderobe looked about the same size as the bedchamber. Light stone flooring led up two steps into a massive white-porcelain tub so big that four people could have lounged comfortably in it. Candles cast warm reflections of light across the steaming surface of the water and earth-tone walls. I took a deep breath. The light yet full scent of vanilla wafted up from the steaming water of the filled bath. I hurriedly stripped off my clothes and was about to bound into the tub when I remembered my armor. I growled and balled my hands into fists. It just wasn't fair.

I yanked one of the folded, embroidered towels off the hook behind the garderobe door, scampered back to my room, and did a quick wipe-down of my gear. I didn't get into all the grooves, and there were swashes of dust that I missed, but I wasn't about to take time to go back over all of it. I shrugged. It was just going to get dirty again tomorrow, right?

Old Red would have made me finish until it shone.

I paused, rolling my tongue across the back of my teeth. I played with the soft cloth between my fingers—now stained brown instead of peach—then looked to the ceiling, blinking until the blur of tears sharpened back into candlelight. I took a deep breath and methodically went over each piece of armor until it shone like new. I smiled.

Old Red would be proud.

CHAPTER
NINE

I sank down in the water until only my eyes showed. The water burned; it was almost too hot to handle. Yet I didn't dare move, as it felt wonderful against my muscles and released the tension in my neck. I glanced at my rippling reflection in the now-murky water, glad to be able to see my face—not the false image of Vestro's—staring back at me.

For a heartbeat, I didn't recognize myself. Pale, hollow-eyed, older than I remembered.

A stranger.

My throat suddenly tightened. I pressed a hand over my mouth, but it didn't stop the sob that tore loose. Hot tears spilled into the water, mixing with the steam until I couldn't tell where one ended and the other began. My shoulders shook, and I curled forward in the tub, trying to hold myself together as everything I'd held back since Damewood came crashing over me. The smoke, the screams, the sky falling, my family scattered, Maurdruik's hard eyes, Andrew's grief.

I gasped, dragging in air thick with steam, and let it out in a broken sound I didn't recognize as my own.

For the first time since fleeing the castle, I let myself cry.

THE WATER HAD COOLED to a tepid blanket, but I stayed, too weary to move. My skin had puckered, my eyes swollen and chest sore from crying, and the candlelight had blurred into gold smudges against the stone.

The faint sound of wood scraping stone stirred me. I tensed at the whisper of hinges and felt the cool night air spill through the open window. My breath caught until the soft rhythm of the steps reached me. I recognized the bare footfalls; soft, steady, deliberate.

Vestro.

I sunk lower in the water but didn't bother to cover myself.

The quiet footfalls stopped behind me. For a moment, there was only the hush of the cooling bath and the slow thud of my heart.

I felt him there, waiting.

"Ves," I whispered. Just his name.

A whisper of cloth moved behind me, and warmth settled across my shoulders as Vestro's arms slipped gently around me. Strong, steady, and wordless. He didn't ask what was wrong. He didn't need to.

I let my head fall back against his warm chest, the weight of the day spilling out in a shuddered breath.

"You're going to get your clothes wet," I whispered.

He let out a short snort. As if my even mentioning it was ridiculous.

My hands floated uselessly until he caught one and lifted it free of the water. His thumb traced slow circles into my palm, kneading away the stiffness he already knew was there. Heat spiraled out from his touch. A sob shuddered through me at the simple tenderness of it. Gods, I hadn't realized how badly I needed someone to just... hold me.

He reached for the sponge, dipping it into the water until rivulets cascaded down his wrist, then drew it over my arm in languid strokes. Warmth slid over my skin, following the sponge's trail as he passed across my shoulder, then grazed my collarbone.

His hand paused there.

Not pulling away. Waiting.

I didn't move, so he continued.

His motions were unhurried, almost reverent; he had long ago learned how to piece me back together whenever I fell apart.

But not like this. This... this was new.

I closed my eyes and relaxed against his touch. The line between care and something deeper blurred, not from habit, but from the simple fact that neither of us stepped back.

When the sponge drifted away, bobbing in the water, his hands remained. His unspoken vow of devotion tucked into every pause, every touch that lingered past necessity.

Light. Careful. As if he wasn't certain he was allowed.

His fingers traced the familiar lines of my body with the quiet certainty of knowing where I held tension, where I carried grief. He followed my breathing, pausing when it caught, continuing when it eased. Each glide, each press, was not exploration, but attention.

His lips found my temple. He pressed a slow, careful kiss against my temple.

I didn't pull away.

His warm breath found my ear, whispered, "I've got you."

As if he ever needed to even say it.

Then he leaned deeper into the water. He slipped an arm beneath my knees and another around my waist, lifting me as though I weighed nothing. Cool air wrapped me as the water rushed away, slipping down his arms and tunic, and soaking the tiled floor when he pressed me to his chest. I shivered and let myself fold into his arms, too hollow to resist.

Vestro carried me to the bed and set me down with a gentleness that undid me more than the tears had. Without asking, he tugged the sheet around us both, then hesitated — just a breath — before drawing me into his space.

I closed the distance for him.

His body fit close, his chest brushing mine, and the weight of him pressing close, with every line of his body fitted against me as though he meant to anchor me in place. He'd always stolen space; always nudged closer, snuck the barest brushes of touch; but tonight, I didn't mind. Tonight, I needed it.

Vestro's arm stayed wrapped around my waist, holding me there, like he knew if he let go, I might break apart. The heat of him sank through the sheets, wrapping me as thoroughly as the blanket itself. His scent of horse sweat, leather, and that faint wild note—like flowers crushed under hooves—enveloped my senses, slipped between my parted lips, and gently caressed the parts I'd buried further than his hands could reach.

I ran my hand down his side.

He went still.

Just for a second.

Then he exhaled, slow and careful, and let himself stay.

It was a reaction I'd never noticed before. He shifted, drawing back slightly as if afraid the closeness might be too much.

My breath shuddered out, too exhausted at the moment to wonder why or to care. I felt my limbs grow heavy, but I fought against the weights pulling at my eyes.

"I don't want to go with Maurdruik," I whispered into the dark.

Vestro stilled, then shifted, and his hand found mine under the blanket. He didn't ask why. He didn't argue. He twined his fingers through mine. Kissed my knuckles.

"How early do you want me to wake you?"

"Before dawn," I whispered. My eyes closed. "We need to be gone before the others..."

"Then before dawn it is."

He helped me roll to my other side, and he spooned me from behind, his body cupping mine so no space existed between us. His palms slid slowly over my arms, gently working all the knots in my shoulders and neck. "Sleep, Nadia. I have you."

Each stroke of his hand pulled the weight of the day further from my bones until I floated in the warmth of his embrace. I fit against him as though I'd been shaped for the space against him, his heavy breath steady at the back of my neck.

A perfect circle. A perfect friend. A perfect horse. If he'd been human, he'd have been the perfect man for me.

Too bad he's not.

I closed my eyes, falling into the calm of Vestro's arms around me, and I let myself believe, just for a moment, that everything would be all right.

CHAPTER
TEN

A rooster crowed before dawn—two full hours before dawn, in fact—and I jerked sideways, slamming my elbow into Vestro's ribs. He grunted, rolled off the bed, and muttered something about plucking feathers as he stepped into his clothes, half-asleep, and then stalked downstairs in the dark to the kitchen to scrounge up something for breakfast. I quickly pulled on my tunic and boots, repacked our bags, and was ready to go when he returned. We made the best of the meager breakfast: stale bread, bacon drippings, and bitter coffee so black it left mud on my tongue.

Still, we were out the gates and a mile up the east road before dawn, and there'd been no sign of Maurdruik. A small miracle.

My stomach growled through the long wait for Andrew and the group and then for Damien. Andrew wasted no time chastising us both for leaving the group. I bit my tongue and apologized, though Damien ignored me entirely.

≈

THE MILES PASSED IN MONOTONY. We traveled for hours without a single problem in sight, the scenery placid and unchanging. The land rolled by gently, dotted with clumps of oak and hornbeam trees, the colorful patchwork of tilled hills and farmland. The air hung heavy with summer thunder, and the wind that had begun the night before remained, stirring up the dust around the horses' hooves and tugging at our cloaks. The quiet of the land was broken by the occasional screech of red-tailed hawks circling high overhead and the snort of our horses.

By evening, we found shade in a glade of firs. The full boughs of the towering trees high overhead created a natural canopy, and sunlight filtered down through the branches in spotted shafts. Tall clumps of brush and flowering bushes covered the moss-strewn ground. The sounds of the horses' hooves were lost in the high-pitched chirping of birds and the chatter of squirrels. A warm breeze slipped through the leaves that swayed to the rhythm of a silent hymn. The smells of old wood and animals drifted in and settled heavily in the stillness of the small glade.

Andrew and Corbin laughed over some private joke, the sound grating after hours of silence.

I slipped away with Vestro, eager for a moment to myself. I dismounted and led Vestro a way off from the group to a small clearing ringed in tall hedge-like bushes so that I could clean myself up. The air was cooler here, but the sweat beneath my armor clung sticky and sour. Gods, how the men managed to go days without bathing was beyond me. Just a few hours sealed in steel left me cringing at my own stink.

I unbuckled the straps, one by one, until the harness sagged and fell away. My leggings and tunic followed, the damp fabric peeling from my skin. Vestro shifted somewhere behind me and stretched his sore legs, using an extra washcloth to wipe the effects of the change off his skin.

I wet my washcloth with the waterskin, the cool droplets sliding over my knuckles before trailing down my forearm. I dragged the cloth across my face, then along the line of my throat, cutting a clean line through the salt and grime and leaving a cool trail between my breasts. My muscles loosened under the slow relief, and for a moment I allowed myself to savor it.

When I looked up, I caught Vestro watching me.

"What's your problem?" I said. "You're supposed to be playing lookout."

A flush rose in his cheeks, and he turned sharply away. His reaction struck me enough that I paused mid-wipe.

What the hell? Vestro had seen me naked many times before. I snorted and then paused. *He's been staring at me a lot lately.*

That was new.

"Nadia," Vestro hissed, his voice sharp and low. "Someone's coming."

My gut clenched. My armor lay in a heap on the grass. "My armor—"

"Hide!"

I scrambled behind the ring of large bushes and faced the clearing in the direction of the men. I crouched down, my knees together and arms hugging my chest as I peered through a break in the hedge. Not that I had that much to hide, but my breasts were just ample enough that I had to be careful. I winced as something nipped at my leg. I smacked at the annoying insect with the washcloth. A second bite followed the first. I looked down.

I'd just squatted right next to an anthill. My frown cut my face in two. The last thing I needed was an ant biting my naked ass. I peeked back through the bushes at Vestro standing alone.

He better not be pulling my leg, or I'll—

Heavy footsteps rustled through the grass just out of sight beyond the clearing.

I looked at Vestro just as he managed to quickly shove his legs through his pants. He turned away just as Andrew appeared through the trees with a wineskin in his left hand.

Andrew started when he saw Vestro, his armor rattling, and

grabbed the hilt of his sword. Then he paused and looked down at my discarded armor by Vestro's feet.

"Strange," he said, almost under his breath. "To see a knight stripped from his steel." His eyes narrowed, curious. "You stand taller without it."

I pressed lower behind the hedge as ants crawled mercilessly over my thigh. I moved slowly, trying to shift away from the anthill. My knee caught on the bush, and it yanked the branches, rustling the leaves. Andrew looked in my direction, and I froze, praying I was still hidden from view.

"I slouch," Vestro said quickly, drawing Andrew's attention around. He dipped his head, letting his hair hide his black eyes.

Dread suddenly weighed heavy in the pit of my stomach as I looked down to Andrew's hand still resting on the top of his hilt. *If Andrew were to catch on, he'd run Vestro through before I had time to stand.*

Andrew studied Vestro for a long moment. His gaze flicked back down to my armor, then up again, searching. He tipped the wineskin to his lips, and the sour scent of fermented fruit drifted across the clearing. He took a casual step forward then slightly to the side, watching as Vestro angled his body so the trees threw half his face into shadow, offering Andrew only his profile.

I caught the look on Andrew's face. *Oh, shit. He's testing him.*

Andrew took another drink from the wineskin, slow and deliberate. "Your horse. He belongs to the princes, correct? I remember him well enough at Damewood. Striking animal."

Vestro's lips curved faintly. "Yes, she sent her prized stallion on this quest to help save her kingdom."

Andrew nodded but looked unsatisfied. "And why would she do that?"

"I am in her favor."

I couldn't help but smile. I could tell Vestro was really enjoying his bragging session and seemed bent on bruising Andrew's over-inflated ego.

Something flickered across Andrew's face. Disbelief? Jealousy? His fingers brushed his crown again, a twitch quick as breath. "A fine beast, certainly. But in the end, it is not the horse. It is the rider." His eyes darkened as he stared hard at Vestro's back. "And I am not easily bested."

Vestro's smirk sharpened, his black eyes catching the fractured light. "I've heard of one who does."

"Really?" Andrew said, grinning. "I very much doubt that. Though I pray you, tell me."

"The Princess Nadia."

My name cracked through the clearing like a whip. Andrew went still, his shoulders locking. His hand twitched toward his crown again, but stopped halfway, fisting at his side instead. For the first time, his smile vanished entirely, leaving the planes of his face bare.

I'm going to kill Vestro for bringing my name up.

A smirk tugged at the edges of my mouth. Still, the shithead was right. In all the years racing as kids, Andrew had never beaten me atop a horse. I knew it was a sore spot in the man's inflated pride.

Andrew's face twitched.

"And...what," he asked slowly, the words weighted like stones, "would bring you to that conclusion, Sir Aidan?"

"I'm just repeating what I've heard, Sire. It's fairly common knowledge around Damewood." Vestro bowed his head respectfully and then turned away.

Andrew's eyes narrowed. "Face me, knight..." His voice carried more curiosity than suspicion, but the weight of command pressed behind it.

"Tell me, how did you manage to face the princess after she left you behind in the wake of her stallion?"

Andrew's smile pulled thin. "I do not seem to recall such events."

Vestro's mouth twitched. "Strange. I remember the orchard fields. The last turn before the river ford. You lost your stirrup in the mud and nearly dropped your reins."

I stifled a laugh behind my fist, heat rising to my cheeks. Of course, Vestro remembered. He had been under me that day, his hooves pounding the ford while Andrew's horse flailed to catch up.

And then the guilt followed just as fast. I shouldn't enjoy watching Andrew cut open. Not like this.

Andrew froze, his jaw clenching, a muscle ticking hard beneath the skin. The wineskin sagged in his grip, then went taut as his fist closed too tight around it, the leather creaking. His smile stayed, but it looked carved there, stiff and bloodless.

"Time we headed off." He turned sharply, crown flashing as he stepped through the grass. "See that you do not tarry, Sir Aidan."

I felt more than saw the pure pleasure rolling off Vestro's form as he crossed his arms. "No need to wait for me. I'm sure my mount will have no problem catching up to yours."

Andrew's posture stiffened, and there was a nearly indiscernible tick in his long stride, but he recovered quickly and vanished into the trees, the brush swaying shut behind him. The clearing fell silent save for the whisper of wind in the firs.

I let out a long breath I hadn't realized I was holding. My knuckles ached from where I'd bitten down to stifle my laugh.

Vestro turned then, catching me through the hedge. His grin was already waiting for me, dark eyes twinkling with mischief.

I shoved through the brush, swiping at the ants crawling up my leg, then socked him hard in the arm. "What the hell was that?" I hissed. "You baited him like a dog."

He tilted his head, his lips curling. "Tell me you did not like it."

"I—" Heat pricked my cheeks. "I shouldn't have liked it."

Vestro's smile broadened. "Then consider it a guilty pleasure." He reached for my breastplate, holding it open as if to remind me how easily he slipped into the role. "He carries himself as though no one has ever beaten him. Perhaps it is good to remind him otherwise."

I slipped back into the armor, the leather straps tugging snug against my shoulders. "You enjoy making him look small."

"I have known him since he was small." Vestro bent close, fastening the last knob with careful fingers. His touch lingered a moment before he stepped back with a grin that was all teeth. "What? I cannot have a little fun? I spend most of my days keeping you alive. Let me enjoy myself occasionally."

I swatted his arm, but the corner of my mouth betrayed me, tugging upward. "You call baiting a king *fun*?"

"I'd say for Andrew it's a lesson in humility." His eyes glowed, satisfied. "And watching him squirm was worth every second."

I pulled the last strap tight myself, shaking my head. "You're impossible."

He only chuckled, low in his throat, and didn't bother to deny it.

The air suddenly felt too still. No birdcall, no squirrel chatter, not even the soft creak of branches in the forest. The silence pressed hard against my ears.

"Do you feel that?" I whispered.

Vestro's head turned slowly as he scanned the trees, every line of his suddenly taut. "Yes." His voice was low, careful. "Stay close."

CHAPTER
ELEVEN

A rustle slid through the undergrowth, wet and heavy. The hairs at my nape prickled.

"Ves—"

The brush exploded. A scaled body whipped across the clearing, green-black coils thicker than a man's waist. A human torso rose from it, skin slick and gray, eyes burning yellow above a mouth full of fangs. The hiss split the air like a blade through reeds.

"Get down!" Vestro barked.

I dove. The naga's strike tore through the space where I'd been standing. Its tail lashed, smashing the bushes I'd just crouched behind. Ants scattered across the moss in a frenzy. I rolled, my armor clattering, and dropped my sword.

The naga turned, hissing, its tongue lashing. Its eyes fixed on me.

Vestro growled, stepping in front of me, my blade already gleaming in his hand.

I shoved at his arm. "I don't need a guard, Ves!"

"You'll forgive me if I disagree," he muttered, not moving.

The creature's hiss split the air. The naga surged forward again, the scaled coils slamming through the bushes and snapping branches. Vestro caught the strike on his blade while I ducked under the lash of its tail.

"Gods—" I choked as its tail clipped my side. Pain flared under my ribs. "Damn thing fights like a battering ram."

"Eyes on its neck," Vestro barked. His voice came out strained and deeper than usual.

It caught me off guard. I glanced at him, noting the way he turned the sword in his hand like second nature, and the shift in his posture that looked more suited to one of the King's Guard than my kelpie.

The naga shrieked, the large head whipping sideways. The stench hit me next—rot and fish oil, sharp enough to sting my nose.

"Lovely," I spat, gagging. "As if it weren't ugly enough—"

The naga coiled again, fast as a whip. Vestro shoved me aside as the creature leaped forward. His blade carved across its shoulder, and black ichor splattered the moss. He dropped to one knee and swung up, my sword cutting through the damp air, nicking along the slick underside of the naga's jaw.

The serpent recoiled, its hiss cracking higher. A low hum trembled through the clearing.

Not a hiss. Not a breath. More like a pulse. It started low, and then swelled until the air itself seemed to hum. The clearing vibrated, hard enough to make my teeth ache.

The naga's yellow eyes locked on me, the red tongue darting as the vibration thickened. The vibration jammed behind my eyes, buzzing like a thousand hornets.

"Nadia!" Vestro's shout was ragged. He staggered a step, shoulders hunched as he dropped my sword and put his hands to his ears.

The naga suddenly turned and slithered off toward the clearing. The sound faded as it disappeared.

"What the fuck..." I straightened and pointed. "Ves, it's headed to the other men."

I grabbed my fallen sword and bolted for the tree line, brush clawing at my legs. Vestro ran beside me, but when we broke into the clearing, he skidded to a halt at the edge of the tree line.

"Nadia, come back!" he barked. "I can't—"

I didn't stop.

The clearing stretched wide, sun glaring down on pale rocks. The naga coiled there, tail draped across the moss. At its base, a soldier lay sprawled in the dirt, head twisted backward, throat ripped ragged. Blood had already browned in the heat.

The serpent reared above him, half-human torso gleaming, a black collar clasped at its throat. A tiny red light blinked steadily against the pale skin.

And the men...

Their horses stood at the oak edge, reins dragging. The riders had dismounted but not by choice. They stood scattered, motionless, eyes glazed, staring raptly at the creature.

Andrew stood at the edge of the main clearing, sword half-drawn. His eyes were open, but vacant, glassy, reflecting nothing. His chest rose and fell in a shallow rhythm, like he was sleepwalking through a dream.

Beside him, Damien's dagger hung loose in his grip, tip resting against his thigh. His lips moved soundlessly, as though muttering to ghosts.

Trea leaned forward in his saddle, his reins slack in his hand. His horse stood rigid, ears flat, nostrils flared—even the animal trapped in whatever this was.

The air vibrated harder here. My armor rattled faintly, each rivet buzzing like a wasp. The sound made my stomach churn, bile crawling up my throat.

"Saints preserve us," I whispered, but the words sounded like someone else's voice, warped and dull in my own ears.

Behind me, Vestro's cry tore through the trees. "Nadia! Come back!"

I turned toward him, but he didn't follow. He stood just inside the tree line, one knee bent, hand braced on his thigh, every muscle shaking with effort. His mouth moved, but the hum drowned the words before they reached me.

The hum pressed harder, drilling through my skull until my eyes watered. The very air shook with it. My breastplate rattled against its straps until each rivet buzzed like a wasp trapped inside the metal.

From the tree line, Vestro's voice cut sharply across the clearing. "The collar—go for the collar!"

I whipped my head toward him, confusion flaring as the hum rose, pressing in on my temples until I felt my skull would crack.

My chest harness shifted. A faint whirr trembled through the inside of my helmet, and a single, piercing beep cut across my skull.

And then the hum vanished. Ripped out of the world in the space between heartbeats.

Silence slammed down on my ears. The silence hit with so much force that my balance slipped. My vision wavered. My ears rang with nothing. The branches moved overhead, but there was no sound from their movement. My breath pushed in and out of my chest without a single note. Even my heartbeat felt distant, muted behind the armor.

"What the..." I said the words out loud but heard nothing.

Something in the armor had activated. A hidden function Maurdruik never explained. The suit sealed the world off, shutting out every sound around me.

I was the only one still conscious.

I lifted my head and forced myself to take in the clearing.

Andrew stood nearest the front. His sword was raised halfway. His eyes were open but vacant, the light in them drained. His mouth hung slightly open, jaw slack. His chest moved in shallow, steady lifts. His fingers locked around the hilt, the tendons in his arm rigid.

Damien's dagger hung in his hand, the blade touching his leg. His lips moved, forming words that carried no sound. His jaw moved in steady pulses. His posture held, but there was no reaction in his eyes.

Corbin sagged in his saddle. His reins slipped through his loose fingers. His horse trembled beneath him, muscles shaking under the strain. Foam collected at its mouth. Its eyes rolled upward, unfocused.

I stepped back. My boot pressed into the moss. Still no sound.

Wind pushed through the clearing, but the branches shifted in total silence. Andrew's cloak lifted at the edges. Damien's hair stirred. None of it reached my ears.

I turned toward the tree line.

Vestro stood inside the shadows, one knee buckled. His hand braced against his thigh. His mouth shaped my name, but the silence swallowed it. His eyes were wide and beginning to glaze. His shoulders shook. His chest strained with every breath.

He was slipping under the hum, too.

My lungs burned, but the noise of my own breathing never rose.

If the suit hadn't blocked the sound, I would already be frozen beside them.

It's only me now.

And if I hesitated, everyone in the clearing would die.

The serpent lunged.

Its body crashed through the moss, earth erupting in clumps. I twisted aside, steel flashing, and the tip of my sword carved across the slick underside of its neck. Black ichor sprayed. Hot, sticky, liquid spilled across my armor and dripped into my visor and onto my skin. I nearly wretched at the stench as it filled my suit.

The naga reeled back, coils snapping, trees bowing under the force. I ducked and rolled across the moss wet with blood. She flicked out her arm quicker than I could move, and her fist caught me under the jaw. The blow rocked my head back, sending a sharp pain down one side of my neck, making my ears ring, and sending me flying ten feet across the clearing. I ducked my head and rolled as I landed, slapped my hand against the ground to take most of the impact.

I struggled to right myself in the armor. Even with Maurdruik's alterations, the armor was awkward as hell when trying to roll off my back, making me feel like an upended turtle. I finally managed to straighten up and brush a clump of moss from my shoulder. I gripped my sword with both hands and jerked my head down in a quick nod, lowering the visor of my helmet with a clank.

My sword wavered, too heavy in my hands even despite the armor's assistance. My legs were shaking, and if it hadn't been for the suit I probably would have been on my knees. My chest tightened as I drew breath, each inhale scraping inside my ribs. The adrenaline was wearing off, and I knew I didn't have much time left.

The naga coiled, jaws opening again, fangs bared.

I jammed the blade upward, every muscle screaming. The point drove through the soft hollow under the naga's jaw, punching out between its teeth. The serpent convulsed, whole body arcing, coils writhing skyward.

I shoved with everything I had left, forcing the blade deeper. My arms burned, and my lungs seared as I screamed—and then the weight gave. The naga collapsed, the massive, scaled coils buckling onto the earth. The body twitched once before lying still.

When I looked up, the men were gasping, blinking, life flooding back into their faces. Andrew lurched forward, Damien staggered, and Corbin tugged at his reins.

I lifted my visor and swiped a shaking hand across my mouth, chest still shuddering.

If not for the suit, I would be among them.

And since Vestro was a demon... why had he fallen, too?

A chocolate muzzle bumped me from behind, and I turned to see Vestro, again in horse form, staring at me.

"What?" I said.

Vestro snorted and pushed me aside. I struggled to keep my feet as he moved past me to the naga's corpse. He pawed at the naga's neck until the black collar slipped to the ground. Then he reared up and slammed his hooves down on it, crushing the little black box into tiny, cracked pieces until the little red light went out.

"Ves, what—"

The men staggered, gasping like men dragged half-drowned

from a river. Damien pressed a hand to his temple, cursing under his breath. Corbin clutched his reins, blinking wild-eyed.

Andrew swayed, then squared his shoulders, his jaw clenched tight. His sword lay forgotten in the dirt, but he ignored it, his gaze fixed on me.

For a heartbeat, he only stared. Then his chin lifted, his voice rough but steady. "Well struck, Sir Aidan." He jutted his chin as if the words cost him. "We are in your debt."

I planted my sword point-down into the moss, drew myself taller, shoulders squared inside the armor. Let them see strength. Let them see a knight who had faced the serpent alone and prevailed.

Pride flared through me, hot and fierce, sharper than the ache of bruised ribs and bloodied hands. For once, it was mine. Not borrowed from Andrew, not shielded by Vestro.

Mine.

CAMP THAT NIGHT hovered with an uneasy quiet. The scent of burnt flesh and wet scales still clung to the air, heavy and metallic. The squires worked wordlessly, clearing a circle of trampled ferns while Trea coaxed life into a fire with a single spark from his flint. Shadows of the trees loomed long and uneven, their branches swaying above the patch of earth still darkened by spilled blood.

Corbin helped Andrew strip the last armor plate from his shoulders with a grunt and set it carefully against a fallen log.

Andrew lowered himself beside it, keeping it within reach. His tunic clung damp to his back, and he set his crown on the log beside his gauntlets to run his hands through his hair. The firelight caught the sweat on his throat and the hollow of his collarbone; I shouldn't have noticed, but my eyes lingered anyway. I caught the faint tremor in his hand as he reached for his wineskin. He leaned back with a low exhale that seemed to take the weight of the day with it.

The sound slid through me, low and tired, and somehow too intimate for comfort. I swallowed down the lump in my throat and looked away from his gorgeous profile.

What is wrong with me right now?

Damien sprawled across a bedroll, boots kicked off, humming some mocking tune under his breath. Jonathan, the taller of the two trackers, pulled out a pair of dice and set them on a flat stone, and started a game with his partner. The mood lightened, if only slightly.

And then there was me. Still standing in my armor like a damn moron with my helmet under one arm.

Every strap on my armor felt tighter now that I wanted it off. The underpadding clung to my skin, soaked through with sweat and salt, and the air trapped beneath the plates turned staler with each breath. I shifted, trying to find a way to sit that didn't bite into my ribs.

Gods, I want to take this damn suit off.

But I couldn't. Not here, not with all of them watching. One loosened strap, one wrong angle in the firelight, and my secret would bleed out faster than I could lie.

When I moved to sit, the sound of polished steel grated against itself, sharp enough to draw every gaze. The firelight flickered across their faces—first confusion, then surprise, then something like concern. No one spoke, but I felt their eyes linger just long enough to burn holes in my armor. The plates pinched at the wrong angles when I tried lying on my side, and the straps dug into my ribs when I rolled onto my back. Each breath echoed in the hollow breastplate, shallow and metallic, bouncing back at me in quick, tiny bursts. Sweat gathered where the leather lining met my skin, cooling too quickly, then burning again when I moved. I shifted once more, trying to find a position that didn't feel like I was lying on knives.

Godsdammit.

Andrew leaned back on the log, the wineskin dangling loose in his hand, and let a crooked grin slip through the exhaustion. "Too proud to shed the plates, Sir Aidan?" he drawled, voice rough but amused. "Or worried we'll all find out you're prettier than the rest of us?"

Damien didn't bother glancing up from his knife. "He's guarding his virtue," he said mildly, flipping the blade and catching it by the hilt with lazy precision. "Can't blame him. You get handsy when you drink."

Saints save me. I bit back a sigh. *They nearly died today, and it still comes back to their damn dicks.*

I rolled my shoulders, forcing my voice down to that low, easy drawl they all seemed to share. "If your aim's anything like your stamina, Majesty, I'm safe enough."

That hit home.

Corbin whooped, then clapped a hand over his mouth as if he'd gone too far. Darren doubled over, wheezing. Damien actually laughed, short and sharp, as he stuck his knife into the dirt beside him.

Andrew's grin widened, tipping his head toward me, wine glinting on his lip. "Stamina's the one thing I've never been accused of lacking."

Andrew's words landed harder than they should have. The way his mouth wrapped around the rim of the wineskin made my pulse stumble, heat curling low in my gut. A part of me hated that I noticed—but I hated that part of me liked it more.

I bet you haven't.

The guard Benjamin barked a laugh. "Careful, Sir Aidan. Say that again, and he'll try to prove you wrong!"

That sent them over the edge. Trea wheezed with laughter. Damien just shook his head, smirking into the firelight. Andrew laughed hardest of all, coughing as wine splashed down his wrist. He licked the wine from his skin, a flash of tongue and firelight, too quick to be deliberate yet too slow to ignore. My breath caught before I could stop it, and for one dizzy heartbeat, I couldn't look away.

Fucking gorgeous man.

"Bastards," Andrew managed between laughs, smiling into the rim of the wineskin. "Every godsdamned one of you."

"Can't argue with that," I muttered.

The laughter eventually faded, giving way to the creak of the tree branches above and the soft hiss of the dying fire.

A heavy hoof clipped against the soft ground. Vestro's dark form appeared at the edge of the firelight, his silhouette all shadow and sinew. His ears flicked once, catching the stillness of the men that followed, then again toward me. The faint glow of embers traced the curve of his flank, gilding him in dull copper light as he clopped past Andrew. His tail whipped out, catching the king in the face as he passed.

"What the fuck?" Andrew wiped at his face, his graceful arrogance interrupted.

I hid a smirk as Vestro circled behind me, his velvet nose snorting gently at the base of my neck. With deliberate care, he lowered himself to the ground and folded his long legs to settle at my back.

He stretched into a warm, breathing wall and turned his head toward me, one dark eye fixed and expectant.

I huffed through my nose. "Show-off," I muttered.

I leaned back, the plates of my cuirass scraping against each other, and pressed into him until my back met the solid curve of his ribs. His warmth radiated through my armor, calming what little fire still lingered beneath my skin. The faint, rhythmic rise and fall of his breathing steadied me—slow and steady.

The fire popped once, scattering a brief shower of sparks. I half-opened my eyes in time to catch Andrew watching from across the flames, the awe and confusion plain on his face before he quickly looked away and took another drink from his wineskin.

No one spoke. The silence thickened, settling around us like another blanket. Somewhere beyond the ring of firelight, an owl called once and went quiet.

Vestro let out a low breath that rumbled through his chest and into my spine, grounding me. My eyelids grew heavy, and the world shrank into his warmth as I closed my eyes and drifted off to sleep.

CHAPTER
TWELVE

The earth moved.

It rolled under me like a beast shrugging off riders, the ground groaning in long waves that made my teeth ache. The air pressed tight against my lips, thick as mud, and my chest heaved uselessly against the crush of my breastplate. I tried to turn my head and couldn't. Black eyes opened in the dark. Not human—too wide, the pupils dilating until nothing remained but bottomless pits. The naga's eyes. They floated above me like twin wells, and I slid toward them, down, down. Coils closed over my ribs, each ring tightening a finger's width, just enough for panic to bloom. When I tried to kick, my body didn't move. My body didn't belong to me.

Paul lay on his back by the rocks, head twisted wrong, a grin on his dead face as if he'd finally heard the punchline. Andrew crawled toward the naga on his knees, sword forgotten, lips moving in a prayer he did not know. The collar at her throat pulsed—red, red, red—each blink driving the fire closer until the heat blistered the skin at my cheeks.

I jerked awake, my heart in my throat, and found myself reclined near the edge of camp at the base of a large, wide pine. I kept still as the blood rushed through my ears in gushing waves, muting all sound. After several deep breaths, the rush subsided, and the sounds of the night trickled into my consciousness.

The dream didn't let go all at once. The ground still thrummed, after-shocks shivering along my spine, but the black eyes faded to ordinary shadows between trees. The weight at my chest resolved into the simple fact that I had slept in my armor like an idiot because I could not take it off in front of the men. The strap at my throat dug because I hadn't loosened it. I found the buckle with my thumb, wrenched it sideways. Cool air mercifully slid along my neck, licking at the sheen of sweat covering my skin.

My vision cleared, and the shapes of camp swam back into place. Saddles dark against trunks. Andrew's pile of armor beside his bags. Outlines of men scattered on their bedrolls, turned toward the slight heat of the dim fire. No one looked my way. No one had heard the way the nightmare had raked its claws through me.

I pushed up onto my knees, moving slowly so the plates wouldn't clatter. A soft roll of cloud smothered the moon; the clearing was the color of old pewter. Men snored with the deep regularity of the dead. I turned my back on them and walked toward the trees.

A STREAM I hadn't noticed from camp whispered somewhere ahead, its glint of water a thin line through the trees.

I found it soon enough, though I followed the small stream through the trees as far from the group as I could manage. The last thing I wanted was for someone to walk in on me as I undressed. I reached the edge of the stream, where the water bubbled up from between a large group of boulders partially overgrown with ferns peeking out of weathered cracks. The blue water trickled down the rocky outcrops, white foam splashing off the stone and clinging to the soft moss and leaves of the nearby bushes and ferns.

A frog jumped into the pool, sending ripples across the surface of the crystalline water. It surfaced and floated with its large head poking above the water, the emerald eyes staring at me as I struggled out of the armor padding. The frog's wide mouth opened, smiling.

I paused and regarded the frog for several moments, accompanied solely by the ambient sounds of the waterfall and the quiet descent of the sun. I bent down slowly and brought my hands closer to the frog. I tensed up my shoulders and then quickly reached out. The frog lazily dipped out of sight as my hands grabbed at the water, the splash sending disturbed ripples dancing across the surface.

Too slow.

A twig snapped behind me. I spun around with a fist-sized rock in my hand. I let the rock slip from my fingers into the water behind me when I saw Vestro leaning casually against one of the pine trunks, picking at his wet hair as he watched me.

Something tight in my chest loosened at the sight of him. Tears pricked my eyes, and I blinked them away.

"Ves..."

Vestro pushed away from the tree and plodded toward me. He was naked and still slick from his change, and moonlight glinted off his tanned skin. He gave me a comforting smile and opened his arms. I leaned against his chest and let him wrap his arms around me.

"I couldn't breathe," I said.

He nodded slowly. "You all right now?"

"I hate sleeping in this thing," I said, dipping my chin toward the cuirass.

His gaze skimmed the buckles and then my face. "You are safer in it."

"I know." I pulled at the collar of the armor. "It still felt like I was suffocating."

"Want to bathe? It will help."

I thought about it and then nodded. I began turning the knobs of the armor, and Vestro's fingers moved deftly, helping me unbuckle and set aside the pieces. The weight on my shoulders lifted with each piece he lifted away and took my first deep breath as the cool night breeze hit the damp fabric of my tunic.

I stripped off my clothing before carefully stepping into the black water. The stream felt good on my feet, and I stepped farther into the water. Cold gripped my ankles, then my calves, soothing the welted skin where the armor had pinched.

I continued until the water reached me mid-thigh, then bent my knees and brought a cupful of water to splash across my face and neck. I gasped at the chill touch, but I kept splashing my arms and chest until the heat under my skin eased. I didn't turn as I heard Vestro walking into the water after me.

"It's cold," Vestro hissed. "Here, let me wash your back for you."

He splashed away the last of the slime from the change and then gently rinsed my shoulders and back. I shivered as rivulets of cold water trickled down my skin.

"I hate sleeping in the armor," I said. I began to shiver and hugged my arms around my chest. The suffocation crawled back up my throat, and my eyes scanned the dark tree line. Shadows danced in my vision, red eyes appearing and disappearing, then floating along the moonlit water. Laughing at me.

Vestro's arms wrapped around me, hugging me into a circle of warmth.

I let my shoulder rest against his. I wasn't subtle about it. He was warm where the night had gone cool, and the way his body steadied mine without engulfing it eased a knot I hadn't realized I was still holding. We stood in silence for a while, letting the water gently roll across my thighs.

"You're safe, Nadia. It's over," he said. "But it's OK to be scared sometimes."

"I'm not," my voice rasped. "I just..."

My control spiraled. Red eyes and blinking lights crowded my vision again. I suddenly felt small in Vestro's arms, and I turned and leaned my face into the crook of his shoulder.

Vestro touched under my chin and lifted my gaze to meet his. The dimple between his brow deepened; his eyes softened the way they did when I said something I didn't think mattered but did to him.

"What do you need, Nadia?" His eyes searched mine, steady. "What can I do to make it better?"

My chin trembled. "I'm not breakable."

"I know."

"Then stop treating me like I am."

His hand trailed down my arm and closed around my wrist, gentle but solid, and he guided my palm to his shoulder. I felt the heat there, the slope of his muscles, and the way his breath hitched as my hand slid up to the back of his neck and curled into his hair.

I needed something to hold. Something steady I could steer before my emotions spiraled again. Vestro had always been that rock, grounding me, keeping me safe.

I met his dark eyes and recognized the want I'd been pretending not to see.

"Kiss me."

He didn't move. He studied my face, and something dark swirled in his eyes. The fine crow's-feet at the edges deepened, then softened. He leaned until his lips hovered at my ear.

"Show me what you need."

I leaned my body up against his, and his bare skin acted as a warm blanket against the chill of the night. I pressed my bare breasts against his chest, and I felt his body react.

Something screamed in the back of my mind to stop, but I ignored it as I pulled him closer and pressed my nose into the hair behind his ear. I became surrounded by his scent of horsehair and wildflowers, and the familiar smell loosened the tightness in my chest. Vestro's warm breath brushed my ear, sinking into my skin and quickening my heart.

This is Vestro. What am I doing?

I blinked and moved to turn, to tell him to go away, to tell him... anything. He stilled, his eyes on me and body tense, loyally waiting for my command. My heart clawed its way up my throat, and it took all my self-control to keep my eyes above his waist. I'd seen Vestro naked countless times... but never like this. Never poised and ready, where the need between my thighs made me notice how beautiful he was, and his proximity and the size of him made me squirm and squeeze my legs together in anticipation.

He's a demon. I can't... I shouldn't be doing this.

But we had crossed lines before. A stolen kiss, a wandering touch, soft hands in the bath. His hands had comforted me and pulled me back from the edge countless times, serving me whenever I'd asked of him.

My heartbeat roared in my ears, and my mind raced with every rational reason why I should walk away and get dressed. But I needed control again. I needed to break whatever grip this dread had on me.

I reached out and brushed the fingers of my right hand across his stomach. I traced the jagged edges of the white scar on his abdomen, the hand-sized star drawing my attention.

I finished tracing the scar and let my hands slide down his sides, following the muscles to the dark hair below. Vestro made a low rumble deep in his throat and swallowed hard as my hands slid further down. My heart crawled out of my throat; I'd never touched a man like this before, and the idea of holding his warm skin in my hands made something slick drip onto my thigh.

I paused. His expression told me everything, but I asked anyway: "Can I..."

Vestro let out a chuff of air and nodded without speaking.

I smiled, drinking in the pleased and slack expression on his face as I slid my hand down the length of him, gliding to the dark curls at his base. I was amazed at how soft his skin was, like velvet, and I let my fingers play and tease along his length. Vestro closed his eyes and tilted his head back, his breathing quickening. The thrill of my hands holding so much power over him heightened my excitement, and I fought to control the urge to just pounce on him. My hands steadied as I touched him, felt him stiffen and thicken even more as I cupped him, controlling the pace and pressure of every touch. His body shuddered under me, slowly stealing away the tremors that had been plaguing mine.

Vestro wasn't what I needed right now, but he could give me what I needed to make the dread go away. To quiet the screams and shut away the red eyes at the edges of my vision. I needed heat, hands, and weight—something to drown the naga's coil still rattling my ribs.

I parted my lips to tell him this wasn't about him, that it was only need clawing through me. But words tangled in my throat, and I choked them down. Two tears trailed down my cheeks, and Vestro kissed them away without a word.

I leaned forward and gently kissed the middle of Vestro's chest, then moved my kisses in small circles to the left side. My tongue flicked out against his dark nipple as I continued to gently stroke him. I gently sucked and nibbled at the soft skin until the nipple hardened and raised between my teeth.

I hooked my free hand behind Vestro's neck and drew his mouth down to mine. He tasted like spring water and mountain air, and I slid my tongue across his lower lip. When I deepened the kiss, he answered but didn't drive; he matched my every move, letting me set the pace and letting me feel the exact point where my want overtook fear. The ache built between my legs until it was almost painful, and I squeezed my legs together, feeling the slick heat already gathering there. My chest ached and I let out a choked sob.

Vestro pulled away from my kiss and cupped my lower back with one hand. "Nadia, tell me what you need."

I wanted this, no, needed it. But I knew I shouldn't have it.

A princess lying with a—no.

Don't name it. It's not a rule that will save me tonight.

"I need to feel better," I said, my voice just above a whisper.

He nodded. "I serve you in every way I can. Let me do this too." His thumbs stroked my skin. "Let me make it better tonight."

I nodded, my aching need and emotions battling for control as I leaned against him, wanting to roll in the warmth radiating from his body. "Just for tonight."

I deepened the kiss, and he let me. I shifted my weight to straddle his thigh, rubbing my slick center against his leg, and he braced his hands at my sides, steadying me but unmoving, as if afraid that one wrong motion might break the spell.

His restraint burned hot on his face. I reached down, took his wrist, and guided his hand between my legs. He didn't move; he only looked up at me, his dark eyes questioning as his breath rushed through flared nostrils.

So, I moved instead, slowly and deliberately, and pressed myself against his still hand, grinding against the roughness of his palm to feed the ache blooming low in my belly. My breath caught as I rocked again, feeling the steady weight of him beneath my touch; his quiet strength that never pushed or demanded, only waited.

Every shift of my hips sent sparks crawling up my spine. Vestro stayed motionless beneath me, the muscle in his jaw flexing, his breath stuttering in shallow bursts as if he felt every ripple through my body.

"Please," I whispered, though I wasn't sure who I was begging— him, or myself—to keep going. "I need…"

I pushed Vestro's wrist toward his thigh, turning his palm up, and he accommodated me by bending his knee and shifting his weight to brace his arm. His face was guarded as he watched me.

I wiggled my hips to press his fingers against the heat between my legs, tracing the slick heat there until the tension in my body quivered into an ache. Then, slowly, deliberately, I reached down and guided two of his fingers inside me. Vestro's body went rigid beneath my hands; his breath catching. But he stayed still, even though his muscles trembling with the effort of restraint.

I moved against him, rocking my hips, and feeling the rough glide of his skin inside mine. The pressure built with each stroke, and I increased my pace until every breath came out in quick, raspy rushes. Vestro didn't push deeper or pull away, but I felt the tension in his body crackling like barely-controlled lightning. The world narrowed to the slide of his fingers and the raw edge of control that hovered between us. My body burned, and my mind went blank so that nothing else existed aside from Vestro.

My knees shook, and Vestro's hands patiently steadied me. My nails bit into his arms when heat flooded low and tight inside me. He made a raw sound against my hair that tipped me closer to the edge I wasn't supposed to find.

Not like this. Not with him.

I loosened my grip, but the idea of letting him go ripped something raw from my chest, and I threaded my fingers back into his hair and pulled him into a deep, lip-bruising kiss.

Time slipped as everything dropped away.

The boundaries we'd placed and the lines we'd never crossed blended and faded as a raw hunger curled and lapped at my insides, soaking my core in liquid fire that dripped and burned everything it touched.

And then I wanted more.

I *needed* more.

I cradled Vestro's face in my trembling hands. He blinked twice and then anchored his hands at my hips as though to steady me from the tremors that ran through my body.

"Nadia?"

"I need this," I gasped. "Just for tonight."

A flicker of sadness crossed his face and vanished. "I know."

I stepped off his hand, his fingers leaving a wet trail on my inner thigh. Then I led him toward the bank, past the wet sand to the cool grass brushing against our skin. He spread my cloak and then sat, his chest rising and falling, watching me with a kind of fragile awe as I sank to my knees before him. My heart hammered as I climbed into his lap and straddled him.

"Take what you need," he said softly, his voice steady even as his fingers trembled where they traced the line of my waist.

I closed my eyes as I lowered myself onto him. Every motion was careful, my breath snagging as unfamiliar muscles tightened and burned. I moved painfully slow, giving my body time to understand what it had never done before. Each slow inch felt foreign; stretching and sharp at first, then melting me with heat that built until pain and pleasure tangled too tightly to tell apart.

Oh, gods. I can barely...

I'd imagined what it would feel like, but imagination had never carried weight, or breath, or the slow push of something real. This was the moment the stories never warned about. The part where pain and pleasure argued over who would win.

A low sound escaped Vestro's chest, rough and reverent. I gasped as my body adjusted, tightening and easing until he was sheathed fully inside me. My thighs trembled. My palms slipped against his shoulders. The air felt too thin, too bright. I breathed out slowly as I felt myself stretch and shudder, and I almost collapsed around him. My muscles clenched and my pulse raced until it drowned out all other sound.

Holy shit, and I haven't even fucking done anything yet!

Vestro didn't move, waiting for my command. His arms trembled with restraint, and his body shuddered as I finally rested deeper against his thick base. His eyes searched mine as though asking for permission to breathe. Vestro's thumbs traced slow circles at my hips, the small motion grounding me while the rest of the world tilted.

"Put your hands to the side," I whispered.

He obeyed, placing his palms flat on the ground.

I pressed my brow to his, forcing air into my lungs as I let myself settle, feeling the deep ache begin to ease and welcome him. I didn't speak. I only nodded.

Yes, yes, I want this.

I shifted slightly, testing, and the pressure changed into something sweeter and warmer. Every nerve in me sparked awake as a tremor ran through me. My breath hitched, a startled gasp breaking loose as the ache gave way to warmth. I tried again, felt my own wetness slicken his skin, and then warmth spread through my belly and legs as I marveled at the feeling of him below me, and how his heat made my center melt and mold around him.

My pulse found its rhythm first. It guided me, small and stubborn, until movement came naturally. Something my body already knew how to do even if I didn't. The world narrowed to the slide of skin, the tremor in his breath, and the slow coil of something raw building deep inside me.

When I rolled my hips, testing, heat rippled through both of us. Vestro made a low sound and his head tipped back, baring his throat to the night. I watched him, marveling at the way the moonlight caught the tendons in his neck, the way his lips parted, the way he breathed my name as if it were sacred. The sight of him open and undone in his surrender to my touch made my chest ache. The tremor in his fingers as they bunched into my cloak betrayed the effort it took for him not touch me or thrust upward. His breath came uneven, the sound almost a plea he swallowed before it could escape.

I had spent my whole life obeying orders, rules, and bloodlines. But here, no crown weighed on my head, no oath bound my hands. Here, alone with Vestro, I was only skin and heartbeat, claiming the space between us as mine alone.

For once, no one decided for me. Not duty, not fear, not a man's hands.

Just me.

"I'm choosing this," I whispered. I pressed my lips to his neck and spoke against his skin. "I'm choosing you tonight."

Vestro's breath hitched, a soft, worshiping sound. He didn't speak. He only nodded once, black eyes wide and catching the starlight, as if afraid that saying anything might break the moment.

My pulse thudded low and heavy, echoing through my bones. I wound my fingers into his long dark hair, pulling gently until his face tilted toward mine. Our breaths mingled, hot and ragged. I pressed my forehead to his and moved again, finding the rhythm, the steadiness, and the power.

My hips set the pace, and he let me. The line between fear and want snapped and fell away as I controlled the way his body moved, shifting my hips to touch only the right places that stole his breath. I watched his face as I rode him, the way his breathing labored, and a sheen of sweat gathered on his upper lip. Every motion hit somewhere between hunger and hurt, between wanting him and wanting the memories gone.

A tremor ripped through Vestro's body, and his hands suddenly slid up my back, rough palms tracing the length of my spine, leaving gooseflesh in their wake.

Then he froze, as if realizing he'd broken the rules.

I should have stopped him. I should have kept the arm's-length rule in place.

But I didn't. I didn't want to.

I turned my face toward his and nodded, just once. I felt the balance shift between us. I knew what it meant, and I let it happen anyway.

Vestro's breath brushed my cheek once, soft, almost relieved, as if in thanks.

Then he began to move, slow at first, careful, as though afraid I'd break. When he met my rhythm, the muscles in his stomach tightening as he thrust into me, our bodies moved together in a perfect, trembling balance. I felt something I'd locked away deep inside me tear open in equal parts of pleasure, sorrow, and something like home. His breath caught on my name, just a whisper, before it dissolved into a groan that vibrated through my chest.

My heart flipped when I felt him shudder beneath me, holding back, trembling with restraint. The power over him I held—his trust, his surrender—sent a pulse of hunger through me so sharp it almost hurt. I bore down on him, tightened my center as I ground my hips. His release hit like a shudder between us; he quaked and cried out my name, and I covered his mouth with mine, taking his release against my lips. I kissed him through it, taking everything he gave until my vision exploded in a burst of starlight and a wave of pleasure ripped under my skin.

My rhythm faltered as my muscles spasmed, and my legs gave out, and I nearly collapsed against his chest. I felt the wave slip, just before the crest. I met Vestro's eyes, desperate, and he grabbed my hips and moved me against him, guiding me, pushing me faster and faster back up the wave until I couldn't breathe and the world shattered around me.

I cried out against his neck, a wordless moan that broke into his skin as a half-sob, half-surrender. The sound wasn't just release but release of everything: the fear, the ache, the years of pretending I didn't need or want this. That I didn't want *him*.

Because I did. *Gods, I did.* Fuck I wanted him so bad. I wanted to push all of him inside me and roll around together in the golden glow as the climax broke me into a million pieces and pressed me back together into something finally whole. I wanted him not just tonight but every night he curled up beside me, picking up my broken pieces, and I finally understood—it was never just tonight. I'd loved him in every breath I'd ever taken beside him.

I clung to him as the tremors took me, shaking through my spine and into his chest until I couldn't tell which heartbeat was mine.

His arms came around me, strong and steady, holding me upright while the rest of me dissolved. My cheek pressed to the curve of his shoulder, just resting. His skin was slick with sweat, and I felt his chest rise and fall, every breath syncing with mine. The air stilled, and all that remained was the faint taste of salt and river and something achingly human.

Vestro's hand came up, fingers brushing the back of my neck. "Nadia," he whispered, but there was nothing left to say.

I pressed a hand to his chest, feeling the steady thud of his heart. I didn't want to move. Not yet.

The night hummed quietly around us: the faint drip of water

from the riverbank, the soft rasp of grass against our legs, and the scent of his skin and a feeling I didn't want to name. Yet in the stillness, the truth slipped through like breath: I had chosen him. Not by accident, not out of loneliness, but because every part of me had already been reaching for him all along.

I leaned my cheek against his shoulder, tracing the line of his collarbone with my thumb. His muscles eased under my touch as if he'd been holding his breath for a century. He was beautiful like this: quiet, strong, wrong for me in every way that mattered. The moonlight wrapped him in silver, softening every edge and making him seem almost human.

I wished, with a sudden ache that hollowed my chest, that I could keep him like this forever. Not as a secret or a sin, not as something forbidden, but as something possible.

The wish broke the spell. The cool air crept back in, chasing the warmth from my skin. I drew a shaky breath, sat up, and smoothed a strand of his hair behind his ear.

"Thank you," I whispered. The words were too small for what he'd let me take.

He nodded, his eyes heavy with understanding as if already mourning what was already lost. His eyes watched my mouth, and his lips trembled as he moved forward, stopped, and then gently pressed his lips to my brow.

"You should go back," he said, his voice rough. "Before someone wakes and finds you missing."

"Always the sensible one," I said, softer than I meant.

"Hardly." He paused. "Do you feel better?"

I pressed my forehead against his and closed my eyes. "Yes."

He pressed his cheek against mine, and he nodded against my hair. I felt the relief bleed through his skin as his shoulders relaxed. He pressed his lips against my temple and held them there for several breaths before leaning back. When he looked up, his boyish grin was back in place, though it looked forced.

He helped me stand, then stepped close, his gaze dark and his hair falling around his eyes. For a moment he looked like he'd speak, but instead he touched his thumb lightly to my jaw, bowed his head, and stepped back into the trees.

For the first time since I started the journey, I felt grounded and refreshed, but beneath it, an ache opened in my chest.

The water whispered against the shore, sliding over the stones in a steady rhythm. I wanted to hate it for moving on when I couldn't.

"Shit."

It all felt unreal—too quick, too quiet, like waking from someone else's dream.

I'd just had sex for the first time.

To a demon.

And fuck, it had felt amazing.

But it wasn't only a need. It was *him*—Vestro's patience, his devotion, and the quiet way he understood every part of me I tried to hide. And I wished, with a sudden, stupid ache, that the world had made him human, just so I wouldn't have to let him go.

I stared at the place where he'd vanished into the trees. Maybe I'd gone too far; maybe there was no way back.

I shuddered as I stepped back into the cold water and pushed the thoughts away. I rinsed the evidence from my skin, careful, efficient, erasing what I could. The slickness between my thighs, the tremor in my hands. Then I dressed, fastening the armor piece by piece until the weight settled over me again. I turned the last knob on my breastplate, locking it into place. Then I froze and looked down.

Where is the second gauntlet?

I spun around, almost falling over in the weight of the suit, and searched the ground in the dim light. I picked up my cloak, shook it, threw it aside. I searched through the damp brush, careful at first and then in haste, trying not to rattle my armor. My vision blurred and I blinked the tears away. My hands were small, no doubt those of a girl, and there would be no way to hide one arm the rest of the trip. If I couldn't find my gauntlet, that would be it.

"Looking for something?"

I froze, my heart stopping as I waited for the barrage of accusations. When they didn't come, I let out a breath and stood up. I turned around slowly, hiding my bare hand behind my back. Not really wanting to face who was behind me.

Peter stood nearby, not close enough for me to clearly see his face but enough to catch the glint of moonlight off my polished gauntlet held under one of his arms. He stared at me through the darkness—like a parent who'd caught a mischievous child stealing from a jar of lemon drops. I frowned at him. He was only fourteen, and in the armor I stood over a foot taller than him, yet he still made me feel the part of the red-handed little thief. He walked through a clump of tall grass toward me, his face coming into focus as he neared.

Peter grinned, and the moonlight sparkled off his mischievous eyes.

I blinked. It wasn't what I had expected. "What?" I said.

"How did you do it?" he said. "This whole time everyone thought you were really a knight. How did you do it?"

"I don't know what you're talking about."

"Come off it. I know it's you, Nadia."

My stomach lurched. *Fucking hell.*

"You're not going to tell anyone," I said.

"Just 'cause I'm younger than you doesn't automatically make me the tattletale of the group. It's King Andrew that you must worry about." He winked at me. "He's going to be in for a big surprise."

"Well, I'm not planning on giving him that chance." I looked at him. "You don't sound rattled."

Peter shrugged. "You seemed a little off from the first time I met you. And," he grinned, "I recognized your horse. You let me ride him last summer my dad and I were visiting Damewood, remember? It was hard since his eyes look different now, so it took me a while to place him, but I did."

Damn, Vestro is going to be my undoing.

I took the offered gauntlet from Peter's outstretched hand. I slipped it on and snapped the knob into place without looking. I had to admit that it felt better knowing someone else knew my secret. Even if it was Peter. I smiled at him, grateful in fact that it *had* been Peter.

Peter clapped his hands.

"But forget about *your* disguise," he said. "Where can I get a horse like Vestro? Is he really a demon?"

"Peter, what?" I choked on a mouthful of air. "How—"

"I was behind the horses taking a piss when this naked guy just appeared between the trees and started walking toward me—well, toward the horses. I don't think he saw me at first, so, I finished and hid behind the nearest tree, waited to see what he was up to."

"I thought you were some big, tough prince," I cut in, crossing my arms. "You didn't try to stop him? What if he'd been a horse thief?"

"I wasn't armed, and my pants were half down." Peter said, a little defensively, making his voice squeak. "Shut up, Nadia. Let me finish." He froze at his outburst, as if remembering who he was speaking to.

I smiled and shrugged, dismissing it.

"Anyway," he said. "This guy comes around near the horses, and I'm watching him, you know, to see if I should try to stop him or something. Then his face came into the light, and I recognized him as you—not *you*, but the *knight* you. Sir Aidan. I was about to turn and go back to bed when he started to...to change!" Peter shook his head. "I swear on my dog's life that it was the most weirdest, strangest, most awful sounding thing that I'd ever witnessed."

"Yeah, well—"

"The guy changed into a *horse*, Nadia! I mean, it looked like his chest was going to explode before he got down on all fours. And that...sludge that dripped off him. Disgusting. It took me a moment to recognize him—the horse, I mean. When I did, I walked out from behind the tree and walked towards him. I don't know if it's possible, but can a horse look embarrassed? Or was it just my imagination?"

"No, he tends to do that." I could only imagine the look Vestro was going to give me when I ripped him a new one for not being more aware of his surroundings.

"He put his head down and I patted him as I passed, then I started walking back the way he'd come to find you." He stepped closer. "Why are you here?"

"Like you, I just wanted to lend my hand at saving the kingdoms. Andrew might not agree, but I have just as much stake in this journey as you two."

Peter nodded. "I know what you mean about King Andrew. Sometimes I think he wishes I wasn't on this trip either. He thinks I'm too young. He doesn't let me keep watch and never asks for my opinion." He paused, peering up at me. "What do you think?"

In all honesty, I agreed with Andrew. I didn't think Peter belonged on this journey either; it was dangerous and the kid hadn't even started shaving yet. But I wasn't about to say it. Not when he stood staring me in the face, almost begging for approval.

"How about this," I said, glancing sideways at him. "You keep my secret, and I'll try to get Andrew to lighten up to you. Sound like a plan?"

Peter nodded and held out his hand. I clasped it and we shook on it.

"Go on back to bed," I said. "I'm going to go wake up Damien for his shift of watch."

"Oh, he's already up," Peter said. "He wasn't in his bedroll when I got up to piss."

My stomach flipped. *If Peter had seen Vestro, does that mean...*

"Good night, Nadia."

"Aidan," I said quickly.

"Oh, that's right," Peter said, blushing slightly as he walked off toward his bed. "Sir Aidan."

"Please don't slip."

"I won't. You don't have to worry about me."

I took a deep breath and glanced at the darkness. Nothing

moved. The chirp of a cricket cut the misty dawn, and I jumped. I closed my eyes and hugged my arms to myself, suddenly cold and very tired.

THIRTEEN

We rode into Mauve with the setting sun at our backs. The dying light cast ribbons of crimson and orange across the cloud-speckled sky, painting the tall pines and illuminating the town with a warm purple glow. Hence, the very original name. The town was small, cozy in a way. The houses all had thatched roofs and exposed beams. Sheep pen fencing wove between the inns, and two main stables that were shared between all the common areas backed up against a row of trees that helped block the easterly wind.

Andrew immediately dismounted as soon as we arrived at the stables, muttering about needing a drink. His fingers twitched at his side, restless, before he forced them to still against the saddlebag. Corbin arrived at his elbow and directed the king inside.

I frowned as I watched them go. The need in Andrew's voice sounded too familiar, too practiced. Lately, it seemed there was always a drink waiting for him.

I took my time shedding Vestro's gear. While the others dropped their saddles and threw hay onto the stall floors, I pulled out my curry comb and gently brushed the dust from his back and sides. His flank twitched under my touch, and he nickered softly at me.

"You rode well today. I'm sure you're tired" I scratched his nose. "But why don't you stay out here for a while?" I said. "Make sure everyone's asleep before you come in, all right?"

Vestro snorted and flicked his ears. I frowned, hoping he would listen to me. Though with Vestro, I could never tell. Exhausted, I quickly brushed off some mud from his coat and headed to the inn. I wasn't even sure why I bothered in the first place; the mud would just slide off with his change anyway. It just felt right, I guessed. I readjusted my bags on my shoulder, quickly exited the stable, and pushed open the inn's front doors.

I pushed the inn's front doors open, and a warm wall of air reeking of sweaty men and roasting meat blasted my face. My stomach flipped and growled at the smell of food, and I looked down to make sure I had my coin purse with me. I stepped inside and let the swinging doors flap shut behind me. I glanced around the large room, trying to locate my party.

The high ceilings were open-beamed and hung with chandeliers made of antlers, with a candle burning at the edge of each point. Animal heads—deer, bear, wolf, and demons—adorned the wood-paneled walls. Two large, stone fireplaces in opposite corners sent light across the walls, casting eerie shadows across the gaping mouths of the stuffed heads.

I shook my head and glanced around the tables scattered around the large room. Farmers, merchants, and knights alike drank and jested, clinking their glasses together as they laughed and sang along to the merry flutist dancing atop the center table. Serving girls in dresses too tight and too low around their bosoms moved quickly from table to table, dropping down rounds of drinks and collecting used glasses. The heat in the room weighed down on me, and I shifted uncomfortably inside the stifling armor, searching.

There!

I spotted Peter's young face in the crowd, seated near the fireplace against the paneled wall. The platters were already half-cleared: roasted fowl and seared pig bones piled high among baskets of rolls and mugs of ale. Empty cups littered the tablecloth, only to be whisked away and replaced with fresh ones. Damien stood beside the table, loading food onto a plate before covering it with a cloth napkin. He caught my eye, gave a minute nod, and then slipped upstairs.

"Knight."

Andrew strolled into view with a woman on each arm, his grin already softened by wine. Too softened, too soon. The room seemed to bend toward him, laughter rising to match his, but all I could hear was the easy slur in his voice—like the cup had met his lips long before I had even crossed the threshold. He looked...relaxed. And entirely too pleased with himself.

He inclined his head toward me in greeting, lips quirking. "You took your time. Again." His amused tone was calm but edged with challenge, as if daring me to object.

One of the women leaned in close, whispering against his ear. He chuckled, a warm, practiced sound, and his hand drifted to her waist —casual yet claiming. The other woman pressed her hand against his chest, and Andrew rewarded her with a light brush of his lips across her knuckles before turning back to me.

"Join us," he said, gesturing with a hand that still held the curve of the woman's hip.

The woman flashed me a wide smile and detached herself from Andrew just enough to lift her skirt to one side and sway her hip toward me. "Join us, Knight?"

My face burned, my eyes boring into Andrew. I couldn't care less about the women, or their choice in profession. I hated the smug way Andrew held himself, the unshakable assurance that every man should admire him for this display. He wore arrogance like a cloak.

And the worst part? It fucking suited the bastard.

"Sir Aidan." Trea's voice cut across my thoughts. "Will you be joining us for dinner?"

"I…" My stomach twisted. I shot another glance at Andrew. "No, I think I'll retire."

Andrew dipped his head toward the blonde, murmuring something that drew a peal of laughter. His touch on her back appeared measured, just enough to keep her near, just enough to be seen.

"Sir Aidan?"

I turned sharply.

Abernathy held something in his hand. "Your key," he said, squinting.

I accepted it with a curt nod. "Thank you."

I started to leave but paused beside the squires. Corbin gnawed at a chicken leg, startled when he noticed me watching. He choked down a bite, gulped ale, then smeared grease into a stained napkin.

"It seems your master enjoys tavern company," I said, my voice tight.

One…two…three…

Corbin hesitated, swirling his drink. "Sometimes. Especially since his father…"

Four…five…

"And tossing coins at strangers eases his grief?"

His mouth opened, shut. "No. But it keeps his mind from other things."

Six…seven…eight.

"Some king," I muttered, "to throw coins at the first woman who bats her eyelashes."

Corbin bristled, surprising me with the force of his reply. "He is honorable! How dare you say otherwise!"

Darren pretended to be interested in the bottom of his mug.

I arched my brow. "He is your king, not mine." The disdain in my tone could have sliced steel. "I'll speak as I please."

Corbin's bravado wilted, and he sank back into his chair. "Forgive me. I spoke out of turn."

"Corbin." Andrew's voice carried across the table, smooth and just a shade too relaxed. Wine softened the edges, but the authority still lay beneath. "What room?"

"Nine, sire."

Andrew repeated it softly to the blonde at his side. She giggled, draping herself against him as though she belonged there.

I exhaled hard, the sound sharper than I meant, and forced myself to look away. No use standing there seething like a fool. I gave Trea and Peter a curt nod, then turned toward the stairs. My boots felt heavy against the tavern floorboards, as though every step dragged the weight of my temper with it.

On the way out, I paused by the kitchen door and ordered two plates to be sent up. Better than sitting at that table pretending I had the stomach for company. The smells of roasted meat and baked bread curled through the air, mocking me with the reminder that I'd eaten nothing since morning. I should have done as Damien had—slipped away with food in hand before the spectacle began.

Instead, I was left with the bitter taste of smoke and laughter ringing in my ears, and the image of Andrew's easy smile burned into the back of my mind. A king's smile, practiced and polished, as though even his vices were a performance.

I clenched my fists, then released them, steadying my breath. No matter. Let him play his games with tavern girls. I had no intention of being one of his playthings.

I WAITED in my armor until the kitchen maid dropped off dinner just as my bath became ready. The town seemed a little behind the times, and instead of turning a knob I had to wait for the fire underneath the iron tub to warm the water. Once the maid left, I sighed in relief and began unbuckling my armor.

I'm so looking forward to a warm meal and a good scrub.

A loud crash came from down the hall. Angry voices seeped into my room through the bottom gap of the door. Something slammed against a wall, rattling the single window. Someone cursed, followed by the sound of scuffling and dragging across the floorboards in my direction.

"What the hell?"

I leaned against the door, my ear to the door. The muted sounds vibrated through, and I could hear the smack of something hitting flesh.

The iron tub hissed and spat as the fire beneath coaxed the water warm, and I considered minding my own damn business long enough for me to wash my hair.

A shout rattled the window. Another crash followed, then a string of curses muffled by the walls. The fight approached from down the hall—louder, meaner, sharper. The voices became distinguishable. My stomach sank.

Of course. Andrew.

I cursed under my breath, strapped my breastplate back on, and slid into my gauntlets with quick, angry jerks. One last glance at the untouched plates of food twisted my gut. Potatoes and bread, roast and butter—already cooling.

Always him. Always now.

By the time I stepped into the hall, the noise had swelled. The two women from the tavern below burst from the door down the hall—bright dresses, flushed cheeks, hair tumbling loose as they ran. They almost bowled me over in their rush, skirts tangling as they squealed past. I didn't need their panicked whispers to know where they'd been.

I looked around, wondering why the others weren't present, before stepping up to room nine. I pounded my gauntlet against the door. "Prince Andrew, open up."

No answer—only more shouting. Corbin's voice, frantic.

Andrew roared, his voice raw and breaking. "I'll not have some farmer call my father a drunkard—"

A thud. A muffled cry.

I shoved the door open.

The room lay in wreckage. Clothes strewn, maps torn and crumpled across the floor, saddlebags gutted and tossed aside. A crooked row of empty wine bottles crowded the nightstand.

Corbin crouched, pressed against the wall, his cheek already swelling purple, his arms thrown up in defense. Andrew loomed over him, fists clenched, chest heaving. He turned when I entered, shoulders rigid, and eyes blazing.

"Haven't you heard of knocking, Knight?" He snapped, but there was a slur at the edge of his words.

"Since when did kings beat their squires?" I shot back.

Andrew turned away, his shoulders a solid knot of tension. He backhanded the bottles off the nightstand.

I turned to the squire. "Corbin, what the hell happened?"

The squire glanced at Andrew. "Someone at the tavern... said Riverwind fell with the king. And its heir is just the king's echo—wine, women, and a crown too heavy for a boy who won't lift it."

Andrew's face twisted, blotched red with drink and rage. "He said I'm just like him." The words tore out raw and low, as if dragged against his will, and for the first time I heard no arrogance at all—only hurt.

Something inside me clenched. I knew that tone too well; the edge of shame, the kind that came from old bruises no crown could hide.

Memories I'd tried not to keep clawed their way up before I could shove them back down: the sting of wine in the air, the echo of anger through stone walls. My throat tightened.

With a sharp jerk, Andrew drew his sword. "Never fucking repeat that."

The steel sang in the dim light, but I barely saw the blade. I stood rooted to the spot, staring at Andrew.

For a moment, he looked every inch the king he pretended to be; straight-backed, jaw locked, wrath sparking in his eyes. But then the cracks showed, even through the slur from the drink. His stance faltered, just slightly. His throat worked as he swallowed. His nostrils flared like a man drowning for air. And his chin trembled ever-so-slightly, just enough that I couldn't look away.

Time slowed. My chest tightened. I didn't want to see this. *Not Andrew.* Not the one who was supposed to swagger through every storm with unshakable pride.

And in that flicker of a moment, it wasn't the insufferable king standing in front of me, but the boy I'd once called my best friend. The one who used to laugh with and hold me before the crown hardened his smile. The one I comforted when his father's drunken rage had left him bruised and reeling. Seeing Andrew now, raw and broken, hurt worse than I wanted to admit.

Then the blade in his hand and the wine on his breath shoved the memory back where it belonged.

But that's not him. Not anymore.

I stepped to my right, and he mirrored me, eyes sharp but movements sluggish with drink. My throat tightened.

"I'm not crossing blades with you tonight," I said quietly.

Andrew's shoulders coiled, and he lunged anyway, a jab more reckless than measured. I slid aside and caught his swing on my gauntlet, shoving his shoulder as he stumbled past. His sword clattered across the floor. He cursed, scrambling after it, and I let him. Any other time, I would have laughed or needled him with a sharp remark.

But not now.

Not when I could see the desperation in the way his hands shook on the hilt.

Not when I was desperately fighting to not cry.

Andrew came at me again, quicker this time, his blade arcing wide. I blocked the blade with my right arm, dropped to one knee, and drove my fisted gauntlet into his unguarded belly. Andrew's breath burst out in a harsh gasp as he folded, the sword slipping free of his hands. I held my breath at how fast he dropped his sword and crumpled around my fist. I sometimes forgot that the armor magically added strength to my movements, and for a minute I worried that I'd really hurt him. I caught and held him for a heartbeat, then let him roll to his side, curling against the floorboards, clutching for air.

I stood back, chest tight, my own breath ragged. Sweat traced down my spine, but all I felt was the weight of silence pressing down on us both. Words raced through me; mockery, pity, comfort, fury... but none took shape.

Andrew's eyes lifted, glassy in the candlelight. Anger burned there, but so did pain. And beneath both, a flicker of something I hadn't seen since we were children; *Fear.*

For one breath, I almost spoke. Almost told him he wasn't his father. Almost reached for the boy I used to know.

Instead, I turned on my heel, leaving the words unsaid, my silence heavier than any blade.

"Sleep it off."

The words lingered in the thick air. It took me a moment to realize I'd even spoken. I blinked and felt hot tears slip down my cheeks, and once again I was happy for the magic disguising my face.

I tore down the hall, boots heavy against the boards, every step creaking too loud in the silence. The sound chased me just as much as the image clung like smoke—the king on his knees, trembling. My chest ached for the boy I'd known, and I hated myself for wanting to reach for.

FOURTEEN

Someone screamed. Again, and again.

My eyes popped open to an orange-hued ceiling, and I sat up in bed, the sheets piling around my waist. The cool air brushed against my bare skin, and I shivered and looked around in the strange light. The bed beside me sat empty; Vestro had never come in last night.

Screams came from outside. High pitched.

A child.

I leaped out of bed and snatched my sword leaning against the bedside table. I reached for the doorknob and stopped. I looked down. *Damn.* I had my sword—important—but not clothes—*equally* important. It felt wonderful to know my priorities in a crisis.

I propped my sword against the door jamb, fumbled through my bags and slid into a set of underclothes.

From now on I'm just going to sleep fully dressed.

I pulled a tunic over my head and had one arm out when the screaming outside escalated. I straightened up and walked to the window as a whistling sound pierced the night. I reached up to move the curtains aside as the sound grew.

What in the world...

A deafening boom ripped through the night, rocking the walls and floor of my room. I screamed, throwing myself to the floor, arms locked over my head. Curtains tore, igniting in orange flame that chewed upward, spitting sparks at the ceiling. I spun around. The window had exploded. The drapes hung in tatters, tiny flames licking at the torn edges. A stream of black smoke slipped in through the busted window, reeking of burning grass and hair.

I looked up to see a strange, fist-sized, metal ball lob through the broken window. It landed with a thump on the floor just inches to my right and then rolled to a stop below the window. A tiny wick stuck out from one end, and I watched, entranced, as the little flame at the end sputtered and crackled, eating its way toward the ball.

My instincts screamed at me, and I snapped back to the present. I dove for the small object, the metal casing warm and surprisingly heavy in my hands, cocked my arm back, and chucked it as far as I could out of the window. I leaned forward to watch it sail through the orange sky as it arced and fell, landing on the flat roof of a silver-smith across the street.

Several heartbeats passed, and nothing happened. Then the roof of the silversmith exploded. The walls peeled outward in jagged shards as if some great hand had torn the building apart. A ball of fire rose and billowed out from the center. Heavy wood beams screamed as they splintered and spun skyward. Heat rolled against my face, hot enough to sting my eyes.

Oh, fuck this.

I shoved my legs into trousers and practically jumped into my armor, twisting the knobs and shoving my helmet on as I hurried out the door.

Trea stood in the hallway buckling on his breastplate and helmet. Andrew stumbled bleary-eyed out of his room in underwear and stockings, leaning against the wall for support. He glared at me when his eyes focused.

"The town is under attack!" Trea barked, voice cutting sharp through the chaos. "We need to leave, now!"

Corbin and Darren appeared from their masters' rooms, their arms burdened with bags and gear. They looked around in desperation. Abernathy came skidding around the corner with Benjamin, so close to the armed soldier that I was surprised Benjamin didn't just throw him over his shoulder and carry him. Five doors away, Peter stuck his head out of his room, his face was pale and his eyes round in the orange glow. His hand trembled as it gripped the door jamb. He looked near ready to throw up.

The screams outside built. The choking smell of smoke wafted up through the floorboards.

"The inn is on fire," Abernathy's voice squeaked as he stumbled down the stairs, trying to put both his boots on at the same time. "We need to get out of here!"

I quickly ducked back into my room and fetched my bags, then hurried after them. Peter slipped going down the stairs and I caught his arm before he fell. He glanced back at me in thanks, but I pushed him forward, yelling for him to keep going. I started to lag a little behind, my arm-full of supplies making it hard to shimmy down the stairs in the armor. Andrew appeared to my right as he fixed his crown and hefted his sword. He gave me a disappointed look, snatched one of my bags, and hefted it over his shoulder.

"Thanks," I mumbled.

He grunted and shoved me forward, propelling me out of the inn doors and into the street. Peter stood just outside the doorway, his face slack and eyes wide with fear.

He shouldn't be here. Why the hell did Andrew ever agree to bring a kid?

Chaos filled the streets. Dogs and chickens fled. Villagers ran in their nightclothes, faces ash-gray, eyes wide white. Fire consumed storefronts, signs blistering as paint melted in rivulets of color. Bodies lay strewn, mouths open to the flames. Blood crept between stones like ink spilled on parchment.

I glanced up as large embers drifted down from the roof of the inn. I spotted my window—red light bathed the inside of the room, and flames licked greedily at the tattered curtain remains.

The twang of a bowstring caught my attention. Damien stood in the street, his feet planted and back straight as if nothing could touch him. His cloak billowed black, bowstring whispering as arrow after arrow vanished into smoke. His eyes glittered with something unholy—half hunger, half delight—as he drew and loosed arrows with the calm of a man plucking a harp. He met my eyes as he reached into the quiver strapped on his back.

Cold trickled down my spine as I stared at the solid black eyes staring back at me. Eyes as solid black as Vestro's.

Then the moment broke when Damien looked away to grab another arrow from his quiver, nocked it, and sent it flying through the dark.

The smoke is playing tricks on me. Damien isn't...

"Corbin, fetch the horses," Andrew ordered, his eyes focused on his shoulder plates as he had trouble buckling the last strap. "We need to leave."

"We can't just leave!" My voice rang too loud, too raw. I slashed my arm toward the street. "They'll all die!"

Andrew's head whipped toward me, his mouth opening for some sharp retort.

"Sir Aidan," Trea panted. "We are on a quest to retrieve Cipher, and we can't help anyone if we fail to—"

"What kind of a king are you?" I screamed at Andrew. "As a new king you should know the people mean everything to a kingdom."

"Do not dare to judge me, Knight!"

I rounded on him. "You're a coward, just like your father!"

Andrew froze, color draining from his face. For a heartbeat the world itself seemed to pause; the fire crackling, the screams, even the smoke-laden wind stilled. His jaw flexed once, twice, his lips parting as though to answer, but no sound came. My stomach twisted, a sick feeling of regret at the low blow rising in my throat. But my anger swallowed it and pushed the feeling down.

Andrew's voice came low and dangerous. "I should have your head for such an outburst."

A scream sounded off to my right. I turned to look, and my heart stopped.

A toddler lay in the dirt, dress torn, hands clawing at the cobbles as her legs kicked uselessly. A wolf demon—like those that had attacked me as I fled Damewood castle—crouched over her, shoulders twitching with the promise of the strike. Its muzzle glistened red.

Oh, please no.

I yanked free my sword, the scraping of metal against the scabbard piercing through the sounds of madness around us.

"You want my head, King," I shouted, baring teeth. "Then come and get it!"

I pumped my legs as fast as I could. My armor came alive and seemed to move on its own, the sound of the whirring joints propelling me forward at double my normal speed. I roared as I lifted both arms overhead and swung my sword down two-handed. The blade caught the monster in the spine between the shoulder blades. It howled and snapped at me, the yellow eyes flashing as it fought to keep its feet. I rammed my knee into its skull. Bone crumpled with a sickening crunch, folding inward. Blood fanned hot across my armor, spraying me through the eye ports. I blinked, and for a moment pink tinged my vision became tinged in pink.

I yanked the blade free of the body and quickly scooped up the child in one arm. She sobbed, trying to crawl inside the gaps of my breastplate, tiny nails scraping against the steel for safety. I shifted her weight on my arm to hold her higher against my chest, ran back to the inn steps and held her out to Peter. His face paled even more, if that was possible, but he took her and held her to his chest.

"Stay here and keep her safe," I said.

Peter nodded. I smiled behind the safety of my helmet. Now not only was the child safe, but Peter would hopefully be kept out of trouble. I looked at the others. Damien watched me from the shadows, his eyes hidden, and lifted his chin in what I deemed was approval.

Andrew set his jaw.

"Swords at the ready!" Andrew's voice snapped like a whip. "Benjamin, Gregory, with me. Trackers, watch our backs. Trea, get your prince out of here."

The chaos immediately shifted, reshaped. Andrew's voice cut through panic, pulling threads into a pattern. Villagers who had been wailing blindly now moved in lines, guided by his barked orders. Damien smiled, a wild gleam in his eye, and took off running after a pair of growling shadows.

My chest tightened. I hated how steady Andrew sounded while my own heart tried to crawl up my throat. The initial adrenaline had faded, and the reality of the destruction unfolding around us began to weigh on my shoulders. The air grew heavier, and I found myself struggling to catch a breath.

Settle, Nadia. We can do this.

Buildings on both sides burned, painted storefronts sending plumes of colored smoke high into the lightening sky as beams collapsed and villagers fled in every direction, carrying children and wrapped bundles of prized possessions. I spun to the right as I caught sight of two figures in gold cloaks tossing more metal balls into what looked like a butcher shop before disappearing down the opposite alley.

I ran full out, kicking the suit into full gear, and sped after them with my head down as twin eruptions practically lifted the entire building off its foundation. The buildings collapsed behind me in a scream of timbers. Butcher hooks and bricks rained down. I coughed dust through the slits of my helm.

Several mouthfuls of teeth leaped out at me as soon as I entered the shadows of the passage, and I quickly spun and sent my sword in an arc, my armor whirring as my blade cleanly sliced all three demons in half. I righted myself and stood panting in the buzzing silence, looking around.

The alley pressed in around me, shadows clinging to the stone like damp moss. My sword felt too heavy, my breath too loud inside the helmet.

The shadows of the alley seemed closer than a moment ago, the blackness seeming to stretch and reach out to me. I turned to leave the alley and halted mid-step, spinning around. Yellow eyes blinked in the dark. One pair, then three. Then ten. Low growls braided together into a single note, so deep it vibrated in my ribs. The sound filled the alley until it felt like the walls themselves were snarling.

My blood-covered gauntlets felt slick. I adjusted my grip, but my sword hilt slipped anyway, and I fought to keep under control. My throat squeezed tight, every swallow scraping raw.

Gods, how many of them are there?

My heart raced as the shadows crept closer, their outlines forming as they left the protection of the buildings' walls to circle closer. Their wiry black hair bristled over the protruding spines of their high-arched backs. Their paws and wolf-like muzzles dripping with bloody chunks of flesh. Long, black claws clicked against the cobblestones as the ring closed about me, the circle shrinking with every step.

My head jerked back, and I nearly dropped my sword in surprise at the sudden appearance of a figure in a gold cloak. The hooded figure stood, swiveled its head, and then stepped from the dark shadows into the light of the burning shop. I froze and focused all my attention on holding back a terrified scream.

The cloak parted just enough to reveal a body upright like a man's but bent and warped. Broad shoulders hunched forward, and long legs were jointed backward like the wolves surrounding it. Fur bristled along its arms, thick at the wrists where clawed hands flexed open and shut. Its face was wrong, terribly wrong: one half lupine, muzzle dark and wet, eyes glowing blue like cold fire. The other half had no face at all, but a jaw of shining steel, plates riveted together and pinned into flesh with black bolts. Each clench whirred like gears grinding stone.

My breath stuck in my chest. I couldn't look away.

The creature tilted its head. Dog-like. Curious. Mocking. The metal jaw caught the firelight, scattering it in glints of unnatural blue. The sound of its breathing scraped across the whir of machinery, a grotesque duet.

I struggled to breathe through the lump in my throat that threatened to strangle me. I stared at the creature's jaw, at the polished metal so shiny that it was almost blue and reflected every crackle and pop of the inferno behind us. Recognition cut. I'd seen that same type of metal once before.

I'm wearing it.

"You are the one who escaped from Damewood," the creature said, its voice resonant and metallic, like words dragging over gears. The jaw clicked with every syllable. The cold eyes blinked, and flicked from my armor to my helm, narrowing as if trying to stare inside the eye ports.

My mind raced as I stared at the bipedal demon in the gold cloak of The Holy. I remembered something Damien had said at our last meeting with Maurdruik:

'The Holy gave them their brains... Without The Holy's meddling, the demons would still be dumb beasts. They made them smarter, meaner.'

I swallowed as things started to come together. The assassins at the castle had been demons. Demons were now attacking the outlying towns throughout each kingdom, using weapons and fire in ways I'd never seen or heard of. But how? And why?

My eyes flicked to the demon's metal jaw, my mind reeling.

'What I did to that suit of yours has been a banned practice from the kingdom for centuries, Maurdruik had said.'

The armor. *Our armor.*

The armor was the answer. But to what?

A furred hand lifted toward me, claws extending and lengthening to three times their original length as I stared. "I was told you had a tendency to run off by yourself, making the job difficult," the deep voice chuckled. "You should have learned to pick better company, Princess. It might have saved your life."

My knees locked. My sword wavered. The world tunneled to that half-flesh, half-steel face. I could hear nothing but the grind of its jaw, see nothing but those eyes—one wolf, one...*machine*. My breath hitched higher. Machines were things of stories. Even Old Red had said so; nothing but scary stories to keep kids in line. To provide old wizards something to muse over.

They weren't supposed to be real.

The circle closed tighter. The wolves padded forward, claws clicking on stone, hot breath wafting through the gaps in my armor. Their teeth gleamed wet.

My body refused to move. I wanted to scream, to run, to fight—anything—but I was stone.

Frozen.

I was told...

The demon's steel jaw whirred, widening in a parody of a smile.

A sword hissed out of the dark and punched through the creature's furred neck. The world cracked apart as time and sound returned to me in a dizzying rush. The half-wolf choked, eyes bulging, then crumpled in a twitching heap as the blade yanked free. Wolves yelped as the longsword sang through the air, felling them in sprays of blood.

And through the circle's collapse came Andrew.

He didn't just stride toward me—he stormed. His sword a burning arc in the firelight, each swing precise and vicious, cleaving the demon wolves aside as if they were nothing. His bright eyes blazed through the ash smeared across his face, his jaw set like iron. His gold hair gleamed red in the fire. His silhouette stretched tall and sure in his obsidian armor, and larger than life. The kind of exaggerated figure bards would sing about for decades to come.

My breath burst free in a sob I swallowed too late. Relief hit me so hard my knees threatened to give out.

Andrew turned to me; proud, arrogant, and an absolute egotistical ass by the smug look on his ash-covered face. Yet, at that moment, I forgave him because he represented everything the world meant when they said *knight in shining armor.*

Gods be damned, and he came to rescue me.

It took everything in me not to just drop my sword and launch myself into his arms.

Andrew sneered at me. "I know you admire my work, Sir Aidan," he drawled, his voice cutting sharp and steady through the chaos, "but get off your fucking ass and help."

It was enough to break the trapped princess spell, and I was suddenly the knight again. My body remembered how to move. The fear didn't vanish, but it bent, reshaped into fire in my chest. I roared and swung, blade flashing, armor screaming with me.

Side by side we cut down the pack. Andrew's blade rose and fell in sweeping arcs, mine darted and struck where his left openings. He fought like a castle wall; I struck like lightning. Together, the demons didn't stand a chance.

When the last one broke and fled, the alley reeked of blood and smoke. Dozens of furred bodies scattered across the cobblestones, steam rising off their torn bodies.

Andrew lowered his sword, chest heaving, sweat streaking his brow. He looked every inch the king he pretended to be. And in that moment—gods help me—I was glad he was there standing just an arm's reach away.

Andrew wiped his forehead, eyes scanning bodies, then jerked his chin for me to follow and we started back toward the inn.

I trudged behind him, my head down and my mind a mess. I couldn't think straight, and I fidgeted under the sudden heat of my armor. The harness itched against me, the straps digging into my shoulders and slowing my movements. The helmet was stifling, and I undid the chinstrap and slipped it off over my head. I gasped at the rush of cool air that seemed to slam against my face, drying the sweat sliding down my temples.

My head jerked up as I noticed that Andrew had slowed to walk beside me and then settled when I remembered the projected disguise over my face. Andrew watched me through the corner of his eye as we walked, his mouth set in a hard, tight line. Ash smeared against his forehead and a splattering of blood across his left cheek. He glanced to his right at the villagers in the streets gathering as we passed the burning inn, then back at me.

"That was a good call, Knight," he said softly. "Defying me to give them hope."

I peered sideways at him as we neared our waiting companions. I nodded.

Andrew's voice grew firm. "But hope without order dies fast. Remember that."

Yeah, I can get behind that.

I looked away from him as we reached the bottom steps of the inn. The villagers had mostly put out the fire at the inn, and only fat plumes of black smoke billowed out into the pale sky above the town. Peter stood behind Benjamin and the trackers, hugging the little girl close. She latched onto him like a baby possum, sobbing into his shirtfront. The young prince looked so lost that I wanted to run to him and pick him up, hug away the fear and hurt in his eyes just as he hugged the little girl. I opened my mouth when a woman ran up to him, begging for the child. Peter looked away, and the moment was lost.

"Where's Trea?" he asked.

"Don't worry," Trea muttered, limping up to us. "I'm not dead yet." He waved us away before anyone could say anything. "I just pulled something in my leg. Happens when you start getting old."

I let my shoulders relax and rolled my head back, stretching my neck. The stench of burning paint and flesh permeated the dawn sky, filling my lungs and crowding out all thoughts from my mind. I focused on my breathing as I straightened up and glanced around the street. The explosions had ceased.

Andrew nodded and sheathed his sword. "Corbin, Darren," he said. "Go fetch the horses. We need to move."

The two squires made it halfway down the street before something clicked in the back of my head.

Vestro!

I dug my heels into the earth and pumped my legs as fast as I could toward the stables. I didn't care if the men saw me run. I'd deal with their questions later. Those demons had been everywhere, killing everything in their path.

Please, Vestro, please be safe.

The two squires looked over their shoulders as they heard me coming, and they stopped as I rushed past them. My lungs burned and I nearly toppled over as I finally stumbled through the stable entrance.

Darkness filled the stables. The dawning light filtered in through the high window slits, dimly illuminating the upper eaves of the building and silhouettes of numerous wood stalls. The stable boy lay crumpled in a bloody heap near the closest stall, his head connected to his neck by a mere thread. A musky, sulfuric smell hung heavy in the air. I covered my nose and stepped around the body toward the back of the stable. The farther in I walked, the stronger the smell became.

"Vestro?" I whispered. "Hey, Ves? Are you there?" My heart raced when no answer came.

Horses whinnied in their stalls, tossing their heads about nervously, their hooves thumping against the straw covered ground. I passed Trea's and Darren's horses, and Abernathy's blue. The rank stench intensified so that I had to breathe through my mouth. Even then, it didn't help much. My vision blurred as tears threatened to spill over. I neared the end of the aisle.

Please be in your stall...

There was a growl to my left. I froze, every muscle in my body tense. Out of the corner of my eye I caught two pinpoints of yellow.

They blinked. Once. Twice. Then they doubled in size as the demon leaped for me. I screamed.

The sharp edge of a shovel came down across the demon's back, severing the creature's spine with a sickening, wet crack and spraying blood everywhere within a four-foot radius. I jumped back and tripped over my own feet, pinwheeling my arms as I fell into the door of a stall. I slid to the floor, losing my sword in the process. The weight of the armor pulled me down, and I struggled to roll off my back. I looked up at the sound of the shovel clanging as it was tossed against a pile of old tack. Vestro bent over me, his smooth face speckled with blood. He smiled and offered me a hand, pulling me to my feet.

"You're all right!" I managed. I hugged him as best I could—not worrying about my armor getting in the way. "I was so worried. When you didn't answer…"

"I know," he said. "Sorry. I heard you come in, but I didn't want to give my hiding place away before I got the bastard." He pursed his lips. "You were worried about me?"

I shot him a look. "Of course I was," I said, noticing the way his eyes brightened and creased at the corners as he smiled. "You're my best friend."

He smiled, soft at first, then guarded. "I'm fine. I heard the attacks start and stayed outside to look after the horses. The demons came inside, and they got the boy before I could react."

"You need to shift, the others will be here any minute," I said. I took a deep breath. "I'm so glad, I…I didn't know how I was going to go on without you."

Vestro smiled sadly, something I couldn't comprehend filling his eyes. He gracefully bowed to me, took two steps back, and began his change. The dark hid most of his change, the shadows acting as a thick curtain that only gave glimpses of movement when he passed into one of the dim patches of light.

He screamed as his back arched and seemed to explode from the inside. Brown hair sprouted from his bare skin, patchy at first, and then in a whispering rush. His clenched hands melted together and hardened into heavy hooves that pounded the dirt floor. He reared up and whinnied, tossed his head and flicked his long tail. He snorted and shook himself, spraying wet goop on the walls of the nearest stalls.

I swallowed and stepped closer. I patted his jaw and leaned my face against his neck, ignoring the wet film on his coat.

"Please don't scare me like that again."

I quickly used the currycomb hanging on the outside of the stall and scraped off most of the slime before the others came in. Vestro nudged me softly, ears pointed forward. I dropped the comb in my knapsack and slipped the bridle over his head, waiting for the magic to turn his pale eyes to turn brown.

Damien stepped into view, followed by Andrew and Jonathan. I heard the others make their way inside, but their faces were lost in darkness. Corbin went right to work on saddling Andrew's horse. Damien watched me, arms crossed as he leaned against the stall door, a twisted grin across his face. The hair on the back of my neck stood on end as I felt his eyes—still dark but human again—study Vestro's form.

What the hell did he think was so interesting?

Andrew brushed up against one of the blood-stained stalls, cursed when he saw the demon corpse at my feet, and then wiped at a smear of blood that had gotten on his armor. Benjamin pulled his horse out of the stall and began dressing it, throwing the saddle onto its back in his haste.

"We need to be off as soon as possible," he said. "Several of the demons got away, and we can't risk sticking around for them to come back with a larger pack."

"Those demons are not the only things I'm worried about." Andrew looked up and stepped aside as Corbin shouldered past him with their gear. His eyes tracked his squire as Corbin dumped the saddles on the ground and started to layer on their horses' blankets. "Someone must have tagged us as the search party for Cipher. It seems too coincidental that Damien saw The Holy members this morning, and then the town is attacked."

"How would anyone even make such a connection?" Jonathan stopped saddling his horse and turned to stare at Andrew. He blinked and looked to his partner, then back to Andrew. "When we signed on, we were told no one was supposed to know that we—or *anyone* for that matter—are traveling in search of Cipher. If the wrong people were to find out..."

"Well, they have," I said. I hesitated at the stares around me and waited for the shuffling of feet to quiet. "One of the demons spoke to me."

"What did it say?" Abernathy spat out. He hiccuped as if surprised he'd spoken up and quickly shut his mouth. But his beady eyes stayed fixed on me, waiting.

I suddenly didn't want to tell them and almost wished I hadn't said anything. My eyes scanned the faces of the group visible in the growing light.

"...You should have learned how to pick better company, Princess."

My eyes halted on the demon hunter, standing directly across from me. Damien looked back at me evenly. Not staring—just looking. His eyes flicked from me to Abernathy, to Andrew, and then back to me. Creases formed at the corners of his dark eyes, visible even in the shadow of his cowl. He ever so slightly jerked his head to the left as his eyes remained fixed on me. If I hadn't been watching closely, I would have missed it.

What is Damien trying to tell me? And what does he know?

"It just knew we were on a mission," I said, my voice low, tearing my eyes away from the hunter.

"That's it?" Peter said. "Well, that's not so bad."

"What about our destination, our plans?" Andrew drilled. "Did it give any indication it knew more..."

"Your highness," I cut in, "that's all it said."

Andrew stood staring at me as Corbin finished with their gear. He reached up and yanked off his crown and polished a smudge with the edge of his thumb. He lifted his hand to place it back on his head, hesitated, and then shoved it into one of his saddlebags. Damien nodded and slipped back into the shadows, leading his black stallion away from the group toward the front doors.

I shook my head and layered on Vestro's blankets and saddle. He stood calmly as I cinched it tight, even lowered his head as I readjusted the bridle in his mouth.

The smell of the monster's corpse became unbearable; my stomach turned in warning. I had to get out of there before I spewed all over the inside of my suit. I gently pressed my heels against Vestro's sides. He didn't complain. I think he wanted out just as much as I did. I felt the muscles in his back below the saddle bunch and quiver as he trotted tight and offbeat, and I could tell that he was using all his self-control not to spring into a gallop.

We started away and the others followed close behind. We passed by burning houses and broken fences. Gutted sheep and cows lay across the streets, their intestines trailed along the stones, making grotesque patterns in pools of blood. A man lay on his back, his throat torn and eyes missing. A woman lay across his chest, her wails echoing throughout the dark alleys.

I lowered my head and looked away. Once again, I felt glad for my armor and the concealment of my helmet.

That way no one could see my tears as we silently plodded through the desolate stretch of street, out of the light of the burned city and into the dawn.

FIFTEEN

The wind whistled across the steep cliffs and whipped our cloaks about us, tousling the horses' manes and stirring up dust in our eyes.

We followed the windy trail leading up to Snakebit Ridge, a high mountain pass running below the crest of Raven Plateau that bordered the southern lands of the Elk Plains. Forty feet below us ran the Warden River, which flowed from the mountain peaks and fed into the central lake, also known as the Well, that provided water and transportation to the borders of four of the five kingdoms, the oceanfront Riverwind being the only one excluded. The lake sparkled like the side of a silver fish in the afternoon sun, catching the rays of the dying light that managed to filter through the thickening layer of clouds, the water's surface flashing blue, white, and gold. Part of me wished I could dive in—wash the dust and sweat from my armor, let the current scrub me clean. But instead, I sat there, clinging to the saddle like a burr, praying the horse didn't slip on the loose stones that littered the trail.

Andrew had insisted this was the fastest way east. Fastest, sure. Safest? Absolutely not. The switchbacks were steep, the wind sharp enough to peel you off the mountain if you weren't careful. Personally, I thought hammering along the lower ground would have been quicker. But, of course, I wasn't the boss.

Andrew's ego had made it very clear who was.

I risked a glance down, gripping the saddle horn so hard I'd leave grooves in the leather. My stomach dropped at the sight of the river's churn below. A sudden gust shoved at me, and I jerked back, heart in my throat.

I looked away from my lunch of day-old biscuits and air-crusted cheese to peer down the edge of the cliff. I gripped the saddle between my knees as hard as I could, until I was sure I'd leave permanent indentions in the leather, and leaned forward against Vestro's neck to get a better look.

His ears flicked back, reading the shift in my weight before I even nudged him. He slowed, steady as stone, letting me settle. Steady and waiting.

A strong gust of wind caught me and threatened to push me over, and Vestro quickly pulled back away from the drop, lifting his head to force me back.

"Always the practical one," I muttered under my breath.

He tossed his head with a soft nicker.

Trea snorted from behind. "Saints, you talk to that beast like he understands you."

I glanced over my shoulder at him, realizing my slip. I glanced past the captain's face to see Damien watching silently.

Damn that man is creepy.

"He's a fine animal." I patted Vestro's neck and dipped my head in acknowledgement. "Excellent breeding."

I looked up ahead to the front of the line at Andrew as he argued with Jonathan. I couldn't hear over the gusts, but I caught sharp gestures and twitching necks—men bristling like dogs in a pen. Wonderful.

"Let's keep moving," Andrew finally bellowed, his voice torn thin by the wind.

The line started moving up the mountain, slowly at first and then picking up pace to match that of a wounded, three-legged turtle. I had nothing to do but grip the pommel of the saddle and follow.

～

HOURS later we came to a wide, level area and stopped to rest. The late afternoon sun had begun to dip toward the horizon, and I hated the possibility of spending the night on this gods-forsaken trail. We dismounted and stretched our sore muscles, aching from gripping the reins and saddles for support against the wind. I limped around in a circle. I groaned with each step, gaining a look from Peter.

"What's wrong with you?" he said.

"My butt fell asleep."

He just looked at me, one eyebrow raised and his mouth twitching. Then he shook his head and turned away, laughing.

Something hit the top of my helmet. *Ping. Ping...Ping.* I glanced up. Another one fell through my visor slits and dripped in my eye. The raindrops came faster, more steadily. *Great.* I shook my head and stepped over to where Andrew huddled over a map with the trackers.

"Now this is fun," I said. "Tell me, Your Majesty, what's next on the agenda? Pneumonia?"

"Shut it, Sir Aidan." Andrew pulled his cloak tighter, cigarette smoke curling in the wet air.

Jonathan snapped the map out of his hand, scowling. "With respect, Highness, *you* chose this path."

"You are supposed to be guides!" Andrew shot back.

The tracker shook his head. "We give options and opinions; you make the decisions."

I threw up my hands. "Could you stop measuring whose... *compass* is bigger, and just get us off this damn mountain?"

The men stared at me like I'd grown antlers.

Fine. Whatever.

Tomas leaned over the map. "We're not lost, just delayed. Left at the next bend..."

The earth rumbled, and the earth buckled beneath our feet. My legs crumpled, and I fought to clear away from the edge of the platform. The horses screamed and reared, one bolting. I crawled out of the way, barely missing the flying hooves, as the Corbin's horse galloped past me. The earth shook again, and a massive chunk of rock cracked, broke off, and fell down the cliff, taking the panicked horse with it.

"Shit!" I yelled and scrambled toward the mountainside of the path.

I couldn't see anything through the rain and falling debris. Men around me yelled and rushed about, their armor rasping over rocks and clanging against their swords. The horses whinnied and shrieked, hooves pounding the ground and banging their saddles against the cliff.

Someone yelled over the noise, "Get away from the wall! Get away from the wall!"

I looked up at the dark shadow of the sheer mountainside slowly materializing through the now pouring rain. Small, dark pebbles appeared through the haze and pelted me as they rolled down the slope, followed by fist-sized rocks, and farther back...

I ducked as a rock the size of my head whizzed past me. The rock could have taken my head right off. My heart raced. The quake continued, and sharp cracks echoed over the cliffs as more rocks fell, crashing into the platform, rolling, and disappearing over the edge to fall toward the river below.

"Help!" a voice shrieked thin and high.

The shaking slowed, and only a few pebbles and chunks of dirt continued trickling down the high cliff.

"Dammit, someone help!" the high-pitched voice yelled.

I hurried over to the edge and carefully peered over. Peter clung to a thin rock ledge sticking out about a foot below the platform we stood on, eyes wide and face pale as his feet dangled in the open air.

"N-Nadia, please!"

My heart flipped. I awkwardly dropped to my stomach and reached out one arm.

"Peter, grab hold!" I screamed. "Someone help me!"

Peter scrambled for my gauntlet and grabbed on, a little too hard, a little too fast. I slipped on the slick layer of mud and fought to keep on the ledge. My heart beat in my ears. I screamed—though I couldn't hear myself, so I wasn't sure if I'd really screamed or if I'd just thought about it. Peter tried to climb up my arm, and his weight pulled me farther over the edge, my armor screeching against the wet, jagged rocks.

"Dammit, you worthless mongrels, someone help me!" I yelled.

My descent quickened and my waist neared the edge when I heard something heavy clank as it fell against my legs, holding me in place. The sudden stop in movement jerked Peter to a halt, wrenching his arm so that he cried out.

"I got you," Trea said as he crawled to lie across me, his weight pinning me solidly. "Someone grab Peter!"

Damien knelt beside me and reached down, grabbed hold of Peter's arms, pulled him higher, slipped his hand through Peter's belt, and hefted the prince over the ledge.

Peter collapsed beside me, his eyes wet and mouth in a perfect circle. He panted and scrambled away from the ledge.

Trea pushed himself off me, and I rolled away to my knees. I struggled to my feet and staggered away from the edge. My head went dizzy for a moment. I leaned against the mountain for support, trying to catch my breath. Peter came up to me and rapped his knuckles on my armor.

"Thanks," he said, the color slowly returning to his face. "I owe you."

"I'll hold you to that, Prince," I said, smiling.

Andrew asked, jogged over to us, his armor clanking as he moved. "Are you two all right?" He looked past me. "Where is everyone?"

We looked around through the thick shower. My eyes frantically searched the horses. At first all I could see were outlines, dark silhouettes through the downpour. I stepped away from the men toward the horses to get a better look, my breath tight. The shapes slowly became clear, and Vestro stared back at me, his ears laid flat and lips pulled back in a grimace. He whinnied at me and bobbed his head.

My heart rate slowed. He was safe.

"Ah, hell," someone whispered to my left.

I turned to look and immediately wished I hadn't. Tomas lay in a crumpled heap near the bottom of the cliff wall, his chest caved-in by a saddle-sized boulder. Blood trickled out of his slack mouth and red, swollen eyes, mingling with the rainwater pooling between his lips. I quickly turned away, my breathing rapid.

"We need to be moving," Andrew said, taking a step back. His face was extremely pale in contrast to the dark armor, and his hair stuck to his forehead and cheeks. "We need to get off this mountain and down to the river before nightfall."

"What are we going to do about..." Abernathy stammered, wiping the rain out of his eyes.

"We've lost Corbin's horse and supplies. We can't afford to take a body down this mountain."

"The road is simple from here," Jonathan said, shaking his head. "We follow this trail straight for another three miles, then it branches to the left before curving right in a steep incline that leads down to the river. We can take him."

"It's hard enough for the horses to travel this road carrying our gear," Andrew said, his tone reserved and all business. "We can't afford to have another horse go over the edge because of—"

"We are not leaving him!" Jonathan yelled, slamming a fist into his other palm.

A low groaning sound and the crackle of falling pebbles stopped all conversation.

The section of ledge under Andrew's feet suddenly cracked and dropped three inches. Everyone froze as he looked down at his feet, and then up at us.

My blood went cold. I tried to move, to say something, but fear of disturbing the fragile hold the rock ledge had on the cliff rooted me to the spot. I considered the weight of my armor, and whether the cracked path would hold.

The section shuddered again, and fragments broke loose and trickled down the side of the cliff.

Damien pushed ahead of me. "Don't move." He inched to the edge, testing his weight. "Someone, grab my hand."

Trea pushed Peter further from the ledge, and gripped Damien's left hand and wrist with both hands, bracing his feet.

Damien nodded and then held out a hand to Andrew. "Slowly."

Andrew's mouth opened and eyes widened as he slowly lifted a hand toward us, rainwater dripping off his outstretched fingers.

The shelf snapped and Andrew gasped as he dropped from view. I stood at the edge, peering down through the rain to catch the end of a heavy splash into the river below us. I spun around at the others as they stood, staring speechless. Since Andrew's landing had made the water, the forty-foot fall was survivable, but with his armor on, Andrew would drown. I turned to Corbin.

"Well, aren't you going to save him?" I shouted.

"I can't swim," he said, his eyes calm.

I frowned. I had expected a little more emotion from the man. Panic, sadness, something. Though I didn't get much. I glanced at Darren. He shook his head. Trea began shedding his armor, but he was slow. Too slow.

No, I'm not losing him!

I dropped my sword and began undoing my armor. The gauntlets came off first, so that my slim fingers were free to fly across the knobs.

"Help me!" I yelled, struggling with my breastplate.

Peter dropped the reins and attacked my knobs, but he didn't know how to turn the dials and just got in the way. Damien appeared and helped, his fingers sure and steady; knowledgeable at how the mechanisms turned. The breastplate hissed and slid open, then dropped to the ground with a clatter. Damien froze in a half crouch. I ignored his shocked stare and the round of curses from the men as I unbuckled the harness from across my chest. I used Damien's shoulders to boost myself up and out of the stiff bottom half of the armor. I tore off my helmet and stripped off my armor padding.

I pointed at Damien. "Make sure you pick up all the pieces for me."

I ran toward the cliff edge in leggings and tunic past the gawking men and then bunched up my legs and jumped.

My heart sank.

Oh, shit.

The water was a lot farther down than I'd thought.

My belly tried to crawl out of my mouth as I fell through the air. I had a moment to realize I wasn't sure if Vestro could even see my shenanigans from where he stood with the other horses, and what would happen when he realized I was missing.

I closed my eyes as the water rushed up to meet me.

CHAPTER
SIXTEEN

I screamed before I hit the water, and the air left me in a hard slap. The cold sucked me under, and the rolling waves from the slow but heavy current filled against my ears and pounded my eardrums. I sank, dazed, then blinked and kicked frantically until I breached the surface. I gasped for breath, spitting out the foul water. It didn't taste as pretty as it looked from far above, and it was freezing. I batted away at the rain falling into my eyes, took a deep breath, and dove down.

I couldn't see much, just vague shapes and bulges in the dark water. It wasn't as deep as I would have imagined, and probably only reached twenty feet in the center. The slow current pulled me across the bottom, and I smacked up against several rocks and sunken logs. It hurt, and for a moment I wondered if jumping to the rescue had been a bad idea. The cold penetrated my limbs, quickly hindering my mobility.

Something glinted in the shafts of sunlight that cut through the darkness.

I kicked my legs out, forcing myself to go deeper.

I fought through the current and came close enough to see

Andrew struggling with his armor on the river bottom near the far bank. He'd gotten his helmet off, and one gauntlet, but his movements were slow and seemed to be slowing as I watched. I kicked my legs as hard as I could, the muscles in my shoulders aching as I swam down to him.

I hooked my feet around a thick branch from a fallen tree to fight the river from dragging me away and fumbled with Andrew's breastplate. He looked up at me, his hair swirling in the water, and even through the murk I could see the surprise on his face. He coughed, letting out an explosion of precious air bubbles.

Don't do that, stupid, I shook my head. *You need those.*

I jerked off his breastplate and unbuckled the first shoulder guard. My lungs ached, and my vision blackened around the edges. I fought with the buckle at his back, but it stuck tight. Andrew's hands moved slower, his fingers clumsy.

Hell, he's not going to last much longer.

Spots dotted my vision. I wouldn't be any good to him if I drowned, too. I bent my legs like a frog and kicked my way up to the surface. I came up gasping, my face numb, and I had to open my mouth as wide as it could go to make sure my numb lips would open at all. The gurgling rumble of the river filled my water-clogged ears and heightened the rasping sound of my lungs. I glanced to my right, spotted a point of reference against the slowly moving bank, and fought the current until I was upstream of Andrew. I took a shaky breath and dove back down.

My arms ached by the time I made my way back to him, my back and shoulders burning despite the debilitating cold whispering promises of sleep to my limbs. My heart skipped a beat as I neared. Andrew didn't move. His head fell forward, his blond hair trailing with the roll of the current, and his arms hung heavy at his sides, weighed down by the stubborn armor.

I attacked his bindings as soon as I reached him and freed him of all the armor save for the chain mail shirt. I tugged with all my might, trying to pull it from him. It didn't budge. I looked down. A tree branch hooked deep into the links, holding him against the current. I pulled at the branch, but it was immobile.

The gauntlet!

I reached down and plucked up the heavy glove and beat it against the branch. The hook bent, bowed, and broke. I yanked the chain mail off, grabbed Andrew under the armpits and kicked off against the large stump. He floated limp in my arms, caught in the water's buoyancy. My head breached the surface, and I pulled on Andrew until he floated face up. I swallowed water as I struggled to tug him along, and my lungs screamed with the aching burn.

The wooded shoreline drifted by as the river carried us downstream, tumbling us about as I frantically kicked toward the shore. I battled to keep Andrew's head above water, losing ground as I fought to keep him with me. My feet finally hit the sandy bottom, and I dragged Andrew toward the muddy bank. I managed to get his upper half out of the water, but I couldn't drag him any farther. My numb hands lost their grip and my legs wobbled beneath me. My boots slipped and I fell to my knees beside him, shivering. I spit out the rain that dripped from my parted lips and onto Andrew's blue face. A dark bruise marred his right temple, and the blue of his eyes dim under his half-closed lids. I put my ear next to his mouth, listening.

Nothing.

No.

I tilted his head back and locked my mouth around his. His lips felt cold, lifeless. I blew out as best I could despite my own aching lungs, and his chest rose with a bubbling sound. I straddled his waist, locked my hands together, and pushed on his chest. *One, two, three.* I counted to ten, then bent down again and gave him more air, my eyes squeezed shut.

Gods, I hope I'm doing this right...One, two, three.

"Come on, Andrew. Breathe!"

I beat on his chest, using all my weight to pump his heart. Panic bit at the nape of my neck as I stared at his immobile form.

"Andrew, please!" I cried.

I felt my last handhold on home slipping away as Andrew's slitted eyes stared back blankly at me; empty as the deep chasm opening beneath my knees. I closed my eyes against the darkness growing at the edges of my vision, grabbing me by the heart and pulling me into nothingness. The river lapped at my legs, mocking my efforts.

My chest jerked with a sob. "Don't die on me like this!"

I threw all my strength against his chest. I slammed my fists down on Andrew's chest, and then pressed my mouth against his again, giving him my air. I blew out as if my soul could crawl from between my lips and into his chest to drag him back.

Andrew's body convulsed, and he threw up river water into my mouth.

I gagged and crawled off him, then turned him onto his side as he coughed up more brown water. I slapped his back and held his wet hair away from his face, trying to wipe away at the thick raindrops pattering against his skin. He wheezed as he gulped in much needed air and curled his legs to his chest, his body trembling.

I stood and attempted to pull him completely out of the water. It was no use. My frozen hands refused to work properly, slipping each time I tried to get a grip.

"Andrew, up!" my voice strained. "Get up!"

I shook Andrew until he became coherent enough to crawl up the bank. I half dragged and half pushed him up to the line of tall pines bordering the bank's sandy shore, and we collapsed together beneath the thick boughs. The trees' thick branches managed to shelter us from most of the downpour.

I peered through the gray curtain of rain, past the muddy bank, to the rolling surface of the river, the black water gurgling in satisfaction at the trouble it had caused us. I could not distinguish where we were in relation to where we'd fallen, or how far the river had drawn us downstream, though I knew it would still take time for the rest of the group to make the slow trudge down the mountain path. I scanned the hazy silhouette of the cliffs in the dimming light and saw no sign of movement.

At least for the night, we were alone.

"You cannot be real..." Andrew rasped, his throat scraped raw. "I-I am dead."

"No, you dimwit." I turned to face him. "I saved you."

Andrew's ribs heaved in a wet cough, his lips still the wrong shade of blue. He convulsed and then pushed himself to all fours and retched. I scooted closer and pulled his wet hair out of his face as murky water spewed from his lips, one hand rubbing soft circles against his back.

He stayed in that position when he finished, eyes closed, as if afraid to move. I used the opportunity to untie his armor padding, tossing the waterlogged pieces outside of our shelter.

Andrew sucked in a deep breath, steadied himself, and then lowered himself to his side. Rain threaded his lashes, and for a breath he only stared—really stared—at me like the world had slid sideways and left him somewhere new. He caught my hand after I finished with the last piece of padding.

"You really dragged me out of the river."

"I know that's not how the story is supposed to go," I smirked despite my shivering. "That the great King Andrew had to be saved by a girl."

He winced, but a reluctant smile tugged at the corner of his mouth. "You'll never let me live this down, will you?"

"Not a chance."

"What..." he paused, a smirk on his lips. "What happened to your hair?"

I instinctively half raised a hand to touch the back of my head. "I... had to cut it. Part of my disguise."

"Your disguise?"

"Sir Aidan."

Andrew's gaze lingered on me, longer than it should have. There was no mockery in it, no swagger. Just awe. "I thought I knew you," he said quietly, almost to himself. "You are not the girl I grew up with." His jaw tightened. "You're... something more."

Appreciation curled beneath my ribs, purring with contentment. I looked away, brushing water from my eyes. "Don't sound so surprised."

A wind rose off the river and slid its cold fingers under my wet tunic. My teeth clicked, and I knew Andrew surely saw it; he pushed himself up—slow, shaky, stubborn—and protectively lifted an arm and reached for me, as if offering warmth without permission would make it easier for me to accept.

For a heartbeat I thought about refusing on principle. Then my shivering body voted to fuck the cold, and I edged closer, my back to him. Andrew's arm came around me, careful and firm, the heat of him startling after the river's bite. I tried keeping several inches of space, only allowing his arm to make contact. Andrew grunted and looped his hand in my belt, gave me a sharp yank, and dragged me across the pine needles until I bumped against him. I twisted my neck to glare at him in warning. He spooned against my back, his grin lazy and unrepentant. His arm slung over my waist, tightening just enough to make me still as he pressed his face into the back small bend of my neck. His heartbeat found the space between my shoulder blades and steadied there. I froze, caught between protesting and melting into the comfort. I closed my eyes and curled to the curve of his body. Timid little butterflies emerged from their cocoons and fluttered against my insides as I settled closer against him.

I'd always loved the way Vestro's powerful body could shelter me, but this was different. I considered the particular weight of Andrew's arm holding me against his chest, the roughness of his unshaven chin against my temple, and the dangerous ease I felt fitting in his embrace. Even waterlogged and ragged, his arms felt familiar and nostalgic. Natural.

I could get used to this, my traitorous thoughts whispered.

I had almost slipped into an exhausted, fitful sleep when strong hands turned me onto my back. I blinked, startled, and looked up to Andrew's confused face staring down at me. Color had returned to his skin, and he studied my face.

"Now, do you want to tell me what the hell you are doing here?" Andrew asked.

I scrunched up my nose. "You're welcome for saving your life," I snapped.

"And what were you thinking, jumping in after me like that? You could have died."

He glared at me, the silence only broken by the sounds of the rain and river.

I opened my mouth to retort, but the words caught as a sob clawed its way up before I could stop it. Tears suddenly blurred the edges of Andrew's face, and once again I saw him underwater, dying under my hands that almost couldn't free him fast enough. I turned my head, pressing a wet sleeve to my cheek as though I could hide it.

Andrew saw. *Of course he saw.* His hand found mine, his grip warm and sure, his thumb gently playing across my knuckles. He said nothing and graciously looked away. No mocking. No arrogant quip. Just that quiet pressure, chivalrous in the way only he could be —pretending not to notice while letting me know he did.

I drew a shaky breath and wiped the rest of my tears on my wrist. "Gods, you're an ass. I should have just kept my cover and let you drown."

The left side of Andrew's mouth twitched in a faint, approving grin.

"So, it was you the whole time," he said. It wasn't a question.

"Yup."

His grin spread, and he shook his head slowly. "I thought I recognized your horse. Only you would try to pull off such a foolish... But how did you manage to—"

"Fool you?" I said. I shrugged against his chest, then shivered.

Andrew lowered himself back to his side, propping his head up with one elbow, and pulled me closer so that our bodies connected in a warm line.

"Wizard magic," I said. "Maurdruik made the armor for me as a gift. So, I could go out and explore the hills around."

A breath sucked in. Recognition. "The demon-slaying knight of Damewood."

I turned onto my back so I could face him and gave a proud smile. "So, you're okay with it?"

"Of course I am not *okay* with it!" He tightened his arm around me. "Just because I may admire your adventurous personality does not mean I condone it."

I let out an annoyed groan. "Enough with the helpless damsel shit."

"You really should not have come." Andrew's face grew serious. "It is not safe..."

"Safe?" I snapped my head toward him. "You'd be dead right now if it wasn't for me."

"Nadia..."

"No! That's all I ever hear—from Maurdruik, from my father, now you. As if I'm just some porcelain doll that'll shatter if you don't wrap me in your protection. It's suffocating and I'm tired of being trapped like a bird in a gilded cage." The words came sharper than I meant, but I didn't pull them back.

Andrew's mouth opened to respond but then paused. A flicker of recognition crossed his eyes. He looked down, as if to choose his words carefully. "You are a princess, Nadia. That means you were born into responsibilities. Your people look to you, and everything you do is watched and judged."

I bit the inside of my lip, swallowing the accusation on my tongue; he was deflecting, shaping a narrative of his own position onto me.

I watched him instinctively reach to touch the crown no longer circling his head.

He dropped his hand and worked his jaw. "When you are of royal blood, you must do what is best for your kingdom. We do not get to just run off after something we want."

The hollow look in his eyes returned, the vulnerability in his voice raw. I swallowed.

"What kingdom, Andrew?" I met his eyes. "My castle was under attack when I left, and half the guards had already been killed before I'd made it past the gates. I don't even know if there's anything left in Damewood." Tears bit at my eyes and I fought to keep my chin from trembling. "So, who exactly is watching over me now?"

Andrew stared at me, his breathing loud as he leaned closer until our noses almost touched. His throat bounced as he swallowed. "I am."

I stared at him, refusing to blink so the water pooling in my eyes could not escape down my cheeks. After a moment, Andrew graciously looked away and ran a hand through his damp hair. He pulled out a pine needle, studied it, and then tossed it away. He wiped at the dampness on his face before looking back down at me, his mouth set in a grim line.

"Thank you," he murmured after a while, the words so soft they almost dissolved into the rain. "For coming after me."

"You're welcome."

A corner of his mouth twitched before he lay back down beside me, nuzzling closer. He wrapped one leg over mine, further binding us in a warm, solid coil. My body temperature seemed back to normal but nestled in his arms the world somehow felt... right.

We lay there listening to the river's low gurgle and the soft percussion of drops in the pine boughs. The world shrank into darkness as the last rays of the sun snuffed out. I turned into Andrew's chest, molding my body into the crook of his arm and pressing my face into his tunic to shut out the darkness. I breathed in the faint memory of cologne that still clung to his skin.

"Explain, Nadia," Andrew asked after a moment. "Explain why you will not accept my proposal."

I blinked at the golden scruff on the underside of his chin. "Andrew…"

He leaned back and gave me a good once over that was part care and part desperation. "I want you as my queen. And with everything happening to our kingdoms, I can protect you. I…"

"I don't need to be treated like a fragile robin's egg!"

He broke off, frustration thick in his voice. "And I don't want to lose my best friend to someone else," he whispered.

The weight of his arm suddenly felt heavier.

"I'm sorry about your father," I said softly.

He went still. The sound of his father's name seemed to cut through the rain. Then his arms tightened around me, and he buried his face in my hair.

"And I am sorry about Damewood," he murmured.

The rain softened, as if even the storm held its breath to listen for my answer. But when I saw Andrew's gaze in the moonlight—respectful and vulnerable—I felt something shift. He didn't just see the princess he remembered, or the knight he traveled with. He saw *me*.

And gods help me, it felt fucking good to be seen.

Heat slid through me, warmth that had nothing to do with his body. It scared me. It thrilled me. My heart beat too loud. His words sent a rush of warmth and terror over my chilled skin. Part of me wanted to lean in, to let his steadiness anchor me. Another part wanted to shove him back into the river. His arrogance had cost me three years of lost time with him, and I resented him for it.

"I don't know if I'm ready," I said, and the truth of it put a tremor in my voice. "For crowns. For vows. For whatever this is becoming. Not yet."

His jaw tightened, then eased. "I can live with not yet," he said. "I cannot live with not at all." His dazzling smile snuck through, and he guffawed. "And I guess I can live with the entire company learning I was hauled out of a river by a girl, if it means you will still be there to mock me for it."

My laugh surprised me, small and honest. "Oh, I will absolutely mock you."

His eyes shone with humor. "I would expect nothing less."

We fell quiet again. He did not push, but I did not pull away. I twisted in his embrace to rest my head on his chest. His arm stayed around me, protective, and only as tight as I let it be. I let it be tight. I let myself be still, just for now, and listened to the steady knock of his heart against my cheek.

Andrew buried his nose in my wet hair, pulling me closer as the rain began to pour, encasing our pine tent in a gray shroud. I felt his heartbeat quicken, and his hand twitched against my side. I looked up to see him staring, and the weight in his gaze wrapped around my throat, stealing my breath.

His eyes stared, intense. "Remember the first time I kissed you?"

I smiled at the fond memory. "I was ten. You tricked me into following you in the old church ruins behind the castle."

A slow, amused smirk pulled at the side of his mouth. "I did not mean *that* kiss."

I blushed against my will. One hot, summer night several years after our first kiss, those same church ruins had been witness to hours spent exploring each other. Touching. Tasting.

My mouth felt dry, and I ran my tongue across my lips. "Andrew," I whispered. "I..."

He pressed his mouth against mine, solid but firm. My lips trembled, uncertain, and then I let them part and Andrew slid his tongue inside. I closed my eyes, and deepened the kiss, remembering his taste. His closeness overwhelmed me, his warmth seeping through my skin. Andrew's tongue played against the roof of my mouth, and a soft moan escaped my throat.

The sound gave him encouragement, and he shifted so that his lips found my neck. He bit my skin gently, and a shudder ran up my spine, making my hair stand on end. Andrew rolled so his chest pinned my upper body to the bed of wet pine needles. I felt myself grow warm and wet as Andrew sucked at the dip in my collarbone. I whimpered at my body's betrayal, caught between wanting to push away and wanting to pull him closer.

I wanted this. My body craved human touch that I'd pushed away, neglected, and only satiated with Vestro's soft, lingering touches.

Vestro...

The memory of Vestro's hands dancing over my skin, and his mouth against mine, my center warm and wet, made me squirm against Andrew's touch. An ache built between my legs, and the sudden intense need caught me off guard, allowing me to breach the surface of reason.

"An...Andrew. Stop." My voice sounded breathy, even to me, and I hated it. I managed to twist enough to put my hands between us and pushed at his chest. "Slow down."

He stilled, eyes searching. His hands slid down to my hips, firm but not forcing, his voice rough with need.

"I will make you happier than any other man could," he said, kissing the curve of my ear. "But tell me, Nadia... do you want this?"

"Andrew, I..."

My world had just been turned upside down. Ripped apart at the seams. Reconstructed as kingdoms fell, roles shifted, everything changing in a whirlwind of dust and destruction.

Except for me. Everyone kept telling me that I had to remain the same. My whole life I had fought against the cage they built for me; a dutiful daughter, and an obedient princess on display. I swore I would never be that. I wanted freedom to make my own choices and fulfill my own destiny.

But here, stripped of titles and walls, I wasn't sure anymore. Freedom felt heavier than chains. Every decision I'd made on this journey so far had been mine alone, and every step felt like I was wandering further from the girl I thought I was. I had wrapped myself in armor of my own making—defiant of control—and still, I felt exposed.

Flashbacks of Vestro beneath me as I rode him, leading his movements, guiding his touch flitted through my mind.

I want that again. I need...

Lying here beneath the storm, with Andrew's eyes holding mine, steady and unflinching, I felt the weight slip. For the first time, I wanted to stop fighting. To lay down the armor and let someone else carry it. Just for tonight.

"I... want to be led," I whispered. "Just for one night."

Andrew's right hand slid under my wet shirt, passing over my chilled belly to play with the hem of my pants, raising goose bumps across my skin. His hand felt soft, probably smooth from years of never having to lift anything heavier than his sword, but strong and surprisingly gentle. His hand hovered there, patient but eager. I stared into Andrew's striking blue eyes and lifted my hips against his hand. Welcoming. Begging.

A low, pleased growl rumbled from Andrew's throat, and he pushed his hand down the front of my leggings. I choked on air, caught between pleasure and surprise as his fingers brushed against my center, found its moist warmth, and explored inside.

For a moment, I couldn't move, couldn't think as his hand twirled magic between my legs. I trembled beneath him and closed my eyes as a wave of pleasure rolled under my skin. Andrew's free hand gathered my hands, laced our fingers together, and lifted them above my head, pinning my arms against the wet earth. He nibbled at the underside of my jaw, licking and savoring my taste, his movements slow and intentional. Experienced.

This wasn't the boy I'd stolen kisses from in hidden corridors, laughing into his mouth when we were caught. That boy had been clumsy and eager; all heat and no direction. The man above me now carried certainty, confidence, a kind of practiced patience that both steadied and unnerved me. He wasn't fumbling in the dark anymore.

He knew exactly what he wanted.

And the gods know that it's me.

"Do you know how long I have wanted this?" he breathed against my ear, each word trembling with hunger.

I moaned as his hand moved faster. Two tears escaped down the sides of my cheek as I released control. Andrew kissed them away, and then locked his hot mouth on my neck, sucking in tune with his hand. My breathing quickened, and my body burned with energy that filled me until I felt ready to burst. I wanted to reach for Andrew, to wrap my fingers in his hair and pull him closer.

"Andrew," I gasped. "I..."

I tried to pull my arms free, but his fingers tightened around mine, holding me firm.

"No," he said, soft but firm. "Let me lead."

Andrew's hand slipped free, his fingers dragging across my skin as he pushed my tunic higher, exposing my breasts. Cold air brushed my skin, and I gasped, the air too thick, my pulse too fast. My nipples hardened in response, and Andrew promptly covered one with his mouth. He sucked hard, rolling his tongue in circles. My body trembled and something small and high-pitched escaped my throat before I could stop it. Andrew hesitated at the sound, his eyes searching my face. For a heartbeat, the hunger in his eyes softened, something gentler rising in its place.

"Hey," he murmured, his voice steady but soft. "Look at me."

I did. My breath stuttered, caught between panic and need.

"You do not have to be afraid of me." He brushed his thumb along my jaw, his expression unreadable except for the quiet steadiness beneath it. "I would never hurt you."

I swallowed and took a deep breath. Then nodded.

When his mouth found me again, it was warm and deliberate, but cautious. Measured. He drew the air from my lungs, slowly and carefully. He watched my every movement and reaction with wonder.

He sucked gently at my breasts, then harder with just a brush of teeth. He rolled his tongue in slow circles that sent tiny tremors racing down my spine. My body reacted faster than my thoughts could follow. A rush of heat, then doubt, then the dizzying pulse of both tangled together.

He released my wrists, the cool air kissing the skin where his fingers had been. I closed my eyes as he slid my damp leggings down my thighs in one smooth, practiced pull. My pulse jumped.

What am I doing?

The fear hit—sharp and irrational. It clawed up my throat, stealing my breath as I trembled beneath Andrew's hands. For all the ways I'd explored my body with Vestro, this was different. Andrew wasn't a demon or safety wrapped in secrecy. He was flesh and blood and *real*.

A real man.

The first man I'd ever let this close. The first who could truly break me.

Andrew must have seen the flicker of panic that crossed my face. He paused and then pressed a soft kiss just below my collarbone. "Breathe, Nadia," he murmured, his voice low and coaxing. "I have you."

Something in his steady tone kept me from falling apart.

Then his kisses resumed, feather-light now, teasing instead of claiming. The ache low in my belly grew unbearable, a throb that pulled me toward him despite the tremor in my hands. I writhed beneath him, caught between want and nerves as my body betrayed me with every shiver. Andrew's eyes darkened again, but the edge of his desire was tempered with care, as if he knew I could break if he pushed too far.

He shifted to his knees, and his fingers found the laces to his trousers. My hands flew to his chest.

"No," I gasped, voice shaking. I tangled my fingers in his hair, pulling him close until our foreheads met. "Not... not this way. Please."

He froze, eyes searching mine as I trembled beneath him. For a moment, neither of us breathed. Then he nodded once, jaw tight, restraint flickering through every line of his face.

"Then let me finish this for you," he said, his voice rough but careful, the gentleness threading back beneath the hunger. His eyes held mine. "Do you trust me?"

I swallowed hard and nodded.

He studied my face as he positioned himself beside me, giving himself a better angle, and slowly slid his hands across my bare thighs, and slipped his hand back between my legs and inside. His hand lingered for a heartbeat, waiting. My breath stuttered, and I nodded again, this time meaning it. He gave me an encouraging smile.

"You are safe," he murmured, the words barely audible over the rain.

He kissed the corner of my mouth before his hand moved again. Slow. Certain. His fingers found their rhythm again, but coaxing rather than demanding. Every stroke deliberate and measured. His eyes stayed on mine, reading every shift, every hesitation, as if he could navigate the war between my mind and my body.

Heat pooled low in my belly, and I felt myself rising with every careful pass of his fingers. My breath caught, then quickened. My body hummed, and it knew before I did that there was no turning back as a wave of pleasure rolled across my skin. My hips tilted into Andrew's hand and a small whine escaped my parted lips.

Andrew's expression shifted from hunger to near admiration. His eyes flickered wide with something like awe.

"Breathe," he whispered again, steadying me when the tremor started in my chest. "Do not fight it. Let me lead you."

His eyes never left mine. He watched me unravel, every gasp and tremor pulling at the corners of his mouth. I felt the tremor in his arm, the tightness of his restraint, as if each wave he pulled from me pushed him closer to breaking.

I moaned when I felt him slide in a second finger, stretching me as he rotated his hand in a wide, slow circle. His thumb swept across my sensitive spot in a rhythm that made my vision blur.

"You are beautiful like this," he murmured, the edge of his hunger softened by something raw underneath. "So beautiful."

I couldn't answer, couldn't think. I gasped, the air too thick, my pulse too fast. My body arched before I could stop it. Andrew leaned forward, his nose and lips pressed into the dip below my jaw, holding me steady through the building tremors that shook my thighs.

"Good girl," he breathed, his lips ghosting against my ear. "Just like that."

"Andrew..." My breath left me in a rush as his hand thrust and rotated, and his name became a lifeline in the sudden explosion of senses that left me floating.

"Let it go, Nadia," he urged, the words a command and a plea all at once. "Just let go."

The words broke something open in me. I shattered beneath him as a sudden wave of ecstasy built within my belly and rolled under my skin. Andrew covered my parted lips with his, swallowing my cry and riding the crest of the wave as I arched my back and let the amazing feeling crash over me.

When the storm inside me finally broke, Andrew stayed with me, steadying me through every tremor until I collapsed against him, spent and shaking. Then, like a gentleman, he sat up and helped me tug up my damp pants before lying back beside me. His hand rested against my hip as he watched my face, a soft smile pulling at his lips. He kissed the corner of my mouth, his breath rough with everything he hadn't done.

"I have wanted to touch you like this every damn day you stayed away from me."

"I'm shaking," my voice trembled almost as much as my body.

He brushed his knuckles along my cheek and pressed his forehead to mine. "Good," he said softly. "Means I did it right."

A shiver ran through me at his words, sharp and aching. I had kept him at arm's length for years, certain I didn't want this. Didn't want *him*. Yet here I was, wrapped in his arms, undone by his touch, and trembling from pleasure only he had drawn from me. I wanted to deny it, to push the truth back into the shadows. But the way he looked at me, the way he spoke about my absence like a wound, made something deep inside me twist into a deep, unsettled knot.

Because, gods be damned, I wanted him.

The taste of him. The weight of him. The way he made me forget every rule I'd built to keep myself safe. I wanted to drown in the warmth of his skin and the steadiness in his hands. To feel that command again, that certainty that I could stop thinking—stop fighting—and just *be.*

For the first time in my life, I didn't crave freedom.

I craved *him.*

And it scared the hell out of me.

THE RAIN SLOWED but did not stop, the fall constant and soothing. I shifted position against our bed of leaves, pressing myself deeper in the crook of Andrew's arm. I watched him in silence as he nodded off, his head propped on one elbow. The bruise on his temple had swelled and made his eye just a tad smaller than the other. He looked young and wrecked and impossibly kingly. I cupped his cheek, running my fingers across the growing scruff of his almost-beard. I grinned. I had never seen Andrew with facial hair before.

I wonder how the lack of personal care time on the journey is eating at his vanity.

I smirked. I liked this new imperfect and dust-streaked version.

Andrew blinked awake and then leaned into my palm, breathing in my skin. "Everything all right?" he asked with a thick voice.

"Yeah," I said, and meant it. But then I watched Andrew out of the side of my eye. "You know this...doesn't mean anything permanent," I said slowly.

The peaceful look on Andrew's face faltered, just a fraction. "I am aware."

"I'm just not ready to make a decision."

"You have made that clear."

We lay together and appreciated the stillness of the dark.

"If you tell anyone I enjoyed this," I said. "I will deny it and throw you back in the river."

Andrew chuckled and brushed back a short lock of my hair behind my ear. "Your secret is safe under the pain of drowning."

"Good." I hesitated and then settled deeper against his arm. "And Andrew?"

"Yes?"

"Thank you." The words surprised me as they left my mouth, but they felt right. "The day of the fire... in the alley. And for tonight."

He didn't answer. He didn't have to.

I tucked my cold hands into the warm hollow between us and breathed in the scent of rain and smoke on his skin. Outside our little tent of pine boughs, the storm quieted to a steady whisper. I closed my eyes as Andrew's heartbeat slowed to match the fading rain.

Slow, certain, and steady.

CHAPTER
SEVENTEEN

The storm broke before dawn, leaving only a fine silver mist beading on the pine needles and clinging to my lashes as I blinked awake. The damp earth exhaled a sharp, mineral smell, mingled with the faint residue of the night's rain. I let my eyes focus on the gurgling river as it lazily rolled past, the surface once again deceivingly sparkling and inviting.

Andrew's steady breath stirred the hairs on the back of my neck. His chest pressed warm against my spine and his arm draped heavily over me. The slow rhythm of his snoring might have lulled me under again if not for the sounds seeping through the trees.

At first, I thought it was only the river talking back to itself. Then I heard it again: metal on metal, the faint creak of harness leather, the sharp snort of a horse exhaling into the cold morning air.

My breath caught. Voices. Low, weary, and closing in.

Panic flooded through me, sudden and hot.

The men.

Gods, they can't see us like this!

The sounds grew louder. Branches cracked under boots. I shoved at his shoulder, harder this time, but he was all heat and muscle and impossible weight.

"Andrew," I hissed, twisting under him.

He only groaned in his sleep, nuzzling against the back of my neck like this was the most natural thing in the world. *Gods, of course he would choose now to be comfortable.* I shoved harder at his chest, earning nothing but a sleepy grunt and his arm tightening around my waist, pulling me closer.

The clink of bridles and voices came closer.

Panic fluttered in my throat. *Please, no, not like this.*

"Shit, shit, shit!"

I wriggled, half rolling, half crawling, trying to pry his arm off me. The motion only made things worse, and his hand caught on the hem of my tunic, lifting it up from my belly. I bit back a curse and froze, breath shallow, every sound in the forest suddenly too loud.

Too late.

The shadows came first, stretching long across the mist. Then the men broke through the line of dripping pines, and I froze.

They stopped dead. For a heartbeat, no one spoke. Even the forest seemed to hush around us.

Trea's expression flickered between relief and discomfort, his eyes darting from my face to Andrew's arm still firmly draped around my waist. Damien stared openly, one eyebrow creeping upward, his expression unreadable but far too knowing. Corbin caught Abernathy's eye, and they shared an odd, silent exchange before it was quickly smothered.

Heat flooded my face. I twisted again, finally wrenching free of Andrew's hold. His arm flopped uselessly against the ground as he blinked awake, confusion furrowing his brow.

"Asshole," I muttered, shoving him aside as I stumbled upright, brushing dirt and pine needles from my tunic with sharp, useless sweeps. My hair clung to my brow, damp from mist and sweat. My boots slid in the wet earth as I stepped away from the tree. Every movement felt too loud, too obvious. I didn't dare meet anyone's eyes.

Andrew stirred behind me, still half-asleep, a low sound rumbling from his throat as he pushed himself upright. "What—" his voice cracked, rough from sleep. I glanced back just as his eyes met the group's.

For a heartbeat, he looked as startled as I felt. Then something shifted. The warmth vanished from his face, his expression settling into that familiar, infuriating arrogant calm.

He rolled to his feet and rose to his full height, the movement smooth and practiced. He brushed off his sleeves, and his measured command restored with every swipe.

He stepped forward, his boots sinking slightly in the damp earth, and placed a steadying but gentle hand on my shoulder.

"She saved my life. Without her, I would be rotting at the bottom of the Warden, thanks to all of you and your lack of action." He scanned the circle, daring anyone to speak against him. "Allow me to formally introduce you to Nadia, Eldest Princess of Damewood."

His words cracked like a whip. No one answered.

Then Peter stepped out from behind Trea, small but defiant, his chest puffed out like he'd just won a tournament. "I knew the whole time," he announced. His chin lifted toward me, eyes bright. "She trusted me with her secret after I figured it out early on. And I didn't tell anyone." Then, too quickly, he added: "And I also knew about—"

"Peter." My voice cut sharper than I intended, and I winced at the way his grin faltered. I forced a crooked smile. "And here I thought you couldn't keep quiet for longer than five minutes."

Nervous laughter cracked through the tension, brief but just enough to break the silence. I stood taller, pretending to ignore the pounding in my chest from the weight of every gaze.

A sharp snort split the air. Vestro's dark form jerked against the leads tied to his bridle strung between two horses. He stamped the mud, ears pinned flat, his eyes locked on me from the edge of the group. He aggressively shook his mane, his velvet lips curling back in what anyone else would call impatience.

But I knew better. I knew the set of his jaw, the snap of his tail, the pointed lift of his head.

He was pissed.

My stomach twisted. I knew the others only saw a restless horse. Yet I saw the accusation written across his equine face clear as words: *You jumped for him.*

Trea stepped forward, breaking my line of sight with Vestro. He quickly unclasped his cloak and looked to me for approval before draping it over my shoulders. I pulled the wool cloth higher up my neck, enjoying the cocoon of warmth and the added level of modesty to cover the dirty tunic plastered against every curve of my body.

Trea bowed at the waist with deliberate respect. "Your Highness," he said, voice low but firm. "You honor us with your courage. I would've given my life before letting you leap into that river had I known." His eyes softened as he straightened, reminding me of Old Red's approving stare. "But I see now you're more than capable of taking care of yourself."

Heat rushed up my neck and I placed a hand on his arm. "Please, don't start bowing. I'm still the same knight who's been cursing your snoring for the past week."

Guffaws from the men to my right. Even Damien's face split into an amused grin.

Gregory cleared his throat and stepped forward, his helm in his hands. Rainwater streaked down his weathered face. He hesitated and looked to Trea as if for guidance.

Regret crossed Trea's face. "Another slide came down on the lower switchback over the canyon," the captain said slowly. "Benjamin and his bay went over. We searched, but…" He shook his head. "No man or beast could've survived that fall."

The air thickened, as though the mist itself pressed down harder. Benjamin had been rough and annoyingly pragmatic, but he'd deserved better than to vanish into the rocks like some nameless casualty.

"I'm sorry," I whispered. I looked at Gregory. "I'm sorry about your friend."

Trea hesitated. "Your packs are still on your saddle. But... your armor was strapped to Benjamin's horse. It's gone."

My lungs constricted, as if someone had sucker-punched me in the gut.

Darren shifted uneasily, his boots sinking in the mud. "We would've tied it to your stallion, Princess. But..." He glanced toward the tether line where Vestro stamped and snorted. "Your horse wouldn't let us near 'im. Not a one of us. He nearly took the 'is arm off when we tried to strap the load to 'im."

Corbin held up his wrist, showing off his torn sleeve. "The beast went wild. We had no choice but to lash him between the greys to stop him from bolting after you."

My stomach knotted, hot and sour. The image flashed sharp in my mind: Vestro thrashing to follow me over the cliff, wild-eyed, while the one thing that tied me to Damewood slipped away with the rocks and rain.

The armor that allowed me my freedom; the shield that wrapped my wants and secrets in a safe, untouchable package that represented everything I wanted to do with my life.

Irreplaceable. Gone.

I rounded on Vestro before I could stop myself. Vestro tossed his head hard, lips peeling back in a violent scream, as if daring me to lay the blame where he knew I already wanted to. The other horses startled, and Corbin and Darren scrambled to tighten the lines strung between them, holding the kelpie in place.

I almost stopped them. Almost told them how much Vestro hated the bridle, how it hurt his mouth, and they were pulling too hard. I wanted to run my hands over his dark coat to reassure him that things were fine, that I wasn't mad.

But I am.

So. Fucking. Mad.

My blood rolled in tune with the tremors rippling along Vestro's dancing flanks, burning the back of my eyes and drawing hot bile into my throat.

My hands trembled as I fought to keep from crying in front of the men.

I felt Andrew's body heat close the distance between us, and I shifted back just an inch to close the distance. I let myself lean gently against the warm wall of his chest, steadying me. Andrew, much to his credit, kept his hands at his sides, preserving subtlety to not draw attention to the comforting act.

I turned slightly and met Damien's eyes across the group. He leaned against a pine, arms folded, that unnerving grin flickering at the corner of his mouth. He stared at Vestro, his dark eyes lingering, studying the way Vestro's ears twitched and dark eyes glared at me with a heat only I could read. The demon hunter's eyes flicked back to me, sharp as a blade, as if he'd just uncovered a piece of a puzzle no one else even knew existed.

A chill that had nothing to do with the rain slipped down my spine. But I glared defiantly back at him.

I'm not in the mood to fuck around right now. So just try it.

Damien smirked and then looked away as if he'd lost interest. I squared my shoulders and lifted my chin as I stepped forward into the mist. Whatever came next, there was no hiding anymore.

THE RIVER'S water still roared in my ears the rest of the day, even after we'd put miles between us and the cliffs. We rode hard along the lower banks, the air damp and sharp with the smell of wet stone and churned mud. The Warden kept close company, rushing fast and cold beside us, as if mocking the foolishness of anyone who thought they could tame its waters.

Andrew rode at the head, straight-backed and back in his role as leader, his cloak snapping in the wind. He spoke little to me, keeping a safe distance to not attract attention. Though every so often he glanced over his shoulder as if just to check on me. That alone unsettled me more than a hundred of his arrogant quips.

I avoided his eyes, though I felt their heat. When our gazes did meet, the smirk he gave was softer than it should've been, not quite the arrogant shield he usually wore. It left me reeling, torn between the relief of last night's warmth and the fresh sting of knowing I couldn't name what it meant.

Vestro seemed to go out of his way to make my travel uncomfortable. He picked up his hooves with sharp impatience, ears laid flat, and pulling at the reins. When the valley opened before us, he danced sideways, as if ready to bolt ahead with me the way we used to—to run out of sight until he could shed the horse's skin in private and breathe as himself. My throat ached from the tension of keeping the silence between us, but I tightened the reins and forced him back into his place. For one, I did not want to get separated again, and two… I wasn't ready to talk yet.

His snort cut through me sharper than Andrew's gaze ever had.

By nightfall we made camp in a low clearing hemmed in by giant pines. Smoke curled thin and gray from the firepit, damp wood snapping in protest as it caught. The men huddled around it anyway, their laughter relaxed and the mood light after our rescue. After the long day of travel in wet conditions, a meal by the fire was a welcome thought. Steam rose off drying cloaks, the wet leather smell mixing with pine resin and the faint metallic tang of swords newly cleaned.

Andrew, naturally, had claimed the choicest spot at the edge of the circle, leaning back against a log like it was carved for his throne. His boots stretched out toward the fire, his goblet raised higher than necessary every time he drank—as though even the ale should bow.

"Careful, Trea," he called across the flames as he chewed on a chunk of jerky. "If your joints creak any louder, we'll have to tie on a bell so the demons don't mistake you for one of their own."

The men chuckled.

Trea rolled his eyes but grunted, "Better to creak than whine every time I lift my sword. If kings are made of complaints, River-wind will outlast us all."

Andrew laughed, loud and rolling, like thunder forced into a smaller sky.

I smiled as I watched his profile in the firelight. His handsome features glowed in the warm light, every word wrapped in the familiar arrogance, the confident mask back in place.

Jonathan pulled off his boots and set them by the flames to dry. He grinned. "Next town we find, first round's on the king, eh? Might even get us a proper celebration with some good company."

A ripple of laughter circled the fire.

Normally, Andrew would have leaped at the chance to spout some crude joke or a boast about which wench he'd charm first. But tonight, his grin faltered just a fraction. A heartbeat's pause. He lifted his waterskin to his lips, buying him a sliver of time.

Then the smirk came back, bright and careless. "Proper is not the word I'd use for my type of celebration."

The men grunted their approval.

But across the flames, Andrew's gaze cut to me, quick and sharp, and the smirk softened for the barest instant. The mask had cracked, just enough for me to glimpse the boy beneath, the one who had clung to life in the Warden and let me hold him steady against the rain. Then it was gone, buried beneath swagger and wine.

I looked away too fast, the heat from the fire suddenly stifling. I'd told Andrew our night together hadn't meant anything. That I wasn't ready. I believed it then. But watching him now, catching that slip meant only for me...I wasn't so sure.

And for the first time, the thought of my future blurred, torn between what I'd always known I couldn't have and what I wasn't certain I could resist.

A sharp stamp broke my thoughts. Vestro tossed his head from where he stood at the edge of camp, ears pinned flat, nostrils flaring as he pawed the dirt, his pale eyes catching the firelight in a way that looked far too human. He had caught me watching. The snort he gave was not impatience.

It was a warning.

The laughter around the fire swelled again, but it sounded far away. Between Andrew's softened glances and Vestro's silent fury, I felt caught in a current I didn't know how to fight.

THE CAMP HAD GONE quiet long before I slipped away. Only the hiss of dying coals and the restless shift of hooves carried through the trees. I pulled my cloak tighter as I made my way through the trees just past the clearing, my stomach knotted, and my chest still raw from the day.

Vestro stood where the trees thickened, half-swallowed by shadow. His dark hair clung damp to his temples, the moonlight plastered to the curve of his bare shoulders. He didn't look up from where he picked at a loose string on his pants, as I approached, but his breathing was harsh in the quiet night.

The smell of wet earth and pine filled the night air, sharp as my guilt. My pulse thudded against my throat.

He finally looked up, and the heat in his pale eyes stopped me cold.

"You jumped," he said flatly. "For him."

I swallowed. I had no defense, not one that wouldn't unravel me. "Andrew would've drowned."

"And what if *you* had?" his voice cracked through the dark, deeper, harsher than I'd ever heard it. "If the river had taken you too?"

The words scraped against something inside me. I wanted to shout back, to tell him it hadn't been a choice at all.

"I couldn't let him die," I whispered.

"You couldn't stand to lose him," he corrected, stepping forward. "There's a difference."

My breath caught. I wanted to deny it, wanted to laugh and push him away, call him dramatic. But my silence was enough, and we both knew it.

"You think I can't see?" his voice rose. "The way you look at him now. The way you leaned on him this morning like he was the only thing keeping you upright." His hands curled into fists, his voice breaking. "That used to be me, Nadia. *Me.*"

The words stabbed deep. My throat closed. "It still is."

"Don't lie to me."

I bit down hard on my lip. My heart was a storm, tearing itself apart. I hated that he could see through me, hated that his words stung because they weren't wrong.

"Why are you the one upset?" I hissed. "I'm the one who lost my armor. The only thing I have left from before this entire fucking nightmare started."

Vestro growled. "You think losing your armor was the worst part of yesterday? They strapped it to Benjamin's horse because I wouldn't let them near me. Because I tried to leap off that cliff after you, Nadia." His jaw trembled. "But they stopped me and tied me between those mares like a fucking animal." He stepped closer, fury radiating off him. "I almost lost you."

For a heartbeat, silence hung heavy, broken only by the hoot of an owl somewhere beyond the trees.

"Vestro," I started, my throat tight. "I have to start thinking of more than just myself. Of my people, of what might be left of them." My voice cracked, but I pressed on. "I can't just keep living like nothing matters outside of us."

Vestro's jaw flexed, and his pale eyes almost glowed as they cut into me. Then his lips curled into something I'd never seen on his face before; a snarl. "How does fucking Andrew help your people?"

The venom dripping from the accusation scorched me. The air

left my lungs in a shudder, like he'd punched me straight in the chest. I staggered back a step as the night tilted.

This was Vestro. My best friend. The anchor who had always steadied me when the world fell apart. And now his words stabbed like a blade between my ribs.

But then the sting curdled into anger. "You don't get to say that!" I hissed. My voice cracked, but I didn't care. "You don't understand what the last few days have felt like. You can't imagine what I'm feeling."

His laugh came out short, bitter. "I understand plenty. Enough to know you're not thinking. You never do when it matters. That's why I'm here. That's why you need me."

"Of course you don't understand," I snapped before I could stop myself. "Because you're not human. And I don't need you hovering over me every fucking second."

My words cracked like a whip, and the moment they left my mouth I wanted to claw them back and swallow them down to a place they could never escape.

Vestro went very still. His eyes widened in shock and then narrowed to slits. The muscle in his jaw jumped, and the look he leveled at me made my stomach pitch.

Silence swallowed us. Even the moonlight seemed to gutter lower, as the night listened.

Vestro turned his face away, as though my gaze seared him. His breath came in uneven, ragged pulls, like each breath took conscious effort. His hands curled into fists at his sides, white knuckled, then opened and clenched again.

I shifted my weight between my heels, uncertain. Guilt coiled low in my stomach, but pride held my tongue. The words had been cruel, despite being true. I'd' never been cruel toward him.

So why does he look like I'd just ripped everything from him?

Vestro finally met my eyes again, and the grief there was raw as an open wound that made me feel like I'd just slaughtered something sacred.

He opened his mouth like he might say more, but whatever truth lived on his tongue, he strangled it down. His lips pressed together, trembling with the weight of something unsaid.

I swallowed hard, my pulse a wild drumbeat in my ears. I wanted to ask. To demand why this truth of him being a demon hurt him so much. But the words caught as I watched his face, the rejection and sorrow swirling in his eyes as they shifted from obsidian to flesh, and I suddenly knew the answer. All his lingering touches, the soft words, and our night by the river...

He wants it too.

And he knows we can't have it.

Yet all I could do was stand there, hollow, as the rift yawned wider between us, dark and bottomless.

"If you were human," his voice was soft but sharp enough to cut. "You'd have never said that... before yesterday."

The truth tumbled out before I could stop it, raw and jagged. "If you were human, Ves, I'd choose you. Every time." My vision blurred, and I let it. "I love you, Vestro. I always have. But you're not. And I..." I pressed a trembling hand to my mouth, trying to keep the sob down.

The admission cracked something inside me, and for an instant I hated him for making me say it and hated myself more for meaning it.

Vestro stood rigid, his face unreadable and still save for the twitch in his jaw. His chest rose and fell too quickly, and his throat flexed when he swallowed hard. His fingers curled like he needed to hold something, anything, to keep from unraveling.

"Don't say things like that," he muttered, so low it barely reached me. "Not if you don't mean them."

"I do," I whispered, though the sound cracked in my throat. "I'd choose you, Vestro. But I can't. And it's time for me to grow up."

His eyes snapped to mine, want and fury tangled into something raw and unnamable. He took a step toward me, his hands clenching into fists, and my whole body went rigid.

For half a heartbeat, I thought he might close the space between us before I could react. And for the first time since meeting the kelpie in my childhood I felt a sliver of something I never thought I'd associate with my best friend.

Fear.

Vestro stopped. His breath hitched, chest heaving once, twice. He shook his head, hard, as if trying to dislodge the moment itself.

"I would have jumped, Nadia." His voice was harsh, scraped raw. "Fuck the world and fuck the kingdoms. Fuck the bigger picture— you go over a cliff, I'm right behind you. Every fucking time." He took another sharp breath, his eyes bright with something that wasn't anger anymore. "Can Andrew say the same? Or will his kingdom always come first?"

The words landed like stones in my gut. I bit the inside of my cheek, hard enough to taste copper, fighting the sob clawing its way up.

I wanted to shout back, to defend Andrew, to deny what Vestro had claimed. But the truth caught in my throat. Because part of me knew the answer.

I blinked against the sudden sting in my eyes and forced myself to turn away. Behind me, I heard Vestro move, the soft step of his bare feet across the damp earth. Then nothing. Just the steady sound of his breath; ragged, restrained, and far too close to breaking.

CHAPTER
EIGHTEEN

The continuous rain had worked itself into everything, swelling our packs with cold, miserable weight.

By the time Roan's red walls shouldered out of the mist, our grain was porridge, our fire starter a lump of useless sludge, and one of the feed sacks had torn itself into a sad, dripping flag from Vestro's saddle. Everything smelled like wet dog and moldy flour.

"We need fodder, lamp oil, wax, and food," Trea said, rubbing his knee where the cold liked to settle. "And a farrier to check Darren's grey. He's off on the near fore."

"I know," Andrew muttered. He'd shoved mint leaves between his cheek and teeth to hide last night's tobacco, but the menthol sweetness did a poor job of masking the wine on his breath. His right hand trembled once on the reins and then stilled, jaw locking. "I am not happy about it, but we need the rest and supplies."

Damien tipped his hood lower. "Roan's also where my old contact listens for Holy convoys. If Cipher moves west, word brushes his door first."

We took the north approach road, but not to be noble about it. The merchants' queue was a living thing—a centipede of wagons and pack mules inching toward the gate while guards in blue-and-brick livery checked crates with iron rods. Beside them stood men in gold-trimmed cloaks, the red circle-and-dot stitched on their backs like a third eye. The Holy didn't bother with rods. They carried black, compact devices I didn't have a name for; angled steel with a small bite of metal where their fingers rested.

They weren't swords. But somehow they felt dangerous.

"Curfew posted," Peter said, voice small as he read the nailed placard aloud: "By edict of the Prelacy and the Council of Roan: sundown bell to sunrise bell—"

"—No gatherings larger than ten," Damien finished. "Nothing scares them more than people standing together."

The gate creaked. Five riders clattered out, cloaks snapping. People flattened against the wall without being told. The Holy didn't look down. They didn't need to. Their symbols looked for them.

"Hold," murmured Andrew. He'd slouched just enough to look like another wet traveler with too much road and not enough coin. Corbin drifted his horse a fraction to the right, gently angling Andrew toward the center of the road where you were easier to count. Helpful squire, that one.

"We cut through the mill lane," Damien said casually, as if suggesting a stroll. "There's a cooper's door three alleys in. From there, we can drop to Thief's Alley and come up near the inn."

"The what now?" Peter perked like a spaniel who'd heard the word biscuit.

"Old tunnels under the city," Damien said. "Used by smugglers, bricklayers, and the occasional person with a poor relationship to the law."

I glanced at Andrew. He nodded once, the decision already made. "We stable fast. No names. We buy what we need in one pass. Then we disappear underground and leave the city as quickly as possible."

Vestro blew steam, ears flicking back, then forward again when my hand found his cheek. I knew he hated cities—too many walls, not enough sky. He reached his velvet muzzle toward my pocket and gave me the most pointed look a horse could give.

I patted his neck, "I know."

At the gate, the guard looked at the pitiful state of us and then waved us through with a bored flick of his wrist. The Holy man beside him didn't bother. He looked through us with the calm indifference of someone deciding we didn't matter. Which was a blessing.

Inside, Roan was noise and color and something sick underneath. Red-brick streets shone slick under the thinning drizzle. Curved tile roofs marched up and up until they seemed to pin the low clouds in place. Banners hung in damp ropes, their colors running. From every second corner a painted symbol of The Holy looked down—the red circle and dot—and beside more than one of those signs, someone had tacked fresh parchment: sermons, edicts, curfews, tithes. Priests in pale robes stood under awnings with bowls for given coins and heads for given blessings. Twice, I clocked city guards and Holy cloaks walking the same beat, shoulder to shoulder. Integration or invasion—sometimes the difference is just whether anyone living there was asked.

We pushed through the main market because there wasn't anywhere else to go. Stalls glowed with gem strands and dyed silk; clever hands turned meat on spits and sold steam by the spoonful. Though my amazement quickly diminished. The colors faded around the edges as women in muddied rags approached us for loose change, holding out hands wrapped in bandages encrusted with dirt and something foul smelling; their faces were bruised, skin pockmarked and flea-bitten.

Andrew gave them each a coin with a gracious smile before sending them away, but my eyes followed their stooped gait as they struggled through the crowd, disappearing under a mold-covered awning near a shadowed alley entrance that crawled with flies and reeked of noxious air. I scanned the buildings behind the merchant carts and became astonished at the number of beggars. Homeless men, women and children situated themselves in rows behind the carts, apparently waiting for any coins or crumbs to fall between the cracks.

A one-armed girl younger than myself, probably around fifteen or sixteen, looked up at me through cloudy eyes as we passed, and I looked away. I wasn't like Andrew. I couldn't look at them and put up a smile like everything was all right.

It's not all right. This is sick. Terrible that anyone must live like this.

"Don't look like it's the first time you've seen this," I told myself. I tried to follow my own advice and failed. Damewood had lanes I'd never looked down. That felt suddenly unforgivable.

The main square stables took all thirty stalls and still smelled like old sweat and burnt hay. We stripped tack quickly and bribed the boy in the loft to find us dry feed. The farrier clucked over Darren's grey, pared his hoof, and set a new shoe with four smart blows. Andrew bought what we needed from a woman whose hands were more scar than skin: wax, tinder, oil, hard cheese, and bread dense enough to last the journey. Trea haggled for oats. I bartered an embroidered sleeve for a small bag of dried apples, which Vestro pretended to disdain before eating anyway.

"Contact's in Low Smoke," Damien said, once we'd divided loads between saddles and packs. "Smoked-meat alley, near the kilns. Two blocks off the main. We don't linger. We listen; we leave."

"Make it fast," Andrew said. He glanced toward the clock-tower at the square's edge. "The longer we stand still, the higher the chance we're seen."

"Maybe the boulevard," Corbin offered, helpful as always. "Faster footing. Easier to—to pass unnoticed in a larger crowd."

Damien's mouth curled. "Bigger funnel is still a funnel."

Andrew's gaze moved between them, sharp and calculating, like a man tracking too many moving pieces at once. "We'll take the smoke lane and then follow Damien through the cooper's door."

We nodded and started off, following Damien's silver hair

through the streets. Low Smoke earned its name. The air tasted like char and old pine. Two men in gold cloaks turned onto the far end of the alley and the crowd rippled the way water does when something large passes under the surface. Damien's hand lifted, two fingers, then dropped. That meant don't look up, keep moving, turn right at the fishmonger with the scar.

Damien halted mid-step, and Peter ran into his back. Everyone bunched up as the line stopped moving and huddled around to see what the problem was. Peter rubbed his nose.

"Damn, Damien!" he said. "You never stop like that in the middle of the road. What—"

"Turn left," Damien said, stepping to his right.

"Why—" Andrew began.

"Move!" Damien said. "Now."

We followed the Hunter down the dark alley. The walls were lined with stacked boxes and trash bins. The last of us had crossed into the shadows just as a loud commotion started in the street. Abernathy held back at the entrance, standing out in the street, looking toward the noises of clopping hooves and a yelling crowd. Andrew grabbed him by the back of the collar and jerked him into the darkness. Damien pushed us back behind a stack of wooden crates. The men huddled about, trying to stare through a space between the crates. I was shorter, so I didn't have a problem finding my own little space.

I wrinkled my nose and grimaced. The wood smelled of rotten apples and cat piss. Something scurried in the shadows off to my right.

A woman screamed as a horse reared, almost barreling over her as she ran forward to throw her arms protectively around a small child, twisting around so that her back was to the rider. The man on horseback shouted down at her to get out of the way and was soon joined by several other riders in matching cloaks. People hurried to press up against the carts or fronts of buildings to avoid being trampled by the sharp hooves. Their cloaks shone gold, a red circle with a dot blazing on each back. In their fists rested strange devices of black metal, compact and sharp-edged, like tools forged for a purpose I couldn't name. The handles bent oddly, with a small piece of steel glinting where their fingers rested, as if a single motion could awaken something deadly inside. I couldn't name the weapon, but I knew the kind of men who wielded it.

Members of The Holy.

"Shit," Damien breathed beside me.

I glanced up at him, then back through the crates. The Holy members were jerking their horses one way, and then the next. Their heads twisted around as they stood in their stirrups and scanned the crowd. It seemed too coincidental that they had arrived at the same time we had. There didn't seem to be any doubt about it; they were looking for us.

But why? I thought they were the ones with Cipher. Why did they want...

"Do they know who the heir is?" Corbin whispered.

"How would they know that?" Andrew snapped at him, his face red. "We don't even know."

Andrew waved him away and turned to Damien. "How do we get out of here?" he said. "The alley's a dead end. I don't want to be caught like sitting ducks if they come this way."

Damien moved silently along the wall behind the crates. He passed several wooden doors and knocked on the fourth one. After a moment, a small window slid open, and quiet words exchanged. The door creaked open, and Damien waved us over. Trea ushered Peter through the door. I moved to follow, and Andrew urged me from behind with a push at my shoulder—firm, not rough. I stumbled, caught off guard, but caught myself.

"Princess!" Abernathy said from the back of the line, very close to a shout. "Are you all right?"

Every head at the mouth of the lane snapped toward us as if

drawn by wire. A horse jerked toward the alley, and the gold-cloaked rider lifted his weapon and held it overhead, the tip pointed at the sky, shouting at the crowd to let him cut through. A sharp crack split the air—hot and wrong—and the crowd screamed and scattered. The Holy rider's device smoked at the nose. He'd aimed high; the shot was a warning, not a kill.

I paused in the doorway to stare at the strange weapon, at the thin line of smoke rising from one end. I froze as the man saw me, shifted the weapon so the smoking tip settled and pointed straight at me. A Holy rider checked his mount, black device rising. He didn't fire. He looked at me.

I blinked. *What is he doing?*

His aim dipped. His eyes narrowed with recognition and a sudden urgency.

For one beat, everything in me went very, very still.

How did he—

An arm hooked around my waist and yanked me backward through the small door, and the lock clicked into place right behind me. Andrew set me down, I almost tripped over Abernathy sprawled on his back across the floor. Andrew stood over him, fists clenched, jaw a hard line. I glanced around the dark room. Dim light snuck in from beneath the cracks of the window frame and under the door, sending thin beams of bright sunlight cutting across the blackness. The light illuminated small sections of the white-painted walls and bare floor that were unadorned with tapestries or furniture. The wall on the left side of the room ended in a sharp corner, dark shadows congregating around the entrance to the hall beyond.

"What the hell is your problem?" Andrew snapped at him. "Trying to get us caught?"

"I'm s-sorry, my lord," Abernathy stammered. "I-I was just—"

"Move!" Andrew barked, jerking his chin toward the hall.

Abernathy scrambled up, tripping over his own boots. Damien was already halfway down the corridor, motioning us on.

We followed in single file through the narrow passage. The dirty walls were close enough that our shoulders brushed them as we passed, and we had to shift our packs off our shoulders just to squeeze through. Somewhere outside, another crack split the air.

"Keep moving," Damien hissed.

Another sound followed; the shuffle of boots, and a hinge whining open. Andrew turned back to reach for my hand, and movement cut across the sliver of light beneath the door.

The next shot came clean through the wall. Splinters burst from the plaster. Andrew ducked, the bullet whining past his ear.

Behind him, Abernathy made a choking sound. He staggered back, one hand rising to his throat as blood squirted from between his fingers, the other grasping at empty air.

"Shit," I gasped.

Abernathy collapsed against the wall, leaving a long smear of red as he slid down it.

Andrew spun, face pale, realizing what happened a heartbeat too late. "No..."

Damien waved him forward. "He's done. Move!"

Andrew's hand reached for me. "Nadia!"

I closed my eyes and took his hand as I stepped over Abernathy's body and kept running. I turned once, just long enough to see blood spreading across the floorboards where Abernathy had stood.

Then we reached a doorway and slipped through. The door slammed behind me, the lock clicking in place. Andrew shifted so that he stood behind me, for a moment his hands shook, and he steadied them by gripping my shoulders and pulling me into a quick but firm hug, and then he stepped back and placed his hand on my lower back as he led me forward.

With Andrew at my back, we quickly walked down a short hall to a dimly lit kitchen. An elderly man wearing a grease-stained apron stood next to a small lit stove holding a heavy wood rolling pin, waiting. The man nodded as we filed in and pointed to a heavy oak bookcase. As we walked closer, I noticed that one end had been moved away from the wall.

Damien's head suddenly popped up through a small round hole in the floor behind the shelving. He pulled himself higher out of the hole to lean on his elbows, pushing a large, circular steel plate with several punched holes farther out of the way. It scraped heavily against the wood floor.

"Unless you like the idea of having a hole the size of a cabbage blown through your chest," he snapped. "I suggest you hurry up."

Damien ducked back down without another word, disappearing in the blackness below. Trea quickly knelt and helped Peter through, then crawled down behind him. Corbin scurried away from Andrew as fast as he could and dove through.

I bent down to follow but hesitated at the absolute blackness below outside of the little circle of light the hold projected. It looked like quite the drop.

Andrew put a guiding hand on my shoulder. "I am right behind you." His thumb drew a small circle on my arm. "Go."

The door down the hall opened, letting in the frenzied sounds from the outside. A woman screamed as something heavy crashed against the floor and several men yelled and fought their way inside.

"You must hurry," the man in the apron said, holding the door open for us.

Andrew pushed me through the opening and dove in after me. I couldn't hold in the scream as I fell through the blackness, with Andrew's hand still on my shoulder. He pulled me against him and twisted below me, taking the brunt of the fall when we hit something flat and solid. The surface gave slightly under our weight, ringing with a deep metallic thump. I grimaced and lifted my head off Andrew's chest.

He lay blinking against the light shining in his face. He looked a little stunned; probably hit his head. Then he blinked and his eyes came into focus. I pressed my forehead against his chest and let out a sigh of relief.

He's OK.

I leaned forward and gave his cheek a soft kiss in thanks and then peered past him into the dark to see what we had landed on. Beneath us stretched a great, gleaming box of gray metal, longer than any wagon I'd ever seen. I craned my neck, following its line into the shadows.

No, not one box. A whole line of them, each joined to the next, perched on small iron wheels that gleamed faintly in the dimness. Dozens of them trailed away into the dark, vanishing around the curve of the tunnel like some endless caravan bound for a destination long forgotten.

Andrew groaned and stirred, and his hands came up to circle my waist. "Are you all right?" he managed, the air still returning to his lungs.

I looked up at the circle of light above us, ignoring his not-so-subtle attempt to pull me into a hug, and spotted a steel ladder hanging down from the entrance. If I had stood and reached for it, the last rung looked as if it would be just a foot or so out of my reach. I frowned. If we hadn't been in such a rush, we could have just climbed down. I heard male voices shouting from above, before the large disk scraped back into place, cutting out all sound and light.

I untangled myself from Andrew and stood, sticking my hands out in front of me and carefully shuffling my feet against the slick surface, the metal denting and bouncing back up as I moved. I couldn't see anything in the dark, but from the sound of our group's footsteps echoing against the floor and walls, the passage itself must have been at least thirty feet wide and close to the same in height.

I cried out as I slipped off the rounded edge of the unstable flooring, and slid down another ten feet or so, hitting the hard, flat ground and landing awkwardly on my right ankle. I picked myself up, testing my weight. It held. I heard Andrew moving about on top of the box, and the sound of his soft landing behind me. I heard his feet scuffling, felt him grab my left hand and pull me forward.

"Andrew," I said, "I can't see anything."

"Just follow me," he said. "This tunnel can't have too many outlets."

The footsteps of the others had all but faded, and I had no way of judging how far behind we were. We fumbled through the pitch-black darkness, our hands searching. The tunnel stank of damp brick and old iron, full of river-rot and long dust. We moved along the side where the wall was honest, and the ground didn't suddenly drop. Somewhere overhead, the city roared and then didn't. My boots shuffled along the floor, cautious, as I fought to find my bearings.

Damp air sighed through the stone walls, carrying the smell of rot and rust. My hands slid over water-slicked stone, the texture of moss and webs making me jerk away before touching for bearings. After a brief and unexpected run-in with a pair of parallel bars that ran along the ground down the length of the tunnel, we kept to one side, Andrew ahead of me, and I could feel his gloved hand brushing against the walls, the scraping sound loud and harsh in the dark. We walked on for what seemed ages, the only sounds being the echoing of our hurried footsteps.

Andrew's hand brushed my wrist, and then his fingers closed tight around mine, commanding. "Stay with me," he said. "I need to feel where you are."

"I can manage," I shot back, too fast, too sharp. Pride stiffened my voice. I pulled away before I could think better of it. I hated the idea that he thought I needed leading like a child.

I felt him pause. His breath caught, sharp as steel striking steel, but he didn't argue. He only shifted a pace ahead, his steps echoing confident and steady.

I followed, refusing to admit the way my heart drummed against my chest.

The passage forked. His steps veered away. I swore I heard him to the left—faint, urgent, just beyond reach. Without hesitation, I turned. When I didn't hear his footfall, I quickened my pace to catch up. I ran my hands along the wall, fingers scraping against rough stone and crumbling plaster.

"Andrew?" My voice scraped out, brittle.

Silence answered.

A soft glow appeared up ahead around a bend.

The glow wavered, like firelight filtered through grime. I slowed, pressing my back to the wall. The damp stone clung to me, cold and wet. Low voices and slurred chuckles carried in the dark, and the scrape of something metallic dragged along stone.

I edged forward, every step too loud in my ears.

Around the bend, the tunnel widened into a pocket of flickering torchlight. Four men hunched together in a loose circle, shadows jerking across the walls as they passed a skin of liquor between them. Their clothes hung in tatters, faces half-obscured by beards and grime. One pawed through a sack at his feet, pulling out trinkets and scraps of food with greedy fingers.

Vagrants.

And they weren't alone. Another shape slouched against the wall; a blade balanced across his knees. His eyes caught the light, sharp and calculating in contrast to the others' drunken haze. He wasn't drinking. He was waiting.

The air turned heavier, pressing against my chest. I froze, heart hammering, realizing too late how exposed I stood at the edge of the light.

My pulse skittered, faster with every breath. I should have followed Andrew. I suddenly missed his voice and warm presence at my side.

Why was I so fucking stubborn?

The men's laughter cracked against the walls, loud and jagged. It carried a sour stench of cheap fermented wine and stale sweat. I shifted back, trying to swallow the sound of my own breath, but my boot scraped grit.

The man with the blade lifted his head.

I froze.

His gaze locked to mine across the dim pool of light, sharper than any steel in his hand. The others followed, their chuckles dying into a quiet that felt far more dangerous. One by one, their heads turned, faces shadowed but their intent clear in the sudden stillness.

The sack of trinkets toppled over. Nobody moved to catch it.

"You're far from home, girl," the words slurred from one of them, ugly with hunger and promise.

Their circle broke, feet shuffling, boots dragging closer, until the tunnel seemed to close behind me with every step they took forward.

CHAPTER
NINETEEN

The air thickened. Sour sweetness slid down my throat, choking me.

"You lost, little lamb?" A voice, cracked and wet, bled out of the dark.

I swallowed, but the lump in my throat refused to go down. My hand went for my sword, but even that motion betrayed me—clumsy without the anchor of my armor, my arms bare beneath the borrowed cloak. I had nothing between me and them.

For the first time in my life, I felt it: how small I truly was. How much the armor had lied for me. How much of my strength had been an illusion forged of steel and the way others looked at it. Without it, I was only flesh. Only a woman. And they saw it.

"Pretty thing, wandering alone," one of them murmured.

I staggered back, the damp wall slick beneath my palms. Their footsteps circled, deliberate. The black was a hand pressing in, trapping me.

I tried to summon my pride, to stand taller, to speak as though I were untouchable. But my voice betrayed me. Thin. Shaking.

"I'm not lost. My...my friends are close."

The chuckle spread between them, sharp as knives.

My chest heaved, my breath hitching in my throat suffocating. I yanked my dagger from my belt and held it in front of me. For the first time in my life, the steel didn't make me strong—it made me small. Slow. Female. I was cornered in ways no blade could fight.

I swallowed, my throat a vice. My hand closed around my blade handle, but the weight felt useless. What had my pride and stubbornness bought me now?

One of the men stepped toward me and came into focus, his shaking belly hanging out from under his cut-off tunic. He held a length of frayed rope between his meaty hands, and his glinting eyes hinted at its sinister purpose. I shied away from him, pressing my back against the wall of the tunnel. He chuckled softly, grinning.

"Don' worry about bein' lost, miss. I'm going to show you how a real man takes care o' a woman."

He crossed the distance between us quickly, his boots thumping on the echoing floor, so fast that my rooted feet couldn't react in time. I stepped back, my chest tight and hands shaking as I held the dagger in front of me. I swiped at him as he reached, slashing the back of his forearm. He cursed and backhanded the dagger away and it fell with a clatter to the ground.

I tried to dart to the side, to run off before he could recover. But another man materialized in front of me, hands out. I skidded to a stop and tried to turn the other way. But the fat vagrant stood there, chest heaving and holding his bloodied arm.

Cold settled into my bones, pulling down on my lungs and suffocating me. My legs trembled as the men closed in, and I struck out with my hands, clawing at faces, but my efforts were pushed aside easily, like a second thought.

I sobbed as terror ripped through my chest. I hadn't realized how much I had relied on my armor while fighting, and I suddenly doubted my ability to take care of myself without relying at all on someone—or something—else.

Maybe Andrew was right...

"Andrew!" I screamed. "Andrew, help me!"

Rough hands caught my shoulders and wrenched me down. The stones scraped my spine, and cold seeped through my cloak as my wrists were slammed above my head. Heavy hips pinned mine, heavy, unyielding, crushing the breath from my chest.

I kicked, clawed, but the weight was too much. My dagger slipped away, clattering into the dark.

His belly pressed against me, hot and slick with sweat, lifting my tunic as he leaned in. His tongue dragged wet across my throat, slow and deliberate. The stench of rot and brine filled my nose. My stomach heaved. I screamed, raw and desperate, but it was swallowed by the tunnel's walls.

Gods, no. Please no.

Another shadow moved in, pressing greasy hands across my mouth. My cries muffled to nothing. I thrashed, my lungs burning with air I couldn't release. The dark swallowed me whole, and I clawed at the edge of a dark abyss as my knees were forced apart and I felt hands at the buttons on my pants.

I felt small. Powerless. No armor, no steel. Just me, and them.

"Andrew!" I tried to scream against the hand. It came out broken, trapped in my throat.

A finger slipped between my lips, and I bit until I tasted blood. The man roared and slapped me hard across the face. My head cracked against stone and sparks flooded my vision.

"You little bitch," he spat. His spit hit my cheek, hot and vile. "Now I'm going to really—"

"Nadia!"

Time stilled. The voice carried like thunder down the tunnel, fierce, raw, unmistakable.

Andrew!

The weight on my chest lifted in a violent heave. The man was ripped away, hurled into the wall so hard that dust rained from the ceiling.

I gasped, air rushing back into my lungs like wildfire.

Andrew stood above me. Feet braced wide, chest heaving, sword dripping red in one white-knuckled fist. His eyes burned wild.

"Stay the hell away from her!" he shouted, his voice hoarse. "Back the fuck up!"

The second man let go of my wrists and pulled a dagger from his belt as he lunged. Andrew's sword sang as it swung through the air, merciless, and the blade sliced cleanly through the man's neck. Andrew stepped back as the head toppled and rolled to the side, followed by the crumble of the heavy body.

I crab-walked from under him and put my back against the wall, grabbing my dagger and bringing it up in front of me. I looked up at Andrew, and it was then that I noticed that he was bleeding. The back of his tunic gaped open, revealing a dark gash that started between his shoulder blades and ended somewhere on his right side. Blood soaked his lower back and trailed down his right leg, sucking his tunic against the wound like a second skin.

I started to reach for him. "Andrew—"

Andrew fought to stay in front of me, his blade swinging through the air over his head with incredible speed, taking down two more of the men.

The others faltered. Then the air filled with curses and retreating footsteps as they scattered back into the blackness.

And then silence.

Andrew's sword fell to his side, and he dropped with it, seizing me in arms that shook as though he'd collapse without me. He crushed me to his chest, his breath harsh as his cheek pressed into my hair.

For a moment I couldn't breathe, not from fear, but from the sheer relief of him. His warmth wrapped around me like a shield, and I felt as if the world couldn't touch me again so long as he held on.

"Are you all right?" his voice ripped out ragged and torn.

I broke then, sobbing into him, clinging as if I'd drown if I let go.

"I'm sorry," he whispered. "I'm so sorry."

I stiffened at his touch and then grabbed fistfuls of his shirt and buried my face in his neck. My body shook as I sobbed, and I pulled up my knees and tried to melt into the warmth radiating through his red-stained shirt.

"I thought you turned left," I breathed. I rubbed my cheek against his shoulder. "And then he grabbed me..."

Andrew cradled me against his chest, and he wiped his eyes against my hair. He kissed my temple and then tilted my face up to meet his, pressing our foreheads together.

"A king's duty..." his voice broke. "A man's duty is to protect. To keep safe what is his. And I let you slip through my fingers." The shame in his voice weighed heavier than his grip.

He kissed me, trembling. "I will never let anything happen to you. Do you understand? Never. But right now, we must go."

His hand found mine, iron tight. His lips trembled as he kissed my knuckles. Then his command was steady again, fierce and unyielding. "I have you now. And I am not letting go."

My hands still shook as he pulled me to my feet. He hugged me close, cradling me against his chest as if to shield me from the air itself, and then turned me away from the bodies littering the ground, keeping me tucked against his side.

He snatched the oil lamp on their makeshift table and then steered me back along the tunnel.

His palm squeezed mine in the dark—steady, anchoring. Every time my breath hitched, his thumb pressed against the back of my hand, a silent reminder that he was here.

I let him lead me through the black.

A LOW MURMUR ahead trickled through the darkness. The oil in the lamp dissipated, and we quickened into a near-run as the light died and collided with someone's back as we rounded a corner.

A tiny spark flared, died, then flared again. A flame bloomed weak and yellow, illuminating the underside of Damien's face. He smirked, likely at Andrew's startled look, but his expression hardened when his eyes landed on me. The skin around his mouth tightened, his gaze lingering just a beat too long before he schooled it flat and gave me a curt nod.

Thank you for not asking.

Damien jerked his chin toward a side passage, his face slipping in and out of the light's reach. "Come on," he said. "We're almost out. The others are already through."

"Where are we?" Andrew demanded.

"It's called Thief's Alleyway," he said. "An ancient travel route that tunnels throughout the city. Most don't know about them, only...a select few." The shadows on his face exaggerated the downturned corners of his mouth as he frowned back at me. "Including undesirables. So, we don't have much time."

We moved quickly through the tunnel and came to a dead end. Damien lifted his small light to shine along the walls and found the bottom of the steel ladder fixed in the stone. The lowest rung dangled just out of reach. He shut the light off. In the darkness I heard him scuff his feet and jump. He hung silent in space for a moment, and then we heard him grunt, his hands grasping the bars and then his boots as he climbed up.

Andrew moved next. I never heard his steps—only felt the absence, the tunnel suddenly emptier, colder.

Terror pricked at the back of my neck. The dark pressed in, heavy. *Empty. Alone.*

"Andrew?" my whisper cracked.

A hand landed on my shoulder. I yipped.

"Sorry," he murmured. "I'll lift you."

His arms cinched around my waist, lifting me as though I weighed nothing. I swayed above him, the memory of rough hands still raw on my skin. My pulse skittered, but his steadiness grounded me.

"Higher," he said gently. His stance braced beneath me, solid.

The steadiness in his voice grounded me, even as shame burned beneath my skin for needing it.

I ran my hands along the wall. I reached out with my free hand and felt the cold, steel rung of the ladder. The chill bit at my palms, real and merciful, and I clung harder than I meant to—proof that I was still here, still alive. I gripped it tightly and pulled myself up. Andrew shifted his grip to the back of my thighs and boosted me higher as I walked my hands up enough to lift a foot to the bottom rung. My boot stuck, and I pushed myself up and out of the way.

I waited, heart hammering, until I heard Andrew's boots crunch against the dust on the ground, followed by his grunt and the clap of his hands against steel as the ladder shuddered under his weight. I closed my eyes and held on tightly as I felt Andrew strain to pull himself up, catch the next rung, and then find his footing.

The ladder shuddered. My foot missed the rung, scraped, caught again. For an instant, the air felt too tight to breathe. My pulse slammed against my throat and the dark rushed in—

"Nadia," Andrew's voice cut through the dark, low and certain. His warm breath brushed my shoulder as he leaned close. "You are fine. You are doing great."

Step by step, I climbed, Andrew's presence below me anchoring each motion. We climbed in silence for what seemed like forever until a crack of light greeted us from above.

I put my hand against the flat steel and pushed up. I gave it all my strength, grunting in the process, but I couldn't move it. Then the circle suddenly slid to the side, and Damien frowned down at me. He reached down and pulled me up and through into what looked like a basement.

The brightness struck like a blow. The sudden openness felt wrong—too much air, too much space. My knees wobbled before I even realized I was shaking. I swayed for a moment, disoriented in the light, and Damien's hands steadied my shoulders. He released his grip as soon as I could stand, and his eyes met mine with a knowing look.

Andrew crawled out of the hole and brushed himself off. He looked as pale and drawn as I felt. He ran the back of his knuckles along my shoulder, reminding me of his presence but graciously giving me space.

Damien sealed the hatch and motioned us on. We climbed narrow stairs, pushed out into daylight so harsh it burned my eyes, then crossed the street to a plain inn. Its blank façade betrayed nothing of the labyrinth below. The thought chilled me.

Was it possible that Damewood held such secret veins? If so, what shadows had I walked over without ever knowing?

Andrew took the lead inside, speaking low with the innkeeper. Soon we were ushered upstairs into a private dining room where the others waited, silent and tense. Trea quickly bolted the door behind us, and we stood in silence for a moment in air that hung ragged with anger and relief.

"That was close," Trea muttered.

"Too close," Andrew snapped, pacing like a caged wolf. His face was tight, his voice dangerous. "Do any of you care to explain how the hell we nearly ended up cut down in the streets? Or how the Holy knew exactly where to look?"

No one answered. Corbin leaned against the wall behind Andrew, calm and silent.

I glanced over at Damien, standing in the left corner of the room nearest the door. His dark eyes flicked back and forth between Andrew, Corbin and me. Corbin seemed oblivious to the stare. It wasn't very different from what he usually did, but Damien seemed to find something very interesting about the nonchalant squire.

Damien must have felt me watching, because he glanced my way and quickly covered his head with his hood. I pursed my lips and looked away.

Andrew's temper boiled over. He slammed a fist against the table hard enough that the wood cracked. "You think this is a game? That we can just stroll into a city swarming with enemies and hope luck saves us?" His voice rose until the rafters shook. "You are men, not frightened children. You fail me again, and I will take your heads myself."

The silence that followed was thick and heavy. Too heavy. Andrew's father's voice echoed in his anger, cruel and sharp. My stomach churned. For once, even I didn't dare speak.

Andrew dragged a hand down his face, muttering curses. Corbin offered him a goblet of wine, which Andrew drained in one pull. One by one the men collected keys, retreating down the hall under the weight of his anger.

I stayed where I was, stiff and hollow. My thoughts spun, circling back to the tunnel, to rough hands, to the reek of sweat and rot. Relief was supposed to feel lighter. Instead, it sat heavy, smothering.

The sudden emptiness of the room made me catch my breath, and I glanced up, only to realize I was left alone with Andrew. I quickly looked away from him, shame flooding my face.

Andrew was still there, watching me. He stepped close, his voice gentler now. "Are you all right, Nadia?"

I nodded too quickly. "Yes. Thank you."

His gaze softened. "Nadia—"

"I'm fine, Andrew."

The words rang false even in my own ears. The truth still clung to me: the scrape of stone at my back, the press of filthy hands, the heat of breath that wasn't mine. I had always believed my armor made me untouchable, that the magical steel turned me into something larger, something more.

But tonight, the reality had sunk in. Without my armor, I had been small and helpless.

Weak.

And Andrew had seen it.

For a moment, neither of us moved. Andrew's eyes searched mine, flickering with something unreadable. Concern, maybe. Longing. Perhaps a little fear. I pressed a palm against his chest, feeling the steady thrum of his heartbeat. His closeness loosened a knot in my stomach. My throat tightened, tears threatening to rise. I hated it. I hated needing him this much.

I suddenly had the urge to run outside to the stables. To the safety that was Vestro. He always knew how to fix things. To fix me.

Before I could pull away, my eyes caught on the dark stain across Andrew's back. His tunic clung wet to the gash I had glimpsed earlier in the tunnel. The blood had dried thick in places, but still welled fresh in others.

"Andrew," I whispered, my voice breaking for a different reason. "You're hurt."

He glanced over his shoulder as if only just remembering. "It is nothing."

"It's not nothing," I said, sharper than I meant. "You're bleeding."

The corner of his mouth tugged into a faint smile, almost rueful. He picked up the bottle of wine Corbin had left behind. "And yet still on my feet."

I ignored him and reached for the torn fabric. "Will you walk me to my room?"

THE CORRIDORS UPSTAIRS WERE HUSHED, and the old wood groaned beneath our steps. My nerves prickled with every shadow, every whisper of wind against the shutters. Andrew kept a hand at the small of my back, steadying me when my breath caught.

We reached a modest room at the end of the hall. A single bed, a nightstand, and a washstand with a small basin of water. The window was shuttered tight, and pale moonlight seeped faintly through the cracks. I shut the door behind us, the click of the latch sounding louder than it should have been.

Andrew stayed near the bed, his shoulders squared, watching me while he slowly turned the wine bottle in his hands as if waiting for me to dismiss him. But I couldn't. Not when he looked like this. Not tonight.

"Sit," I said quietly.

For once, he didn't argue. He set the bottle on the nightstand and lowered himself to the edge of the mattress, the bed creaking under his weight. He watched me in silence as I began unlacing the front of his tunic, my fingers pulling at the ties enough so I could slip the shirt over his head. I heard his sharp intake of breath as he stretched his arms overhead, but he bit down the wince and gave me a reassuring nod.

I found a small stack of clean linens in the washstand cupboard, dipped them into the cool water, and crawled on the bed to sit behind him.

He hissed when the cloth touched his raw flesh. "You needn't—"

"Be quiet," I muttered. "You kept me alive tonight. Let me return the favor."

The cut was not as deep as I'd first thought. The slice ran thinly across his back, cutting an angle from his left shoulder toward his waist, the skin red and bleeding already mostly stopped. The edges were angry and swollen but had already begun to scab.

The memory of the vagrants in the tunnel worried me; while the cut was not deep, their blades may not have been clean. And infection killed just as many as the wounds themselves.

My hands trembled at first, but the work steadied me. Andrew's shoulders eased under my touch as I cleaned his wound. Silence stretched, filled only by his breath and the slow, gentle scrape of cloth. Slowly, my shaking stilled. The work pulled me back from the edges of panic, gave me something solid to hold onto. I let my fingers brush against the damp skin of his back, tracing the paths of invisible but raised scars. The switch marks from childhood that had gone especially deep.

Andrew shuddered under my touch. "You see?" he said softly, after a long while. "You are strong. With or without armor."

I paused, fingers resting gently on his shoulder. My throat ached. "Tonight I wasn't," I whispered.

He caught my hand before I could pull away. His fingers closed around mine, warm and sure. "Then I'll be strong for both of us."

I swallowed hard, blinking against the sting behind my eyes.

Before I could speak, Andrew turned toward me on the mattress and drew me forward until I knelt between his knees, his hands settling at my waist. No pressure, and no demands. Just present.

I let myself lean into him. His chest rose and fell against mine, his heartbeat steady under my palm. The heat of him, the steadiness, felt like shelter.

"I thought I'd lost you," he whispered.

I bowed my head, resting it against his shoulder.

He shifted, wrapping his arms around me fully, tucking me against him in a tight embrace, slow and protective, as though releasing me might unravel him entirely. His lips brushed the crown of my hair, light and trembling. I let myself rest with my cheek pressed to the warmth of his shoulder.

For once, the silence didn't feel dangerous.

After a long moment, he pulled back slightly. His hands lingered at my waist, hesitant. "You should lie down," he said, voice low. "You need to rest."

The thought of being alone in the dark, with the tunnel still echoing inside me, sent panic clawing at my chest.

"Can you stay for a while?" I whispered before I could stop myself.

His expression softened. "Always," he said.

He sat further back on the bed and leaned against the headboard, his boots still on and sword within reach. I hesitated until he lifted his arm in quiet invitation.

I crawled across the mattress and curled against his chest, tucking myself into the circle of his body. He pulled the blanket around me as I curled into the space against his chest. His warmth wrapped around me like a shield.

I felt the tension in him; his back too straight, the edge of discomfort in the way he shifted to keep me balanced against him. But he never complained. Not once. His hand found mine beneath the blanket and wove our fingers together. His thumb brushed the back of my knuckles in slow, steady passes.

At first, I tried to keep still. But the longer I lay there, the more the memories pressed in; the scrape of callused hands, the reek of sweat. My body betrayed me. A tremor rippled through my shoulders. Andrew's arm tightened instantly, anchoring me.

I stiffened again when the wind hissed against the shutters. Andrew didn't hush me, didn't call it foolish. He only stroked his thumb across my knuckles, slow and sure, until I steadied.

I forced my breath to steady. "This must be really uncomfortable for you. You'll wake up tomorrow with half your body asleep."

A silence stretched. Then Andrew's chest rumbled beneath my cheek, a low, half-laugh, half-sigh.

"If it means you rest, I will endure worse than numb arms."

The words loosened something in me. I pressed my face deeper into his chest, hiding the wetness stinging my lashes, pretending I hadn't heard the tremor in my own voice. My fingers curled tighter around his, clinging despite everything I'd said.

He bent his head, lips brushing my hair. "I'll protect you forever," he whispered. His voice caught as if he had more he wanted to say, but he let it die there, swallowed back into the quiet.

I shut my eyes, letting the steady rise and fall of his chest lull me. His arms tightened just enough to stable me, his silence filling the space where the words almost lived as I let myself slip toward sleep.

CHAPTER
TWENTY

I stirred awake to the clink of metal and the faint smell of warm bread. The shutters let in a spill of gray morning light, pale and thin, just enough to gild the edges of Andrew's silhouette as he balanced a wooden tray at the foot of the bed.

Steam curled from a clay cup, and slices of fruit gleamed red and gold in the morning light. My stomach grumbled at the sight of sweet rolls dusted in sugar.

Speaking of sweet, Andrew looked infuriatingly fresh for someone who'd run through tunnels and almost died hours ago, clad in new clothes with his hair still damp from washing and face cleanly shaven. I stared at his handsome profile for probably a moment too long because he dipped his head in an acknowledging nod and winked.

I fought against a smirk as he sat gingerly on the edge of the bed.

There's the Andrew I remember.

I stretched, pulling the blanket closer around me, acutely aware of the space between us and how small it felt compared to last night.

"You'll regret being up this early," I teased.

Andrew shrugged, rolling the tension from his shoulders. "Kings don't get to regret mornings."

The line might have sounded arrogant from another man. But here, half-asleep, it landed softer. He sounded tired, almost vulnerable.

"Thank you," I said finally.

Andrew's mouth pressed tight at my words, but he gave a small nod, as if he'd been waiting for them. He picked up the wine bottle on the nightstand, jerked out the cork, and took a long swallow.

"You should eat," he said, his tone half order, half coaxing.

I grinned. "Since when does the king of Riverwind play the role of a servant?"

His mouth quirked. "Since the king's tomboy princess refuses to take proper care of herself." He picked up a slice of apple and held it out. "Humor me."

I intended to swat him away. Instead, I plucked the apple from his hand and hungrily chewed and swallowed it down. I'd forgotten I hadn't eaten yesterday after the tunnels and just realized how hungry I was. I looked up to see Andrew watching too closely, as if my chewing were the most fascinating thing in the world.

"You're ridiculous," I muttered, reaching for the cup.

"Perhaps." His eyes softened, the arrogance slipping at the edges. "But you are alive. That is all that matters."

The warmth of his leg brushed mine through the blanket. His gaze softened, lighter than I'd seen in days. For a moment, I remembered the way his voice had caught in the dark the night before.

I'll protect you forever...

We ate together in silence, save for the distant clang of buckets in the courtyard below and the muffled creak of footsteps in the hall. He offered me the wine bottle, but declined and stuck to the tea in the clay cup. I reached for one of the rolls, bit into the soft dough, and a cloud of sugar powder cascaded down my tunic, catching the sunlight like snow. I coughed, swatting at it, and Andrew barked out a laugh, unguarded and genuine, that filled the room with warmth.

"Do you remember when you visited for my name day feast?" His eyes glinted as he looked at me. "Just before the ceremony, you dared me to climb out the gallery window, and I nearly tore my cape in half when I fell the last few feet."

I licked powder from my fingers and laughed. "Didn't we sneak back in through the scullery?"

He nodded, grinning. "And somehow ended up in the pantry. By the end, we looked like we had fought a war with a flour sack."

The memory pulled a laugh from both of us. Andrew shook his head, shoulders loosening with it. For a moment he wasn't a king, wasn't hard edges and command, just the boy who'd once grinned through a cloud of flour at me in the half-dark.

"The cooks nearly fainted." I smiled into the roll as I tore off another piece.

Andrew leaned back, shoulders bouncing with laugher. "We left white boot prints halfway to the tower. Wizard Drachier was livid."

"I remember that! Gods, I thought for sure we'd be flogged," I said. The words slipped out before I thought better of them.

Andrew's laugh cut off. Only a flicker, but enough. His mouth stayed curved, but his eyes shuttered, and the boy vanished. My stomach sank. I remembered then; the bruises on his knees from hours of forced praying to the gods for forgiveness, the switch marks, the crown he'd been forced to bear even as a child.

He looked down, his hand brushing once at the bare place where his crown should have sat. "No. You were not," he said quietly. "The crown weighed heavy enough for me that day. My father made certain of it."

The air thickened and pressed close. I held still, afraid that moving might shatter the fragile bridge between us. I suddenly wanted to reach out to him, to touch him and pull him back from the lip of whatever abyss on which he stood.

Then Andrew blinked as if shutting away a memory and reached across the tray, picked up a slice of fruit glistening with juice, and held it to my lips. "Here," he murmured, softer again. "Try this, it is quite good."

I hesitated and then leaned forward and took it from his fingers. Sweetness burst on my tongue, and under it the salt of his skin as my lips brushed his fingertips. The pear dripped onto his fingers as I bit, and on impulse I licked the juice from his knuckle before it could fall. His breath caught and for a heartbeat neither of us moved.

His hand lingered near my lips, and I didn't look away. I didn't want to.

Then his hand shot behind my neck and gently but firmly pulled me to him. The kiss was steady and deliberate. His hand cupped my cheek, rough against my skin, holding me like something precious and breakable. He pulled away just long enough to set the half-empty wine bottle onto the nightstand, and then his other arm circled me, pulling me closer as he shifted closer on the bed, until I could feel the heat of him radiating through my tunic.

His mouth found mine again, and this time there was no hesitation. The kiss deepened, and the air between became thick with heat. I caught his tunic and yanked him closer, so his weight pressed into me.

Gods, I want him so bad!

My fingers curled into his tunic, dragging him closer still. I pressed back into him, my lips parting against his, daring him to follow where I led. The sound he made—half-growl, half-groan—vibrated against my lips and tickled something low in my belly. His tongue brushed mine, tentative only for a heartbeat before the hesitation broke.

His hand cupped my jaw, thumb grazing the corner of my mouth as if memorizing the shape of it. Then his hand slid from my jaw to my throat, his fingers spreading and thumb tracing the hollow there before he gave a slow, deliberate squeeze.

Not cruel. Not a warning.

A promise.

Heat pooled between my legs, slick and ready, and my pulse

jumped against his palm. I knew Andrew sensed it, because his breath broke, rough and uneven, and he kissed me deeper. Hungrier.

I tilted my hips into his, pressing against the building ache in my core. I caught his wrist and guided his hand higher to cup my breast. His eyes opened at the gesture, startled, as though I had just given him something he'd been afraid to take, and his hands roamed and squeezed, pulling at the strings of my tunic.

"Andrew..." I whispered, tugging him back into another kiss. My heart hammered against the cage of my chest.

Andrew shifted on top of me, and the mattress dipped beneath our weight. I hissed as the edge of the tray jabbed against my thigh. Andrew huffed out in annoyance, flicked a glance down, then swept it off the bed with the back of his hand. The tray and cup clattered to the floor, the buns rolling out of sight beneath the bed.

Andrew drew me tighter; his breath ragged against my lips. He pressed his hips against me, letting me feel him hard and ready through the font of his trousers, and I ground my legs against his. For one dangerous heartbeat, I wanted to let it all go; to forget every reason I had to resist and simply give into him.

And in that heartbeat, I remembered the words he had swallowed in the dark: *I'll protect you forever...* The rest had gone unsaid, but I heard it now, as if he had spoken it aloud. *If you'll have me forever.*

And gods help me, if he had asked it then, I probably would have said yes.

The thought struck harder than the heat of his mouth, harder than the press of his hands. My pulse raced, tangled with his, and for a moment I couldn't tell whether the pounding in my chest was mine or his.

Yes.

The words rattled inside me, sharp and terrifying. Not because I didn't want him, but because I did.

So, fucking bad.

And it scared me how much I did.

Andrew's hand came between us, cupping the inside of my thigh and sliding higher. He traced the front of my pants, reverent, steady, as if he already knew the answer I feared to give.

I broke the kiss first and pressed my forehead to his, breath shaking, my hands still fisted in his tunic as though letting go might undo me entirely.

"Andrew, stop," I whispered. The words scraped raw from my throat. "Please stop."

Andrew froze, breath still hot against my skin. For a heartbeat he didn't move. Then, rough and quick: "If you are worried about..." he swallowed hard, voice low and uneven. "Nadia, it is fine. I take the Voidshot every few weeks. Dachier makes sure of it."

He moved to kiss me again, but I turned my head to the side.

Andrew's eyes searched mine, as if desperate to read what had changed. "You do not have to be afraid."

"It's not that," I whispered.

He hesitated, the heat between us shattering into something heavier. His hands slipped from my waist, slow, reluctant, as though each inch cost him. He leaned back just enough to look at me, his jaw tight, eyes fierce in the dim glow.

"Then why?"

"Andrew, I—" My chest ached. "I can't. I just..."

He let out a short laugh, sharp and humorless at first, then softened into something lighter, practiced, as if to spare me. "Of course," he said lightly, though the edge beneath it betrayed him. "You lure me this far, then leave me stranded on the shore. Cruel, Nadia."

Heat rushed to my face. "That's not what I—"

"I know." He leaned back, raking a hand through his hair, every movement restless. "Gods, do I know. You have told me no a hundred times before. I thought—" He stopped, swallowed, and finished softer. "I thought this time might be different. That we were past this."

He's referring to the river. I closed my eyes. *Yes, I can see how he'd think that after his hands had been down my pants...*

"I'm sorry," I said.

Andrew exhaled, sharp, then settled back against the headboard beside me, stretching his legs out and folding his arms across his chest with a kind of frustrated elegance. Even angry he was gods-damned gorgeous.

"No. You are not," he said. "And you should not be." His voice gentled, though the edge still lingered. He looked at my sideways. "Just... do not toy with me, Nadia."

The words stung, not because they were cruel, but because they had a measure of truth.

He glanced toward the bedside table at the half-drained wine bottle. My chest tightened.

Andrew reached for the bottle, swirled what was left, and took a slow drink. He caught me watching. For a moment, he looked like he might make a joke of it, but his mouth closed again. Instead, he set the bottle back down and rubbed the heel of his palm against his temple. He looked...uncertain. Torn. His frustrated gaze flicked to me, but then he reined it in, forcing a crooked smile that didn't quite reach his eyes.

"Gods," he muttered, voice rough. "You undo me. And yet I have not been fully honest with you."

He hesitated, as if the admission cost him more than restraint ever had. His hand twitched upward, fingers brushing again the air where his crown would have been. The small tell set my nerves on edge. My breath caught, a faint chill tracing down my spine.

He hadn't moved, hadn't looked at me. Then, slowly, he pulled something from his tunic pocket, caught my wrist, and pressed his fist into my palm. His knuckles trembled against my skin before he pulled back and let the object fall into my hand.

A ring.

Not gaudy or ostentatious like I would have expected from him. No, it was actually incredibly simple. Something that a I would have chosen to wear myself. The band was made of thin silver, the edges worn soft by time. A dark ruby, small and flush against the metal, caught the candlelight with a muted glimmer. The kind of jewel chosen for permanence, not spectacle.

I tilted my hand to gaze at it in the light, and something on the inside of the band caught my eye. An inscription etched so fine I had to squint to make it out: *My best friend, my love, forever.*

My throat caught. I looked up, but Andrew was already shifting uneasily, watching me with an expression I didn't recognize. His cheeks had gone a little red, and when he licked his lips, I realized that he was nervous.

I stared. My throat locked. "Out of all the things to bring on this gods-forsaken quest," I whispered, almost laughing at the absurdity. "You carried this?"

A muscle jumped in Andrew's jaw. He gave a short, uneven shrug. "It was my mother's." His voice dipped, low, weighted. "The only thing of hers I have left. I made sure I packed it before we left Riverwind. If I had no kingdom to return to..." His eyes flicked to mine, then away again. "I wanted to make sure I kept it for you."

The bed tilted under me. For all the arrogance Andrew cloaked himself in, that confession broke something quiet and unguarded inside him.

"I was going to ask you again that night after the Damewood ball," he said quickly, almost defensively. "But *someone* never gave me the chance. Something about the hour being 'ill-chosen'." He gave me a sideways look, then placed his hand over my wrist. "So yes —I've kept it with me. All this time."

Before I could form words, he rose, drawing me off the bed with him until I was standing beside it. Then he stepped back and dropped to one knee before me, still holding my wrist.

I cleared my throat. "Andrew—"

"Just listen." His grip tightened, then loosened like he was reminding himself not to hold too hard. His voice rasped, rougher than I'd ever heard. He drew in a sharp breath. "My father is dead. I am the only heir to Riverwind. My coronation waits for me upon my return. Last year, my father left orders that I cannot take the throne

237

unless I stand beside a bride. He thought I'd never settle on my own. He put his doubt in writing, with his wizard's hand guiding the ink."

His laugh came out short, bitter, almost a bark. "Imagine it. Your father making his lack of faith into law."

The words stung, and I could see how much it cost him to admit it. Andrew's eyes burned with frustration, with shame, with something too raw to name.

He shook his head. "If I fail to present a bride at my coronation, the council takes power until I am fit. And if power goes to them, I know I will never get it back. They will keep the crown strangled in their grasp until the kingdom rots. Unless..." His grip tightened, steady but not cruel. "...unless you would stand with me. As my bride."

I forced a brittle laugh. "So that's what this is?" I said lightly. Too lightly. "A solution. Secure the kingdom by promising yourself to the bastard of Damewood."

Andrew's temper cracked the silence first. "*Fuck*, Nadia, I am on my knees here and you still cannot see me. You think I chase you because you are convenient? Because I cannot have another?" His frustrated growl ripped out harshly, edged with something dangerously close to pain. "I could fill a ballroom with willing brides tomorrow. But I do not want them. I want *you*."

For just a heartbeat, I caught an expression I didn't recognize on his face. Not arrogance or strategy. Something naked and unguarded that I didn't know how to answer.

He dragged a hand through his hair, shoulders rising and falling. "I will stop asking," he said finally, quieter now. "But I need your answer before this journey ends. Not for my pride," his mouth twisted, "but because my crown will not wait."

He rose, the moment sealed away, and with one last look—one I couldn't quite read—he left, the door shutting soft but final.

I stood in silence, my fist curled tight around the silver ring. It bit into my palm, sharp enough to anchor me as my pulse skidded out of control.

He hadn't pleaded. He hadn't threatened. He had knelt with humility—and somehow that made it worse. He had shown me the man beneath the crown, and I wasn't sure where to put that knowledge.

Andrew was willing to barter his own future to keep Riverwind from tearing itself apart. That was the weight he carried. I had lost pieces of my life to violence and chance, but I had never been asked to choose who paid the price for an entire kingdom.

The thought settled in my chest like a slow, unwelcome truth: wanting was a luxury. And maybe it always had been.

Maybe it was time I stopped clinging so tightly to what I wanted for myself and started thinking of what I owed to others. To my people. To him.

I hesitated, and then slid the ring over my finger, testing. I sighed and sank back onto the bed.

Of course it would be a perfect fit.

Andrew's words replayed in my head, colliding with the memory of that unguarded last look. For the first time, I didn't just see the arrogant boy who'd chased me—I saw the king he was becoming. And the terrifying part was how much I wanted to stand beside him when he did.

TWENTY-ONE

When I finally descended the stairs, the others were already stirring in the common room. The inn smelled like last night: smoke sunk into wood, and spilled ale that puckered your tongue. It looked like someone had tried to sweep but given up on the tracks of boot grit and pine needles littered across the floor and between table legs.

Trea crouched beside Peter at a bench, showing him the safe way to run oil along a blade. Damien leaned against the far wall, arms folded, his eyes half-shut as if he hadn't closed them all night.

Andrew sat at the head of a long table, his posture radiating that he was accustomed to rooms going quiet for him. He barely looked up as I entered and then focused again on the men. Corbin appeared at Andrew's shoulder almost the instant I entered, and he set a cup of wine in Andrew's hand. The rest of us found places along the table, benches creaking under the weight of fatigue. We waited as Andrew drained half of the cup in silence.

Trea spread a map over the long table and weighed it with whatever came to hand: a knife, a stoneware salt cellar, a horseshoe gone smooth with age. He'd even set Peter's crust of bread on the northeast corner; the prince glared and then pretended not to care.

Andrew's hand rested on the map, fingers splayed, the faintest tremor ghosting the knuckles before he bunched them into a fist. He took another drink.

Damien broke the silence first, his voice flat. "We should address yesterday."

Everyone shifted, but no one argued. I pictured the gold-cloaked riders, the roar of unfamiliar weapons, the way one soldier's aim had lowered when his eyes caught mine.

Trea straightened. "Those weren't swords or bows. Whatever they carried…"

"Guns," Damien said. His silver hair caught firelight, making his sharp profile look carved from steel. "The word is guns."

The sound of it sat wrong in my ears, blunt and alien. "Guns?" I repeated, the syllable clumsy.

"They kill faster than arrows, straighter than crossbows, and don't care if you've got steel or leather between you and the shot. At close range, they don't miss." Damien's eyes narrowed at a memory. "One squeeze of the hand," he mimed it, index finger crooked as he pulled, "and you're dead."

My stomach turned. The sound of that thunder still rang in my ears if I let silence stretch too long.

Andrew leaned forward. "And how do you know this?"

Damien's jaw tightened. A pause too long. "Because I've seen them used before. That's enough for you to understand the threat."

Andrew's hand curled against the table. Corbin, silent as shadow, poured into his cup until the red wine kissed the brim. Andrew took it without looking.

I kept my eyes on Damien. His calm never cracked, but I felt the lie in his stillness. He knew more. He always knew more.

Trea grunted. "We need to know where we're headed, and whether we're riding into another trap."

Andrew's eyes flicked around the table. "There are two routes to Ferrington Pass. Direct east is faster, but more exposed. They will expect us there. Or detour north, circle back through the foothills. Slower. Harder terrain. Safer if we do not mind losing time."

"Time is the one thing we don't have," I said. All heads turned. My cheeks warmed, but I pressed on. "If the Holy are moving as quickly as we are, we can't afford to waste days. Not unless we want them at the pass before us. But we can disguise our numbers. Travel at night, take shifts so we don't collapse. Catch them off-guard."

Andrew's mouth twitched, the faintest smile. "Exactly what I was about to propose. A staggered march. We will make speed, and their scouts will not expect us to risk night travel."

The sting was instant. He hadn't been about to say it. I knew it. The words were still warm on my tongue, and he'd taken them as if they were his. My shoulders tensed, but I forced my jaw still.

Across the table, Corbin nudged Andrew's cup closer to his hand. Andrew caught it, and this time he drank deep. The tremor in his fingers stilled only after the second swallow.

Trea's voice pulled me back. "Night travel doubles the risk of accident. Horses stumble in dark terrain, men fall asleep in the saddle. Supplies run thinner."

"We will manage," Andrew said briskly. "The crown cannot wait on excuses." His eyes met mine, steady, firm. "And Princess Nadia rides behind me," he added. "Between Sir Trea and me. For protection."

It wasn't said cruelly. Not even arrogantly, not on the surface. But the words landed heavy all the same. A cage dressed as concern.

Heat flushed my throat. "I can manage my own seat."

"You'll do as ordered," he said, voice low enough that only those nearest heard.

I stared at him, and he met my eyes. Unyielding.

Trea cleared his throat and looked away.

Andrew's hand tightened around his cup, as he leaned toward me to whisper, "I am not losing you again."

The table shifted restlessly. Corbin coughed into his sleeve. Damien's eyes stayed on the fire. Peter's small hands fidgeted with the hilt of his blade, torn between loyalty and unease.

I bristled, every part of me itching to fight back, but the air was too tight. My words would only clang against stone.

I traced the ridges of the map with my fingertip, pretending to study it, though my eyes no longer saw. Damien's words hung too heavy, like smoke in my chest. Guns. Soldiers in priest's cloaks. Demons with faces. None of it fit cleanly together, and every answer sounded more like a lie wrapped in a half-truth.

Andrew's voice rose again, commanding the group into motion for tomorrow, but I barely heard him.

I told myself I should stay. That I belonged here, at the table, with plans and parchment and talk of kingdoms and heirs. That this was what my father would have wanted, what the crown demanded. But my feet were already shifting beneath the bench.

I stood before anyone could remark on it. The men kept on talking, arguing over provisions and the order of march. No one tried to stop me. Perhaps they were glad to let me slip into silence.

I LEFT the men to their planning and made my way into the stables and down the rows of stalls. The air stung hot in the barn, and flies buzzed around my head in the thick, hay-scented air. Sunlight cut through the barn in bright patches, illuminating the little bits of floating hay and dust. A white mare stuck her shaggy head out of her stall as I neared, and I stopped a moment to scratch under her chin and shoo a fly away from her big brown eyes. She whinnied at me, and more horses answered from farther down the line.

I stepped away from the pale horse, my ears perked. There were voices down at the end of the aisle. I recognized one of them as Vestro's.

What is he doing in human form?

I quickly tiptoed past the occupied stalls, trying not to startle the horses, and stopped just around the corner of Vestro's stall. The voices were coming from inside. I crouched down near the outside of the stable wall, listening.

"You got it?" Vestro's voice, hushed but edged.

"You have the money?" The other voice rasped, hoarse, worn from shouting.

"It's all here." A clink of coins, the tug of a drawstring.

My stomach dipped. Who is he paying? For what?

"I hear you've taken up with humans. And a Hunter." A growl vibrated through the planks, crawling my spine. "Pathetic."

"It's complicated," Vestro sighed. "It'll be over soon."

"Not soon enough. Don't screw this up—we've waited too long."

"Do you doubt me?"

A chuckle, thick and cruel. "Not your skill. Your head, when it matters." A pause. "Keep your priorities straight. We won't take matters into our own hands—again."

Again. The word split cold down my spine.

The boards behind me buckled. Something slammed the wall, rattling dust into my hair. I bit my lip to choke back a sound, lungs burning as I crouched lower. Another scuffle, heavier.

"Tell them not to interfere," Vestro snarled, guttural. "I'll handle it."

"See that you do," the other hissed. "Our fate rests in your hands."

Their voices thinned, but I didn't wait. I edged back, one step, then another, heart slamming in my throat.

I wasn't supposed to hear this. Gods, I didn't want to hear this.

'Humans and a Hunter'—that was us. But why would Vestro—? The second voice was not human. Demon, clear as fire in the dark.

Again. Take matters into our own hands—again.

The siege on Mauve. The fires. The cloaked demon's warning.

No. Vestro would never risk the mission, never risk me. He couldn't—

I backed faster, breath shaking. Ves.... *What have you done?*

The high-pitched screech of the stall gate opening made my heart jump out of my chest. I backpedaled to the door and was just feet away when I saw the two shadows against the back wall of the stable move around the corner toward me. I turned and dove out of the front double-door, landing on my side and rolling to the left out of the line of sight from inside. I scrambled to my feet, my boots sliding in the dirt in my haste, and darted around the corner of the stable and ran through the growing crowd down the street.

I didn't stop running until I'd made it halfway back to the inn. I finally slowed and turned down into a deserted alleyway, tired of trying to barrel my way through the bustling streets. The morning sun filled the street, warming the shaded stones of the buildings lining the alley. Merchants called out their morning wares, and the sweet smells of freshly baked bread and pastries drifted down from the open windows above me. I leaned back against the wall, my breathing heavy and eyes stinging. The back of my shirt stuck to my damp skin, and my knees shook. I rubbed my eyes with the back of my wrist and took a deep breath, squatting and putting my head between my knees, trying to relax.

What if I'm wrong? I thought. *What if I'm overreacting? I mean, it's Vestro! He could have been talking about anything...*

A bitter chuckle escaped my lips, and I shook my head, almost amazed at my own stupidity. There were only so many things two demons could be talking about when it involved an assignment and our particular traveling group. But what exactly he was supposed to do, I could only guess. I took a deep breath and stood up, one hand brushing against the warming stones of the laundry, then left the alley and started walking back toward the stables.

I guess there's only one way to find out.

How I was supposed to spark such a conversation, I hadn't the faintest clue. My mind raced as I passed cart after cart of silks and baked goods but had not found an answer by the time the tall doors of the stables came into view. My breathing picked up, and I swallowed, trying to slow it down. Vestro was good at picking up on my body language, and I didn't want him to be on the defensive as soon as I walked in.

I wondered for just a moment if I was doing the right thing and hesitated at the doors. I didn't have my sword with me—and it unnerved me greatly. For one, if it came down to a fight, I wasn't even sure if my sword would have done any good against a demon like Vestro. Secondly, it bothered me that I was even thinking about having to fight him. I shouldn't have feared Vestro.

He is not—

I let out a surprised yip. I hadn't realized that I'd passed through the doors and made it down to the end of the aisle. Vestro peeked around the corner of his stall, looked past me, and then walked toward me as he straightened his tunic.

"Are you OK?" he asked. "You look a little pale."

"I'm fine," I said. I swallowed and willed my heart to slow. "I just ran all the way here. I'm a little out of breath."

He looked at me, his eyes intense. His scrutinizing stare made my skin tingle, and I crossed my arms against the sudden chill in the air. I looked away as his black eyes swirled pale and then slid back to black. He took a small step toward me, his shoulders tense.

"You look...different." His head tilted, nostrils flaring the way he did when he was in horse form and the world around us made him wary. "Where were you?"

The question hit harder than it should have. I swallowed and set my hand on the stall rail, wood biting into my palm. "With the others. Discussing plans." My voice scraped thin, even to my ears.

Vestro's gaze narrowed, not angry but searching.

Damn guy knows how to read me too well.

I forced a smile and moved toward him, doing my best to relax my stance. "I came to see how you were holding up. You pushed yourself harder than anyone yesterday."

"*I* am fine." The words came clipped, defensive. Then his shoulders dropped, tension leaking out. "But you...you should not risk coming here. Now that Peter knows, I'm worried we can't hold this up much longer." His jaw tightened. "Damien acts like he's waiting for me to slip."

"Peter won't snitch. And if they found out, it won't matter," I said, too fast. "You're still mine."

His eyes softened at that, but only for a breath. He sniffed the air, then again, slower. His face burned red, the tops of his cheeks flushing until the color edged toward purple. His eyes swirled to the color pale flesh.

"Yours?" His nostrils flared, and he leaned into my ear, close enough that I could feel his warm breath ghost over my cheek. "Then why do you smell like him?"

My stomach pitched. The air vanished from the barn, replaced by the hammer of my pulse in my ears.

He watched me for a long moment, the pale flesh fading back to black in his eyes. His hand twitched at his side, fingers curling and uncurling, like he couldn't decide whether to reach for me or let me go.

I froze under the weight of his stare. My mouth went dry. I reached for him, but when my fingers brushed his sleeve my skin remembered Andrew's hands, and it felt... wrong. I let go and pressed my palm to the stall door, grounding myself against the warm wood.

"I..." The word cracked out and died.

Vestro's eyes narrowed, not cruel, but raw with hurt. He leaned closer, moving dark hair falling into his eyes, voice low and sharp.

"What the hell is that?"

I blinked and looked at him. "What?"

"That." He pointed, his face tight.

I followed his eyes down to my hands, and I realized too late that I'd forgotten to remove Andrew's ring. My cheeks reddened. I unfolded my arms and twiddled my fingers, my thumb playing with the edge of the silver engagement band.

"Last night, after the tunnels, Andrew took me upstairs—"

"Don't even finish," he cut me off, shaking his head and raising his hands. His upper lip curled, and he wouldn't make eye contact. "I don't need to know the details."

"You shouldn't have asked," I shook my head too quickly.

"You come here with his scent across your skin, your hands shaking, and a ring on your finger, and you expect me not to ask?" He snorted. "Why are you here?"

The barn walls pressed in, and the air felt thick. Dust clouds swirled around my feet as I shifted, suddenly restless and trapped in the dark.

My voice broke. "I came because I wanted..." My throat closed on the word. Comfort. Forgiveness. Something I didn't deserve. "Because I don't know where else to go."

Vestro exhaled through his teeth, sharp and slow, and his eyes narrowed with concern as he searched my face. "Something happened last night," he said quietly.

Oh, yes. So fucking much happened last night.

My fingers curled into fists at my sides. They wouldn't stop trembling. No matter how tightly I clenched, they still shook.

The black of Vestro's eyes faded to pale fleshy white, and his brow lowered in quiet fury. He stepped closer, his movement unnaturally smooth, and the air around him seemed to change. I almost felt the shadows condense around his feet as he edged closer, and his shoulders rounded with coiled attention.

"Did he hurt you?" The words were jagged, caught between fury and fear.

"No," I said too quickly, too loud. The horses stirred in their stalls, hooves shifting on straw. "No. He has been...respectful." The last word cracked, and I hated it.

Vestro's eyes searched me, suspicion flaring and then folding into something worse: hurt. His fingers twitched as if to take my hand but fell away, curling into a fist at his side. "Then why are you shaking?"

Because of you. Because of him. Because of all of it.

I felt something wet drip down my cheek, and I wiped it away quickly. The memories of the tunnel flashed back, and I replayed them in my head as my mouth moved of its own accord, softly recounting the night's events of getting lost in the tunnel that led to falling asleep in Andrew's arms. I trailed off, not wanting to finish the story of our morning together. Though after a quick glance at Vestro's stricken face, I realized I didn't have to.

Vestro closed the small space between us, gathering me against his chest in a sudden, fierce embrace. The scents of leather, horse, and wildflowers clung to him, grounding and suffocating me all at once. My hands bunched in his tunic before I realized I'd reached for him.

"It's all right, Nadia." Vestro's arms tightened and I felt his chin tremble against my hair. "Even if you're his, I'm still yours. I'll carry what's mine until you pry it from my hands—or until it kills me."

Vestro's words carved out something raw and aching in my chest. I let out a strangled sob, and he took my face in both hands and bent, slow and deliberate, and kissed me. His lips were warm as they pressed against mine. His kiss was soft yet deliberate and said what he couldn't: that I could break his heart a hundred times over and he would still be there.

"You have me," he whispered. "Always."

Guilt clung at the edges of my heart, whispering that I was stealing this comfort from him, that he deserved better than crumbs of my attention. He deserved more than this half-truth. He deserved someone who could love him fully, without hesitation or shame. And still I clung tighter, selfish as a child clutching a toy I'd outgrown but couldn't give up.

"Ves," I whispered, not sure what I meant to follow it with. *Sorry? Thank you? Don't let go?* The words tangled uselessly on my tongue.

For a moment, the rest of the world fell away. I tilted my head back and deepened the kiss, parting my lips and letting his warmth close around me.

Then I forced myself to step back, my hand resting on the familiar cadence of his heartbeat beneath my ear, steady and unyielding. His gaze followed, still raw, still searching, but he let me go.

I wanted to promise him I would always love him. I wanted to tell him again that he was my first choice—that he always had been.

But I can't ever have him. Because of what he is.

And it's not fucking fair.

"We're leaving soon," I said softly. I wiped my eyes with the back of my hand. "You need to shift before the others arrive."

Vestro stared at me for so long I thought he might refuse. Then he gave a single weary nod and turned to step into the shadow of the nearest stall.

He paused at the open door, and his hand gripped the wood so tightly that the wood creaked beneath his white knuckles. He kept his profile to me as he spoke, low and rough: "I would burn the world before I lost you."

He slipped back into the stall without a word. The scrape of hooves and muffled cry followed a heartbeat later, and when I stepped in after him, he stood already there in horse form, dark coat gleaming, eyes still too knowing.

I reached for the brush on the rail, my chest loosening as I dragged the bristles down his neck in long strokes. He shifted his weight, leaning into it, and I smiled despite myself. "There's my pretty boy."

His ears flicked at the sound of my voice, and I felt the rumble of breath when he exhaled, warm against my cheek. I smoothed the line of his tack, fussing more than I needed to, because the rhythm of caring for him steadied me.

I kissed his nose and slipped the bridle into place, brushing a bit of hay from his mane. "There we go," I murmured. "Back to how things are supposed to be."

When things made sense.

The stable doors banged open, and the men filed in, Andrew at their head, posture squared and voice already sharp with orders. His gaze cut straight to me, then softened—too much for my liking in a public setting, like he'd forgotten for half a heartbeat that we weren't alone.

Vestro's ears flicked back, then forward again, a mischief I knew too well glinting in his eyes.

Andrew smiled and stepped close, reaching as if to brush his fingers against my arm. Before his hand could touch, Vestro tossed his head and shoved it between us. The move was deliberate, a bump hard enough to make Andrew rock back on his heels.

Andrew's jaw flexed. He tried to brush it off, but when he tried to step around to me, Vestro swung his hindquarters with lazy precision, forcing Andrew to side-step or take a hoof to the knee.

"Your horse is insufferable," Andrew muttered.

Vestro let out a sharp snort, ears flicking forward like he'd won some private game.

I bit down a smile and patted Vestro's neck. "He's a bit of a joker," I said, though the words sounded far too pleased.

Andrew's gaze lingered on me, unreadable, as he adjusted his gloves. "Keep him steady, then."

"I always do," I said, softer than I meant to.

Vestro flicked his tail, flicking it against Andrew's chest as if to underline the point.

"Stop showing off," I scolded Vestro, loud enough for the others to hear. I swatted at his shoulder, though my hand lingered in the sleek curve of his neck a moment too long. "Anyone would think you're trying to be difficult on purpose."

The men scattered to check packs and tighten straps. Trea brushed past with a wink that told me he'd caught more of the exchange than Andrew probably realized. Damien didn't bother to hide his smirk as he leaned against a post, his silver hair catching the light. Corbin, though—his eyes lingered over the top of Andrew's saddle, flicking his gaze from me to Andrew to Vestro as if he were taking notes for some test I didn't know was coming.

I ignored the odd squire and turned my attention back to Vestro, tugging the cinch into place, and then smoothing a hand down his glossy shoulder. He leaned into the touch with exaggerated weight, enough to press me closer, enough to make Andrew take an involuntary step back to keep his boots clean.

Vestro's ears twitched, forward then back, his equine version of a grin. I pressed my forehead to his for a moment, whispering so low only he could hear. "You're impossible."

He snorted, a puff of hot air against my cheek that felt suspiciously like laughter.

I moved to swing up on my own, boots braced against the stirrup, but Andrew stepped forward before I could.

"Allow me."

His hand extended, steady. It hadn't been a request.

I bristled at the eyes that turned our way. *So much for keeping things quiet.* Though, to be fair, for as long as Andrew had been courting me, I doubted it really made a difference. *They'll all probably assume it anyway at some point.* I didn't want to make more of a scene, so I nodded. Andrew's grip was firm around my waist, and he lifted me with ease.

As I settled into the saddle, Andrew's hand didn't fall away. His gaze caught on the band circling my finger, the glint of the ruby winking in the morning light. The breath that left him wasn't quite steady. He gently took my hand, and brushed his fingers over my knuckles and the ring as if to remind himself it was real.

For a fleeting heartbeat, his kingly mask slipped. The corners of his mouth twitched, the barest flicker of a proud grin threatening to break free before he forced it back under control. But I saw it. I felt it.

And I loved how it made me feel.

Vestro stilled beneath me, the restless flick of his tail going quiet. His ears pinned back, head lowering, as though the weight of Andrew's touch carried through me into him.

Andrew straightened, the warmth of his hand finally leaving mine. His expression was all composure again, voice cool and commanding. "Stay close to me."

I nodded, though my throat was too tight for words.

Andrew lifted his eyes to mine, the softness already shuttered away, replaced by something clipped, kingly. "My lady."

He smiled and patted Vestro's neck before he turned.

Vestro's body tensed under me, the ripple of muscle betraying his temper.

I smoothed my palm over his neck, whispering low. "Easy."

But inside, I wasn't sure which of them I meant.

CHAPTER
TWENTY-TWO

The thinning air sliced through my chest the higher we climbed, as though the mountain was trimming me down piece by piece until there was nothing left to breathe with. The trail wound upward like a scar carved into the cliff, shale loose underfoot, every step threatening to slide back down into nothing. I pressed my legs to Vestro's sides, urging him onward. He responded with a powerful surge, as if the strain of the climb meant nothing. I tightened my fingers around the reins, but my gaze studied the way his ears pinned and flicked. He hadn't looked at me since we left town and hadn't even so much as tossed his head my way.

My hand pressed into the heat of his neck, feeling the twitch of his muscles under the glossy coat. He wasn't spooked. He was too tightly coiled for that, too controlled. But I could feel the storm in him, muscles humming as though he wanted to throw himself off the trail just to have something to fight. His ears flicked back, nostrils flaring with each gust of air, as though some scent traveled the wind I couldn't sense.

"Easy," I whispered. "We're almost there."

Andrew's voice floated back from the front of the line, "We intercept before they reach the pass. If they get through..." He didn't finish. He didn't have to. We all understood the stakes at hand.

His stallion tossed its head, snorting.

Andrew squared shoulders. "We strike fast, break their formation, and take the chest then get out of there. No hesitation."

My pulse quickened, fingers tightening on the reins. "Then I'm with you."

Andrew's head snapped back, eyes narrowing on me. Not with his usual smug glint. This was something colder. Controlling. "No. You stay back."

I blinked. "Excuse me?"

"You do not have your armor anymore."

"Neither do you."

"You are not as strong as a man."

His words cut as if he had reached out and struck me. My lips parted, but nothing came.

What the hell, Andrew?

Andrew held up a hand, as if he could push down my building anger. "One strike, Nadia. One stray shot, and you will break. I will not risk you." His tone softened on the last word but was still heavy enough to smother me. "Not this time."

Heat burned up my throat, humiliation sharp as fire. I wanted to bite back, to remind him that I had fought since before he could grow a proper beard, that I had bled beside him, not behind him. But the truth—damn it, the truth—sat heavy: he was right. Without the armor, I felt bare. Too small. Too slow.

My jaw clenched until it hurt. "Fine."

He gave me one last searching look, as if trying to confirm the leash would hold, then turned to the others. "Trea, Damien, you're with me. Peter, guard the ridge."

Vestro shifted beneath me, a rumble through his chest, his ears twitching back like he could hear the protest I swallowed. I smoothed a hand down his mane. "Don't give me that look. Apparently, I'm fragile."

~

WE CRESTED the ridge just as the convoy appeared below. A line of Holy riders moved with surgical precision, black cloaks neat, rifles gleaming in the low light. Their formation was tight, no wasted movement. At the center the cart trundled, chest lashed down, the lock catching the sun.

Damien leaned forward, voice quiet and sure. "Middle cart. Guards heavier than usual. Eyes ahead, not above."

Andrew's jaw flexed. "We drop. Hard, fast. No stragglers."

He gave the signal, and they plunged down the slope. Gravel scattered, horses thundered. Shouts rose from below as rifles angled up.

I stayed. Watching. My chest heaved with the kind of breath that had nowhere to go. My hands ached from how tightly I clutched the reins. Every part of me screamed to dive into the chaos, but I stayed. Because Andrew told me to.

Vestro stamped, ears pinned. He hated it as much as I did.

The clash below was all steel and fury. Andrew cut through soldiers with vicious grace, his stallion shoving bodies aside. Damien slipped through the fight like smoke, his knives quick and merciless. Trea was the anvil, blows crashing down heavy, Peter's arrow whistling from above to cover him.

I could only watch, burning, every nerve in my body itching for the fight.

Then a hissing sound like steam from a kettle, sharp and cold, slid down my spine. The hair on my arms rose before I even turned.

The shadows peeled away from stones.

Figures emerged, eight, maybe nine. All different. All...wrong.

The first was wolf-like, hunched, lean, its jaw stretched too long, teeth clicking together with a sound like bones snapping. Another followed, reptilian, scales glistening, its tail lashing the dirt until sparks spat. Behind it, a brute loomed, hulking, taller than two men stacked, arms knotted like twisted oak. And then it was too human, at first glance. Too human until the joints bent too far, the elbows folding wrong, the eyes ember-red and glowing.

They weren't mindless beasts. They weren't wild like I'd imagined. The demons moved like soldiers, disciplined, their voices rumbling with command.

One pointed directly at me. "Destroy it." His voice cracked the air like stone splitting.

Another's gaze found Vestro. His sneer curved like a knife. "Traitor."

My stomach dropped.

I didn't wait for the explanation. I yanked the reins, heels digging in. Vestro bolted, carrying us back down toward the battle below. We reached the edge of the convoy just as a rifle cracked. The chest shook loose, tumbling from the cart, slamming onto the stone road. Guards scrambled.

Vestro reared with a scream, hooves smashing rifles to splinters, scattering men. The chest split on the rocks, wood splintering.

Cipher tumbled free.

The artifact gleamed in the dust, plain and small, and yet it pulled at me as though my bones had been carved for it.

I was off Vestro before I thought better of it, my hands closing around it. The smooth, cold metal of the tiny device pressed into my palms. I shoved it into my tunic pocket, against my ribs, as a thrill seared into my skin.

We got it. We actually got it!

Andrew turned to glare at me, his eyes furious. "What the fuck are you doing here?" he yelled. "Get out of here!"

The Holy captain roared, "Take the girl! We need both of them alive!"

My heart flipped. *Both of them? What does he...*

The demons snarled, blades flashing. "Kill them. End it now!"

Both sides advanced in a rush. And I stood trapped in between.

What. The. Fuck.

The clash swallowed me whole. Holy rifles cracked, gunpowder burning my nose. Steel clanged, shrieks echoed. Demons pressed in, their movements disciplined and merciless. Bullets shattered stone off the cliff wall, sparks spitting. Cloaks snapped as they moved in their drilled formation, sabers glinting when the rifles ran empty.

I dropped to my knees and rolled out of the way as a shadow lunged in my direction.

The nearest demon was wolf-like, with long teeth bared in a snarl that rattled in its throat. It hit the nearest Holy soldier full-force, claws ripping through the man's chest plate. Another reptilian demon followed, the gray scales catching the sun, a tail whipping out to snap a rifle clean in half. The Holy staggered but recovered quickly, his saber cutting in precise arcs to rip through the scaled flesh.

More poured in from both sides.

A hulking brute, taller than two men, its arms knotted like twisted oak, slammed a Holy soldier into the dirt, bones crunching. A figure too human at first glance flickered in the melee, joints bending wrong as its arm stretched unnaturally to hook another soldier from behind.

The air filled with the wet sounds of steel in flesh, snarls, screams, and rifle cracks.

Andrew rallied us like a general on the field. "Hold the line!" His voice carried far, cutting above the chaos. He carved through one of the wolf-creatures, his sword biting deep. His stallion surged forward, the warhorse striking out with its hooves and moving as one with his rider.

Damien dismounted and slipped past him, silent and terrifying. His blade caught the glint of light, and a demon's throat opened, spraying black blood as the body folded soundlessly. Another swung at him, but Damien ducked low and rose behind it with a thrust that sank home. His calm was wrong, unnatural, while the rest of us fought to breathe.

Trea planted himself near Peter, sword steady, every swing a shield to keep the boy alive. Peter's arrows whistled past, shaky but true enough to sink into a demon's side. He shouted in triumph, then yelped when a reptilian tail cracked too close.

Gregory shouted, swinging his mace wild, but the hulking brute demon caught him full in the chest. His cry cut short as claws raked across him, throwing him into the dirt. Trea's roar shook the air as he lunged, cutting down the large demon with a stab through the gut, but Gregory lay still, blood pooling under him.

My stomach lurched. The smell of iron infiltrated everything, thick and choking.

Vestro was suddenly beside me, fury in every line of his body. He reared, hooves smashing a Holy rifle to splinters, then slammed down on a demon's skull with a sound that made me gag. He twisted, his body a weapon as he bit, kicked, and stuck with his front hooves, keeping me out of reach. He bent a knee and lowered his thick neck, and I quickly scrambled up onto his back.

But the press was too much.

A demon's claws hooked into the front of my tunic and yanked me off Vestro's back. The world tilted, slammed, and the hard ground knocked the breath from me as I rolled across the earth. Pain burst white-hot, in my shoulder, and my ribs screamed where Cipher pressed under my tunic, cold and unyielding against my chest.

I scrambled for my sword, but the demon's shadow blotted out the sky. His eyes glowed like coals buried deep in ash, and his mouth curled with something worse than hate. A blade gleamed in his hand, slick and dark, its edge aimed for my throat.

"Nadia!" Andrew's voice cut through the din.

I looked up to see him fighting his way toward me, sword flashing, blood painting his face and sleeves. He cut down one soldier, shoved another back, and his horse plowed through the melee like a battering ram. He was close enough that I could see the strain in his jaw, the sweat darkening his hair, and the desperation in his eyes as he reached for me.

But then the Holy line shifted. Two more soldiers surged at him, empty rifles swinging like clubs. Andrew's horse screamed as the butt of a gun smashed against its shoulder. Andrew reeled, blocking and swinging his blade, shouting my name again, but he was shoved sideways, his blade locked against theirs.

His face fell in horror when he realized he couldn't reach me.

The demon standing above me raised its blade higher.

I froze. Every instinct screamed to move, but terror rooted me to the ground. The world funneled to the glint of steel above me and the hiss of breath through teeth that weren't human.

"Andrew!" my voice broke.

The blade began its arc.

A scream unlike anything a horse should make ripped raw from Vestro's chest. It shook the air and split the battlefield. Even the Holy soldiers faltered mid-swing.

I turned, half-blind with panic, and watched Vestro shift mid-leap in full view of everyone present.

My heart flipped.

He just fucking jumped.

For me.

Vestro's form shuddered in the air, collapsing inward, twisting bone and sinew. Muscle reshaped. Skin split and folded. Hooves split into hands and his mane shrank away into dark hair. The smell of hot iron and brine stung my nose as flesh tore and knit in the same instant. In a blur, he was human. His chest heaved as he landed hard, splitting the rocky ground with the impact. Blood and slime from his violent shift streaked down his bare skin that trembled with unbridled rage.

He hit the demon above me like a tidal wave. Ripped it off me with one arm, lifted its crooked body overhead, and slammed it down hard enough to splinter bone and spatter skull across the dirt. The body twitched once, then stilled.

Vestro whirled on the next demon, his eyes burning. "Don't fucking touch her!" he roared, his voice raw.

Around us, the battlefield faltered.

The demons snarled. "Traitor."

"You'll doom us all," one hissed.

Vestro answered by seizing a fallen sword and spreading his stance, low and grounded. His grip tightened on the pommel, as if testing the weight, and then he struck.

The blade cut a clean diagonal through the air, splitting the nearest demon's chest open in a spray of dark blood. He pivoted, weight rolling through his hips, and parried a saber strike with a ringing crack. Before the soldier's arm could recover, Vestro riposted, thrusting straight through the man's sternum and wrenching the blade free in a single, practiced motion.

A reptilian tail lashed at him. Vestro dropped his shoulder, rolled under, and severed the limb mid-snap, ichor spraying hot across his chest. He rose with a brutal upward stroke that drove the blade through the creature's torso, then booted the body free with a soldier's efficiency.

Another wolf-thing lunged. Vestro sidestepped, let its momentum carry past, then hooked its hind leg with his foot and drove the point of his sword clean through the base of its skull. He ripped it free, flicking gore from the steel in the same motion; a soldier's tic, as if some ingrained part of him expected the next opponent already coming.

My breath stilled as I watched Vestro cut through the surrounding crowd of demons and soldiers alike with unbelievable skill. He moved like a man who had trained with a blade for decades. Every cut precise, every motion exact. Brutal. Efficient.

Human.

Terrifyingly human.

And I realized I didn't recognize him.

Andrew had always been a skilled swordsman, honed by tutors and the battlefield.

Damien was fast and efficient, inhuman in his own quiet way.

But Vestro... Vestro was something else. This wasn't just demon strength or speed. This was history. Years. Decades.

Vestro fought like he'd lived his entire life with a blade in his hand.

And I'd never known.

Time seemed to pause as I looked up and saw Andrew locked in strain against a Holy soldier. He stared over his sword at Vestro, and his face shifted from disbelief, to recognition, and then to fury.

The demons broke first, their discipline unraveling. Their commander spat a curse, and they vanished into the rocks.

The Holy reeled back, wounded, smoke curling from their rifles, and then stilled. Not one raised a blade against Vestro. Their captain's eyes cut to him, narrowing with something I couldn't name at first. Not fear. Not shock.

Recognition.

Then the captain shouted for report, jerked his horse around, and the remaining Holy members spurred off hard toward the Pass.

And then it was over.

CHAPTER
TWENTY-THREE

The air hung thick with iron and smoke, and the breeze caught and spread the copper tang of blood. Vestro staggered, chest heaving, blood streaking his temple, sword still slick in his grip. His legs buckled and he dropped hard to his knees, bare shoulders trembling, skin streaked with grime and blood.

I moved before anyone else. I yanked my cloak free and draped it over him, tugging it closed around his shoulders, covering as much of him as I could. My fingers shook on the soft wool as I crouched to face him.

"Ves, you stupid bastard," I whispered. "You scared the life out of me."

He looked up at me with eyes dark and raw. "I told you I'd jump," he rasped.

My heart clenched. I closed my eyes and pressed my forehead to his as I pulled the cloak tighter around him. For one fragile moment, the battlefield fell away. It was just the two of us, close enough for the others to see the bond but not understand it.

Steel rasped.

Vestro's head jerked up. I followed his gaze and froze.

Damien stepped forward, sunlight catching in his silver hair, his knife in one hand and sword in the other.

"Kelpie. I had an inkling, but I needed to be sure." Damien's tone was light, almost conversational, but every word crawled under my skin. His head tipped and his gaze sharpened. "And not just any kelpie. That was the killing discipline of a man who's drilled for decades. So, tell me, demon, who honed your blade? And who did you serve when you learned how to wield it?"

Vestro's jaw clenched but he said nothing.

"He's different," I hissed as I stood and hefted my sword. "He saved me. He's loyal to me."

Damien's smirk thinned. "Loyalties can change when survival demands it." His eyes cut to Vestro, gleaming with cruel amusement. "If they haven't already."

I stepped in front of him, planting my feet, sword up. My shoulders squared. "You will lower your weapons at once."

Damien's boots ground the dirt as he shifted his stance. "Demons are to be hunted and killed on sight. You know the old rules."

"And my rule is no one touches him. Do so and I will kill you. If he proves a danger, then I'll deal with him myself."

Damien didn't blink. Then his mouth twitched in that infuriating amused curl of his as he lowered his blade.

Vestro's hand trembled as it brushed my leg. His eyes were glazed, breath ragged, the cloak sliding from his bare shoulders. He leaned into me, cheek pressing weakly against my thigh, the touch protective even in his collapse.

"Well?" I lifted my chin at the circle of men. "Do you mean to threaten me too?"

Peter's dagger clattered to the stones. "Well, I already knew."

Every head swung his way.

He flushed, and his ears burned red. "What? I thought it would be obvious by now." He gave a small shrug, then added, almost off-hand but loud enough to cut, "Honestly, I'm surprised you didn't spot it first, Andrew. You're with her enough..."

The tension cracked, just enough for me to take a breath.

Trea's sword lowered next, confusion written deep in his eyes.

Andrew's face twisted as he stepped closer to me. Fury and betrayal fought to control his expression. His lips curled. "You would protect him? You would side with this—this thing?" His voice cracked into a half snarl, half plea. "After everything?"

"He's not a thing." My throat burned. "He's mine."

Andrew recoiled physically as if I'd struck him. He turned on Vestro, voice low and trembling with undisguised rage.

"You think I do not remember?" His gaze burned into Vestro, his eyes building and lighting the pyre under Vestro's knees. "Nadia whispered about you for years. I laughed it away. I thought she had invented someone to keep her company. But it was never a game, was it? All along, it was *you*."

My grip on my pommel slipped. I rotated my sword between my hands, wiping my sweaty palms against my thighs. I had been nine years old when Vestro came into my life. I'd been lonely, and having a secret guardian who always watched over me made me feel safe. Vestro had been the only one who listened to my cries without judgment. He had comforted me.

Andrew's hand slashed toward Vestro as he shouted at me. "You let that demon make himself essential to you. Always there. Always waiting," he spat. "He made sure you never learned how to sleep without him watching over you."

Vestro's shoulders stiffened. His jaw clenched, a flicker of pain crossing his face.

I swallowed hard, heat pricking behind my eyes. Andrew was twisting the memory, warping something pure into something ugly and foul.

I wanted to scream at Andrew that he was wrong, that what Vestro and I had wasn't the same as what Andrew and I shared, that it had never been the same.

"Vestro is different," I said, my voice cracking.

Andrew turned away, spun back. "Gods..." he choked, shaking his head hard as if to fling the memory out. "I fed you sugar cubes from my hand. I let you near. I—" His mouth twisted, rage and revulsion warring in his voice. "I trusted you with her."

My heart lurched. I remembered that afternoon in the stables; Andrew's boyish grin smudged with sugar, his laughter carrying over the straw. Vestro had dipped his head in patience, a quiet sentinel even then. The memory, once warm, now twisted in my chest until it burned.

Andrew's face twisted; he looked ill. "Every stumble, every dream, every fucking moment we shared together, Nadia. He was fucking there. Always between us. Don't you see that? Demons poison everything."

Andrew's words hung in the air like smoke—thick, choking, impossible to breathe through. I opened my mouth to speak, but nothing came.

Vestro's jaw tightened, the muscle ticking. His knuckles whitened, then forced loose again. At last, he raised his eyes to Andrew, steady but pleading without words. His voice broke the silence, low and heavy. "Yes, I watched. Both of you. Because you mattered to her happiness. I chose to guard you as well, even when it was not my duty."

Damien's head tilted, tone mild but cutting. "Duty. That's an oddly specific choice of words."

Andrew's fist crushed the hilt of his sword, leather squealing under his grip. His voice came out raw and spit flecked. "You were not guarding. You were making yourself indispensable. You let her lean in until she forgot there were others who could hold her. Who could protect her."

Flashes of memory from the other night on the riverbank stuck. I closed my eyes and saw him below me on the riverbank, his presence surrounding me, filling me, as he gave me everything.

When I opened my eyes, Vestro was already watching. I flinched.

And in that heartbeat of hesitation, I knew he saw my doubt.

Vestro's eyes widened, frantic. "No!" his voice rose sharply, breaking. "Nadia, listen to me. I only wanted you safe." His words tumbled faster, ragged. "But over the years, I just... Nadia, I..."

To my left, Trea shifted. His stance widened, and his shoulders bunched as he moved quietly, circling wide behind Andrew.

Andrew's face contorted, foam at the corners of his mouth as he stepped closer. "Do not fucking say it." Andrew's entire body shook with fury. "You do not get to claim her! You cannot feel anything for her. You are a fucking parasite, a vile abomination of shadow. You do not care for her; you *feed* on her trust. Every breath you stole was a breath *I* should have been there to give."

Andrew's hand shook over his pommel, murder in his eyes.

Cold settled in the pit of my stomach as realization hit.

Andrew is going to kill him.

I saw it. One more breath and Andrew's control would fail.

Vestro did not move, his eyes only for me. I saw my reflection in his obsidian eyes, and the struggle on my face. Defeat filled Vestro's features, and he lifted his chin, exposing his throat as if inviting Andrew's blade. His stillness mocked Andrew's fury more than words ever could.

"If you will not see it, Nadia," Andrew spat, eyes blazing, "then I will cut the truth out of him."

Steel rasped as he yanked his sword half free.

"No!" I lunged forward, slamming my palms into Andrew's chest.

At the same instant, Trea fell on him. The old captain hooked one forearm hard across Andrew's chest and clamped his other hand over Andrew's sword wrist. With veteran precision he wrenched backward and down, driving his weight into Andrew's spine, forcing the blade toward the ground.

The three of us collided in a crush of heat and rage. Andrew roared, thrashing between us, chest hammering into mine as Trea pinned his sword arm tight against his own ribs, levering the joint until the half-bared steel screeched against the scabbard and stuck.

Heat rolled off Andrew like a wildfire. His heart thundered under my hands, pounding wild as a war drum. "Get the fuck off me!"

"Think, boy," Trea growled in his ear. "Would you spill more blood here? Look at yourself."

But Andrew didn't hear him. His glare burned past me, locked on Vestro. Inch by inch, his sword slipped free, even under both of us, his arm strained higher, the steel shivering in the air.

And for the first time, Andrew's rage truly scared me.

"Andrew, look at me," my voice cracked, raw. I seized his face in my hands, driving his chin down to force him to see me, not Vestro. His burning eyes flicked down, like a storm held closely in check.

My voice cracked, desperate. "If you care for me at all, don't kill him. Please. Whatever he's done, whatever lies you think he—" My throat closed, but I forced the words out. "Spare him, and I am yours. I choose you. But do not take him from me."

The words ripped through the clearing.

Andrew's silence became a void, waiting to collapse. The sword trembled between us, his arm still straining against Trea's hold.

Behind me, Vestro broke. "Nadia!" his voice cracked. "Don't. Don't give yourself away for me. I..."

I glanced back as Vestro's words choked off to see Damien's dagger tipping Vestro's chin up.

Damien's mouth curved up in a lazy, sardonic smirk. "Careful, pet," he drawled. "Best not push your luck."

Vestro froze, his eyes burning into mine with everything he couldn't say.

"I promise," I whispered, tears streaking down my face. "I promise, Andrew. I am yours."

Something in Andrew cinched taut.

The silence that followed cut like glass. No one moved.

Then, with a guttural snarl, Andrew wrenched against Trea's grip one last time. For a breath, I thought he would finish the draw and split my world in two. Instead, he rammed the blade home with a metallic screech, the sound echoing off the cliffs.

His chest heaved and his eyes burned as he slowly and forcibly removed his trembling hand from his pommel. Trea held his hands up, giving him his space. Andrew ignored him and staggered past me, his eyes never even registering Damien as he approached Vestro.

And struck.

Andrew drove his fist bare-knuckled into Vestro's face, with all his weight and fury behind it. The crack of bone on bone snapped through the clearing. Vestro's head whipped sideways, blood streaking his mouth as he reeled back and caught himself against the ground with one arm.

I felt the impact in my own bones.

"If you so much as touch her," Andrew spat, voice ragged, "I will slit your fucking throat."

My stomach clenched. For a heartbeat, I wanted to reach for Vestro, but I froze. I believed him. No, gods help me, I *knew* he was telling the truth. Yet Andrew's words gnawed like a splinter, the doubt they planted sharp enough to sting.

Vestro straightened slowly, sorrow carved into his face. His eyes found mine and held until I had to look away.

"Enough," Trea barked, the old captain's voice brooking no argument. His hand clamped down on Andrew's arm and steered him away toward the horses. Surprisingly, Andrew let him.

For a moment it seemed finished. The clearing sagged under silence, the fight draining out of everyone by inches. Blood dripped. Smoke curled from charred corpses. The stench of sulfur and iron turned the air foul. No one dared speak.

I looked behind me. Damien's smile was gone, eyes narrowed as if weighing what he had just witnessed. Corbin stood rigid, unreadable, but his gaze lingered on Andrew's retreating back.

Vestro's hand lifted, trembling, reaching toward my leg as though to thank me for standing between him and death. The gesture was so natural, so much a part of us, that once I would have leaned into it without thought.

But the image of Vestro, not a loyal protector, but a demon

always beneath me, waiting patiently, in the shadow—between my legs—rose unbidden, sickening. And Vestro's skill on the battlefield still unsettled me, made me wonder what other secrets he held after all this time. My breath stuttered and I stepped away, shying from his touch. For the first time in my life, I wasn't sure if I wanted his hands on me.

The hurt in Vestro's eyes gutted me, but I let the silence stretch as I wrapped my arms around myself, trying to ward off the sudden cold seeping into my bones.

Then came the hoofbeats.

Slow. Heavy. Each strike of the metal shoe a war drum against the rocky ground. Not a charge. Not a show. A measured cadence that pulled every gaze. Andrew returned on his stallion, his tall shadow stretching long across the bloodied ground. He loomed above us from the saddle, elevated, his fury shoved behind a cold mask of command.

"He walks free only because you begged for it," Andrew said, his voice low and rumbling like heavy iron dragged over gravel. "But mark me, if he steps out of line, I will kill him." His gaze swept the circle of men, daring any to contradict him. "And hear me, all of you; he is never to be alone with her again. Not without an escort. Not without my sanction."

The words fell like stones into a still pond, the ripples widening through the clearing and echoing against my skull. Trea gave the smallest nod. Peter swallowed hard, his wide eyes darting between us as if hoping to find a crack in the tension. Damien met my gaze and cocked his head, his lips twitching with amusement, as if questioning my obedience.

Vestro stayed on his knees in silence, his jaw set, and shoulders squared. Blood welled from the split in his lip, dripping down his chin. He did not bother to wipe the blood. Instead, his eyes followed Andrew's hand as it rested on the pommel of his sword before looking at me.

I took a step forward. "Andrew—" I started, anger flaring.

Andrew's hand cut me off, palm raised. The sharp, kingly gesture burned deeper than any words.

He spurred the stallion closer. The horse's muscles quivered, steam curling from its nostrils.

"It is my place as your future king to protect you," he said firmly. "And I will do so until my dying breath. Even if it means protecting you from yourself." He leaned down and held out a hand. "Nadia."

Just my name, spoken like command, like inevitability.

I felt the weight of every gaze pressed on me. Damien's sharp, Trea's steady, Peter's wide-eyed, and the others guarded and tense.

My hand hovered at my side, trembling. My lips parted, breath shaping the start of it; defiance, refusal, the promise that I didn't need him to pull me up like some helpless damsel.

I can ride myself, I wanted to say.

But then my gaze landed on Vestro. His chest heaved, bare and battered, eyes fixed on me like a wound that would never close. And Andrew's words splintered and twisted through my chest. *Demon. Parasite.* I didn't believe it. At least... I didn't want to. But now, the thought of taking Vestro as a mount, having him between my legs as I had a thousand times before, curdled dark and wrong.

And I'd just made a bargain, I reminded myself.

I faltered as shame rose to my cheeks. My hand lifted, slow and traitorous, and slid into Andrew's grip. He hauled me up behind him with unyielding force, the saddle creaking, the heat of his back closing around me like a cage.

The stallion shifted beneath us as it adjusted to our weight. Andrew's hand settled heavy on my knee, possessive. The heat of his hand burned through the fabric of my trousers. Claiming. Final.

Across the clearing, Vestro's eyes flared. The raw desperation that had cracked him moments ago smoldered into something harder, darker. He said nothing, but the set of his jaw was voice enough to let me glimpse the anger burning below the surface.

I drew in a breath. "He's hurt, Andrew. Give him time to—"

Vestro's reply came low, steady, the corner of his mouth ghosting something like a smile though it did not reach his eyes. "It's fine, Nadia."

I felt Andrew's back flex against me, but he didn't look back. "Then he can catch up." His voice cut cold as steel. "I am sure your mount will have no problem keeping pace."

Vestro stood and swayed. Then, with a shudder he let my cloak drift to the ground, and his form buckled and broke, collapsing back into hooves and chocolate hide. The scream of bone and sinew twisting still rang in my ears as the stallion stood where he had been. He tossed his head, his milky white eyes bright with something more than pain.

Hate.

Damien strolled past Vestro's trembling form. He gave Vestro's muzzle a soft but sharp cuff as he bent to fetch my discarded cloak, blocking Vestro's line of sight and drawing his attention from Andrew. An attempt to break the tension.

"Try to keep up," he said, his thin smile cutting and humorless.

I looked around at our quiet party. Peter's horse was nowhere to be seen, so he mounted behind Trea. Corbin lashed my tack to the back of his horse.

Andrew's stallion reared and surged forward, and I wrapped my arms around Andrew's waist to keep balanced in the saddle. His body was heat and iron, and for a shameful, stolen moment I let myself sink against him. His strength was a fortress. His heartbeat was steady. Safe. Human.

Every jolt of the horse's stride echoed the crack of Andrew's gauntlet against Vestro's face, the press of steel I had held to Vestro's throat.

Andrew shifted, one hand closing over mine, giving me a gentle squeeze. The gesture was small and almost tender, but it burned like a brand. *I will protect you, even from him.*

Part of me wanted to believe him. To let that vow be enough.

I pressed my cheek to the back of Andrew's shoulder to hide the tears burning my eyes.

CHAPTER
TWENTY-FOUR

Blightwood loomed ahead like the jawbone of some ancient beast, its black iron spikes angled toward the reddening sky. The walls cut against the bruised horizon, sharp enough to draw blood from the low-hanging orange clouds. Lanterns sputtered along the gate, their yellow light only managing to stain the dusty road below. The rest of the city crouched in darkness, silent and watchful. Even the trees of the surrounding forest seemed to shy away from the walls, leaning their branches away from the imposing structures so that those along the tree line were bent and shriveled.

But after the hellish morning we'd had so far, I thought the brooding city and its potential to supply soft beds looked unfucking-believably beautiful.

Vestro, now dressed and in human form, walked close to my side as we entered, almost touching, with his hood pulled low. He looked like he wanted to fold into himself and vanish into the folds of his cloak. Every clang of the gate made his shoulders twitch; every echo of boot soles turned his eyes sharp before he forced them back down. I hated how Vestro seemed to shut down a little more with each step.

Damien's unreadable gaze slid to him more than once, but he said nothing and kept his distance.

I tugged on Vestro's shirtsleeve. "You're fine, Ves. They won't touch you."

He glanced at me, then immediately turned back to the quiet town streets. "I don't really want to stay in the city," he whispered. "I can wait outside, catch up with you in the morning."

I balked at him. "And what if things go sideways? We *never* separate."

He looked ready to argue, then swallowed it down and nodded. Though the dimple between his brow deepened as he pressed himself closer to my back.

Inside the inn, the clerk slid four brass keys across the counter, their handles polished to a dull shine by years of passing hands. Andrew scooped them up with practiced indifference, handed keys to Trea and Damien, then turned with the third pinched between forefinger and thumb.

"Your room," he said to me, his voice too sharp for such a simple sentence.

I moved to take the key, but he pulled it back before I could. I furrowed my brow, unsure of what he wanted.

"Thank you?" I said after a moment.

Andrew didn't move. His gaze flicked past me to Vestro. "He stays with the horses."

Heat shot through me, faster than thought. "He's not an animal."

A muscle jumped in Andrew's jaw. His hand rose halfway toward the place his circlet used to sit and jerked back. He looked at me, hard, then down at the two remaining keys in his palm, weighing them.

"There are two rooms," he said at last, voice clipped. "One for me. One for you." He dangled a key from his fingers, deliberate. "If you want him to have a room, then you share mine."

Vestro's head came up fast, hood slipping back just enough for me to see the flare of his brow. "Nadia—"

"Ves," I cut him off sharply. "I'm not sending you to the stable."

The silence thickened. I felt every eye on my back.

Andrew's mouth curved into something not quite a smile. He pressed the key into my palm, his touch lingering just long enough to reinforce his point.

Vestro's jaw worked as I turned and handed him the key, but no sound followed. He stared at me, the weight of his anger and hurt burning hotter for the words I'd stolen from him.

ANDREW WALKED me to our room, then, like a gentleman, left me so I could have privacy. I scrubbed the road from my skin in a quick basin bath, dressed, and quickly washed my other clothes and hung them on the edge of the tub to dry, and went down to the common room. The hall pressed in warm and loud, a hundred voices ricocheting off cherrywood panels and black-beamed rafters. The fire in the great stone hearth spat sparks that glowed and died before they hit the flagstones; the smell of roasted meat and spilled ale clung to the back of my throat.

I found Vestro waiting by the entrance, shoulders tight beneath his cloak, head bent as though the floorboards might be safer company than any eyes in the room. I felt him stiffen beside me as we crossed the room. His hood shadowed half his face, but he tilted it lower still, keeping his eyes down and hidden from view. When a man at a nearby table laughed too loud, Vestro flinched and drew his cloak tighter, as though the sound itself might strip away his cover. His hand twitched once at his side like he wanted to bolt.

I touched his sleeve and steered him toward the long table in the corner Andrew had claimed. I made certain to tuck Vestro on the inside, with me between him and the room. He settled, but uneasily, his shoulders locked, eyes darting everywhere but at the other patrons. I could almost feel his concentration as he kept his gaze black, not letting that pale ripple slip through.

He settled into his seat, but he never looked comfortable. His hands stayed very still in his lap, eyes everywhere and nowhere at once.

Across the table, Andrew's gaze cut sharp as a blade. He glared openly at Vestro as he drained his ale.

Trea finally broke the silence. "Gregory didn't deserve that."

Andrew looked away from Vestro and his jaw worked. "I did not think we would lose so many," he said quietly.

"He knew what he signed up for," Damien cut in, not unkindly.

Corbin gently plucked the empty mug from Andrew's hand and set a fresh one on the table. "Let's drink to staying alive."

Andrew hesitated, then took it. His hand shook faintly.

I swallowed hard and looked away. Looking for a distraction. I peered sideways at Vestro, who hadn't moved.

"Eat," I murmured, sliding a plate toward him. When he didn't move, I pulled a basket of bread closer and nudged a piece until it touched his fingers. He finally took it, the brush of his skin against mine careful.

I fussed without thinking; angling the bowl of stew closer, making sure he had a spoon, adjusting his cloak so it wouldn't drag through his food. His hood had slipped back far enough for me to see the hollows beneath his eyes. He gave me the ghost of a look; exhausted, but softer for the fussing.

Andrew's mug paused halfway to his lips; his jaw tightened as his eyes lingered not on Vestro, but on me; on every small adjustment, every time my hand touched the edge of Vestro's cloak or shoulder. He lowered the mug a shade too deliberately, the thud against the table louder than it needed to be. The edge of his mouth twitched, but it wasn't a smile. More like he was trying to keep something down. Then he took another drink. Longer this time.

"Princess," Trea said, lifting his own mug with a small grin, "the lad's been talking about you all day." He tilted his head at Peter, who flushed and ducked lower over his plate. "Tell me, how does a girl like you manage to tame a kelpie?"

"I didn't." I smirked. "We... came to mutual terms."

"Aye." Trea tipped his mug toward Vestro, a look in his eyes that said he understood more than he said. "Then you've my respect. Takes grit, riding with men who don't trust you."

Vestro went very still, then inclined his head.

Corbin leaned close to Andrew, muttering something I couldn't catch. Andrew's eyes flicked to Vestro, then to me. His jaw flexed. The mug in his hand tilted again, and he drained it near to empty. He reached across my side of the table and reclaimed the bread-basket I'd nudged toward Vestro as if it were his by right. He tore a piece free, the crust splitting with a sharp sound, and leaned back with calculated ease. His elbow bumped his goblet and almost sent it off the edge. He caught it too fast, and the grip left his knuckles white.

Vestro's hand stilled above his spoon. Slowly and deliberately, he looked up and met Andrew's gaze.

They held it.

Andrew settled back, lounging with casual authority. Vestro didn't move at all, his fury held tight beneath the surface. The space between them hummed, charged and brittle, the stare stretching longer than was comfortable.

Andrew's hand closed around his mug and slammed it down.

Hard.

The crack of wood on wood split the tavern like a whip. Ale sloshed over Andrew's knuckles, foam spattering the scarred table. A faint tremor buzzed through his fingers, but he didn't wipe the spill, didn't seem to feel it. His gaze never left Vestro. He didn't speak.

He didn't need to.

Nearby patrons glanced toward our table, curiosity flickering across their faces.

Vestro was the first to look away. He dropped his gaze and tipped his head beneath his cowl, hiding his eyes from the room. His chair scraped back with a violent rasp that cut through the tavern's laughter. He didn't look at me. Didn't look at anyone. He turned and strode for the door, his cloak snapping behind him. The door banged shut hard enough to rattle the windowpanes.

Andrew leaned back, one hand draped possessively near mine, the other curling around his mug. He moved to drink from the mug again but then seemed to think better of it. A flick of irritation crossed his brow.

I saw it then; the stiffness in his shoulders, the tremor at the corner of his mouth, and the way he blinked slow and heavy just once. Andrew's mask was starting to slip.

My stomach twisted. "Why'd you do that?"

Andrew took a long, slow swallow of ale, set the mug down properly this time, and lifted his gaze to me with kingly patience. "Do what?"

Infuriating ass.

"You know exactly what." My voice rose as I stood. "You've all been so cold to him, so damned cruel, and for what? Because you don't like the sight of him at my side?"

Peter's fork clinked against his plate. "He really did save us," he said softly.

"Aye," Trea agreed, eyes on the door.

"You do not see the danger in your little game because you choose not to," Andrew said, tone like a gavel. "Sit down."

Oh, now that *pisses me off.*

"You don't command me," I hissed. "And he's earned his place by my side."

"Funny thing about place." Andrew's gaze flicked to Vestro's empty chair, then back to me, narrowing. "Some do not know when they are in one that is not theirs."

I placed both hands on the table and leaned forward until I was just inches from Andrew's ear. "Or maybe it's those at the head of the table who think they get to decide that for everyone else."

A tremor touched his fingers but then vanished as he lifted the mug. "I thought you and I understood each other better than this. Or am I mistaken?"

It cut deeper than I wanted to admit. I dropped my voice for him alone. "You're not mistaken, Andrew. But don't force me into a corner. You might not like the outcome."

His eyes searched mine, too steady, too sure. Firelight flickered across them; then he looked away and drank as if nothing had passed.

I pushed my chair back, the scrape loud enough to turn heads. "Enjoy your drink, Your Highness."

The mug was halfway to his lips again. He didn't answer. Just drank.

I left before he could answer, every step burning with the words I didn't say. I kept my shoulders straight, my stride purposeful, as if I were bound for the stairwell and the hall of rented rooms. Let him think I was retreating to bed.

THE INN'S heavy door slammed behind me, shutting out the warmth and the clatter, and the night air rushed in sharp and cold. It bit my cheeks and cleared my head, leaving me shaking more from the inside than the chill. I pulled my cloak tighter and glanced around. The street was quiet, shadows long under the weak lanterns swaying from their hooks. My eyes searched the pale-yellow squares of light projected from the inn windows. I caught sight of a winking flash across the street, just outside of the light, and a pinpoint of red in the darkness. I frowned as I trudged in the direction of the tiny, round light.

Vestro came into focus as I neared, leaning against the hitching post in front of the stable, his long legs crossed at the ankles. He seemed lost in thought and didn't acknowledge me until my boots crunched close enough on the gravel to give me away. He jerked his head up, eyes pale and guarded, then frowned and looked away again, hiding his hand behind his back.

"You left fast," I said softly.

"Didn't feel like being the evening's entertainment." His voice sounded tired. "Easier to let your king win than let the whole room know what I am."

"He's not—" The words snagged in my throat. I didn't know what Andrew was to me at the moment, and I did not want to even open that can of worms right now. "I hate the way they look at you," I whispered.

"I'm used to it."

"Well, I'm not." My jaw set. "They'll just have to get over it."

That earned me a real look. Direct, unflinching, enough to set the air buzzing between us.

A familiar stench wafted in the air. I jerked my head around.

Then I saw it behind his back: a pinprick of red, glowing, fading, glowing again.

"Ves, are you—are you smoking?"

He flinched, then showed me the cigarette between two fingers. "Stole it from Andrew's stash yesterday." His shoulders hunched, guilty. "I just... needed to breathe."

"You could breathe by not letting him get to you."

"That would require him not trying." He took a long drag. He held the air in his lungs for a long heartbeat, then exhaled smoke, curling it into the cold night.

I frowned at him. "You know I hate that smell."

"Doesn't seem to stop you from being near the boy king."

I looked away toward the inn, then back to him. I really didn't want to get into this tonight.

Vestro took one last drag, then dropped and smashed the butt into the dirt with his boot heel. It made me feel a little better.

"You want to come back inside?" I said. "I can order another piece of pie."

Vestro's face softened. He blew a trio of smoke rings and looked away. The smoke rings meant he'd smoked before—more than just a few times to get that trick down.

Before this journey, I'd thought I knew Vestro inside and out. What else have I been wrong about?

"No," he said. "I need to cool off out here."

"What's up with you right now? Usually you're a little more..."

"Poised?"

"That works."

"Nothing, I just...I just don't trust some of the men. I don't..." He shook his head. "I'm tired. That's all."

"You've been using that excuse a lot lately."

"I know." He let out a shaky laugh and then gave me a sloppy grin. "Really, though. I am tired. The long days on the road have kicked my ass, and I'm a little on edge now that my cover's blown."

I frowned at him. He really did look worn, and it wasn't a look I was used to seeing on him.

I gave him a hug, leaning my head on his chest. "You sure you don't want to come in?"

"I'll come in later." He half-heartedly returned the hug with one arm and kissed the top of my head. "Go back before Andrew explodes."

I held the hug, focusing on his heartbeat, before pushing away and crossing the street back to the inn. I felt his eyes on my back.

I climbed the steps to the inn and found Corbin leaning against the doorframe. Watching. I jumped and took a step back.

"Sorry, Princess," Corbin said quickly, his hands up. "I did not mean to scare you."

"*Startle.*"

"Pardon me?"

"You startled me," I said. "But you don't scare me." I smiled at his serious face. "I'm just messing with you, Corbin. You've been around Andrew too long, relax a bit."

The squire let out a self-conscious chuckle. "Fair enough."

The torchlight caught the pale lines of his face, too young for the haunted way his eyes flicked past me toward the street. "You may want to wait before going back inside," he added, lowering his voice. "His Majesty is... displeased. About you rushing outside."

"After Vestro, you mean," I said.

Corbin hesitated, then nodded once.

I gave him a smile I didn't quite feel—it was the most I'd ever heard him speak at once. "Then I suppose we're both avoiding tempers." I glanced across the road, toward the darker outline of the stables, where a faint light glimmered through a slat. My chest tightened.

He must have gone inside the stable.

Corbin followed my gaze. "It seems you've got a good eye watching over you," he said carefully.

"You mean Vestro? He's been with me for years."

His lips pressed together. "Has he...said anything? About the mission?"

"Why?"

"Curiosity," he said too quickly. "It unnerves me—that we chase this key token without knowing much about it. Or the heir. Makes a man wonder if he's protecting the right one."

I stood silent. I didn't know what to say as I tried to process what had spurred our conversation in the first place. From what I'd seen so far, it wasn't like Corbin to assert himself like that.

Yet he had *shown a little streak of his temper when I'd questioned Andrew's honor.*

Still, this little exchange didn't fit into the profile I'd painted of the man. It seemed out of character, and it bothered me. Most squires were devoted to their masters and never questioned their duty regardless of the circumstances. And they *never* voiced their concerns with members of the courts.

Corbin's intense eyes searched my face. He'd pushed away from the doorframe to stand straight. Though he wasn't a big man, and physically not imposing in the least, I didn't like the sudden closeness—even if it was only a difference of a few inches.

I drew my cloak tighter. "If you've questions about duty, Corbin, you should take them to your king."

A shadow stretched across us, heavy in the doorway.

Andrew.

His presence cut like a blade, silent but commanding. His gaze moved once between me and Corbin, lingering on the squire too long. "Strange hour for small talk, Corbin. Do you not have duties to finish?"

Corbin bowed his head, but not before his eyes slid toward me once more, unreadable. Then he backed into the dark, boots crunching quickly down the street toward the stables.

The porch sagged with silence.

Andrew stepped closer, crowding my space, as he struck flint against steel and the end of a cigarette glowed red. He drew in a lungful, the smoke curling pale in the lantern light.

The sharp scent wrapped around my throat, familiar and unwelcome. I took a step back, ready to head inside. I was done indulging men and their vices. "Really? Drinking the tavern dry wasn't enough for tonight?"

Andrew's eyes flicked to mine, unreadable, then down to the cigarette. He dropped it and ground it under his boot, the gesture almost gentle. His fingers lingered a moment too long, then drifted upward almost touching the space where his crown should be. Then fell. "Satisfied?"

I arched my brow. "Almost."

"You think I would not notice you slipping outside to him?"

My pulse hitched. "I don't need your permission to breathe."

"You do not need to be alone with him either." He stepped closer, his movements smooth but too deliberate and the wine still hot on his breath. "He is not safe."

"He's saved me more times than you've ever known." My voice rose. "You don't get to cage me, Andrew."

His jaw locked, a tremor flicking through his jaw. "I am not caging you. I am protecting you. There is a difference."

"You don't own me."

For a heartbeat he faltered. His voice, when it came, was lower. Rougher. "You are mine to protect, Nadia. Whether you like it or not."

A silence fell, taut as a drawn bow. Andrew stood closer than was necessary, the heat of him cutting the chill. His breath wasn't steady. His fingers twitched again. He looked like he might say something else but couldn't find the words.

For a moment, I thought he'd say something more, but then voices cut through the night.

Low at first, muffled from the stable yard. Words sharp, too fast to catch.

Andrew stiffened beside me. "Stay here."

He strode down the steps, and I followed, my cloak snapping in the wind.

His arm shot back, his hand firm around mine. "Nadia, go back."

I should've listened. I Should have let Andrew stand between me and whatever waited. But then I heard Vestro's voice break through the dark.

I yanked free and ran.

TWENTY-FIVE

The night pressed colder the farther I stepped from the inn porch. I meant only to follow the faint sound of raised voices, but the trail drew me past the lantern light and toward the darker shape of the stables. The air was sharper there, thick with the musk of hay and horsehair. The stable lamps burned low, their oil almost gone. Shadows hunched long across the straw-littered floor.

I heard Vestro say my name, his voice rough with anger. My breath caught, and I quickly pushed inside. The horses stamped and tossed their heads at the commotion, their reins jangling against the rails. Corbin's voice carried sharp through the haze.

"—not part of the job!"

"Then do your fucking job," Vestro snarled, "and let me do mine."

I rounded the corner to see Vestro pinning Corbin against a post, his fist cocked, blood dripping from his knuckles. Corbin's nose was a mess, his lip split, breath ragged.

Andrew barreled in behind, his sword already drawn. The glint of his blade flashed against the yellow lantern light as he stepped instinctively in front of me. My pulse thundered. Only then did I realize I'd drawn my own sword too, my hand white-knuckled around the hilt.

"Vestro!" I barked.

Vestro's eyes snapped to mine. His fist tightened, his arm trembled with anger. "Get out of here, Nadia."

"Don't you dare." My blade lifted, the point glinting in the swaying light. "Flex your arms at me again."

He froze, fury knotting his features. "He deserved—"

"Enough!" My voice cracked through the stall.

Both men jerked their heads toward me.

Andrew strode closer to the men, filling the walkway with his shadow. His gaze swept once over the scene, then landed on his squire, flat and cold. "Explain."

The silence stretched, brittle. Corbin straightened, sleeve pressed against his bloody mouth. "A misunderstanding, my king," he said, too quickly. "Nothing more."

Vestro's eyes shifted once from Andrew's blade to my face.

Andrew moved, just slightly. His sword tilted, the point lowering toward Vestro's chest. It wasn't a strike, but the intent was there, inches from being realized. Vestro's weight shifted back a fraction, his belly low. His fingers splayed, palms open, instinctively placating.

"Andrew, don't." My hand shot out before I could think. I pressed my palm to his arm, halting the blade's slow drift forward.

Andrew's jaw tightened, his eyes flicking down to where my fingers curled against his sleeve, then up to meet mine. A question hovered there, unspoken.

Vestro's entire body flinched, and his eyes homed in on my hand on Andrew's arm. He masked it by straightening and setting his jaw, but his fists clenched harder.

"Please," I whispered.

The weight in Andrew's arm eased, though the tension in him did not. Slowly, as if reluctantly, he lowered the blade. The lantern swung once, casting all four of our shadows long across the stable wall.

Andrew stared coldly at Vestro. "Your take?"

Vestro's jaw flexed, the black of his eyes faded to milky white for just a heartbeat. "A misunderstanding," he echoed, his voice rough.

My stomach twisted. "That," I said tightly as I pointed to Corbin's face, "was no misunderstanding."

Andrew's gaze lingered on them both before he flicked a hand toward Corbin. "Outside. Now."

Corbin bowed stiffly and turned on his heel to leave. But as he passed, he shot Vestro a nasty look and muttered, "Keep your leash tight, demon."

Andrew's arm shot out, cuffing Corbin hard across the ear. He shoved him toward the doorway faster.

Vestro shook, his rage barely bridled. He lunged half a step in Corbin's direction as he passed. I planted my palm against his chest and shoved him back. Vestro stumbled back in surprise, and tripped over his own feet, landing hard on his butt. He struggled to right himself as I stood over him and put my sword to his neck.

Vestro's breath came hot and ragged, fury pouring off him in waves as glared up at me. But it wasn't fury alone. There was something else beneath it, something dark and uncertain I couldn't name.

Something that scared me.

"Do not touch Corbin again," I said between clenched teeth. "He already gets enough shit from Andrew without you adding to it."

Vestro's jaw flexed as he met my stare. "Tell him to stick to his job," he growled, low and even. "If he keeps stepping out of line again, I'm going to answer."

The meaning landed cold and precise. For a heartbeat, the room folded back to earlier that day in the mountains, the way he'd torn through those demons like playthings, the sudden slither of something feral under his skin.

For the second time today, I didn't recognize him.

Vestro's eyes narrowed as he tried to rise. "You—"

I pushed my blade forward so the point kissed his skin. He didn't stop, testing me, and I let the tip break through. A fat bead of blood welled and slid onto the steel.

Vestro looked at me as if I'd grown a second head.

"You really would," Andrew murmured from the doorway. Not disbelief, but cold measure.

I set my mouth in a tight line. "I don't bluff, Andrew."

The stable went silent, broken only by the restless shift of hooves.

Vestro swallowed. "Are you that angry with me?"

"Angry is not the word." I shook my head. "I don't know what your problem is lately. Yes, your secret's out. But you've been acting like the whole world is against you."

Vestro barked a humorless laugh. His eyes blanched to a milky white, squinting under a deeply furrowed brow. "If you haven't noticed, it is. We're traveling with a demon hunter and a king who hates my kind. And you expect me to be... gracious?"

"Andrew's father was just murdered. So, what the hell do you expect him to feel toward demons? Of course he's going to hate them."

"It's not murder if it's the cost of a war," Vestro spat out.

My heart stopped. I held my breath as I focused on the drumming in my ears. The earlier fight was forgotten. Inconsequential. Corbin and Andrew meant nothing, their faces blurred at the edges of thought. I blinked and stared at Vestro's suddenly very-black eyes.

For a long beat nothing moved. The low scrape of straw under hoof and the faint tick of a loose rein reduced to the smell of sweat and hay and the iron tang of blood. The stable narrowed to the thin line of my blade and the frightened pulse at Vestro's throat.

Andrew's boot cracked against the gravel, deliberate and slow. He moved like a man pacing himself; every step exact, as if he knew one wrong move would tip too far. He stopped a pace behind me, the shadow of him folding over my shoulder until his presence was weight against my back.

The scrape of flint broke the silence before the soft hiss of fire. The tip of his cigarette caught, and it flared bright orange in the dark. Smoke curled from his mouth, ghost-pale against the shadows.

He didn't speak. He didn't need to. The anticipating tremor in his hand and the steady drag and long exhale of smoke in Vestro's direction said enough.

Something hot and cold at once slid under my ribs. My fingers clenched so hard around the hilt of my sword that the wood bit into my palm. My knees trembled, and the world pitched sideways for a breath. The air thinned to a pinprick. I could feel the heat of Andrew behind me, the press of his dark authority, and it made my throat constrict.

"What did you say?" I whispered.

Vestro's face flushed and his lips turned white around the edges.

I brought my sword up again, this time pushing hard enough against his neck to force him onto his back. I stepped closer so that I stood over him. My chin trembled as I stared at my best friend, and I suddenly realized I didn't know him at all.

"What did you say?" My voice came out thin, dragged just along the edge of panic.

"I-I didn't—"

"Choose your next words carefully." I pushed the blade a fraction deeper.

Andrew's shadow leaned in, close enough that the smoke curl from his cigarette brushed the back of my neck. His boot shifted forward a fraction, a small, measured sound that promised what he would do if I failed to keep order.

Vestro stared past me, to anywhere but my eyes. "Some of us are tired of hiding. Tired of watching our kind hunted. There are... factions declaring that they will no longer hide away and wait for their enemies to come after them."

His words slid like oil across the straw, thin and slippery, refusing to take shape and make sense.

My breath snagged. "Factions," I repeated, my throat raw. "And those enemies being the rulers of the five kingdoms?"

"Among others," he said.

"And what is the ultimate goal of these demons?"

Vestro hesitated.

Andrew moved without sound. His hand closed over mine; steady, but firm enough to press my knuckles into the hilt. Too tight. He held it there just a second too long before dragging in a slow breath through his nose. His restraint had teeth. He took a long drag on the cigarette, the ember burning red against the shadows, and leaned into my shoulder, the weight of his chest pushing my arms down a little harder so my sword bit into Vestro's neck a little deeper, and two lines of blood slipped out on either side of the blade.

Andrew breathed out forcefully through his nose, and smoke curled out around his face slowly and deliberately. "Go on."

Vestro's neck bounced. "They want to level the playing field by going after the Cipher and are willing to do anything to keep it from reaching the pass."

"You mean like setting the fires," I said, "and the assassination attacks." I took a deep breath and wiped at my eyes when Vestro nodded. "Is that what came to Damewood?" My voice cracked on the name. "Is that what stole my home from me?"

Vestro's face tightened. He hesitated, lips parting, closing, then pressing white. He tried to sit up, but he stopped when I pushed my sword harder against the bottom of his jaw. He made a choking sound and went still, the blood leaking from the wound on his neck. Only his eyes moved as he stared up at me.

"Nadia, I was not part of that, I swear."

"But you knew!" My vision blurred and I fought not to blink. "You knew, and you didn't say anything. You could have prevented..." My words trailed, swallowed by the dark and the restless shifting of the horses.

"No. There was nothing I could do to stop it. All I could do was guarantee your safety by getting you out of there."

"You could have told me. Or Old Red, or Maurdruik."

Vestro's eyes swirled milky white before shutting back down to black, and the dimple between his brows formed before he forced it away.

But I saw it.

Damn, I saw it.

"Old Red addressed you directly when we left Damewood," I said slowly, trying to keep my emotions in check. "Do they both know about you?"

The silence that followed was worse than a confession. The blade quivered in my grip, my arm trembling with the weight of all I wanted to demand but feared I already knew.

My heart nearly stopped. "Did you *all* keep it from me?"

Vestro shook his head. "Not the captain."

Maurdruik.

"How long has Maurdruik known?" Rage built behind my eyes.

Vestro's face twisted like he was going to be sick. "Maurdruik tasked me with guarding you. He also tasked me with guarding Cipher... if it ever surfaced. I was meant to keep it out of the Holy's hands. Even if it meant running with you and never looking back."

Something inside me tore apart. My chest constricted until I couldn't breathe. I could still picture the first time I'd laid eyes on Vestro. The flash of his black mane as he galloped from the river, the cold bite of fear before I reached out to touch him and thought he'd chosen me. That first look and our bond, every memory I'd held sacred, all of it had just been a stage.

A fucking lie.

Vestro coming into my life wasn't fate. He'd been assigned.

I lowered my arm.

Vestro's head drooped, and then he rolled to all fours, slow and deliberate. Straw clung to his trousers and Corbin's blood smeared across his knuckles. He kept low, his shoulders hunched, and head bowed, as he crawled slowly toward me, his movements cautious and trembling.

The tip of Andrew's cigarette flared beside me, and Vestro flinched from the light, shying like a startled horse. He crept forward anyway, inch by inch, his breath uneven, palms slipping in the straw until he was close enough that the scent of flowers and horse fur filled the space between us.

When his fingers reached my ankle, they shook. Warm. Familiar. A touch that once meant safety.

Now, it made my stomach twist.

"So, that day in the river," I said slowly. "Was that all a setup?"

"Nadia, please understand..." his words rasped out. He shook his head. "Just at the beginning. But then, it changed. I... changed."

Rage ripped through my grief. I screamed and swung my arm. The hilt of my sword cracked across his cheek with a sickening crunch. Vestro fell back, eyes wide as the flesh above his cheekbone split and blood spilled down his face.

"Don't touch me!" My voice tore from me, ragged and broken. "You don't fucking get to touch me! Not after this!"

Vestro staggered back into the straw, breath heaving, one hand braced against the ground as if the whole stable tilted around him. His pale eyes burned with something between agony and shame.

Andrew shifted forward then, silent and absolute. He didn't acknowledge Vestro, he didn't need to. He pressed a hand to the small of my back and guided me forward toward the door, his palm broad and still. I felt the tension in his arm as we walked, the pulse of his restraint in every measured step. Steadying me or staking his claim, I couldn't tell.

Frankly, I didn't fucking care.

Behind us, Vestro's voice cracked the air. "Nadia!"

I half-turned, eyes burning. The sob caught in my chest came out as fury. "Not now!" I screamed.

Vestro's hand fell useless to his side. He stood there in the lamp-light, blood drying on his jaw, the echo of my slap still raw on his cheek. The sound that followed wasn't language, just a low sob that cut off as Andrew steered me out into the night.

CHAPTER
TWENTY-SIX

Andrew's hand stayed at the small of my back as he guided me, quiet and firm. The night air hit sharp and cold as Andrew guided me out of the stable. I hadn't realized I'd been holding my breath until it escaped in a ragged hitch. My chest tightened and vision blurred at the edges. It took everything in me to keep them from spilling.

He stopped with me just beyond the threshold. His hand shifted from my back to my arm, firm and grounding, then lifted to catch my chin. His touch was careful, steadying me, forcing my eyes up to his.

His gaze held steady, but there was a flicker beneath the calm, a faint tightening at the corner of his mouth and a hard gleam in his eyes. Not exactly triumph. Something colder. Something certain.

My breath hitched again. Andrew's hand lingered, holding me steady until I stilled. Then he let go, slow, deliberate, leaving the choice in my hands.

I glanced back once. Vestro still stood inside the stable, his shoulders sagging against the post. His pale eyes met mine, hollowed, before Andrew's hand found its way again to my back and gently pressed me forward.

The lantern's glow pooled over the street as we crossed. Inside, the inn's warmth wrapped around me, thick with ale and heavy smoke. The floor creaked beneath our boots, each thud too loud in my ears. Conversation faltered as we neared. Damien's eyes followed us like a drawn bowstring. Trea's jaw tightened, unasked questions pressed behind his teeth. Peter bent low over his plate, but his quick glance betrayed worry. Even the squires froze when they saw us.

Andrew didn't slow. He walked straight through the press of stares, his hand still at my back. At the corner table, a half-full bottle of wine sat between the men. Andrew reached for it without a word, fingers closing around the glass neck, and plucked it off the table as we kept moving.

The stairwell groaned under our weight. My hand slid along the polished rail, but my fingers shook too hard to keep steady. Every creak of wood, every rustle of Andrew's cloak, the slosh of the wine against the bottle rang sharp in my ears. My pulse beat loud enough I swore the hall could hear it.

At the end of the corridor, Andrew slid the key into the lock of a door on our right. The metal turned slow, precise, the tumblers clicking in the hush. He nudged the door open with his shoulder, the hinges sighing against the frame under his weight.

He led me into the dark room and shut the door behind us. He pulled a matchbook from inside his tunic pocket and lit the taper candle waiting on the nightstand. The wick guttered and threw soft gold up the walls.

Andrew closed the door behind us with a soft click and slid the lock shut. He walked to the bed and dropped the key on the nightstand. He lifted the wine bottle in his hand. His jaw tightened as he uncorked it and raised the bottle directly to his mouth. The swallow was long, deliberate, and aggressive. His throat worked as the bottle tipped, wine sloshing against glass. When he lowered the bottle again, it was no longer half-full. Not even close.

The silence after was deafening, only broken by the faint drip of wax from the candle and the creak of floorboards as Andrew shifted his weight. His knuckles stayed white around the bottle's neck before he set it down hard on the nightstand.

He took a deep breath and then turned to me. "Nadia..."

I pushed past him, and I barely made it into the washroom before the tears came. They fell hot, bitter, burning my skin. I pressed my palms to my eyes, but it did nothing to stop the flood of tears and emotion that poured out as I sat in the empty tub and wrapped my arms around my knees. Betrayal and grief tangled sharply in my chest until I thought I might choke on them. The sobs broke out of me, sharp and ugly, echoing off the stone walls. I pressed my hands to my face and cried until my body gave in to my grief.

WHEN I FINALLY RETURNED TO the bedchamber, I found Andrew sitting on the edge of the mattress, his sword across his knees. The near empty bottle of wine dangled from one hand. His posture was rigid, but his eyes were bloodshot and glassy as he stared through the wall like he was seeing ghosts.

"I can take my own room," I said softly. "I don't need—"

"A proper guardian would not leave you unprotected," he said, without looking at me. "Especially not tonight."

A part of me wanted to bite at the word *guardian*. To say it wasn't a title he could drape over himself like a cloak simply because he thought he looked good in it. Another part wanted to sink into the bed and sleep for a week and let the world crash down around me and just fucking burn.

Instead, I unpinned my cloak and draped it over the chair. I spotted a smear of dried blood near the fastening that had darkened to brown.

Vestro's blood.

"I'm fine," I said, softer. It came out defensive anyway.

Andrew let his eyes run down me, evaluating.

Heat shivered through me in a line. "Don't look at me like that," I whispered.

"Like what?" His voice was low, the room small enough to hold it close.

"As if I'm broken."

He looked away. "You can take the bed."

"I can sleep on the chair," I said.

He shook his head and didn't bother to dignify my stubbornness with an answer. He stood and picked up my cloak off the chair, shook it out and hung it on a wall hook. Then he yanked off a blanket from the foot of the bed and tossed it over the chair.

I reached for him. "You don't have to..."

"Nadia." He didn't raise his voice. He didn't need to. "You will take the bed."

The way he said my name slid something small and sharp into me. I didn't argue, and I climbed up and sat on the edge of the mattress because arguing would turn this into a contest I didn't want to win.

He nodded once, half-satisfied, and dragged the chair a handspan farther from the bed like he was drawing a line neither of us needed chalk to see. He kicked off his boots and unbuckled his belt to lean his sword in arm's reach against the wall. He draped his cloak over his shoulders and dropped into the chair and stretched his long legs out, crossing them at the ankles.

He looked inconveniently good that way; uncomfortable on purpose, his chivalry worn on his sleeve like steel pauldrons instead of charity. Though I noted the way his knuckles trembled faintly as he lifted the bottle again to his lips.

I pulled off my boots, tossed them under the window, and slid beneath the blanket and let the cool of the sheets steal heat from my skin. The bed smelled like linen and cheap soap, but it helped cover the tang of wine wafting from Andrew's direction. I turned my face to the pillow and breathed through the ache in my chest until it dulled enough to ignore.

Andrew let the silence hold. Maybe he was being kind. Maybe he didn't trust what would come out if he broke it. The candle guttered, recovered, then steadied into a small, steady flame. Below us, a laugh rose and fell through the floorboards. Somewhere down the hall a tankard thumped a table, and the inn sighed the way buildings do when they settle after a long day of holding people up.

I rolled onto my back and stared at the low ceiling. The knot in the timber above the bed looked like a dark, open eye. A black demon eye. Silently judging me. I couldn't stop listening past the door for footfalls, to the floor's low groan, and to the spaces between sounds. Every absence became a shape my mind pressed into Vestro: out there in the dark, in the stables where the hay kept a different kind of warmth, where the night pressed closer. The memory of his face in the lantern light, tight and unreadable, wouldn't loosen its grip.

The silence stretched until I heard the tick of the candle's last drips. Shadows climbed the walls. Outside, the wind found the seam in the shutter, and the thin whine that leaked through made the room feel emptier than it was.

I pushed the blanket down, pulled it up again. My shoulder ached; a bruise along my ribs throbbed in time with my pulse. I shifted onto my side and curled my knees to my chest.

The chair creaked as Andrew shifted. "Go to sleep, Nadia."

I shut my eyes because he asked, not because I wanted to. The chair complained again as he tried another position. After a while, his breathing evened into a slow tide.

I turned my face into the pillow and whispered, "Idiot," but I wasn't sure if it was meant for him or me.

Probably both of us.

Likely all of us.

I STIRRED awake to the faint clink of glass against teeth.

The room smelled like damp wool and sour wine, sharper now

than before. I lay on my side, staring at the seam where the wall met the ceiling, counting the cracks because it was easier than counting the ways my life had split open.

I instinctively felt across the mattress, reaching for Vestro's arm so I could wrap myself in his warmth and chase away the shiver nipping at my ribs. Needing that layer of comfort to remind me I wasn't alone and that everything would be fine.

My hand met cold sheets.

I lifted my head and looked around.

That's right. I was alone in the bed.

The shutters let in only a thin smear of moonlight, but it was enough to catch Andrew's silhouette hunched in the chair by the door, the empty wine bottle balanced between his knees.

I pushed up on one elbow, watching the way his hand shook when he lifted the bottle and set it back down. He muttered something under his breath, ragged and slurred.

"Andrew," I whispered.

His head snapped up. Too quickly and too sharp. "Go… go back to sleep," he rasped. "I will keep watch."

"You'll ruin yourself sitting like that all night." I pushed the blanket aside and sat up. "The bed is big enough for both of us."

His jaw worked. He rubbed at his temple, then at the place where his crown should have sat. "No, it would…it's not right."

He leaned back, head tipped against the chair, the gold of his hair catching the glow of the candle. For the first time, I saw how thin his mask had stretched; his eyes bloodshot, jaw unshaven, the normally proud lines blurred by exhaustion, wine, and heartache.

I gauged the small amount of wine left in the bottle. Tried to recount the number of glasses he'd had at the table before the shit had hit the ceiling.

"It isn't right to let you sleep like that," I pressed, rising to my feet. "Come to bed. Please."

For a long moment he only stared at me. His fingers tightened around the wine bottle neck. His voice cracked when it came, low and rough, the words slurred by the wine still thick on his tongue.

"He was always so close to you," he whispered. "Tell me true, Nadia. Did he... have you?"

The breath locked in my chest. That wasn't what I was expecting. *Shit. What am I supposed to say?* My mouth felt thick and dry. *No... Actually, I had him.*

Though I doubt that will go over any better.

My silence answered for me.

Andrew's entire body stilled. His jaw clenched until the muscle jumped, then his mouth twisted as though the taste of the words sickened him.

He lurched to his feet, the chair legs screeching across the floorboards, and the bottle fell from his fingers with a clatter and rolled across the floorboards. His hand braced the wall, unsteady. His fists curled, opened, then curled again, his body trembling.

I watched as his anger hit first, hot and immediate, sparking in his eyes. Then disgust followed, his lip curling as though he couldn't bear to imagine Vestro's hands on me. And finally, shame. His shoulders sagged under the weight of it, his head dropping as if he were the weaker man for even asking.

"Andrew," I crossed the floor to him and caught his wrist.

His skin burned under my palm, trembling with the violence he hadn't unleashed. He pulled away and squeezed his eyes shut. His breath was sharp and unsteady. "I should have known." His voice broke. "Should've kept you from him. But my arrogance pushed you away..."

"Andrew, look at me." I forced his fist open with both my hands, holding his fingers between mine. "You did nothing wrong."

He nodded. "I should've killed him." He rubbed the heel of his palm over his eye, like he could scrub his thoughts away. He pulled away. "Fuck. I shouldn't... shouldn't be near you. Not like this."

"Come here." I held my hand out.

He blinked hard and stared at my fingers like they would bite. "I smell like a tavern."

"I don't care," my voice came steadier than I felt. "Please."

He raised his eyes slowly. The fury had gone hollow, leaving only something raw and vulnerable. "Nadia."

The way he said my name made something in me pull tight. Something had broken in him, and the crack in his normally polished attitude threw me off balance and further tilted my world sideways. I hated seeing him like this, defeated and blaming himself for something I had chosen to do willingly.

I took Andrew's hand and gently tugged him toward the bed. He let me lead him, his steps heavy and stumbling. At the edge of the bed, he hesitated as I slipped back under the sheets. But then the mattress dipped beneath his weight, and though the space between us was deliberate, his presence was undeniable. His body heat seeped across the sheets, brushing the edge of my skin. It was ridiculous how much steadier his closeness made me feel; just the confirmation of another human pulse within reach, someone who could share the silence and prove I wasn't alone.

"See?" I whispered into the dark. "Not so difficult."

I closed my eyes and forced myself to take deep, slow breaths. The bed now smelled faintly of smoke and mint, and underneath it the sharp edge of Andrew and sage replacing the wild flower-and-fur scent I'd grown used to. For years, Vestro's warmth had been a constant presence, curled around me like a shield. He'd been the hearth I hadn't realized I grew to depend on. And now... now that comfort felt farther away with every step he took into the shadow, and without his presence, I felt small and alone.

I wanted to reach across the bed and take some of Andrew's warmth for myself. My fingers twitched against the blanket, stopping halfway. The space between us felt dangerous; like thin air hovering over a drop I couldn't see the bottom of.

I'd never shared a bed with a man. Not really. Not like this.

Vestro had been all shadow and silence, comfort without weight;

a warmth that never asked for anything in return. Andrew was different. The heat coming off him had gravity, pulling me under like a raging river's current, promising things I wasn't sure I was ready to want.

My breath caught, and heat rose in my cheeks. Even without touching him, I could feel the shape of his body in the dark, every inch of distance stretched tight as a bowstring.

I curled my hand beneath my chin and tried to hold still. My pulse wouldn't listen. It thundered in my throat, tripping over itself, pushing me closer to a choice I didn't want to name.

"Do you mean it?" Andrew asked quietly. "What you said today. That you choose..."

If Andrew had asked hours before, while I rode behind him on his stallion and I kept looking over my shoulder for Vestro, or when he'd acted like a complete ass at dinner, I would have said no. That I'd only agreed to marry him to save my best friend's life.

But the truth was... I wasn't sure anymore.

I'd found myself drifting from Vestro even before he'd jumped for me. Ever since I'd jumped for Andrew something had changed inside of me, too. Maybe it wasn't about jumping anymore; maybe it was about loosening my grip on the reins I'd tied around Vestro for so long. Reins I'd used to keep us steady, to keep *myself* steady.

But tonight, watching Vestro peel back dark layers I hadn't even known were there, I felt those reins slipping through my fingers. And somewhere between the letting go and the fall, I realized my choice had already been made.

My lips parted before I could think. "I think so."

Andrew turned toward me, searching my face. The air between us seemed to move. I could almost taste the heat of his skin. I heard the tremor that wasn't in his voice but in the space between us.

My chest hurt. Every part of me fucking hurt. My chin trembled, and I felt myself shrinking inward, wanting to curl into a ball and sob and forget that my false sense of security had shattered with Vestro's unveiled truth. I wanted something solid to hold onto, something that could drown out the ghosts in my head.

Not some*thing*. Some*one*.

It should have been Andrew comforting me. I should have let him take the role of knight in shining armor and rescue me from my thoughts; a role I knew he would gladly take up. But the truth was I needed to steady him first, or I'd fall apart watching him crumble.

My heart pounded in my chest. I knew what would happen if I reached for him; what it would mean if I let that line I'd drawn blur. Because there was no going back from this. Not after this night.

So, I did.

My fingers brushed his sleeve, then his skin. The current caught me before I could pull back, and I shifted closer to press against him and slipped my hands to the sides of his face. Then I kissed him because I couldn't stand the fracture in his voice, and because the tide of him had already dragged me too far from shore to pretend otherwise.

For a heartbeat, Andrew froze. The air between us trembled with heat. Then his hand caught the back of my neck, and the dam burst. His lips met mine with a desperation that stole thought, tasting wine-slick and rough, and every ounce of grief, rage, and want poured into the motion. The stubble on his chin scraped my skin, grounding the kiss in something wild and real.

He rolled to his elbows above me. I felt the firm wall of his chest through his tunic, and the muscles in his arms bunched as he circled his arms around my back. His strength startled me; the sheer physicality of him. Of a real, actual man. He shifted position, and my thigh rubbed against his front, I felt him harden against me through the fabric.

A jolt shot through me before I could hide it. My breath caught; my body went rigid against him.

Oh shit, this is real.

Andrew felt it. His eyes flicked to mine, dark and questioning, a flash of the same restraint I'd seen by the river when he'd realized how easily he could hurt me.

His hand stilled. "Nadia?"

But I shook my head, the sound caught somewhere between a gasp and a plea. I rubbed my leg across his front again. "Don't stop."

His breath stuttered. He braced a hand to either side of me and hovered there, as if the wrong angle might shatter the moment.

"I am not gentle tonight," he warned. His arms trembled. "I-I don't know if I can be."

I arched beneath him, refusing to flinch. "Then don't be."

He stepped off the bed. His hands shook, clumsy as he tried to pull at the laces of his tunic, the fabric twisting in his fingers. I caught his hands, steadying him, and drew the cloth over his head myself. He let me lean forward and undo the laces at his waist, his breath breaking against my cheek, and his heart drumming beneath my palms as he stepped out of his pants.

The flicker of the candle flame painted him in bronze and shadow, every muscle taut, every scar catching light like a story carved into him. His chest rose, broad and steady, the tight lines of his stomach flexing as he crawled onto the bed. My throat tightened.

Gods, he is fucking gorgeous.

The sight of him made heat pool between my legs, and I felt a low ache begin to build and slick.

Andrew trembled as I kicked off my pants and I slipped my tunic up and off, baring my breasts to the air.

I pressed his trembling hands flat to my waist, pulling him closer until the blanket tangled around our legs. I kissed him again, slower this time, giving him something steady to follow. He took his time, his palms savoring their sweep over my ribs as if committing every inch of my body to memory. Goosebumps rose in the wake of his palms as they slid over my breasts, the brush of his calluses textured enough to make my nipples harden in response but soft enough to leave me aching for more.

"Andrew..."

I tried to breathe, but his lips stole the word, his tongue sweeping past mine, his will swallowing mine whole. His grip shifted, fingers threading into my hair, tilting my head exactly where he wanted it, deepening the kiss until there was nothing but him and his strength and certainty. But then he pulled back just enough to let his breath caress my cheek.

"Look at me," he rasped. "Tell me you want this."

My pulse hammered against my skin. The words lodged in my throat, but I forced them free, hoarse and desperate. "I do. I want this."

His jaw flexed. He pressed harder. "No. Me. Tell me you want *me*."

"I want you," I breathed.

The sound had just left my lips before his mouth seized mine. His kiss was a wave crashing onto the beach, rough and consuming. Every shift of his tongue, every nip of his teeth was deliberate, practiced. His hand slid down my spine, urging me closer, angling me until I fit against him exactly the way he wanted.

I caught his wrist before he could rise. "Wait." My voice shook, unsure of itself.

His eyes flicked up, glassy and raw. "What?" he rasped.

"Lie back," I said.

He blinked once and then moved to obey. He fumbled for balance, one elbow sliding off the mattress before I caught his wrist to steady him.

We both froze. His eyes met mine, glassy but sharp enough to register embarrassment. A small, broken laugh slipped out of him. Then he sank back into the mattress with a low exhale and a smooth grin.

I hesitated. My body moved before thought could catch up, acting on an old reflex that was half muscle memory and half self-defense. The last time I'd been touched like this, I'd been the one on top. Vestro had let me move the way I needed, slow and certain, and it had felt like safety. Maybe if I did the same now, I could keep that feeling and pretend for a moment that this wasn't breaking me open.

The thought of Vestro alone hurt.

But tonight, I didn't want to hurt.

I wanted to feel.

So, I climbed over Andrew, one knee braced on either side of his waist. The heat of his bare skin pressed between my thighs like a question I didn't know how to answer. I hovered there, my center slick against his skin. I trembled, feeling him hard and ready pressed against my lower back, and realizing how reckless a move this could be. His hands rested lightly on my hips, but there was nothing light in the way he looked at me.

"Nadia," he murmured, his voice rough. "You don... you don't have to..."

"I know." I swallowed. "I want to."

I rotated my hips, feeling the shiver that ran through him when my wetness brushed his stomach. He drew a sharp breath, head tipping back against the pillow. His hands trembled once before settling again. The feel of him was amazing, but as I looked down at him I suddenly lost my bearings and hesitated, unsure what to do next. Andrew smiled softly and saved me.

"Come closer," Andrew managed after a moment, the words caught halfway between plea and instruction. "Let me... just closer."

Heat rolled through me. I moved, clumsy, uncertain of what he wanted as his hands pulled my hips higher, until I was straddling his chest and my knees framed his face. "Here?"

He grinned. "Not quite."

I yipped in surprise as his hands cupped my ass and jerked me forward. I caught myself against the headboard and stared down at him in a mix of excitement and horror as I watched him scoot further down on the bed, so my thighs framed his face. His breath hit the inside of my thighs, warm and unsteady.

"That's it," he whispered, slurring slightly. His fingers flexed against my hips before he pulled my hips closer. "Right there."

The first touch of his mouth was hesitant, tasting more than taking. His concentration showed in every pause, every careful adjustment; his drunk focus turned devotional. When I spread my knees wider and rocked forward so I sat deeper, the sound that broke from him was half-groan, half-curse.

His mouth found me like he was starving, every flick and press of his tongue a vow. He worshiped me with unsteady reverence, his mouth working and sucking at my center like it was the only thing keeping him tied to this moment.

I moaned and threw my head back as he slid his hot tongue inside, and then focused his attention on the tiny, sensitive mound at the top. His mouth worked against me, chin dragging in a maddening rhythm, and the texture of his soft beard heightened the sensation as a warm, coiled tension built. My muscles tensed, and an uncontrollable quiver took over my right leg. My head grew light, and warmth spread in my belly as tiny waves of pleasure lapped under my skin.

At one point, Andrew's rhythm faltered; the next breath hitched into a quiet but self-directed curse.

"Fuck," he muttered, jaw tightening as he fought to steady himself.

I brushed his hair back from his forehead. The small moment of human clumsiness of him undid me more than any precision could.

Gods help me—I am in so much trouble.

Andrew paused. "Don't...don't move," he whispered, as if he needed a second to breathe. Then he found me again, and the drag of his tongue turned rougher, slower, more deliberate.

"An...Andrew..." Waves of pleasure pounded behind my eyelids, washing through my chest in ragged bursts.

When my legs began to shake, he broke away long enough to catch his breath, voice hoarse and uneven. "Stay with me. I got you." He gripped my thighs tighter, slightly shifted the angle of his mouth, and dug in deeper.

The tiny waves built in intensity and frequency. My breath hitched, and my hands shook as I grabbed fistfuls of his hair. My body spasmed against him, and he growled in pleasure against my skin.

The world narrowed to that heat between my legs, the hitch of his breath, the steadying hands that kept me from slipping as the wave broke. I gasped and trembled above him until strength left my thighs.

I slid off his face and straddled his waist, my legs trembling. Andrew let out a pleased moan and sat up long enough to wrap one forearm around my waist and roll me to the side. The world tipped and caught, and I landed on my back with a startled breath.

Andrew followed, a heartbeat slower than sober. He swayed for a moment, planting his hand on the mattress beside my head to steady himself, and then his weight pressed against my chest. His eyes searched my face. The sloppy edge of a smile across his lips tugged at his wet mouth before resolve erased it.

He wiped his face clean on the sheet and then kissed me, and I tasted myself and the faint bite of wine on his lips. He tried to swing a knee across the mattress and misjudged the edge; the bed frame thudded. A rueful breath, almost a laugh, then he steadied himself with a palm by my ribs.

Then something shifted. A sound tore from him, low in his throat, and his body surged against mine, not polished or practiced, but primal. His hands, clumsy a moment ago, closed around me with startling force, hauling me under him. The kiss turned urgent, consuming, as though some dam inside him had finally broken.

Then, with a guttural sound, he moved. In one motion, his arm banded around my waist, and the next heartbeat, I was on my stomach. I yipped in surprise at the strength in his arms. The mattress dipped under his weight as he crawled over me. His chest pressed to my back, and my cheek sank into the sheets as his mouth found the nape of my neck. His lips trailed kisses down my neck and to the back of my shoulder. His teeth scraped at my skin, biting a little too sharply with teeth, and then pulled back as though he realized he'd gone too far. He leaned forward and ran his stubbled chin against my jaw, raw and tender.

"You're mine," he growled. His breath scorched my cheek. His hand caught my jaw, and he leaned into me until my eyes met his. "No one else can have you."

Andrew steadied himself on one arm. The other hand slid under my stomach, drawing me up against him until I felt every hard line of him. He leaned forward to lick a hot, wet line up my spine. His palm flattened as he cupped and rubbed between my legs, fingers splaying to hold me open and ready.

"Say it again," he demanded as a finger gently tested my opening, then slid easily inside. "Say you want me."

I squirmed under his hand as his finger moved with aching patience, tracing a rhythm that made my thighs tremble with a sudden, aching need. I tried to turn around to face him, to reach for him. But his hand on the nape of my neck pressed me down, trapping me face down against the bed. My breath caught as the warm length of him replaced his hand, teasing at the edge of me, not quite entering.

"I want you," I gasped, the words fractured as they tore from me. "I want you, Andrew."

He moaned low, guttural, and pressed forward. I gasped and my body went rigid as he entered. He didn't rush, but the entry wasn't gentle. I bit back a cry as he continued to push until he reached his base, and my body screamed and writhed against him as he rocked his hips in a slow circle, making room and slicking himself down. He moaned as he rolled his hips against mine, my wetness guiding him deeper, before he started to thrust.

"You feel amazing," he rasped. His body trembled against me. "So, fucking good..."

His rhythm faltered, broken by the haze of wine, and he growled in frustration, clutching tighter at my hips as if gripping harder might anchor him. He ground into me with a force that made the bed frame shudder. His arm cinched tighter around my waist, holding me steady as his pace quickened, relentless and sure.

For a heartbeat, I fought back against the building current beneath my skin. I tried to twist, to roll Andrew under me, to take back the rhythm. My hands reached back for his chest, straining against the muscles in his arms, my hips pushing for control. He only groaned, low and guttural, driving deeper, faster, as though my defiance fanned the flames of his hunger.

"No," he rasped, harsh and certain. "Not tonight. Tonight, you are mine."

My vision narrowed to his strength, his heat, the merciless certainty of his body against mine. Every nerve ending lit, every breath burned, until all I could do was cling to the sheets and let him take me apart.

Then, just as the fire in me began to crest and tremors shook my thighs, he pulled out and shifted again. I gasped as he left me, my body screaming with unsatiated need. He flipped me onto my back a beat clumsier than he meant to. The mattress jolted, my lungs emptied, and then he was above me, all sweat, heat, and burning eyes.

"For years," he rasped, voice ragged with hunger, "I have wanted this."

He slipped off the mattress to stand beside the bed. He caught my hips and dragged me effortlessly to the edge. My thighs burned with need as my legs and ass dangled over the side, spread by the unyielding grip of his hands.

He moved like he meant to claim me, like his body had rehearsed this moment in dreams, and now he was dragging it into reality, all slow heat and unrelenting purpose. Each motion carried a promise I'd feel tomorrow in every breath, every aching muscle.

And gods, I want it.

I wanted to be unraveled by him.

Andrew's kiss tasted of salt and wine, the mix intoxicating, dizzying, making me want to roll in his skin until I forgot where he ended and I began.

He pressed into me again in one smooth, devastating motion, and then his hips began to move. Merciless. Precise. Every thrust a collision that rattled through my ribs and stole the air from my lungs.

His right hand hooked beneath my thigh, yanking it higher over his hip until I was wrapped around him completely.

His mouth tore from mine, breath ragged, almost a growl. "You let him..." the words fractured, broken by fury. His hands clutched too tightly at my hips, dragging me against him. "But he can't..." He stopped, breath shaking. "He can't give you this."

The words scorched through me. I wanted to resist, to take back even a shred of control. But my body betrayed me, arching and floating helplessly like a twig down his raging river. A thrill ran up my spine; at the power he wielded over me with every thrust.

Andrew's body moved with mine in a rhythm that burned and blurred, heat building until it roared in my blood. His grip tightened, and his breath stuttered hot against my cheek. The world faded. I felt my heartbeat in every place he touched, as though he were pressing the memory of him into my skin, stroke by stroke, so I'd never forget where he'd been.

"Gods, Nadia," the words poured out, raw and unguarded. "I love you."

My heart lurched, staggered, as if it didn't know whether to soar or collapse.

He buried his face in my neck, shuddering, his breath against my skin. "Gods... so much. So, fucking much."

The confession tore out of him, not with pride, but something deeper. Older. Like a river finally breaking past its dam. And gods help me; I didn't push him away. I pulled him closer.

Because I was broken too. Because anger and grief twisted inside me and healing him was easier than facing what I'd lost. I wanted this. I wanted *him*. I wanted the love in his words, even as fear pressed sharp under my ribs. Fear that if I answered, if I let myself believe it, I would be lost in his current.

Because I loved him, I did. But the memory of Vestro's arms, his whispered vow that he'd burn the world before losing me, clawed up my chest like a ghost. I loved them both, and in loving them both I knew I would break one, or maybe both, before the end.

I silenced the thoughts with my mouth, kissing Andrew hard, because answering wasn't possible. Not tonight. Instead, I held him tighter, grounding him in my own brokenness. I kissed the side of his face, his temple, and his jaw, unable to stop myself. My fingers threaded through his hair, clinging as tightly as he clung to me. Heat and shame and longing all tangled until I couldn't tell one from the other.

Andrew shifted his grip again, wrapping one arm around my waist and lifting me just inches off the bed as he crawled back onto the mattress, still sheathed inside me, and set me in the middle of the bed as he covered my body with his. He reached between us and placed his palm on the small, soft mound just below my stomach, his hand warm against my skin, and pressed his weight into it as he thrust.

My eyes rolled at the new angle and feeling of fullness. Each thrust filled my skin, stretching and molding me to his will, to his strength. I leaned my head back as he locked his mouth to the side of my neck and sucked in tune to his thrusts. He covered one of my breasts with his hand, and he rolled my nipple between his thumb and forefinger.

"An...Andrew..." I tried. I couldn't form the words.

I couldn't think.

Only feel.

Andrew's hand tightened over my breast, and his fingers pinched nipple, hard, as he gently bit at my neck.

Release suddenly tore through me, not just pleasure, but a rupture. My cry broke against his shoulder, raw and breathless, as my body splintered around him in waves too vast to contain. He followed with a strangled groan of my name, his body seizing as he thrust deep one final time, burying himself to the hilt as though he could brand me from the inside out. I felt his warmth fill me, spilling fire that coated every nerve, and I melted beneath him, completely undone.

The world spun soft and distorted. My lungs strained for air. Andrew's weight sank over me, heavy and real, anchoring me as the echo of him trembled through every muscle.

We lay there, tangled together, as the storm of him still whispered through my skin.

That was when the fear crept back in, sharp and sobering.

I had thought wanting Andrew was like taking a leap of faith, but this wasn't falling into love. This was an ocean current stronger than I'd imagined, dragging me into depths I hadn't prepared myself to face.

"Did I hurt you?" he asked, his voice husky and small in the dark.

His question lingered in the air, fragile and uncertain, and something in it made my throat close.

"No," I said.

My hands dug into his back, clinging to him because I didn't know how to hold myself steady otherwise. Not passion. Not surrender. Just a desperate need not to be swept away.

He shifted above me, lifting his head. His mouth brushed my temple, softer now, and when his glassy gaze caught mine there was no trace of doubt left in him. His lips curved, slow and sated after finally crossing the finish line he'd been chasing for years.

"I know," he whispered, his voice thick with relief. "I love you, too."

Fuck.

I didn't answer. I couldn't.

Andrew let out a breath that felt like a promise and settled his weight beside me, chest rising and falling against mine. His arm curled around my waist. The motion felt final. Like my silence had answered for me. Maybe it had.

He shifted once, just enough to press a kiss to my temple. Then his breath deepened. His body softened. The strain in his shoulders unwound as the wine and exhaustion dragged him under.

I stayed still. My hand traced the shape of his shoulder, memorizing the slope, the heat, and the way his heartbeat slowed beneath my fingertips. He slept without fear. Without weight. And I was glad for that, even as I lay wide-eyed beneath the hush of his breath.

Because I did want him. Not just his body. Not just this moment.

I wanted all of it. I wanted to believe that wanting was enough.

But an ache lingered; feeling like I'd stepped into the tide and couldn't see the shore anymore and a slow awareness that something wasn't finished. Not guilt. Not even doubt.

Just the quiet knowing that someone else's arms had held me first. That another promise still lingered in the air, unbroken, even if unspoken.

A memory of softer hands. Of vows made in shadows. Of a love that asked for nothing but waited anyway. Even if I knew that love would remain unrequited because of what he was.

I pressed my nose to Andrew's neck, breathing him in like I could ground me to the riverbank if I just didn't let go.

And when my eyes finally closed, it wasn't peace that came.

It was the hush before the current pulled me under.

CHAPTER
TWENTY-SEVEN

Pale morning light pushed through the shutters, gray and thin, softening the room's jagged edges.

I stirred. I ached between my thighs, a languid heaviness that pulled me deeper into the mattress, caught between lingering pleasure and hinting pain. I wrestled with the blanket tangled around my legs, rolled onto my side, and pulled the blanket higher to cover myself. While being naked last night had been perfectly fine with all the wonderful tricks Andrew had shown off on my willing body, laying quietly beside a very real and very naked man was... something I was going to have to get used to.

Andrew lay beside me still fast asleep, his head tipped back and mouth slightly parted. His chest rose and fell in an even rhythm, the faint rasp of a snore vibrating low in his throat. One arm was thrown wide, the other tucked against his stomach as if even in sleep he needed to hold fast to something.

I traced the perfect profile of his face with my eyes, admiring the way his lips curved above his straight jaw and exposed neck. I honestly felt happy that his expression seemed finally at ease. No crown or the stress of our journey weighing him down. Just a man asleep after claiming what he thought was his.

Peaceful. Certain.

And for a dangerous moment, I felt peace, too.

Because gods fucking help me, I had wanted this. Wanted him. Even now, the tide of him lingered under my skin, every breath reminding me of how easily I had been swept away. And it was easy to imagine forever waking up like this. To imagine Andrew's arms as home, his certainty as anchor.

But as the light crept higher, another truth twisted through me.

I had made love with both men now.

And I loved them both.

The words looped in my head, slow and poisonous.

I pulled the blanket tighter around my neck and watched the rise and fall of Andrew's chest, listening to his careless snore. The air between us still smelled faintly of wine and smoke. Sweet, then sour.

The sound of his breath shifted, a groan catching at the end. He rolled sluggishly onto his side, eyes half-closed against the light.

"Too bright," he muttered, voice rough. He dragged a hand down his face, winced, then blinked at me.

When his gaze settled, the corners of his mouth lifted. Slow, sloppy with exhaustion, but certain.

"Good morning, beautiful," he rasped. His hand slid under the blanket and found my hip. "You look... like you belong here."

His tone was soft, but the words landed like a chain tightening around my chest.

His smile deepened, lazy and content. His thumb drew idle circles against my hip beneath the blanket, slow and deliberate, as if mapping territory he'd already claimed.

"Last night proved it," he said softly. "You don't have to run anymore. You're mine, Nadia. You always have been."

The words sank through me. Sweet, slow, and impossible to swallow. My body still hummed with him, but the certainty in his voice tightened something in my chest.

You're mine. Not *I love you.*

I belong...

The air felt too warm. Too still.

My throat tightened. "You drink too much, Andrew." The words came out sharper than I meant. Maybe because they were safer than everything else, I wanted to say.

For a moment, his smile faltered. The air caught between us, heavy with something unspoken. His eyes flickered with a hint of shame before the defiant mask slid back into place.

He chuckled, low and easy, pressing a kiss to my knuckles as though nothing had cracked. "Then perhaps I should find other ways to sate my appetite," he murmured, his mouth curving into a slow smile. "Last night proved you are far better than wine."

Relief flickered through me as the old Andrew I knew flashed me one of his signature smoldering grins, comfortable again in his skin.

Well, at least he's feeling better.

As if to prove my point, Andrew rolled toward me, angling his lips toward mine.

I groaned and put up a hand over his face and pushed him back.

"I'm serious," I said, the words cutting through his charm. "I'm a little worried about you."

For once, he didn't answer right away. His eyes searched mine, red-rimmed but startlingly clear, as though gauging the weight of my statement. Then his grin returned, softer this time, tugging only at one corner of his mouth.

"You should not be." He feigned lightness but did not quite pull it off. He caught my hand and folded it against his heartbeat. "I have survived worse vices than a bottle of wine."

I frowned. "That doesn't make it all right."

He pulled me closer and tucked me under his chin. "Nadia," he murmured into my hair, "with you beside me, everything will be fine. Better than fine."

I closed my eyes, letting myself rest against the warm wall of him, though unease still pricked at the edges of my chest. Despite his confident demeanor, I couldn't tell if he meant it or if he simply wanted us both to believe it.

He pressed a warm kiss on my temple. His voice lowered, raw and unguarded. "I know you do not want to say it yet, but last night proved how you feel about me. And I promise I am going to make you very happy."

My heart lurched.

Gods help me, a big part of me did love him. But my lips parted, and no answer came. Andrew didn't seem to notice. Or maybe he chose not to.

He kissed me again, softer this time, as though sealing something already settled. When he pulled back, his smile lingered, his face content.

Andrew swung his legs over the side of the bed. His shoulders hunched briefly, his hand rising to press against his temple. The wince flickered and was gone in the same breath, hidden beneath the sweep of his hand through his tangled hair. By the time he glanced back at me, his smile was back in place, warm and certain.

I slipped from the bed, dressing in silence, the weight of the night and morning pressing into me with every movement. When my fingers brushed the pocket of my tunic, I stilled. Cipher was still there. Not forgotten. Not finished. Just waiting—like everything else we hadn't dealt with yet.

When I was ready, I stood by the window and hugged my arms to my chest.

"Come," he said, holding out his hand. "They are probably waiting."

I didn't move. "Andrew... we need to talk about Vestro."

His hand stayed outstretched, then lowered a fraction. "No, we do not."

"Yes, we do." The words came steadier than I felt. "There's more to what happened, I know it. He wouldn't have attacked Corbin without reason. He's..." I swallowed, hating how small my voice sounded. "He's not what you think."

Andrew leaned against the bedpost, studying me in silence. The early light caught his eyes, clearer than they should have been after a night of wine. "You are still trying to save him," he said, not unkind, just tired. "Even now."

"I'm not trying to save him," I said. "I'm trying to understand."

"Some men do not deserve the time it takes to understand them," Andrew said quietly.

I shook my head. "He's not just some man. He's saved my life more times than I can count."

Andrew's gaze didn't waver. "And yet he did nothing to save your home."

He let the silence hang there until it bent the air between us, then pushed away from the post. He ran a hand through his hair and then looked back at me, his mouth in a tight, grim line.

"We are short on hands," he said finally. "And he is very skilled with a blade. We... we need to succeed in this mission."

My throat ached with relief I knew couldn't show.

It wasn't mercy; his reasoning was calculated. But it was enough.

"So, you'll let him stay?"

Andrew's jaw flexed. "He stays where I can see him. His oath was to you. That means it is mine now, too." His voice dropped, quiet and deliberate. "Everything that is yours, Nadia. Your loyalty, your safety, your love, is now mine. And I will guard it with every breath from my chest."

I met his eyes. The words landed like an invisible brand. He didn't need to say what we both knew: it wasn't a request. It was a claim. And gods help me, for once, I didn't push back.

I STAYED silent as we moved down the narrow stairs, ignoring the smell of smoke and last night's ale thick in the air as my mind wrestled Andrew's words. The common room churned with clatter and low talk, none of it reaching me. I must have strayed at one point, because Andrew's hand found mine and he gently squeezed my fingers as he led me through the tables.

The scrape of boots on floorboards blurred into the thrum in my head. My body was still his from last night; my thoughts were not.

There had to be more to the story. Too much didn't add up. The demon attacks, the timing, the stolen Cipher... it all circled back to Vestro's warning. If the demons were after it, they hadn't been the ones to steal it. So, who had? The Holy? Damien seemed certain. Maurdruik didn't. I kept imagining the gold-cloaked demon and the riders with their thunder-loud weapons and couldn't make them belong to the same war.

And Vestro... my chest twisted at his name. He had lied. He had hurt me. But he had also saved me, again and again. The fear I'd seen in his eyes last night hadn't looked like guilt; it had looked like a man trapped by his own truth.

And whatever that truth was, it was waiting for me in the stables.

THE MORNING GRAY closed in as we stepped out into the street and made our way toward the stables. Mist hung low across the yard and pooled in the hollows where hooves had churned the earth to mud and pressed damply against my skin. It filled every breath with the scent of rain and iron, leaving a heavy stone ball in my gut. The horses stamped and tossed their heads, uneasy with the changing weather. Someone had left a saddle blanket half-draped over the fence, and the frayed edges sat dark with dew.

Andrew walked ahead of me, his posture straight but heavy with purpose. The fog curled around his boots as if making way for him. The air between us still felt like it belonged to last night, hot and blurred around the edges, but I couldn't let myself touch him. Not here. Not with Vestro waiting in the shadows.

The others were already there when we entered.

Trea adjusted the straps on his pack with mechanical focus, eyes darting from one man to the next. Damien leaned against a fence-post, turning a dagger idly between his fingers. Corbin stood by the water trough, his bags tucked under his arm, his stare sharp and restless as if ready to bite at whoever gave him the chance.

Vestro stood near the far stall, half in the light and half swallowed by shadow. The bruise on his jaw had gone purple and hard overnight, and dried blood still streaked the edge of his cheekbone. Which meant he hadn't shifted last night to heal. His shoulders were squared, but the tension in them betrayed something brittle underneath.

Vestro's eyes found mine and his nostrils flared once as he sniffed the air, and I saw the muscle in his jaw tighten and the brief, raw flicker that cracked through his composure.

I knew it had to be my guilty imagination, but I felt the stall's shadows thicken. I almost saw a glimmer of something move beneath Vestro's skin, and for a heartbeat thought he'd shift right then and there.

Then he blinked hard, and it was gone. His jaw locked, and he fixed his eyes on some point past my shoulder, as if looking at me a moment longer might undo him. But I knew he'd smelled it; Andrew lingering on my skin.

He knows.

Shame slapped me across the cheek, hot and sharp. I tucked closer behind Andrew's shoulder before I could stop myself.

The smell of hay, sweat, and damp leather filled the air, mingled with the metallic tang of the sharpening wheel someone had left turning. It all made the moment feel sharper, suspended, like the world was waiting to see who would move first.

I knew it sure as hell wasn't going to be me.

Of course, Andrew did.

He strode forward and stopped just a few paces from Vestro. He pulled out a cigarette and struck flint against steel. The brief flare of light drew every eye. The cigarette caught on the second spark, the ember glowing fiercely against the fog. He took a slow drag and exhaled, smoke coiling like a ghost between them.

"Despite my own misgivings, the success of our journey comes first," he said, his tone even as it carried through the cold air. "We need every skilled sword that can help ensure that success."

Corbin's head snapped up. "You can't be serious."

Andrew's gaze barely flicked toward him. "You will speak when I ask you to, squire." His voice was mild, almost lazy.

But I knew better.

The tic in Andrew's jaw as he pulled on the cigarette confirmed the restraint bearing down on his chest.

Color rose on Corbin's neck. He bit down on his words so hard I heard the swallow.

Andrew turned back to Vestro, the ember of his cigarette painting faint orange lines in his eyes. "You will stay," he said. "But under my terms."

Vestro's throat worked before he spoke. "Name them."

Andrew took another long draw on his cigarette, dragging out the moment. "You touch one of mine again without reason, and I will put you down myself. No more secrets that endanger her. If you know something, you speak it." He exhaled, blowing smoke that curled between them. "And your oath was to her. That means it is to me now."

Vestro lifted his head at that. The light caught the faint shimmer in his black eyes. "My loyalty is to her," he said, low and certain.

Andrew took one slow step closer until they stood nearly chest to chest. "She is promised to me," he said. "Her safety, her loyalty, and her life now belong under my crown. You swore fealty to her; that binds you to me. You answer to me now, Vestro." He spat Vestro's name out like it burned his tongue. "Every command, every breath, every swing of your blade. It is now mine."

Vestro's jaw tightened. For a heartbeat, he didn't breathe. The smoke shifted between them, catching on the pulse in his throat. His eyes slid in my direction, not quite looking at me, before focusing again on Andrew.

I stepped forward, unable to stay behind Andrew's shoulder any longer. The straw gave a soft crunch beneath my boots as I stepped between the men. I fought against the instinctual urge to reach for his arm.

"Do as he says, Ves," I said quietly. My voice trembled only once. "Please don't leave."

Vestro's gaze caught mine, unreadable. His eyes dropped to my mouth. Recognition flickered, and a faint tremor ran through him that he didn't bother to hide. Then he straightened, steady again, as if nothing had happened. He gave the barest of nods toward Andrew.

"Understood."

The knot in my chest loosened as Vestro turned away to gather my riding gear. At least he was staying.

Damien let out a short, sharp laugh. "Lovely. Nothing wakes you up in the morning like the smell of horse shit and unresolved sexual tension."

I inwardly flinched. *Fucking Hunter.*

Andrew didn't turn or dignify Damien with even so much as a glance, and the silence that followed was heavy enough to crush the humor flat. He reached for the nearest saddle strap, tightening it with a deliberate pull. His gaze slid to Vestro.

"Corbin, give your mount to the princess," he said, his voice even. "You'll ride the shifter."

The stable stilled. Even Damien's face registered surprise before it bled to something darker and knowing. Corbin's head jerked up, his eyes wide and flicking to Vestro. The bruise from last night's fight still colored his jaw, ugly beneath the lamplight.

"Andrew," I stepped closer, lowering my voice so the others wouldn't hear. "That's unnecessary. I can ride Vestro."

He turned before I finished, so close the edge of his cloak brushed my hip. "No."

"Why not?"

"He is staying," Andrew said without looking at me. "But not carrying you."

My mouth opened, but no answer came.

The old part of me, the one that wanted to fight, to throw the words back at him, rose up sharp and hot. But the others were watching. I felt their eyes boring into my back as they waited on edge for a response. The morning already felt brittle. Another fight and everything might splinter.

What was it Andrew had said? That's right...

The success of our journey comes first.

And damn him, as much as I hated it, with everything at stake he was right.

Fucking prince.

All these fucking men and their egos.

So, I just stared.

Then Andrew leaned in, close enough that his breath brushed my jaw. "Because I will not watch him between your thighs again."

My breath caught. The words weren't loud enough for the other men to hear, but they burned where they fell on my skin.

Vestro's shoulders flinched, his hands tightening on the bridle until the leather creaked. He busied himself with a strap, his movements careful and mechanical, as if wanting to do anything to keep his hands from shaking.

Of course he *had heard.*

"Do you even hear yourself?" I hissed. "You sound like—"

"Like someone who remembers the look on your face when you are near him?" His whisper slid lower, cutting, intimate. "Yes. I hear myself."

Heat flared through me, equal parts fury and shame. "This isn't about us."

His gaze dropped briefly to my mouth before finding my eyes again. "Everything about you is about us."

I stared at Andrew as the edges of my vision became watery. "You don't own me," I whispered.

His eyes darkened, a flicker of hurt buried beneath the arrogance. "You keep saying that. But you keep coming back like I do."

For a heartbeat, we just stood there. The world seemed to hold its breath around us, until the sounds and smells of the hay-filled barn faded and I felt myself standing once again at the edge of the dark river rushing past my ankles. Andrew's words hung there, and something in his face cracked just enough for me to see the edge of what he wouldn't say.

Vestro's voice came low from behind me. "After last night, you trust him on my back?"

Andrew straightened, his face hardening back into the king the others expected, and reality snapped back into place. He didn't turn to face Vestro. "You two will manage."

The tension that followed was physical, almost as visible as the fog outside. Corbin hesitated, jaw tight, but moved to obey.

Vestro's restraint showed in the smallest ways; the tremor in his hands, the steady exhale that came before he turned and unbuckled the bridle with careful precision. He draped it over the nearest door and stepped into the stall's shadow. His folded clothes appeared on the lip of the stall door, dropped with a heavy sigh.

The sound that followed was familiar now: the crack of bone, the wet slide of shifting muscle, the painful hiss of breath through clenched teeth. I stood still as I felt the men behind me flinch. I straightened my shoulders, refusing to let them see even a hint of reaction to Vestro's transformation. Steam curled out into the fog, and the scent of ozone wafted sharp in the air as the sounds faded.

Vestro emerged from the stall in stallion form, his coat shining wetly and milky eyes swirling with anger as he glared at Andrew. The muscles in his withers jumped, and his ears pressed flat against his head. He expelled a hard snort and met Andrew's gaze squarely.

324

The corner of Andrew's mouth twitched, the movement barely perceptible. "Corbin."

Corbin flinched. Then he moved and carefully settled the blanket and saddle across Vestro's wide back and adjusted the saddle strap. He kept his body angled, never crossing behind Vestro's hind legs and eyes flicking up every few seconds as if expecting to be struck by the sharp, heavy hooves.

Corbin's hands shook as he slipped the leather bridle over Vestro's nose. The bit clicked softly against Vestro's closed teeth, a quiet sound that somehow filled the entire stable.

For a moment Vestro didn't move, and I held my breath as Corbin's trembling hand pressed against Vestro's lips to guide the bit deeper.

Then slowly and deliberately, Vestro opened his mouth and took it.

His gaze never left Andrew's.

The act was obedience. The look was not.

The air shifted with something dark and unspoken.

Andrew's jaw flexed once, a tiny betrayal of breath. "Mount up," he said finally, voice flat, measured.

Corbin obeyed after a short hesitation, and swung stiffly into the saddle. Vestro did not move, as if he didn't even register Corbin's weight on his back.

I forced myself to take Corbin's horse and tightened the reins myself. My hands shook, though I told myself it was the cold. Andrew thought this was control. I knew it was fear dressed as command; his jealousy peeking through his carefully placed facade. I mounted without a word, because another argument would only break what little thread of peace still held.

Even though it felt like everything around me was shattering beneath my fingertips.

Andrew turned his horse toward the doors without a word.

Numb, I kicked Corbin's horse to follow.

The cold air outside the stable nipped at my neck and numbed my hands, but it was nothing compared to the bite of silence as I fell in line. Even as the world began to breathe again, I couldn't shake the sense that the real fracture hadn't come last night, or in the stable.

It had come just now, quiet and decisive; the moment Vestro bowed to Andrew's command, and I let him believe my silence was consent.

TWENTY-EIGHT

"This forest is not supposed to be here."

Andrew's voice was too calm. The kind of calm that shuts everyone up as they turn and look.

I sat astride Corbin's docile horse beside Peter, watching Andrew, Damien, and Trea bend over the map spread across a saddle. The inked lines of the map gleamed faintly in the light. Rivers and ridges mapped where there should have been an open plain. Yet in front of us, a wall of black trees rose from the ground in jagged formations, stretching across for miles before the edges blurred and disappeared in shadows.

Andrew's hand trembled as he put a cigarette to his mouth. The flame caught, throwing a brief flash against his jaw.

Jonathan had skipped out on us upon our arrival in Blightwood, saying that he wasn't up to traveling with demons. That might have been part of the reason, but I thought he was just tired of everything we'd been through and scared of what might lie ahead. Regardless, it meant we were without a guide, leaving Andrew in charge of our course. And after reaching the edge of this hellish forest, I was seriously starting to doubt his navigation skills.

Trea glanced between the map and the horizon, his brows drawn tight. "We must be off course."

Andrew's face turned a darker shade of red, and his eyes narrowed as he glared at the map and his hand twitched to the empty space where his crown sat. "We have been heading straight east for the past four hours. Look at the fucking sun! If we had gotten off course, then it would not be at our backs. I am telling you; this forest is not supposed to be here!"

"So, what? The trees spawned overnight?" Damien snapped. "Unless your wizard's map is shy."

"Regardless of how it got here," Trea cut in, "we need to decide on our next move. We've been standing here for nearly an hour debating already. We're losing valuable time."

Andrew tossed his half-depleted cigarette down and ground it into the hard dirt with his heel. He ran his free hand through his hair. He yanked the wineskin off his saddlebag and took a long, hard drink.

"How wide do you think this runs?" he asked, the cigarette bouncing between his lips.

"Well, considering it's not on the map," Damien snapped, "there's really no way to tell. From here it looks like a few miles, but there's the chance it might spread out the farther we go."

"Adding wasted hours if we were to try and go around." Andrew pulled out another cigarette and lit it before looking back up.

"Like the hour we've wasted debating this," Peter muttered to my right.

To my right, Vestro suddenly became agitated and dipped his head, his lips pulled back and ears flat. Corbin gave the reins a hard jerk to bring Vestro's head back around.

"Don't do that," I snapped.

Corbin ignored me.

I dismounted without thinking and wrapped my fingers around the reins so Corbin could not pull on them. "He doesn't like it."

Vestro swished his tail and pawed at the hard earth, his tongue noisily working at the bit. He jerked his head to the side and tried to turn left away from the trees. I patted his neck, running my hands through his wild mane.

"It's all right," I whispered, leaning forward over his long neck. "He won't do it again."

Vestro flicked his tail and pawed at the ground again and shook his head. The muscles in his back twitched, and he whinnied and bumped my chest with his nose.

A chill crept up my lower back.

Oh shit, he's trying to tell me something.

"Andrew," I called out, my eyes still on Vestro. "Andrew?"

I felt Andrew's heat appear at my back before his hand found my waist and steered me a step farther from Vestro, pushing his shoulder between us.

Vestro snorted and danced to the side, his distress clear.

Andrew considered him for a long moment and then looked back to the trees. He looked ready to say something but then took a controlled breath and flicked his cigarette butt away.

"We do not have a choice," he said slowly. "The sooner we get started the sooner we will get through."

Against my better judgement, I turned back to Corbin's horse without a word. I didn't like it, but I knew Andrew was right. We had to get to the pass, even if it meant running blind. Because if we didn't continue... if we didn't make it in time...

My fingers pressed against Cipher in my pocket. The tiny object feeling heavier than it had that morning. I closed my eyes and ran my hand down the horse's warm neck, trying to convince myself that it was Vestro's coat beneath my fingers.

Breathe, Nadia. We're going to be fine.

But the coat wasn't as sleek. The muscles not defined in the same, familiar curve.

I am going to be fine.

Andrew's arms circled my shoulders, and he hugged me to his chest. His heart beat against my back, and the steady rhythm helped to calm my nerves. I let my hand drop from the horse's neck, and I leaned my head back against his shoulder. Andrew's stubbled chin brushed against my cheek as he pressed a kiss to my temple.

"Are you all right?" he whispered.

I nodded because there really wasn't anything else to say.

He frowned against my hair. "I have faced enemies with less power than your silence, Nadia." He stepped to the side so he could see my face. "Talk to me."

My eyes slid past him to Vestro, and I caught Andrew's face darken.

I shook my head. "I just want this journey to be over."

Andrew frowned, and then his hands circled my waist and lifted me into my saddle. He sighed and laid a hand on my thigh.

"Soon," he promised. "We are almost there."

He gave my thigh a gentle squeeze and forced a small smile before stepping back and mounting his own horse.

"Stay right behind me," he said.

I felt movement to my right and looked up as Vestro and Corbin appeared at my side. Vestro's shoulder gently nudged my knee, and he bobbed his head as if to say, *yes, I'm still beside you. Even now.*

Corbin tried to pull on the reins to steer Vestro away from me, and Vestro quickly turned his head back and snapped at his leg. The look the squire shot me made it clear he got the point and let Vestro stay at my side.

I nodded in thanks at Vestro and slowly pushed my horse to trudge behind Andrew into the forest.

THE HUMMING HAD STARTED ALMOST IMMEDIATELY.

I gazed around through the trees as we rode. I could hear it, like the constant buzz you get in your ears when you're alone for too long in an empty room. The crushing silence that always comes with the presence of nothing. In fact, there was nothing, save us. Not a thing moved. There were no animals, no birds. I peered closely at the trees as I followed. The trees were shiny, glinting in the shafts of sunlight. The light breeze didn't even rustle them, although it did stir up the dust that had settled in a fine layer over the even ground. The leaves were flat and hard, sticking out at sharp points. All of them were the same monotonous green, no changes in tone or shape, and no fallen needles could be seen. And it was quiet.

Except for the humming.

I shook my head. The trees were definitely making the racket. I looked over at Vestro, and his ears laid back flat against his skull, his trot stiff. I could tell he was unhappy, but whether it was for the same reasons as mine I wasn't sure.

I sighed and looked ahead. The path appeared wide and clear, bordered by tall evergreens that pointed our way to the visible light of the valley beyond. We'd been riding through the strange forest for three hours already, and we had yet to run into something that breathed. I studied the trees closer as we rode. There was no resin, no loam. I closed my eyes and took a deep breath, hoping to catch that light, yet musky, scent of pine. I sucked as much air into my lungs as possible, but I wasn't rewarded. There were no smells that signaled life at all, just the sharp scents of freshly pounded copper and oiled armor. I jolted upright at the piercing sound of metal screeching against rock.

Corbin's horse reared and screamed.

"What the..."

The men had stopped as well. The horses in front shuffled their feet, lifting their hooves uneasily, clearly nervous, their teeth clicking against their metal bits. I stood up in the stirrups to get a better look. My jaw dropped.

The forest was...different. The entire view seemed to have shifted so that there was now a wedge of trees in the middle of the road, dividing what had earlier been a wide path into two separate forks. The shallow valley wasn't visible in either direction, making it seem as if it never had been.

"You have got to be shitting me," Andrew said. He drew his sword and glanced back at us, his kingly face drawn tight.

Steel rasped against leather as the men drew their weapons, the sound echoing off the trees and back to me. I quickly followed suit, and kneed Corbin's horse a little closer to Andrew. Andrew twisted in his saddle, glancing over his shoulder at me.

"Stay close," he said.

"You don't have to worry about that," I said. I had no urge to be alone in a forest that spontaneously switched out roads.

Andrew's head swiveled left and right as he studied the two paths. He reined his horse toward the left, then changed his mind and kicked the horse forward to the right.

I quickly moved to follow, keeping just behind Andrew. The forest shifted again, trees seeming to pick themselves up from their roots and...roll? The nearest trees hissed and hummed as they lifted six inches off the hard ground, revealing four wheels where there should have been roots. The wheels spun with a high-pitched whir, and the trees rolled from their original positions to recreate the scenery. Even the spiky underbrush had switched places with each other, following the path of the moving trees and shifting into a new pattern.

The men behind me yelled and the horses screamed as the trees closed in. The path thinned until we were forced to follow in single file. Andrew led the line, his horse picking its way between the metal trunks. I rode behind him, close enough that the hem of his cloak brushed my knee. Corbin and Vestro rode directly behind me, and the others followed just out of reach.

The forest pressed closer until the branches scraped our shoulders. The hum thickened, vibrating in my teeth. Several yards ahead, a small, square-shaped clearing beckoned us, and we pushed the horses harder to reach it before our path disappeared. Once inside, we pulled them to a stop to regroup.

Shiny, black vines sprang up from holes in the ground near the line of trees, crisscrossing over themselves. They pulled tight, creating a pulsing fishnet-like barrier between the gaps in the trees.

"We're trapped!" Peter squealed, holding tighter to Trea's waist.

His own nervousness seemed to pass to the other horses. Darren's mare danced around, unsettled, and he clung to the saddle to stay upright as the animal bucked. The movement startled Damien's and Trea's horses, and they fought to keep the animals under control and away from the throbbing vines. Trea brought his horse around so he could grab Darren's reins to steady the terrified animal.

"Shut up for a moment," Andrew snapped. "Let me think."

The forest stopped moving. It stood as still as before. The men milled about, turning their horses first one way and then another, yelling back and forth over the constant, low hum, pointing their swords and bows at the trees.

Andrew hesitated, the skin around his eyes taught as he looked at me, and then at Vestro. An internal struggle played clearly across his face; his mouth twisted, and color spread up his neck before he squared his jaw and slipped his royal mask back in place.

"Nadia," he said flatly, his voice perfectly measured. "Swap mounts with Corbin."

My head jerked up. "What?"

"Swap mounts." Andrew breathed hard through his nose. "Just until we are out of this forest." He glared at Vestro. "Then Corbin will take the shifter back."

Corbin held the reins tighter. "Sire?"

"Did I fucking stutter?"

Corbin scrambled off Vestro's back and quickly stepped out of reach. I breathed a sigh of relief and slid off Corbin's saddle and practically leaped onto Vestro's back. I felt a weight lift off my shoulders as my knees gripped the familiar indentions in the saddle's leather. I patted my right hand down Vestro's neck, and the warmth of his coat under my fingers helped to settle the tremor in my limbs.

Andrew watched in silence, his eyes following my every movement. His mouth pressed into a tight line, but he did not move to interfere. He nodded once I settled and then looked directly at Vestro.

"Stay on me," he said, and then his voice lowered. "If you see an opening out, take it."

Vestro's ears flicked toward Andrew, and then he bounced his head in acknowledgement. Andrew nodded once and then turned away and kneed his horse forward to assess our surroundings.

My heart surged at the realization.

Andrew knows Vestro would do anything to keep me safe.

Even in the event Andrew wasn't around to do it himself.

I urged Vestro forward, and despite his ears flattening back, he clopped up to Andrew's side.

I placed my hand on Andrew's arm. "We're making it out of here. Together."

Andrew considered me for a moment and then smiled. He took my hand and pressed my knuckles to his lips. His breath warmed my skin as he held the kiss for a long moment before releasing me. "Together."

Vestro suddenly went still and lowered his head with his legs braced wide apart. I reached forward and patted his neck, but he did not respond. I flipped the reins, but he'd taken the bit between his teeth and didn't move.

"Vestro," I whispered. "What is it?"

Vestro whinnied and lifted his head, his eyes fixed on the skyline and keeping himself as still as possible. Only his ears flicked back and forth, listening.

Listening to what?

I stood up in the stirrups and leaned forward, straining to listen.

Horses' hooves, the creak of leather, heavy breathing.

Focus, Nadia, what am I missing?

My frown deepened. I couldn't hear anything...except the humming.

The humming. It's getting louder, more frantic.

"Andrew," I said slowly, carefully.

"Hold on, Nadia."

"Andrew," I said, a little louder.

"Nadia," Andrew waved me off. "I said hold—"

"Andrew!" I yelled, leaning forward in the saddle. "We need to leave right now! Something's coming."

The men turned to stare at me. I pointed past them to the tree-tops. It looked like the trees were beginning to move again, but this time their leaves were swaying and reshaping... No. The trees weren't moving. Something was coming out of them. Several dark clouds shifted and morphed as they emerged from the shiny tree trunks and rose to swirl above the tree canopy. The clouds blew toward us, the humming growing to a dull roar as the cloud particles took shape.

My shoulders slumped and my throat constricted as realization hit. They weren't clouds.

They were bees. Thousands of them.

I opened my mouth to yell, but nothing came out. Horses screamed as the men wheeled them about, the bits tearing at their mouths as the trees picked up and rolled around again. The vines sucked back into the earth, and the path spread out ahead of us until it was ten-feet wide. The men kicked their horses forward, cursing as the clouds descended on us.

"Holy—"

"Shit!"

"Move!"

Vestro leaped forward, and I gripped the saddle between my knees.

Andrew spurred his horse on, and Vestro's pace quickened to match. I glanced around at the trees. Thousands of bees appeared out of holes in the trunks, holes that slid open like eyelids and screeched each time they moved. The bees swarmed around us. I swung my sword to fend off the nearest few. It clanked each time I hit one, a little ping lending proof of my aim.

The fly when I met Andrew on the road had pinged, too.

This isn't right... isn't natural.

Something stung at my leg, and I gasped as I looked down. One of the bees had landed on my calf, and it was stinging me through my leggings. The little gray body glinted, shiny as the trees, and the wings were like mini silver spoons. Not like a normal bee at all. It poked a thick needle into my skin, and immediately my calf seemed to catch on fire, an insatiable itching quickly spreading across my skin. I batted at it, trying to knock it away, and kicked my heels into Vestro's sides.

"Are you all right?" Damien yelled, his voice barely audible over the buzzing as we sped through the path.

"I'll be fine," I yelled back.

I grimaced with each of Vestro's long strides, the jolts sending fire through my leg. I reached down to scratch at it, but we were moving too fast. Though it itched like hell, keeping my butt in the saddle for the moment seemed like a much better idea. The bees were everywhere. They flew around in circles over our heads, trying to land and sting, and I fought to keep the bees off Vestro.

"Hurry up!" Andrew yelled.

He veered to the right as the forest shifted again, releasing more of the strange, shiny bees. The humming was so loud it was hard to think, even harder to ride in a straight line. I looked up to see light appear at the end of the newly made path, showing the green valley beyond. I spurred Vestro on harder. The end of the forest couldn't have been more than a few-hundred yards away.

The forest shifts every few minutes. We can make it out in time...

Andrew's horse pulled up beside me, and he backhanded a trio of bees flying straight for my head. "Almost through, Nadia," he shouted. He looked away for a moment as Damien's horse passed us. "Keep ahead of me and get out!"

Several vines shot out of the earth ahead of us and wrapped around Damien's horse. The Hunter yelled as the animal fell, and he jumped from the saddle and rolled away. The vines whipped out, caught Damien by the ankles, slithered up his legs like writhing snakes, and jerked him across the ground toward the trees. He cried out and dug his gloved hands into the ground, but his strength was no match for that of the forest.

I pulled on Vestro's mane, and he veered toward the Hunter. I lifted my sword. Andrew spun his horse around and screamed at me.

"Nadia!" he shouted. "Get out! That's an order!"

"We can't leave him!" I yelled back, though somewhere in the back of my head I was wondering if maybe he was right.

Several more vines shot away from the shiny trees to block my path. Others wrapped around Damien's arms and chest. Panic welled in my stomach as the vines seemed to multiply and envelop his entire body. I pulled Vestro to a stop, and meant to get down from the saddle, but my legs wouldn't move. I stared at the strange vines. They seemed so familiar. Vines that weren't natural, weren't...real.

Vines like I'd seen in Maurdruik's lab.

I gripped my sword with my shaking hand and met Damien's eyes through the crisscrossing creepers.

Suddenly the vines went still, and Damien had a moment to catch his breath. Then, just as suddenly as they had stopped, the vines tensed around the bulk of the demon hunter. Damien screamed out as the vines slowly began to crush him.

A blurred form flew past me as Andrew's horse leaped over a hurdle of vines. Andrew jumped from the saddle toward Damien, his sword held high and ready. Several quick swings ended in flying sparks as his sword bit into what I'd thought were vines.

Vines aren't supposed to spark. What is going on?

I scrambled to get a grip on the reins and hold on when Vestro reared and screamed. A new wave of bees emerged from the trees. Vestro bucked as several bees landed on his flanks, but none seemed to be able to latch on long enough to sting.

Andrew finally broke through the vine-cocoon. Several of the vines hissed and slipped back into the holes. Damien spilled out, gasping for breath. There were red welts across his face, and his eyes were a little unfocused. Andrew helped him to his knees, snatched up the fallen travel bags, and then quickly mounted his horse. Vestro galloped closer, and I held out my hand for Damien. Damien ignored my hand, grabbed hold of the saddle and mounted up behind me. He wrapped his arms firmly around my waist as we rode, leaning forward over me, pushing my head down.

"Damien—" I started.

"Shut up," he panted. "Lean forward over his neck and cover your head."

A metal bee rushed past my nose, and another buzzed near my ear. I bent down as Damien said, and he threw my cloak over my head, protecting me from the onslaught of mini metal demons.

Suddenly, sunlight poured over us, and I peeked out from under my cloak to see that we had emerged from the forest. Vestro didn't stop and followed Andrew and the others for a quarter mile or so down the valley. We finally slowed to a stop to look around, listening. There was no sign of the bees. No humming to betray their presence. I pushed my cloak back and sat upright in front of Damien.

We walked the horses to the center of the valley, enjoying the green of real grass that crunched under our hooves and the occasional call of a pheasant. I breathed out a sigh and let a bit of the tension in my shoulders relax. I stretched my leg out and rolled up my pant leg. My calf was swollen and burned beet-red. I scratched at it, and Damien thumped me on my back with the heel of his hand.

"You shouldn't do that," he said.

I twisted around to glare at him. "You try getting stung by one of those... those monster bees and not scratch."

Damien pursed his lips and dismounted in a single, smooth motion to walk beside Vestro. He rolled up his left sleeve. There were two welts on his arm, the skin just as red and swollen as my calf. I clamped my jaw shut and looked at him, silent. Plus, he had getting squeezed by sparking, metal vines under his belt. The red welts on his face had mostly disappeared, there were just a few scratches here and there, serving as reminders of the encounter. That was three points to the demon hunter.

"Should I start saying something nice about you now, or do we have time?" I asked.

"On the bright side, if I die of anaphylaxis, I won't have to walk to the pass." Damien grinned and winked at me before gently taking Vestro's bridle and leading us after the others.

WE STOPPED at the small grove a few miles away from the strange forest.

I hesitated a moment before entering the shade of the trees, not wanting to let my guard down in case more of those devilish bees were around. I looked up, studying the trees. The giant oak branches swayed gently, and the creak of old wood mingled with the whistling of birds and the rapid thumping of a woodpecker. Vestro seemed calm, even going as far as nibbling on grass, and it made me feel a lot better.

I unsaddled Vestro and quickly checked him for stings. Lucky bastard didn't have any. I patted his neck then limped off to be by myself. He flicked his ears and nickered after me, but I waved him away and slipped through the trees.

I sat on a log just out of sight of the men, removed my boot and rolled up my leggings, revealing my swollen calf. It was red, bumpy, and hurt like a bitch. I attacked it with my short nails. It itched so much I didn't think I would ever get rid of the burn. I leaned to the side and grabbed a handful of mud near the base of the fallen tree and pressed it against my skin. The coolness helped for a few seconds, but then the fire flared back.

"That looks like it hurts."

My head jerked up as Andrew stepped through the trees, a wine skin in one hand and a small leather satchel slung over one shoulder. I quickly looked away. I wanted to run to him; to have him wrap his arms around me and hold me. My vision blurred.

"I'm fine," I said, my voice meek.

His footsteps rustled through the leaves, and I felt his shadow across my face. I clenched my teeth together to keep my chin from trembling as I brushed the mud off my hand and resumed scratching my leg. He squatted beside me and bent his head, trying to look up into my face.

"Nadia?" He reached up to touch my cheek.

"Please, go away," I said, scooting farther to the left on the log.

His hand brushed my shoulder, and it felt as if he'd knocked something down inside of me. My eyes welled up and my shoulders hunched forward. My chin trembled, and my hands shook as I covered my eyes. The log moved as Andrew sat beside me and wrapped his arms around me. I stiffened for a moment and then relaxed against his chest.

Andrew kissed the top of my head and rubbed his cheek against my hair. "It is over, Nadia."

I tried to pull away, to turn and wipe my nose, but Andrew's arms tightened around me.

"Just stop," he said. "Let me hold you."

"I thought Damien was going to die. And I just froze and stared while you—"

"Nadia," Andrew said, pushing me away and holding me at arm's-length. "You are a strong, and amazing woman." He kissed my forehead. "But you do not always have to be the hero."

I guffawed and shook my head, rubbing my eyes with the back of my wrists. I managed a tight smile. "I guess I'm supposed to leave that to you?"

"Yes. Let me protect you."

We sat silent for a long while, and then Andrew unstopped his wineskin and took a drink. I bent and scooped up more dirt and slapped it on my skin. I reveled again in the fifteen-or-so second break it gave me.

"Quit scratching it," Andrew said.

"Bug off, leave me alone."

"You are going to make it worse." He shook his head and grabbed my arm. "Here."

"Let go of me!"

"Here!"

He shoved a vial into my hand. I stopped pulling away from him and looked at the small glass bottle stopped with a tiny white cork. I shook it and liquid swished around inside. I looked sideways at Andrew. He might have enjoyed pumping himself full of poison, but I was never very fond of the idea. And I didn't care to start.

"What is it?" I asked.

"Rosewart oil. It will stop the itching, but you cannot scratch while it starts to work."

I glared at him from the corner of my eye and uncorked the tiny bottle. The sharp scent made my nose wrinkle. I shook my head and shoved the vial at him.

"No way."

Andrew snatched the vial from my hand, knelt in front of me, and used one hand to scrape away the layer of dirt on my calf before splashing the oil over the sting. It burned like he'd dribbled molten iron across my skin. I yowled and tried to jerk away, succeeding only in slipping off the log and landing hard on my butt. Andrew grabbed my ankle and held my leg in place as he poured more of the oil on the wound and then blew on my skin to help ease the burning.

I ground my teeth as he worked. I wanted to hit him, but I didn't want him to stop blowing. The bastard was right that it actually helped. So, I begrudgingly leaned back against the log and let him work. Andrew watched me as he blew, his mouth inches from my skin and eyes twinkling with humor.

I narrowed my eyes. "Stop looking at me like that," I said.

Andrew kissed my ankle. "Like what?" he asked, his voice low as his hand slid up my thigh.

Heat pooled deep in my stomach, traitorous and alive. I caught Andrew's wrist but didn't push him away, feeling the slight tremor beneath his skin. I smirked. "For someone so noble, you're terrible at self-control."

He leaned in closer, his eyes heavy. "If you knew what I dream of doing to you the next time I have you in bed, you would stop calling me noble."

Oh... hell.

I did my best to conceal my grin, knowing by the twitch in my lips I failed miserably, so I turned my head away and covered my mouth with one hand. My heartbeat ticked up several notches and heat crept up my cheeks.

I could only imagine what was going on in that pretty head of his. But just the thought of his hands flipping me over again made me want to giggle like a silly girl.

And *that* I hated.

Andrew winked at me, satisfaction at my reaction clear in his eyes, as he went back to blowing on my leg. I frowned when his lips brushed against a clean spot on my calf, higher up than the last kiss. I pulled away just enough so that he couldn't go any higher.

"You really are a pain," I sighed.

"Stop pretending that you do not enjoy it."

I rolled my eyes, but the smirk at the corner of my mouth betrayed me. "Maybe."

He gave a short laugh, low and rough. Then his expression softened as the humor fell away. He gently set my foot down and then took a seat on the ground beside me.

"You scared me back there," he said. "When you turned around instead of running."

I swallowed hard, staring at the dark stain the medicine left on my skin. "I couldn't just leave him."

"You could have died."

"So could you," I shot back. "You came back."

"I will always come back for you. Even if it means my life."

For a moment neither of us spoke. The sound of the wind rustling through the oak branches filled the small space between us.

I became acutely aware of the heat radiating off his arm, and I caught myself unconsciously leaning into him.

"And then what of your people?" I asked softly.

Andrew's fingers brushed the side of my jaw. "When I am around you, you make me forget I am supposed to be king."

He leaned in and pressed a kiss to my cheek. His nose bumped against my skin, tilting my face toward him and he cupped my jaw and kissed me. His mouth was warm and soft, and I let his tongue part my lips and slip inside. I closed my eyes and leaned into him, relishing the golden warmth that began to tug at my insides and build low in my belly. I felt myself drifting, falling, and I let myself lean into the comforting strength of his arms. A soft whine escaped my throat before I could stop it.

Damn this man. Every time he touches me, I forget which way is up.

My hands found his chest and then slid up to grab the hair behind his ears so I could pull him closer. Andrew's chest rumbled with satisfaction, and one hand cupped my breast as he deepened the kiss.

A bird startled above us, jerking me out of the spell. I pushed away to catch my breath, blinking against the sunshine. I cleared my throat and willed my heart to slow.

"Don't think you can win me over by touching me," I said.

Andrew's grin was slow and maddening. "No. But it is the only time you stop pretending you do not want me to."

"You're an insufferable ass."

Andrew leaned closer, his breath warm on my cheek. "I know from firsthand experience that you love this ass."

I bit back a laugh. *Yes, actually, I do.* "You have too high an opinion of yourself."

"Apparently not nearly high enough," he said, leaning back casually against the log. "Not after the way you said my name last night."

Heat shot straight through me, and I hated that he could see it. "You don't fight fair."

"Fair would give someone else a chance." He shot me a half-smile. "I am not that generous."

Andrew winked at me and stood. He brushed dirt off that gorgeous ass of his and then offered his hand. "Come on, before someone finds us and ruins my reputation."

"Yours?" I asked incredulously, slipping my fingers into his. "And what reputation might that be?"

He pulled me to my feet in a single, solid motion. His free hand caught my lower back, steadying me, and he gave me a wide, shameless grin.

"The one you are currently destroying."

We followed the trail through the trees in silence save for the soft rhythm of our boots in the dirt. Andrew's thumb traced slow circles against my skin as if to remind himself I was real. And I didn't pull away.

My fingers brushed the pocket of my tunic, and the weight there drew my attention back to our mission like a deadly hook. Cipher felt solid and unforgiving against my skin. A reminder that the world did not pause just because I wanted it to.

I slowed, then stopped altogether.

"Andrew."

He turned at once, the humor fading from his expression as he looked at me in question. I drew Cipher free and held it between us, the metal dull in the dappled light, heavier than it had any right to be.

"Hold this for me," I said quietly. "I can't keep track of everything right now."

For a moment, he didn't speak. He just looked at it—really looked—then back at me. Whatever he saw there sobered him completely and his expression steadied. He closed his fingers around the small device and met my eyes.

"You don't have to," he said simply. "Not by yourself."

Without another word, he opened his satchel and tucked Cipher inside, securing the clasp with deliberate care before his hand returned to my back, just as sure as before.

Something in my chest loosened. And I didn't pull away.

We stepped into the grove. The others looked up, a half-circle of weary faces and restless horses. Sunlight fell in sharp stripes across the clearing, catching on dust and sweat and the faint shimmer of auburn in Vestro's dark chocolate coat.

Vestro lifted his head when he saw us. His ears flicked forward; pale eyes locking on where Andrew's hand held mine.

Andrew slowed but didn't stop. His thumb dragged once across my knuckles before he lifted my hand and pressed my fingers to his mouth. The kiss was brief and clean, the scrape of his stubble catching the edge of my skin.

The gesture was soft and tender—except for the way his gaze lingered on Vestro when he did it.

Vestro's tail flicked once, the sound sharp in the quiet. His nostrils flared.

Then he turned away, hooves shifting restlessly in the dirt.

CHAPTER
TWENTY-NINE

We continued through the forest along a wide, overgrown trail. I rode double with Andrew, since we were short a horse after Damien's had been lost, and it made more sense than having him ride with another man. I didn't mind having Andrew's steady heartbeat against my back, but the tension shedding off Vestro when the hunter smiled and saddled him was... awkward, to say the least. At least Andrew hadn't said anything when I fastened Vestro's bridle for Damien, leaving it looser than Corbin had it around his nose.

Not that Damien cared. He let the reins fall uselessly in his lap, so his hands were free to hold his bow at the ready as the forest darkened around us. He nocked an arrow and winked at me.

"He knows what he's doing," he'd said.

After that, no one spoke as all eyes were fixed on the forest around us. The air stunk of decay, and I had to cover my nose with my sash to keep the bile down. Tall, dying conifers stood like gigantic columns beneath the dense canopy, and were covered in black moss and draped with heavy vines slick with humidity. Shafts of sunlight cut through the darkness like spears gliding through water, illuminating tiny clusters of pale mushrooms and stiff moss. A golden moth flashed past, bright as a coin in a beam of light, then vanished back into blackness.

Glowing eyes peered out from the misty darkness, watching and sneering as we zigzagged our way along the winding path through the twisted labyrinth. Something screamed in the blackness above, and a shower of leaves and twigs tumbled down around us.

I flinched, clutching the front of the saddle. Andrew's arm came around my waist to steady me, his breath close against my ear.

"Easy," he murmured. "I have you." His hand didn't move until I found my balance again, and then he turned sideways in the saddle toward the others. "Keep up," he said. "It might be hard to find you if we get separated."

"Stay in the order you're in now," Trea said from the rear of the line. "This way we can best keep track of everyone."

Several times we ran into walls of giant fallen tree trunks or obstacle courses of twisted vines and had to work to cut a path around to make it easier on the horses. We steered clear of the many bubbling-hot springs that appeared on the sides of the path below outcrops of boulders. The sulfurous-smelling water sporadically sent columns of steam shooting above the overhanging canopy that singed the leaves and caused the steaming water to drip from the branches in an odious, yellow rain.

We came upon a gray, stone wall, which I thought seemed very out of place in the middle of the forest. It must have been ancient; most of the stones were broken and crumbled so that the wall stood no more than two feet tall, and less in some patches. Vestro hesitated, and I felt the tension drum through his body.

Vestro slowed beside Andrew's horse as we approached, his ears flicking back and muscles bunching under Damien's knees. His unease was impossible to miss, and he snorted and pawed at the earth.

As we passed the line of stones, a thin metal pole sprouted up from the ground next to the wall. I felt Andrew tense against my back as we paused to watch. The top of the pole opened like a flower, little black plates rotating outward to reveal a glass circle in the middle that reflected my surprised face. A little red light to one side of the circle blinked.

Vestro reared, making Damien almost lose his seat, and struck out with his front hooves, knocking the device off the pole in a sputter of sparks. The glass circle shattered, and the light went out, and Vestro's heavy hooves stomped down on the metal flower-like object, crushing it flat. He bared his teeth and looked up at me and snorted.

Andrew kicked his horse forward, and I had to clutch at his waist to hold on as we quickly rushed away.

THE GROUND GREW soft and squelchy the deeper into the forest we went, and we wound way across the flat waterlogged marsh land in zigzagging patterns, aiming for the patches of craggy ground with large, platform-like rocks that allowed for a brief moment of rest. The horses' sharp hooves sunk easily into the mire, and several times they stumbled to their knees. We eventually had to dismount and lead them, so that there was less stress on their legs. Damien slid off Vestro's back and unbuckled my gear. Then, Vestro disappeared behind a trio of trees to shift to human form. When he reappeared, tying the front of his pants and fixing his tunic as he walked, he didn't speak to anyone and just slung my saddle over his shoulder.

"It looks like there's another outcropping a way out," Trea called back as he scouted ahead. "Once we get there the horses can rest."

Vestro shifted his weight from one foot to the other and then stepped around Andrew and reached over to squeeze my shoulder. He smiled down at me, though the smile didn't reach his worried eyes.

Andrew's head turned at the gesture, his mouth hardening in a grim line.

Vestro's hand closed around the pack strap on my shoulder and lifted the bag off my arm and added it to his own. As if to mask the earlier touch.

"Ves, you don't have to," I started.

He gave a single, short jerk of his head, silencing me.

Andrew lifted his chin, then turned away. "We need to keep moving."

A low, deep shudder rolled through the trees. Then the forest trembled. Everyone grabbed at something for support as the ground bucked beneath our feet. Peter stumbled and fell, Trea reached back, pulled him upright, and steadied him.

"You good?" Trea said.

"Yeah," Peter said, his voice breathy. "What was that?"

"An earthquake?" Darren said, his frightened eyes darting around the ground.

Vestro shook his head. He licked his lips and looked around. "That wasn't an earthquake."

I glanced at the others, then around them out into the dark, swampy forest. Every shadow seemed alive.

What in hell else could possibly be that big to make such a ruckus?

Damien crouched, his head tilted toward the ground as he listened, his brow furrowed and dark eyes intent.

The color drained from his face.

"Run to the rocks," he said. "Now!"

The rumble started softly beneath the mud, then grew until it sounded like the world was cracking open. The ground quaked again as we started to run, forcing us to our knees as we fought to lead the terrified horses to the safe spot. I slipped on a patch of slimy moss and went to one knee, and Andrew grabbed my upper arm and jerked me to my feet, pulling me along with him. I glanced over my shoulder at the squires, each trying to pull the horses along, and my eyes went round as a monstrous, silver worm-like creature breached the muddy ground behind them like an earth-bound whale, sending clumps of moss and mud flying into the surrounding trees, and then burrowed back beneath the surface to tunnel its way after us.

Oh shit!

My breath came in hoarse gasps as I ran. The rocks were so close, yet the sticky mud made it hard to run. Andrew slipped on a slick patch, and we both went down, landing hard. Vestro was right there. He dropped my saddle and yanked us to our feet, pushing us forward. Tears stung at my eyes as panic set in and weighed my limbs.

We must make it to the rocks.

We have to.

Peter shouted out in warning, and I dared a glance over my shoulder.

The ground exploded on our left and the creature burst from a massive, gaping hole, lifting Andrew's horse into the air. Close up, I saw that the monster's long body was divided into rings of shiny metal casing that reflected the shafts of light. Metal armored plates slid across one another as it moved, and clear slime—like the slime from Vestro's changes—lubricated the joints so it glided through the marsh. The horse screamed as the massive maw lined with a dual layered circle of spinning, serrated teeth, snapped shut and cleanly split the horse in half.

I screamed and fell backward as a shower of blood spattered the boggy ground around me. Vestro immediately bent and pulled me away toward the rocks with one arm.

Peter struggled to pull his horse along, and then the animal reared and bucked until he let go of the reins and it took off into the marsh. Peter tried to go after it, but Trea grabbed his collar and roughly jerked him around toward the rocks.

"Leave it, boy!"

The metal worm loudly beeped several times, then slipped back into the ground. Several seconds passed, and the only sounds were those of our feet dragging through the squelchy mud, and the occasional grunt as one of the men tripped and fell to his knees.

I'd just started to breathe easier when the rumbling began again, softly at first and then louder until it built to a thunderous roar that nearly blocked out all other sound.

The rocks were just up ahead, the wide, flat-topped boulders jutting up from the mud like safety platforms. The sturdy soil between the rocks housed much newer and stronger trees than those in the surrounding swamp, the healthy branches hanging out over the marshy ground nearby.

The monster closed in faster than before, and we quickened our pace, though even then it seemed as if every step took a lifetime. Andrew suddenly cried out and fell behind. I glanced back at him, but Vestro grabbed me around the waist and lifted me into his arms, holding me against his chest as he ran.

Behind me, Trea shoved Peter forward with both hands. "Move, damn you!"

Peter stumbled, breath ragged. "You don't have to..."

"Shut up and run." Trea's words broke at the edges. "Run, Peter!"

I was just losing hope when suddenly the rocks were right there. The men in front quickly stepped up and pulled the remaining three horses onto the large slate slabs at the bottom.

Trea stopped at the edge of the rocks and motioned for everyone to pass him to higher ground. "Circle up! Keep your footing! Don't you move from up there, Peter!"

Vestro shifted his hold around the waist and hefted me up high onto one of the boulders in the center, as far from the marshy ground as possible. I glanced around.

"Andrew!" I called out. "Where's Andrew?"

I turned to see Andrew on his hands and knees, struggling to dislodge his leg that was sunk knee-deep in the sucking mud several yards back. He looked up, fear plain on his face as the worm closed in, the large tunneling body visible beneath the muddy surface.

"Oh gods, Andrew!" I screamed.

"My leg," Andrew yelled. "I'm fucking stuck!"

"Andrew!" I yelled above the roar. "Someone, do something!"

Corbin didn't move. He watched Andrew as he held onto his horse's reins with a distant look on his face, almost...anticipating.

Anticipating what?

Peter's breath hitched. "He'll never make it." He took a step in Andrew's direction, but Trea grabbed his shoulder.

"Let me help!" Peter shouted. He tried to jerk free, but the old soldier refused to yield. "If I keep hiding behind you," Peter shouted. "I'll die a coward."

"You'll die faster if you don't," Trea snapped back. "Stay here while I..."

I turned away, not hearing them. My entire body shook, and I fought to keep my footing as I tried to slide down the tall boulder without breaking my neck.

The metal worm-like monster burrowed closer, the large body pushing aside the sludge and small bushes in its path. My lungs ached as I turned one way and then the other, looking for something that would help. My eyes landed on Vestro, and I opened my mouth and reached for him.

"Ves... Please."

My voice had been no more than a whisper; my throat didn't seem to want to work, and I knew that he couldn't hear me over the rolling thunder of the approaching beast. But his eyes said that he'd understood, and his face tightened before looking away. I closed my eyes, letting two hot trails of tears slip down my cheeks as I felt the ground begin to crumble beneath my feet.

I can't watch this...

I don't want to lose him. Not like this.

Vestro's low, frustrated growl sounded to my left, and then ended with a barked, "Fuck!"

My eyes snapped open as Vestro rushed past me, back toward the marsh. I watched him deftly leap across the rocks and then up into one of the thick trees. He hesitated for a moment, gripping the limbs carefully to gain balance, then scooted his way out on a thick bough extending above Andrew.

I sucked in my breath and pressed my lips together. *Yes, thank you.*

The worm dipped deeper, the rumbling intensified, and then the world cracked open beneath Andrew. Mud and water exploded upward as the ring of teeth tore through the surface. Andrew shot up with the spray, flailing for balance, but the serrated circle was already closing.

Vestro swung down from the branch, one leg hooked tight around the wood, the other braced hard for leverage. His upper body dropped low, muscles straining as he reached down, clamped his hand around Andrew's upper arm, and hauled him clear of the ring of spinning teeth. The pull wrenched Vestro sideways, and tree bark splintered under his grip as the branch bowed several inches under their weight.

The worm's jaws clamped shut over empty ground, then opened again, the circle of blades whirring just above the surface. Waiting.

Andrew dangled in the air, gasping, his face white and mud dripping from his clothes. Vestro's arm shook from the strain, every line of his body taut and trembling.

"Pull me up!" Andrew demanded, panic edging his voice. "Fucking pull me up!"

Vestro twisted his head toward me. His eyes found mine, dark and unreadable. For a moment, he just looked, and everything around us froze in that single, suspended beat. Something flashed behind his gaze, cold and deciding.

He didn't haul Andrew higher.

Mud slid down his arm, slicking their joined hands.

Then Vestro's grip began to relax—slow and deliberate.

Vestro's hand slid inch by inch from Andrew's upper arm to the crook of his elbow, muscles flexing with careful control. Andrew twisted upward, his eyes wide as his free hand reached for Vestro's arm, trying to gain leverage. "Vestro..."

Vestro didn't answer. His eyes stayed on mine.

The slide continued, measured and merciless, until his fingers wrapped around Andrew's wrist. He held him there for a heartbeat. A second. Then eased his grip the smallest fraction.

My chest seized. I opened my mouth, but no words came.

Vestro, no...

The worm beeped frantically and dove beneath the mud. It slammed into the roots of the large tree, shaking the trunk, and both men cried out as Vestro's legs slipped. He caught himself at the last moment, still clinging to Andrew. The worm breached again, its circular mouth opening and closing with a shrill, grinding whir.

"Hit the buttons!" Vestro yelled. "Shut it off!"

"Buttons?" Trea yelled. "What the hell are—"

"The red blinking lights!" Vestro shouted, his voice cracking with strain as he fought to hold Andrew. "Push them to turn it off!"

I held my breath as the worm rose higher, inching nearer to its dangling victims. I scanned the metal ridges of its body, looking for red...*There!*

On the second ring of metal below the open mouth were three raised, red dots the size of gold coins in a row, blinking simultaneously.

Those must be them.

"Lift me higher," Andrew croaked, staring face-down at the moving black pit below them. "Fuck! Pull me up!"

Damien grabbed his bow, nocked an arrow, and let loose. The barb went straight to the mark but bounced harmlessly off the metal body. Trea loosed one right after, sparks flashing as the iron tip glanced off the metal and away.

"The fucking buttons, dammit!" Vestro screamed. His upside-down face grew red and contorted as he struggled. He had both hands wrapped tightly around Andrew's arms, but the weight seemed to be getting heavier, and the branch creaked under his boots as his legs began to slip. A guttural sound tore out of him—half snarl, half human—as he tried to reposition his grip on the tree. "Shut it down!"

My hands flew to my mouth as I heard the low, but frequent

cracking sounds ripple across the marsh as the branch began to fail under their weight.

I'm going to lose them both.

I sucked in a breath, my entire body trembling. A high-pitch wail built in my throat as I gazed across the marshy ground churning as the worm slowly raised higher. Toward the man that loved me with every ounce of his being. To the one that I couldn't have yet still gave me everything. Even this last act of sacrifice.

I met Vestro's eyes.

His black eyes said everything as he stared back, his face drawn with resignation. Even as his legs began to slip, his grip tightened, refusing to let Andrew go.

Not for Andrew's sake.

For mine.

The truth burned an aching hole through my chest, hollowing me out until the air leeched from lungs and laced the edges of my vision with darkness. The rocks beneath my feet faded, and I felt myself falling into the darkness that threatened to swallow me.

It was always for me.

Every move.

Every breath.

Every lie.

Tears slipped down my cheeks and my chest convulsed.

"I'm sorry," the words slipped out, even knowing he couldn't hear me. "Please, don't leave me." I slid down the boulder, the rough surface scraping against my skin, and landed hard on the craggy ground. The world came back into focus in a rush, and I caught my balance, my body tensing as I gauged the distance between me and the tree.

"This is it," Peter whispered beside me.

I spared him a glance. "What?"

Peter hesitated, and then eyes flicked down to Trea.

"I can do this," he said. Not bravado, just conviction. He bent and filled his arms with several fist sized loose rocks. Then he carefully stepped down the craggy boulders toward the edge of the marsh.

I reached for him, but he slipped away before I could grab hold of his arm. "Peter! Don't!"

Trea glanced over at us from across the platform and his eyes went wide. "Peter, get your ass back up on those rocks!"

Peter paused long enough to glance back at Trea, his eyes bright in his young, mud-streaked face, and his jaw clenched.

"Don't," Trea rasped.

Peter shook his head once. "If not me, then who?"

Then he ran straight for the worm.

"Peter!"

Peter slipped in the mud, righted himself, cocked his arm back and sent a stone flying toward the worm. The rock hit with the metal siding with a sharp ping and bounced off harmlessly.

"Peter!" Andrew's shout cut through the noise. "Fall back! Do you hear me?" The command carried across the swamp, sharp and clipped, but there was fear buried under it. "Godsdamn it, Peter, go back!"

Trea stumbled off the rocks after him, boots sinking deep into the mud with every step. "Peter!" Trea yelled, his voice cracking.

"It's okay, Andrew," Peter called out, calmer than his almost fourteen years should have allowed. "It's going to be okay, Andrew."

Peter paused and took a deep breath, sighting down his arm as he aimed and tried again. The stone struck true with a solid thump, and one of the button's lights dimmed, blinked, and switched off. The worm beeped and slowly whirred to a stop.

No one moved, no one spoke. The silence hung thick enough to choke us. Trea faltered and slowed to a stop as Peter turned back to us with a grin from ear to ear.

I threw up my hands and let out a sob of relief.

Then the beeping started again, and the two remaining buttons started to flash. Faster this time.

"Peter," Trea yelled. "Get out of there! Peter!"

"Run!" I screamed, lunging forward before I realized I was moving. My boots hit the mud, the suction catching at my feet.

Then an arm clamped around my waist and jerked me backward and dragged me back onto the rocks. I twisted in the strong grip to a profile of silver hair.

Damien.

His bow dangled from one hand, his voice low and sharp against my ear. "Don't," he said. "He's too far."

"Let go!" I struggled, my fingers clawing at his sleeve. "Dammit! He's just a kid!"

Damien's grip only tightened. "You'll die, too."

The metal worm twisted and bowed like a giant wave as it came whirring down toward Peter. The young prince froze, and the rocks slipped from his fingers and sank into the mire.

"Peter!" Andrew roared, his voice breaking.

I dug my fingernails into Damien's arm as I screamed, "Run!"

The giant mouth closed, and Peter disappeared from view as the worm swallowed him and dove down below the surface.

I stared at the black hole in the ground and screamed, over and over again.

Damien dropped his bow and wrapped both arms around me, guiding me carefully to my knees as my legs gave out. I screamed until my throat was raw and the sound finally broke into silence.

Then the worm's head reappeared, the two blinking lights flashing at us like a giant slap in the face.

Trea went still. His shoulders hitched once, then his face twisted, and the sound that came out didn't belong to rage at all. It tore from somewhere deeper, raw and wordless, until it became a roar that shook the air.

He drew his sword and charged.

"Trea don't!" Darren yelled. "Your sword is useless!"

"You killed my prince!" the old soldier screamed. "You took my prince from me!"

Trea yelled and leaped to the side as the monster came at him, the whirring teeth narrowly missing his legs. He hit the mud hard, rolled, and came up running. Like a madman, he clawed his way up the metal side, mud and blood mixing as his hands dug into the grooves between the plates. The worm beeped and rocked its head back and forth. Every slide of its armor shredded skin from Trea's hands until blood streamed down the silver casing.

Trea jammed his sword between two of the plates just behind top of the head, and bright yellow sparks surged around the blade. His hands were now shredded, pulpy messes, and he struggled to hold his grip. So, he wrapped one elbow around the exposed blade to keep from falling as he reached toward the button panel.

"You bastard!" he roared and brought his hand down.

The light on the first button died. The worm shrieked and reached toward the tree, teeth spinning inches from the men dangling above. Vestro howled, twisting his body to pull Andrew closer. Andrew lifted his legs as high as he could, clutching at Vestro's arms.

Trea struggled to hold on, and the elbow around the sword poured blood down his side.

"Peter," Trea said, his voice hoarse, so faint above the loud whirring that I could barely hear. "This is for you."

Trea swung his body and kicked at the worm, his boot hitting the last button before the blade cut through his arm, searing it away at the elbow. He cried out as he fell and landed on his back with a wet slap into the mud.

The button blinked, once, twice, and then faded. The worm froze. The rotating teeth slowed and finally stopped, the whirring and beeping noises cut off.

Then with a groan, the monstrous body tilted and dropped like a felled tree to smack into the mire, crushing Trea beneath it.

Silence followed.

The stillness pressed in, heavy and absolute except for the wet *blurp* of the mire or the horses' nervous whinnies.

The men beside me stared into the mire, their faces gray and eyes vacant. Darren's shoulders trembled before he turned away and huddled against a boulder.

Vestro shuddered. His legs slipped from the branch, and he dropped with Andrew, landing in the mud on top of the king. Andrew groaned and clutched at his ankle with one hand and his ribs with the other.

Vestro pushed himself to his knees, his breathing hard and mud streaking down his neck.

"You're a heavy bastard," Vestro muttered, his voice hoarse.

Andrew winced as he groaned and rolled to his knees. "I think you cracked a rib when you fell on me."

Something inside me snapped. The scream that ripped from my throat was half sob, half prayer.

Damien let me go.

I didn't think. I just ran.

The mud pulled at my boots, every step a fight as I practically clawed my way across the marsh. Vestro's black eyes watched me from his knees, mud-slick and breathing hard, blood running down from a cut in his arm. I aimed for him without thought, a sound caught somewhere between his name and a sob tearing from my throat.

But before I reached him, Andrew heaved himself upright and to his feet. His bad ankle buckled, yet he leaned into my way caught me as I collided with him, his arms clamping around my waist and dragging me against his chest. The impact knocked the air from both of us, and we dropped to our knees.

"Nadia..." Andrew's voice cracked. He crushed me tighter, burying his face against my hair. "Gods, everything is all right. I have you."

I clung to his shoulders, shaking as a sob wracked my body, the smell of smoke and blood thick between us. His body trembled with exhaustion, and for a heartbeat I let him hold me, my fingers twisted in the torn fabric at his shoulder. A mixture of relief and grief burned through me so hard that it hurt.

Then I looked up.

Vestro knelt braced just behind Andrew, his chest heaving, eyes locked on me. The sight stopped my breath cold. Mud streaked his jaw, trailing down the line of his throat, and his hands—Gods, his hands—were still raised halfway, caught between instinct and anticipation.

He'd been ready to catch me.

The air between us felt too thin, stretched over something raw and unspeakable. His fingers curled once, like muscle memory fighting itself, then lowered by slow degrees until they hung useless at his sides.

The movement undid me.

There was nothing dramatic in it; just that quiet, terrible lowering, like watching a stone sink into a calm but deep pool. Lost and out of reach. His shoulders trembled as he drew a breath that looked like it hurt to take. I watched every inch of him scream to move, to reach for me; how every inch of him didn't.

And that restraint was somehow worse than if he'd broken.

I could see the war behind his eyes; the pull to cross the space between us, to rip me out of Andrew's arms and damn the consequences. And I could see him stop himself, jaw locking, breath shaking, swallowing the ruin of it all.

Because I knew him. *Really* knew him. I'd felt those hands steady me through storms, patch my wounds, and lift me when I couldn't stand. I'd watched them destroy and protect in the same heartbeat and then touch me in a tender worship that until now I hadn't recognized for what it was. Calloused palms that never once hurt me.

Until now, when they fell away.

And in that slow collapse, I knew exactly what it cost him.

He wasn't cold. He was breaking.

And the only thing holding him together was the distance between us.

Andrew's grip didn't loosen, even as I reached past him. My hand found Vestro's arm, and my fingertips brushed the slick, warm line of blood. The contact jolted through me like a current, his heat running up my arm and tingling across my skin. The air between us tightened, humming with something I didn't have words for.

Vestro's gaze caught mine, his dark eyes pained and unguarded. His hand lifted halfway, hesitating. Then his fingertips lightly grazed my wrist. His fingers trembled, almost reverent. The touch was fleeting, but the world went quiet around us.

For one breath, I felt safe.

Whole.

Then Andrew's voice cut through the peace. "Nadia."

Quiet, but low and warning.

Andrew stood, pulling me up beside him. His hand closed around my waist and moved me back a step. The shift was small but sharp enough that I felt the possessiveness in it; the invisible line being drawn. "We should move," he said quietly, the edge beneath the calm unmistakable. "It is not safe here."

Vestro slowly rose to his feet, the muscles in his arms corded and bunched. His jaw locked and voice flat. "No. It isn't."

Andrew's gaze lingered on him a moment longer, cool and precise. "You have my thanks," he said, his tone measured. "For your service."

Vestro's mouth twitched with a mixture of anger and contempt. He stepped forward, close enough now to see the pulse beat steady and strong at the side of his throat. "Don't convince yourself I did that for you."

The air between us drew tight, thrumming with everything we couldn't say.

Because how could I speak when the words would ruin us all?

I couldn't say that when I thought they would fall, I felt something in me break clean through. That the world had narrowed not to Andrew's voice or the screaming or the sound of the worm tearing the earth open—but to Vestro. To the thought of losing the one person who had always stayed close enough to catch me.

And now he stood in front of me, alive and wrecked, and I didn't know how to look at him.

So, I said nothing. Because if I spoke, it would all come out: the fear, the anger, the want. The ache of knowing that I loved two men for entirely different reasons and hated myself for both.

Vestro's gaze stayed on me, unflinching, and for a single breath I thought he'd say something—*anything*—to shatter the silence strangling us.

But he didn't.

He just breathed once, shallow and ragged, and then turned his head the smallest fraction away.

My hand fell back to my side, shaking. Andrew's grip tightened around my waist, grounding me in the wrong kind of safety.

I swallowed hard, tasting salt on my lips.

Corbin appeared at Andrew's elbow, reaching forward to assist, but Andrew smacked his hand away.

"Now you want to fucking help?"

Corbin shied away, then held out a wineskin. Andrew hesitated, then snatched it and drained the last mouthful of wine and grimaced and then tossed it aside. He grimaced but then took Corbin's offered shoulder and the help to limp back toward the rocks.

I hung back hoping to have a moment alone with Vestro, but he walked past me toward the horses without looking back.

I pressed my lips together and trudged behind him.

I deserved that.

Damien looked up as I neared, his dark eyes flicking between me and Vestro, but he smartly didn't say a word. He held the reins to Trea's gelding and dipped his head toward me. "Princess."

I nodded and took the reins, but the massive horse was too tall, and the stirrup out of reach. Vestro's hands suddenly appeared around my waist without asking. He gently lifted me into the saddle, making sure I settled before he let go. I forced a smile, but it was hard when the heat of his hands disappeared, and I was left with an aching cold.

I watched him as he tied the salvaged packs to the saddle.

Andrew approached. Vestro shot him a single glance before walking away. So, Damien helped Andrew mount up behind me. The horse shifted under our weight, the big square head dipping patiently. Andrew grimaced and wrapped his arms around me to stay steady.

For once, there was no teasing or flirting to accompany the arms around my waist.

The absence made everything worse.

"Let us leave this cursed forest," Andrew said. He paused, looked over his shoulder at the fallen monster, then down at the churned-up mud surrounding it. "We... we are running out of time."

We only had three horses left, so we took off at the fastest pace the men on foot could manage. Damien mounted the gray gelding and took the rear, with his bow out and ready. Darren and Corbin lashed what supplies we could salvage to the third horse and huddled as close to the animal as possible without getting trampled. Vestro had refused the idea of a mount, walking ahead through the mire, the reins of our horse looped loosely in his hand. He glanced back at me several times, his face unreadable in the dimming light.

No one said anything, not to each other, not about Peter or Trea. Words were useless in times like this; they couldn't explain the uncertain fear that nipped at the back of our necks, or the aching pain weighing down on our shoulders.

No. Words could not make sense of what we'd just lost.

I swallowed and hunched my shoulders, leaning back against Andrew's chest. His arms tightened around me, his cheek brushing my hairline as his left hand covered mine. His fingers traced the ring absently, as if reminding himself it was still there.

That this was all real.

I turned my face into his neck, ignoring the thick smear of mud on his collar. His warmth steadied me; his heartbeat was a slow, deliberate rhythm against my back.

I said nothing. The silence between us said enough.

CAMP THAT NIGHT reeked of ash and worm rot, a sour-sweet stench that clung to our gear no matter how the campfire smoke curled or how many times I rubbed my palms against the grass to wipe away the mud. We did not have a lot of water to spare, so bathing away the splatter of horse blood and marsh ick was out of the question. I tore through what was left of my pack for a clean tunic, hoping a change of fabric could muffle the scent of death.

It didn't.

Damien had coaxed a small fire from damp wood, which was a miracle as everything around us dripped with moisture. The ground. The sky. Our faces.

Mostly our faces. They'd stayed wet since we left the muddy gravesite of Trea and Peter behind.

The flames sputtered, throwing uneven light across faces hollowed by grief as we settled into our cloaks for a restless night of sleep. Darren lay apart, hunched over Trea's sword, his shoulders heaving soundlessly, as if he could still anchor himself to the man who had wielded it.

Vestro sat off to the edge of camp, just inside the circle of firelight. His bare shoulders were streaked with blood and dirt, the lines of him carved in shadow. He sat too still. Too quiet.

I knelt beside him with my waterskin and a linen cloth, and he reached for me in the way he always did.

But when his hand brushed my wrist, I pulled back. Just slightly, but enough. The motion caught him mid-breath. Something behind his eyes cracked, then went still.

I kept my hands busy, dabbing at a shallow cut across his ribs, pressing cloth against it with more care than I wanted to show. His jaw tightened, but he didn't speak.

The worm's scream still rang in my bones. And I couldn't stop replaying the look on Vestro's face when Andrew had stumbled in the creature's path.

"You said it was okay," I whispered, the words sharper than I meant.

The air between us shifted. He didn't ask what I meant. He didn't need to.

I wanted him to say something. To take it back, to tell me I was wrong, to tell me that none of this was okay. That Andrew wasn't the right choice.

He didn't.

Vestro's head bowed, hair falling forward to shadow his expression. "I know." His voice was so low it barely carried.

The sound of it hit harder than a shout.

I finished checking him over, confirmed that most of the blood wasn't his, and then wiped my palms on my pants and stepped back. I stared at him a moment longer, unused to the cold space between us. When he didn't look up, I turned and walked away.

The fire crackled behind me, the sound thin and tired. Just like everything else in the clearing. My body moved on its own, putting one foot in front of the other, leading me toward the only other shape still upright at the edge of the light. Each step felt heavier, as if I were wading against a current drawing me back into a pool of all the shit that we hadn't said.

Andrew leaned against the rough bark of a pine, shoulders bowed, one hand pressed to his temple. The other hung limp, an empty wineskin dangling from his fingers. His head tipped forward, hair shadowing his face, but when I stepped closer, his eyes lifted.

"You okay?" I asked quietly, the words sounding wrong in the hushed darkness.

His mouth twisted. "Headache." The word came out clipped, bitten off, but his grip on the wineskin betrayed him. The empty leather creaked under his fingers.

He shifted when I sat beside him, wincing as he pulled one leg close. His ankle was swollen, a dark bruise blooming above the boot line.

"Let me see," I said.

365

Andrew's lips pressed thin, but he let me kneel and roll back his pant leg and wrap the joint with what little cloth we had left. My fingers brushed his skin, and he sucked in a sharp breath through his teeth as I bound his ankle.

He forced a smile. "Thank you."

I started to answer, but Andrew's eyes stared past me, fixated on the fire. The light caught the edges of his clenched jaw and the tightness around his red-rimmed eyes.

His fingers twitched once against the wineskin.

"Two men are dead because I brought us this way," he said finally, his voice rough. "I should have seen the signs. The ground... Everything was wrong."

His knuckles whitened around the leather. The words came out like he was talking to himself. Not a confession. A calculation.

His gaze flicked toward the dark. "Peter was their only heir." He looked up at me then, ghosts in his eyes. "I just ended the line of the Elk Plains."

"Andrew—"

I reached for his arm, but he lifted a hand to touch that spot just above his temple and shook his head, short and sharp. His jaw clenched tightly, as if he could muscle the grief back down.

I lowered my hand and looked away, only to catch Vestro watching. The firelight caught his eyes and turned them to embers, and the weight of his stare pressed on my every motion.

I let out a heavy sigh, dropped the waterskin and remaining linen strips beside Andrew and stood.

I'm too tired for all this shit.

I just can't.

I spread my cloak near the fire, exhaustion dragging at my bones. I settled against the hard ground slowly, forcing my body to relax inch by inch as I tried to ignore the tremor building in my hands and pulled my knees to my chest.

The grass rustled behind me, and Andrew eased down, his weight sinking to the earth beside me. His arm slipped around my waist, slow and careful, drawing me back against him. He pulled his cloak over our shoulders, tucking most of it around me. The heat of him found me instantly, and I closed my eyes and breathed in his familiar scent of smoke and sage.

I shifted so that I fit better against the curve of his body and rested my head on his shoulder. I let myself lean into the warmth of another human being; let the touch alone ground me so I didn't slip into the dark hole gnawing at my chest.

My breath evened out, but my mind didn't.

The quiet didn't erase what had almost happened. The shadow of it clung close, pulsing behind my ribs; the memory of metal teeth, of the earth splitting open, and of the heartbeat I thought I'd lost. For one awful second, I'd already mourned him.

Now it pressed against me, steady and alive. I held still, afraid that if I moved, the moment might slip.

I opened my eyes. Across the clearing, Vestro sat half in the firelight, shadow cutting his face in two. Grief, fury, and shame flickered across his features with the shifting glow.

Andrew's breath deepened, and he shifted in his sleep. His arm tightened around me like a shield. Maybe it was protection. Maybe possession. It didn't matter; his warmth burned all the same with the echo of everything we'd survived.

I met Vestro's eyes, and I shoved my fist in my mouth to quiet my sob as my breath hitched.

And maybe everything we hadn't.

The fire crackled low. I let the heat swallow the noise in my head and closed my eyes, pretending to sleep.

Because pretending was easier than choosing.

THIRTY

Morning came too quickly. The sky hung low and gray, heavy with ash and haze. No one had slept well. Vestro had disappeared somewhere off in the forest before sunrise, and Andrew had excused himself to sit alone at the edge of camp. Darren's eyes were red-rimmed, and even Corbin's endless complaints had burned down to silence. What little we'd salvaged from the marsh only half-filled two packs, and the weight of that loss hung heavier than the air.

So, I sat alone near the depleted fire, wrapped in my cloak. Trying to quiet the whirlwind of thoughts harassing my senses as I tried to make sense of where my head and my heart collided, and where they threatened to rip me apart. I used the edge of the wool to wipe at the crusty layer of mud on my skin that just didn't seem to ever want to rub away. My eyes burned, and my stomach growled, empty of both food and hope, and the morning all-around felt pretty fucking miserable.

Damien broke the quiet first. He ground his boot into the dirt.

"Three days. That's what we have to reach the Pass." His tone was flat, but the words cut through the quiet. "After that, the gates close, and every soldier in Ferrington will be waiting."

A band tightened around my chest. Three days to reach the pass and finish our task. Then we could go home.

If there is a home waiting for us at all.

I felt a presence at my side and lifted my chin toward the shadow as Vestro slowly squatted beside me. I blinked at the relief that flooded through me, unaware that I'd been holding onto a feeling of dread in case he finally decided that this entire mission—*that I*—was too much effort and he'd just say *fuck it* and never come back.

I'm not even sure if I would blame him.

My chin trembled but I held the bastard in check and swallowed my tears down.

Vestro simply looked at me for a long moment. The fine lines at the edges of his eyes seemed deeper this morning, weariness pulling his skin tight. He held his fist out, knuckles up, waiting. I hesitated but then held my hand out. Vestro lowered his hand to mine, letting his touch linger, before relaxing his grip to let something small and soft fall into my palm. He trailed his fingers against mine as he let his hand fall away.

A small, sad chuckle escaped my trembling lips at the sight of the meager handful of wild blackberries in my hand.

Of course, he'd gone to find me something to eat.

Of course, he was looking out for me like he always has.

Guilt for ever doubting clawed at my chest.

I felt Vestro's calloused thumb brush away the tear on my cheek before I realized it had fallen.

"Always the practical one," I whispered.

He gave me the ghost of a smile. "Hardly."

I held the seven blackberries between us. "Did you eat already?"

He smirked. "Yeah."

"Liar."

I leaned toward him slightly, and he cupped the side of my head with one hand, bent, and pressed his forehead against mine. The tension in his shoulders escaped through his sigh as he held me there, breathing in the air between as if were a lifeline. He pulled back just enough to look into my eyes before he let his hand fall, and he stood and stepped back. His eyes slid toward Andrew, and I tensed as I followed his gaze.

Andrew never even looked our way. He sat a little apart, elbows on his knees, and rubbing at his temples. His face was pale, his jaw tight. His hand tapped against his knee, his fingers flexing, as if searching for something to hold. Then his hand went up too sharp, to fix the crown that wasn't there. The stress tell I'd come to recognize.

I clocked the truth then. The wine skins were empty. His building headache wasn't just from fatigue or strain.

It was withdrawal.

The word hit hard, cold, true.

Damien stirred the ashes from last night's fire with the toe of his boot. His gaze brushed mine, fleeting and impassive, but in that brief flicker, I knew he'd seen it too. He didn't speak, just turned back to the dying coals as if nothing had passed between us.

The clock was ticking.

And for the first time, it was written plainly on Andrew's face.

THE FLAT-TOPPED PLATEAU ENDED ABRUPTLY, dropping off at a steep angle to border the edge of a massive dry lakebed, the cracked-mud surface running for miles across and twice that distance wide. The air above the pit shimmered too evenly, like the world was trapped behind a sheet of rippling glass; every few breaths the shimmer pulsed and bent the horizon in small waves. Steam rose in spurts from the cracks in the earth, hissing in a rhythm too regular to be natural, the spray shooting up hundreds of feet into the air. The hard dirt surface faded farther into the lake where it softened into white rolling hills of sand and ash.

Wind swirled in visible waves between tall, black poles twice as high as any pine tree. There were multiple rows of these tall poles, spreading out hundreds of feet apart from each other, yet arranged in perfect lines, covering the entire white floor of the lake. Atop each pole perched a wide panel of large, glowing disks; the crowns turned together in an eerie concert, and when they angled the glare struck in spear-like beams that made the sand smoke. I watched a crow wheeling too near a beam and drop from the air, feathers smoking before it hit the ground.

Andrew dismounted and helped me from the saddle. Then he walked to the edge and peered down the slope. He stood near a small, crooked plum tree sapling, the only sign of life that dared come near the hellish wasteland. He rubbed the back of his neck and gazed off across the wide gorge. I stepped forward to follow him, ignoring Vestro's outstretched hand.

I stared past the ragged edge of the plateau, my chest aching with the thoughts I couldn't shake. This journey was peeling us raw. Every mile stripped another layer I hadn't known was there; in Andrew, in Vestro, and in me. And I wasn't sure I liked what I was seeing.

"Are we going across that?" I asked, shifting in the saddle.

"I...the map stops here," Andrew said. "There are no records of anything beyond this ridge. But both Drahcier and Maurdruik had said east, and that," he waved a hand out at the white sands, "is east. I do not know where else we should go."

"The climate should not be this hot here," Damien said, almost to himself. He stepped back from the edge, squinting at the rows of disks mounted on the poles. "This is not a normal desert. Heat doesn't march in straight lines." He let that hang between the poles and the men. "Someone made this to keep us out, or something in."

Vestro didn't answer. The wind kicked grit against his boots and the horses shifted, uneasy, but he stayed rigid, eyes locked on the white expanse below. The glare off the panels caught the amber in his irises and turned it glassy. For a heartbeat, he looked carved from the same sunbaked stone they stood on.

The disk panels rotated with a soft whine, their mirrors sweeping the horizon in perfect rhythm. With every synchronized turn, Vestro's shoulders twitched, as if the sound scraped against a nerve. His throat worked once, but no words came.

Steam hissed near the ridge. The others flinched and stepped back. Vestro didn't. His gaze followed the vent's plume, tracing it upward, then down again, as he mapped something unseen. His hands fisted until his knuckles glowed white.

Damien's glance flicked toward him, a half-smirk fading. "You've gone quiet," he said, trying for levity, but Vestro's stillness swallowed the humor before it reached the others. "You've seen something like this before."

When the next gust passed, Vestro finally blinked. "There's no other way around," he said, low, almost to himself. Then he turned from the edge, leaving a strange silence in his wake.

I inched closer to the edge of the ridge, looking up at the tall poles. I couldn't look directly at the panel of disks; they burned my eyes and left rows of tiny purple circles dancing in front of my vision when I looked away, even with my eyes closed. It was like looking too long at the sun.

Andrew's eyes revealed his disappointment. "We cannot spare the time waiting for nightfall."

Irritability flickered at the edges of Andrew, his responses too quick, too sharp for the situation, and he snapped at Corbin when the gear slipped. The insult was small and ugly, and he caught himself and flushed. He pulled his waterskin from his belt, but his hand trembled as he raised it. The mouth slipped, a trickle of water running down his chin. He cursed under his breath, swiping his face with the back of his hand.

Damien breathed out heavily through his nose as he studied Andrew. "Three days with no taverns in sight, and the worm took half our packs," he said dryly. "Tell me, Corbin, did you manage to save any of His Majesty's favorite tonic?"

Corbin's head came up sharply. His face stayed flat, unreadable, as he adjusted his horse's girth. He frowned and gave a short jerk of his head.

Damien's smirk didn't quite reach his eyes. "Then we'll see how far water carries us."

Andrew's jaw flexed and his eyes narrowed, but he said nothing. He shoved the cap tight on his waterskin, almost too forcefully, the leather crinkling in his fist.

"How much do we have?" I asked.

Vestro checked my bag he'd slung over his shoulder. I had one water skin, and when he sloshed it around, I knew that it wasn't even two-thirds full. Darren pulled out two skins, both only half full. He handed one to Damien. Andrew's hands closed around his own skin in a white-knuckled grip.

A sprout of steam rushed up not far from where we stood. The heat shriveled the tree sapling instantly, the leaves curling and turning black. I glanced at the men's pale and worn faces.

"Maybe we should try to go around," Andrew said, stepping back toward the horses.

The others nodded, their eyes fastened on the hissing sands. They pulled on their reins and turned about. I turned to follow, but suddenly the edge I was standing on crumbled, and I gasped as I slid down the dusty slope.

I ground to a halt about halfway down, caught by a pair of strong arms. I blinked against dust to Vestro's grimacing face just inches from mine. He skidded down the rest of the way, landing with a jolt on the hard lakebed. He jumped out of the way of the tumbling dirt clods, and then gingerly set me down.

"Are you hurt?" he asked, distracted.

He wasn't looking at me. His gaze slid past my shoulder, fixed on the rows of black poles below us. The light from the disks reflected across his face, bleaching it pale. For a heartbeat he didn't breathe.

"Vestro," I said, barely above a whisper. I laid a hand on his chest, and his heart pounded under my palm.

He blinked, once, twice, as though forcing himself back into the present. Then he loosened his hold and set me down, slow and careful, eyes never leaving the horizon.

"Hey!" Darren called down from above us. "You two good down there?"

All the men were crowded around the edge, anxiously peering down through the turned-up dust. Andrew was shaking his head at me. Vestro waved them down.

Vestro gave no answer until the last of the dust settled.

"Fine," he said finally, but his voice was too even and sounded wrong. "It's not that bad coming down, but you might want to dismount first."

The others hesitated, carefully dismounted, and skidded down the ledge. Darren had to jump out of the way as the pack horse stumbled and rolled, and Corbin dumped the entire contents of one bag when he dropped it just before reaching the bottom. I shook the dust off my clothes and out of my hair as the men settled the horses. I fanned my face. We hadn't even started moving yet and I was already sweating. I shielded my eyes and tilted my head back. The heat didn't just glare from above; it pressed from everywhere at once in invisible waves. The disks above us hummed low and constant, the sound vibrating so loudly I felt through my teeth.

We moved at a steady clip, with our goal being to get through this hellhole as soon as possible. The air was hot and dry, sucking the moisture out of my lips and throat. Even the water in the skin at my hip tasted scalded, as if it had been left too long beside a hearth.

The dusty crust of the lake cracked without warning, and Damien's horse stumbled with a scream that sent the others into a frenzy. We were forced to dismount and run alongside them, our boots slipping in the softening sand, so our weight didn't add to their strain.

"Keep them moving," Andrew barked. His voice came sharp and ragged; each command spat like it hurt to speak.

When the mare I rode lurched sideways and a saddlebag slipped off Corbin's shoulder, Andrew wheeled on him.

"Gods damn it, are you blind?" He snatched up the fallen strap, his hand shaking so badly he fumbled it twice before ramming it back into place. His chest heaved, sweat soaking through his tunic, but instead of stepping back he shoved Corbin hard in the chest. "Fucking useless! Do one thing right!"

Corbin staggered back a step, his face unreadable as ever, but his hand tightened imperceptibly on the reins. He didn't say a word. That blankness made the moment worse, somehow, like he was letting Andrew fail.

Andrew's eyes blazed. "Look at me when I am speaking to you!"

Corbin lifted his gaze slowly, steady, almost bored. Andrew's breath hitched with fury, his hand twitching like he might strike him. For a terrible second, I thought he would.

"Andrew," I snapped, my voice hoarse, forcing its way through the heat between us. "What the hell is wrong with you?"

His head snapped toward me, fury cracking raw across his face.

Damien's voice cut through the stifling air, flat and sharp as a blade. "You sound like a man overdue for his medicine."

The words landed like a slap. Andrew reeled on him, teeth bared. "Say that again," his voice tore, half a growl, half a plea. "Say it to my face, Damien, and see how far you walk out of here!"

Damien didn't even flinch. "I just did."

For a heartbeat, all I heard was the hiss of wind and the pounding of my own blood. Andrew trembled, his chest heaving and eyes wild. He spat into the sand, his spit red-stained, and turned away, shoving past Corbin so hard the squire had to step aside to keep his footing.

Tears pricked at my eyes, but the hot air dried them before they could fall.

I told him he drank too much. I should have done something...

I shook my head, mainly to myself. *Why would he listen to me? I ignored him for years. I have no room to talk about being stubborn and self-destructive.*

No one spoke after that. Only the endless slap of boots in sand, the hiss of the hot wind, and the relentless glare of the disks above.

MINUTES, hours, days. There seemed to be no difference. Time dragged on endlessly, taunting us as we trudged through the deepening sand. A wind had picked up despite the clear sky, clogging our throats and throwing sand into our eyes, so that we walked blindly with no way of knowing where we were going or how far we'd gone. The identical rows of tall poles continued on, their endless numbers mocking our struggles as they stood straight and proud against the biting gusts.

My throat ached for water I didn't have. My body trembled with the same exhaustion I saw in Andrew's gait, the tremors in his fingers worsening each time he lifted them.

Fear gnawed at me. Not just of the desert, but of the way Andrew staggered and his temper snapped like a frayed rope.

The desert wasn't just burning us dry. It was peeling him back to something raw and volatile. And in that rawness, I saw a shadow I'd spent years despising. He looked like his father.

And that was the cruelest cut, because Andrew had fought his entire life not to be that man. I'd seen it in the inn, the way one careless word—*like him*—had made his fists clench, his voice breaking with fury. He didn't want to be an echo. He swore he wouldn't.

But here he was, slipping into that shadow all the same. His rage, his trembling, the wildness in his eyes. I loved him, but gods...

I couldn't love his father's ghost. I couldn't survive it twice.

I won't.

I watched Andrew more than I intended as we continued, feeling the heat and something worse curling up under my ribs and burning something that had once been beautiful into something black and twisted.

We lost the gray horse first. The animal just suddenly dropped. We tried to revive it, Andrew pouring some of his precious water on the velvet muzzle, but it was too late. Its hide blistered as we watched though no flame touched it; steam hissed off the skin as if he'd poured water on iron. The horse's flesh smoked in the hot air, the heat sizzling the meat, the open dark eyes swelling and bubbling while we watched. We were forced to spread out what gear we needed between the remaining two horses and hurry on.

An hour later, I slipped to my knees and couldn't stand up. Damien grabbed my arm and hauled me up, but as soon as he let go, I went down again. Vestro knelt beside me. He put a hand to my forehead.

"Nadia?"

"I'm fine," I said, shaking my head. I coughed, my throat as dry as the sand at my knees. I looked up at Vestro as he stood, stepped back, and began unlacing his tunic. "What are you doing?"

"You need to ride," he said. "Here."

He handed me our water skin, and I drank from it. Too much. The skin was too light when I finally lowered it.

"Vestro," I rasped. "You can't. It's too much weight—"

"You don't have a choice, and the other horses can't handle it." He glanced at the men. "Can you look away..."

The men grunted and looked away, all except for Damien. His face was curious below lines of sweat as he stepped closer, watching with that blunt, appraising silence of his. Vestro glared at him, then shook his head and shucked off his pants. I stared wide-eyed at Vestro's bare skin as he bundled the clothes up and stuffed them into my bag, watching as the exposed skin on his shoulders and thighs reddened and almost began to blister immediately. I closed my eyes as he started to change, waiting for his scream, and involuntarily cringed when it finally came. A slimy muzzle bumped my shoulder, and I reached up and gave him a squeeze around the neck.

Damien hoisted me up onto Vestro's bare back, and I felt the wetness of his change soak through my pants so that the cloth stuck to my legs. Vestro whinnied and started off without waiting. The men hefted their gear and followed.

~

THE HUM in the sky above deepened until my skull throbbed.

Andrew staggered a few paces ahead, his gait uneven, one hand pressed to the side of his head as though he could hold himself together by will alone. His worsening cough tore raw through the shimmering air, leaving a smear of red across his knuckles when he wiped his mouth.

He stumbled again, his boot dragging through the sand. He caught himself on one knee, shaking, breath ragged. His hands wouldn't stay still. His fingers twitched and clenched, then opened as if he were fighting some unseen tremor.

"Andrew," I called out.

But he didn't acknowledge me.

I leaned forward and patted Vestro's neck so he would stop, and then dismounted.

I caught Andrew's arm before he pitched forward. His skin felt slick, fevered, and his eyes had that wild, unfocused sheen I'd come to dread. Not the desert. Not just thirst.

Tremors that ran deeper. Older.

He jerked his arm out of my grip. "I said I am... I am fine," his words rushed out. "Keep moving."

"You can hardly stand," I shot back. Anger mixing with concern. "You'll bring us all down with you at this pace. This isn't about your pride, Andrew. It's survival."

Andrew's jaw tightened, his teeth clenched so hard I thought they might crack. For a heartbeat he looked ready to spit fire, to drag himself through the sand just to prove me wrong.

Damien appeared at my side, his voice sharp and unkind. "You can't walk straight. How long until you start seeing ghosts?"

Andrew rounded on him with a flash of teeth, but the effort broke into a spasm that doubled him over, gagging into the sand. When he straightened, red stained his cracked lips.

I turned to Vestro. He had stopped a few paces back, watching, his pale eyes unreadable. He caught me staring and his ears went flat against his skull. He gave a subtle shake of his head.

The first faintest shiver of refusal he'd ever shown me.

"Please," my voice cracked. "I need your help. I can't lose him." My throat closed. "Not to this."

Andrew's head snapped toward me, fury blazing hotter than the disks above as he realized what I was asking. "No," his voice tore, raw. "I will not..."

Andrew's chest heaved as a coughing spell overtook him. He glanced at Vestro, and I saw the revulsion there. Though I wasn't sure if it was for Vestro, or his own weakness.

"Please," I whispered. "Do this for me. For us." I pressed both palms to his damp neck.

Vestro stilled, the tension in his shoulders coiling. Then his gaze flicked once to the satchel strapped across Andrew's chest. The one holding Cipher. He hesitated and then bowed his head in reluctant assent.

I clutched Andrew's arm. "Please, Andrew." I buried my face in his sweat-soaked tunic. "Let us help."

Andrew shut his eyes as a whole-body tremor ripped under his skin. Then, with a sound halfway between a curse and a sob, Andrew let me guide him forward. I lifted his arm across Vestro's back; Vestro's damp coat twitching beneath his weight. I mounted first, straddling Vestro's broad back and looked down at Andrew.

Vestro's hide shivered beneath me. I smoothed his coat down with long, soft strokes of my hands. Soothing him, calming him. His ears stayed flat, his gaze still fixed on Andrew. Slowly, grudgingly, he lowered himself to one knee.

Damien stepped forward and heaved Andrew up, dragging the king's trembling body across the Vestro's back behind me. Vestro staggered to all fours under the double weight. His muscles bunched, and foam flecked his lips, but he bore us without another complaint.

Andrew clung to my waist, silent, his tremors shuddering through both of us. He didn't look at me, or at Vestro.

Vestro carried us forward, in front of the other men, his hooves dragging through the sand. Every stagger shook through my legs. Andrew trembled behind me, clinging more than riding, his head pressed into my shoulder as his body continued to shatter. I whispered to both of them; nonsense and promises I needed to believe.

Anything to just keep us moving forward.

I shook my head and squinted my eyes, searching the sea of white sand.

The white sands glowed, as if illuminated from somewhere below. Nothing moved, and the landscape hadn't changed since we'd started through, save for several black rock outcroppings that had popped up in the last hour like ink drops on a newly pressed parchment.

If only I could use some of that ink and draw us a bit of shade. I won't be selfish, just a single oak that we can all fit under. Or a tent. Or my castle back home...

I licked my lips with a dry tongue and squinted against the glare of the sand. I sat up taller and kneed Vestro a few yards away from the group to get a better look. My breath caught in my throat.

"Rocks," I rasped. My throat was so raw the word barely made a sound.

Damien shaded his eyes. "Or mirage."

It didn't matter. If we didn't find shelter soon, we were all going to die anyway. I steered Vestro toward the shapes, each step another prayer that I my mind wasn't playing tricks on me.

Closer, the heat shimmered worse, turning the horizon to liquid, but the rocks held. And between them sprouted bushes. Green, impossibly green, alive.

We stumbled into the rocks like the last survivors of a battle, half-blind and staggering. Vestro's flanks heaved beneath me, each breath rattling through his body as if the desert itself had wrung him dry. Andrew clung behind me, his weight dragging at us both, his face pressed into my shoulder. The tremors running through him made each of Vestro's steps jolt and shiver.

Just a little farther. Just a few more steps.

I nearly fell off once as Vestro stumbled. He whinnied and struggled to stay upright. We'd only gone a few horse-lengths when he went down again, followed quickly by one of the other horses. It was all I could do to roll away with Andrew so that Vestro didn't land on us.

"Vestro," I said, crawling over the burning sand to his head. "Vestro?"

Vestro's dark coat was covered in large patches of thick white froth, and his chest rose and fell rapidly in deep, rattling wheezes. Foam bubbled from his mouth, and his pale eyes rolled around unfocused. I rubbed his cheek and used my cloak to wipe away at the froth on his muzzle. The sand stuck to the foam, and I struggled to wipe it from him.

"The gelding's dead," Damien said, walking over. He bent down and opened Vestro's mouth. Vestro's tongue was swollen behind his teeth. He shook his head. "He needs water and rest or..." He hesitated and glanced at me. "We need to get out of this heat."

I pushed on Vestro's neck and patted his chest. "Vestro, come on," I said. "You need to get up and change." I looked at Damien then quickly went back to Vestro. "Vestro, get up!"

Vestro whinnied and jerked his neck forward to roll to his feet, but the sand collapsed under his weight, and he fell back on his side. I grabbed onto his mane and leaned back, trying to pull him upright. He kicked his legs, spraying sand, and tried again. Damien and Darren went around to his other side and pushed as I pulled. We finally managed to get Vestro to his feet. He shook himself off and hung his head, his legs shaking beneath him.

"You need to shift," I said. I petted his face, kissed his nose.

Vestro snorted and started his change without waiting for us to turn around, which I took for a bad sign. A very bad sign, considering how he was usually so self-conscious about it. He cried out and dropped to all fours in the sand as he completed his change. I helped him dress as quickly as possible and covered his head with my cloak. The heat dried the slime on Vestro's skin to a flaky crust almost immediately. I used my cloak to wipe away as much as I could, but the act was more care than effective.

Vestro tried to stand and push me away, but his legs weak kept wobbling, and he couldn't get off his knees.

I turned around, searching for a hint of shelter and my heart dropped to my feet. We'd just found rocks. Not caves, or stone huts, or...anything. Just fucking rocks. I felt like I was going to cry. In fact, I think I was; my shoulders shook, and my chin trembled. It was just that all my tears were dried up because we were all so damn thirsty. I plopped down beside a clump of bushes growing out of the rocks. We made it all this way for nothing.

"Dammit!" I grabbed at the sagebrush next to me, jerking it out between the cracks in the rocks and flinging it away. "Piece of shit plant," I said. "If I can't live, then neither will you, you stupid—"

"Nadia."

I froze and turned to Darren. The squire hobbled over and fell to his knees beside me. He swallowed and pointed at the bushes.

"Bushes."

"They're just tiny bushes, Darren," I said. "There's not enough shade to..."

My breath caught in my throat, and I stood so I could inspect the plants more closely. The bushes grew in a cluster that followed a large crack in the rocks, their tiny, round leaves surprisingly green in the sizzling heat. I grabbed handfuls of branches and pulled, yanking them out roots and all. A line of darkness greeted me as I tossed them aside.

Yes! Where there's black, there must be shade, and where there's green there must be...

I pulled out several more bushes and stood back, admiring my pruning skills. The crack cut deeply through the rocks, maybe six feet long and almost three feet across. Plenty of room for me, should be fine for the men to squeeze through. I dropped a fist-sized rock through the opening. A moment later I heard a splash.

Water.

But how far down is it? I glanced back at Andrew and the others. *Only one way to find out.*

I swung my legs over the side and jumped.

I landed with a splash in a small thigh-high pool, and I sobbed from the shock. The cool water felt like ice against my sunburned skin. The water was fresh; it was a heavenly spring in the middle of this forsaken desert. The plunge hit me thigh-deep in the cold, I buried my face in it, drank until my stomach clenched, splashed it against my eyes, my neck, my burning skin.

The cave was small, and the pool covered half the floor, but there was enough wet sand around its edges for all of us to have space to lie down, and a few little alcoves that provided more ground space. I could just touch the low ceiling when I reached up and jumped.

I laughed, wild and broken, the sound echoing off smooth stone walls worn by centuries of flow.

We were going to be fine.

"Nadia?" Damien called.

I hurried back under the opening, standing in the thick ray of sunlight. I squinted up at him.

"Come down," I said. "There's water!"

Darren came through first. Then Corbin and Damien lowered Andrew down in a clumsy half-drop. He landed hard and I dragged him against me as his knees gave out. His lips were cracked, a smear of red staining them, and his hands wouldn't still.

Damien followed and immediately shoved a skin beneath the spring, filling it fast, while Corbin gulped water straight from his cupped hands. Darren sprawled against the wall, chest heaving, too tired to move. For a moment the cave was nothing but desperate gasps as the men drank like animals at a trough.

Vestro followed last, collapsing to all fours when he landed in the water pool. His skin steamed in the cave's cool air, the dried slime flakes falling off his arms. He didn't speak, didn't meet my eyes. Just crawled out of the water and braced a hand to the wall, head bowed, as his chest heaved with exhaustion like he'd poured out the last of himself.

Then Andrew swayed into me. His weight knocked the air from my lungs. I caught his shoulders, meaning only to steady him, but his legs folded, and he slid down into me, pulling me down to the ground.

"Andrew—" I tried to haul him upright, but his head dropped against my chest, his breath rattling against my collarbone. His hands clawed weakly at my cloak, jerking, trembling, unable to still.

The others froze. Damien's eyes flicked over, assessing, but he didn't speak. Corbin shifted his weight between his feet, muttered something about giving space, and turned back to the water. Darren looked lost.

Vestro hadn't moved from where he'd collapsed, still braced with his head bowed against the wall. But I saw the flex of his fingers against the stone, curling hard enough to whiten his knuckles, the muscle in his jaw tightening once before he stilled again. He didn't look at me. Or Andrew. Only the wall.

Andrew's body shuddered in my lap, every tremor jarring through me. His skin was slick, fever-hot, though the cave's shade was cool. His lips cracked with every rasp of breath, a smear of blood painting them dark. His hands wouldn't still; they clawed weakly at my cloak, twisting, clutching, then loosening only to grip again like a drowning man who refused to sink alone.

"Don't..." his voice tore in half, raw and childlike. "Don't let go. Nadia...please."

I pulled him tighter against me, whispering nothing, just breath, because I had no words that could make this better. My heart broke with every shiver of his frame. I'd loved him since we were children, loved the boy who had laughed and sparred and dreamed at my side. And here he was, stripped of crown and mask, unraveling into something raw and broken.

Tears burned the back of my eyes, but none would come. Not for me. Not for him. I bent my face to his hair and breathed him in; sweat, iron, the sour tang of old wine still clinging to his skin. This was not the king. Not the lover. Just the man beneath, and he was breaking.

"Nadia?" his voice cracked, then softened into something smaller. "Don't let go... don't let him..."

The words tangled, breaking apart, swallowed in a sob. Andrew whimpered again, body spasming in my arms. His eyes fluttered open, glassy and wild, not seeing me. His hand lifted weakly, fingers clawing at the air as though something hung just out of reach.

My chest crushed in on itself. To hear him this way, undone and slipping into shadows he couldn't fight off, was almost more than I could bear.

"I'm here," I whispered, clutching his hand tighter, even as tears stung hot in my throat. "It's me. I won't let go."

His lips trembled. "Please..." The rest dissolved into shuddering breaths, his whole-body quaking in my arms.

My arms ached. My entire body trembled with exhaustion, every muscle screaming to give out. I was so close to the edge I could taste the fragile, breathless space where tears wouldn't fall but lived hot and sharp behind my eyes. But I clung harder anyway. If I loosened even a fraction, Andrew would slip through me, and the shadow he'd fought his whole life to escape would claim him.

I lifted my gaze past him to Vestro. He stood in the half-shadow, his shoulders bowed, and eyes fixed on me as they swirled between obsidian and pale flesh. My heart broke all over again as the words formed on my tongue. He had already given so much, and here I was asking more of him without words. I knew it was too much, to have him see me like this, with Andrew crumbling in my arms, and ask him for help when I had nothing left to give.

So, I gave him the only thing I had left: a look that said, *Please. Help me.* A look that said the rest too, the words I couldn't speak: *I love him, too.*

Vestro crossed the wet sand and lowered himself behind me. His chest pressed against my back, steady and grounding, his legs bracing mine so I wouldn't topple under Andrew's weight. He said nothing, but the strength of him at my back steadied me as surely as if he'd wrapped me in his arms.

I leaned back against him, letting out a sigh of relief as my muscles unclenched and relaxed with his support.

Then, slowly, I felt it: his hand brushing my arm. Tentative. A question more than a touch.

My heart clenched. I turned just enough to see his face, and in the dim light caught his dark eyes. They shone now, not with defiance, but with tears. His lips twitched as though words wanted to break free, but instead he bent and pressed a single kiss into my hair, his breath hitching.

He was breaking, too, and still he held me up.

My free hand lifted, almost on its own, until my fingers found the curve of his cheek. Rough with exhaustion, damp with tears, and cool compared to Andrew's fever. I let my palm rest there, holding both men at once; Andrew's hand in one, Vestro's face in the other.

The cave went still around us, disturbed only by Andrew's broken murmurs at my front and Vestro's breath at my back. And me, caught between them, my love stretched so thin it felt like it might tear me apart.

Then Andrew lurched in my arms. His body seized, shoulders jerking, fingers clawing weakly at my cloak as if he were drowning and I the only scrap of driftwood in a storm. His cracked lips moved, words spilling in fragments.

"No more...no, stop..." his voice cracked into a sob, then rose in a raw, broken plea. "Father, I'll be good. I-I'm sorry, just..."

My blood ran cold. He wasn't here. He wasn't seeing me. He was trapped in some nightmare memory, begging ghosts I couldn't banish.

"Andrew," I whispered, shaking him, forcing my face into his line of sight. "It's me. Look at me. It's Nadia. You're safe."

But his eyes rolled glassy, unfocused, pupils blown wide. He sobbed again and pressed his forehead into my chest. "Don't let him...don't let..."

I held tighter, though my arms screamed and my chest ached. Every breath Andrew dragged sounded like it might be the last. My tears burned but would not fall.

Behind me, Vestro tightened his hold around my waist, his silent strength bracing me even as my own bones felt like they might splinter. I felt his heartbeat against my spine, steady and solid, a cruel counterpoint to Andrew's convulsions against my breast.

"Please," I whispered, not sure which of them I was begging. Maybe both. Maybe the saints I wasn't sure if I believed in anymore. "Please don't leave me."

Andrew only sobbed harder. Vestro held me tighter. And between the two of them, I broke silently, my heart pulled in pieces no one could mend.

Andrew gagged suddenly, his entire body seizing. I tightened my hold, but he convulsed harder, breath rattling wet in his throat. Panic shot through me.

Damien was there in an instant. He slid his hands under Andrew and rolled him gently off my lap and onto his side as Andrew retched, shifting away the weight that had nearly crushed me. With quick, practiced movements, Damien tugged off his cloak, rolled it into a thick bundle, and tucked it beneath Andrew's head so he wouldn't choke if he heaved again. Practical. Efficient.

I sagged forward, my empty arms trembling with relief. My hand still clung to Andrew's, but my eyes lifted and caught Damien looking past me. His gaze locked with Vestro's for the briefest breath as something passed silently between them.

Then Damien looked away, back to Andrew, before moving back to his side of the cave.

Exhaustion pulled me down, and I lay beside Andrew, curling into the curve of his body. My arm draped over his chest; my forehead pressed to the line of his shoulder. He was feverish, trembling still, but still alive, and I let myself anchor him, if only for this fragile night.

Behind me, Vestro shifted but kept his distance, as though waiting for me to choose.

My throat burned. I reached back without looking, fingers brushing and then grabbing his wrist. Then I pulled. A wordless plea.

Don't leave me. Don't make me do this alone.

He hesitated, just for a breath. Then he yielded, lowering himself to the sand behind me.

I lay folded between them; Andrew burning in front of me, Vestro steady at my back. My body acting as a fragile bridge between two tides pulling me apart.

Exhaustion blurred the edges of thought, dragging me under as my vision faded and everything went black.

THIRTY-ONE

The cave was dark when I woke, cooler now, the damp smell of stone and water mixing with the sour tang of sweat. My body ached everywhere, heavy with exhaustion. Andrew's chest rose and fell beneath my arm, each breath shallow and uneven, his skin fever-hot against my palm. Behind me, Vestro's warmth pressed close, steady as a wall at my back.

For a moment I stayed still, letting myself feel the strange, impossible peace of being held on both sides. Andrew burning in my arms, Vestro bracing me from behind. The rhythm of their breathing wrapped me in a fragile cocoon, and for the first time in days, my own heartbeat slowed.

I shifted slightly, pressing back into Vestro's chest. His breath stirred my hair, warm and steady, and I let myself sink into it. Into the safety that he'd always been. Into the knowledge that whatever had broken between us had not erased that truth. My hand slipped back, brushing his arm, and he stilled. Then, slowly, the tension bled from him. His presence curved around me, not possessive or demanding, just there, holding me up as he always had.

I realized then how much I'd missed him.

My eyes traced Andrew's face where it lay inches from mine. Sweat dampened his lashes and his lips were pale, yet even now there was something achingly beautiful about him. Vulnerable. Young. The mask of a king stripped away until he was only a man who'd carried too much. My thumb brushed lightly across his temple, chasing a damp lock of hair from his brow.

Caught between them, I felt the contradiction of my own heart; the comfort of Andrew's nearness and the safety of Vestro's steadiness. Neither alone filled the hollow in me. But together, for this fragile breath of time, I felt almost whole.

The thought slid through me like water through cupped hands. Impossible to hold, yet impossible to ignore. My mind tried to clutch at it, to shape it, but exhaustion blurred the edges. Was this constant stability saving me...or undoing me? Did leaning on their strength make me stronger, or weaker than I dared admit?

Andrew stirred. Even in sleep, his body sought mine. His arm dragged weakly around my waist, pulling me closer, his face burrowing into the curve of my shoulder as though he could shield both of us with that fragile embrace. My chest ached at the need in the gesture, stripped of his crown and command.

His lashes fluttered open, and his eyes were dazed and fever-bright, but they softened when they found me. Then as he shifted closer, his gaze slid over my shoulder. To Vestro.

His whole body went taut, the tremor of it rattling through me. Shame flickered in his expression. But before he could pull away, I caught his face in my palm. My thumb brushed across his lips, silencing the protest he hadn't voiced. I leaned forward and pressed a kiss to his brow, letting my lips linger on the salty taste of his skin. Grounding both of us.

"Stay with me," I whispered.

Then I turned slightly, not away from Andrew but toward the other weight at my back. My other hand lifted, slow and sure, until my fingers rested against Vestro's arm. My cheek followed, pressing my face against the solid line of his forearm.

"Please."

The air thickened. Andrew's jaw eased beneath my thumb, his body shuddering once before he yielded and pressed closer, his face turning into my hand as if to soak up my comfort. Behind me, Vestro's breath steadied, and he leaned into my touch, bracing my back. Neither pulled away. Neither denied me.

Nothing moved, save for the drip of water echoing somewhere in the dark, slow as a heartbeat.

But the longer I lingered, the more it ached. I hated the need that kept me tethered. Hated the way my strength frayed until it felt borrowed, drawn from them instead of born of me. If I stayed there, I would dissolve into it, lose myself in the quiet pull of two loves that could never be whole on their own.

I listened to the quiet, to the subtle shift of their breathing as exhaustion pulled them back under.

Carefully, I let my hand slip from Andrew's sleeping face, the crown of his head falling heavy against my arm. Andrew murmured in his sleep, clinging tighter in reflex, but I still managed to slip free from with slow, deliberate patience.

Behind me, I eased from Vestro's arm, feeling the faint tremor of his breath. Vestro shifted faintly, a restless twitch, though he didn't reach for me.

Perhaps he knew better. Perhaps he knew I needed the space.

The cool cave air pressed against my damp skin as I pushed myself upright. My legs protested, pins and needles waking in them as I stood. I swallowed the ache and moved carefully across the stoney ground so I did not disturb them further.

A flicker of orange danced ahead, too steady to be firelight, and I followed it. Damien sat with his back to the wall, his strange little flame cupped in one hand. The light painted the hollows of his face, his expression unreadable as always.

I sank down beside him, my heart still thudding from what I'd left behind. For a long time, neither of us spoke. The hush between us was easier than any words.

At last, Damien shifted the light, and its glow caught in his dark eyes. He didn't look at me, but the smallest crease pulled at the corner of his mouth. "Trouble sleeping?"

The question was dry, typical Damien practical. But something in his voice made it feel like an olive branch.

I pulled my knees to my chest, wrapping my arms around them, and stared at the wavering light in his hand. "Not trouble. Just... too much." My voice was barely a whisper.

Damien turned the light between his fingers. It wasn't flame, not truly — no wick, no scent of smoke. The glow lived inside a small metal case, steady and contained, burning without ash or hunger. The shadows it cast jittered along the walls, wrong and restless.

"That's the way of it," he said, almost to himself. "Too much, too long, and sooner or later something cracks."

I glanced at him. His profile was sharp in the glow, every angle of his face cut in firelight. For once, he didn't wear mockery like armor. There was something rawer there, something I hadn't seen before.

"You sound like you can relate," I said softly.

He didn't answer at first. Just let the glow dim, then flare again. Finally, his lips twisted into a half-smile. "I grew up learning cracks don't always mean weak stone. Sometimes it means something buried wants out."

Damien's eyes shifted then, catching mine in the glow. For a breath, I could have sworn the dark in them wasn't entirely human —something flickering, too dark, too sharp. Just like the night of the fire. But just as quick, it was gone, and he gave me his usual wry grin.

"Go on, Princess. Get some rest before you're the one falling to pieces."

But I didn't go. I sat, staring at him. Finally unafraid of the demon hunter enough to stare into his dark eyes and try to figure him out.

Damien eased his thumb off the wheel and the glow dimmed. He flicked it again, snapping the light back to life, pulsing like a heartbeat. He kept his gaze fixed on it when he spoke.

"You saw, didn't you."

The words prickled down my spine. I didn't answer, at least not out loud. But I knew without asking he was talking about his eyes.

His mouth curled, humorless. "You know, most people would've flinched. Reached for a blade. Crossed themselves or some other nonsense. You didn't."

The cave pressed close around us; cool stone at my back, the water's drip steady in the hush. I found myself whispering before I'd thought it through. "Why would I? I'm in love with one of them."

His eyes cut to me then, dark and glinting with something deeper. A silent acknowledgment.

"I'm not one of them," he said, voice low. "Not fully. Just enough to make priests piss themselves when they look at me." A thin smile tugged at his mouth. "An addition crept into my bloodline. A family legacy, courtesy of my grandfather."

A sudden, cold ball of steel settled deep into my stomach.

So, demons and humans can... breed?

Flashes of bare skin, ragged breath, and Vestro's lips against mine on the riverbank filled my vision.

Oh... fuck me.

I almost snorted out loud at my brain's poor choice of words.

Because Vestro already had.

Damien's eyes narrowed at the corners, like he'd caught something flicker across my face before I could bury it. The look came and went in a heartbeat, too quick to call out, but my hands still trembled as I closed my eyes to steady them.

"Odd line of work you chose, then," I said softly.

That earned a huff of laughter, dry and quick. At least he had the decency to let the subject slide.

"Isn't it? Guess I figured if I killed enough of them..." He flexed his knuckles, his eyes shifting back to shadow. "Doesn't work, though. Nothing ever scrubs it clean."

I swallowed hard. I wasn't sure how I felt about Damien's confession, or the knowledge that my stolen moments with Vestro may not have been as risk free as I'd hoped.

At the same time, I wasn't sure if it even really mattered.

Damien shrugged, the flicker of mirth gone as quick as it came. "Don't expect me to say more. But... it's easier when someone else sees and doesn't look away."

The light in Damien's palm flickered once more, then died as he snapped the metal lid shut, leaving us with only the hush of water and breath. I stayed there a moment longer, knees drawn up, before slipping back into silence. He didn't look at me again.

Weariness pulled at my body, but it wasn't from sleep; my mind was exhausted. Drained. I started to walk back to where Andrew and Vestro lay but then stopped to stare at the space between them.

Not wide. Not hostile.

Just... empty.

Andrew slept on his side, arm curled around nothing, his breathing finally heavy and even. The tremors were gone. His face looked younger and unguarded in a way that twisted something deep in my chest.

Vestro had shifted further away, his back braced against the wall and eyes were closed.

But I knew he wasn't asleep.

His breathing was too controlled and deliberate, the kind he used when he didn't want me to hear the strain beneath it. A faint twitch pulled at the skin near the corner of his eye with every slow exhale, subtle enough that no one else would have noticed. But I'd slept next to him long enough to sense the tremor below the surface. His fingers flexed once against the stone beside his hip, a restless little motion he'd never make in sleep.

He was awake and listening.

Waiting for something he didn't trust himself to look at.

The heat in the cave pressed against my skull until it felt like the stone itself was breathing down my neck. Suffocating. Andrew's snoring, the drip of water, Damien's incessant flicking of the wheel on his little light; all of it crowded my ears. I slipped into the narrow passage beside the spring before I realized I was moving.

Cooler air kissed the back of my neck. I braced one palm against the wall and closed my eyes.

Just one moment.

Then soft steps approached behind me.

I didn't need to look to know who it was.

Vestro had a way of arriving like a shift in air pressure. Subtle, heavy, and far too familiar. His warmth touched my spine before his hands did.

He didn't say my name.

Didn't ask if he could come closer.

He just slid an arm around me, slow and steady, gathering me in the way he always did after nightmares or fights, as if wrapping himself around me was years of baked-in muscle memory. His chest met my back, solid and grounding, the heat of him sinking into places the cold of fear hadn't left.

"You shouldn't walk off alone," he murmured.

My shoulders dropped without my permission, and I leaned into him.

"I'm not alone," I said tightly. "You followed me."

"You're shaking."

His breath moved through my hair, warm against the crown of my head. The rhythm of his chest pressed along my spine. His hand gently rubbed along my upper arm, more soothing than intimate.

Then his hand stilled, and his breath hitched.

He swallowed hard, the sound brushing my ear, and his hold tightened just a fraction. His forehead dipped, grazing the side of my temple as if he needed that touch to stay upright.

An alarm bell jingled in the back of my mind. Subtle, but present. It rang louder as his hands twitched against my arm.

"Vestro..." I whispered, a warning. Maybe.

He didn't pull back.

Instead, his body shifted around mine, instinctive, drawing me with him as he angled to face me. His arms loosened only to guide me gently into the curve of his chest, my hands landing on his ribs out of pure reflex.

The closeness had been innocent a breath ago.

Now it hummed.

His thumb brushed the inside of my elbow. A familiar gesture. A thousand times familiar. But my pulse jumped, and Vestro felt it— his breath shuddered across my cheek.

His nose skimmed the curve where my jaw met my neck, just enough contact and just long enough for the world to tilt. His hand came up and cupped my cheek with the softest, most terrified reverence.

I pulled in a breath to steady myself and tipped my chin up to meet him.

He stole that breath with his mouth.

For a heartbeat, I froze in the warmth of him; the scent of dust and rain falling on wildflowers, the tremor in his lips against mine, and the faint rasp of his breath catching in his throat.

Then he deepened the kiss. His mouth shaped against mine with the kind of hunger he'd never let out before.

Then sense slammed into me.

I jerked back, my breath punching out of my chest as our lips parted. His hands released me instantly, like I'd burned him.

His eyes were wide, wrecked, panic flickering beneath the surface; like he knew exactly what he'd done and exactly why he shouldn't have.

"I can't," I whispered, voice shaking.

Vestro's face stripped bare, like he'd handed me some trembling, fragile part of himself and watched me drop it. Then the stoic mask slammed back into place.

A voice cut the air behind us.

"Well," Damien drawled from the mouth of the alcove, "this seems like an ill-timed moment to explore new and inventive ways to self-destruct."

I flinched. Vestro went motionless.

Damien arched a brow. "Your king is awake. And calling for you. Which, shockingly, is the only reason I'm interrupting whatever this was."

I stepped away from Vestro completely. "Is he worse?"

Damien's expression softened a fraction. "No. Just weak. And aggressively clingy."

I started to walk past him.

Damien turned to Vestro. "Not your turn."

Vestro's jaw flexed once.

I ignored him and rounded the corner to find Andrew sitting with his back propped against the cave wall. His eyes were closed and his head resting back.

I let my boot scuff against the rock as I neared. Letting him sense me before I approached.

His eyelids cracked open, pupils unfocused but searching.

"Nadia," his voice rasped, raw but not broken.

I knelt beside him and touched his face. His skin was still too cool, his cheekbone sharp under the smudge of dried sweat, but the tremor in his hands had faded to a faint flicker. He didn't pull from my touch—but he didn't lean into it either.

Classic Andrew: pretending he's fine while very much not.

"I am not fragile," he muttered, voice low. His jaw tightened once. Twice. The tremor in his fingers stilled.

Only then did he look at me fully.

His eyes were clearer than I'd seen them in years. The striking blue bloodshot at the edges, but alive. The way he looked at me... gods, it hit like a blow. His softened pride wrapped in something that felt dangerously close to relief.

"You stayed," he said. "All night."

A truth he needed to anchor himself to.

"You needed me," I said quietly. "And I care."

His throat worked at that. He shifted his weight again, pulling his legs beneath him. His breath hitched once, but he masked it by running a shaking hand through his hair.

Damien hovered nearby, watching with the patience of someone waiting for the danger to clear so he could mock it later. I'd come to realize that was his way of dealing with stress.

"You're pale," I murmured.

Andrew huffed, a ghost of a scoff. "I have been worse."

He blinked hard, grimaced, and pressed his palm harder into the stone, the muscles in his forearm flexing as he pushed to stand. His knees wobbled. My hand shot out to steadying him.

He stiffened but didn't move away.

For a heartbeat, his forehead dipped toward mine, breath brushing my cheek. Something in him softened, just enough for me to feel the warmth under all that pride.

"I am fine," he said again, quieter. And then, even quieter: "Just... stay close."

I slid an arm around his back and helped him rise fully. His weight leaned into me, warm and solid. *Human.* His shoulder brushed mine as he adjusted his balance, his breath tightening for a moment before smoothing out.

The tremor eased completely.

"See?" he murmured. "Standing."

A quiet smile tugged at my mouth.

Andrew reached up—slowly, as if testing his steadiness—and his fingers brushed my cheek. His thumb glided along my skin, warm and careful, tracing the line beneath my eye. It was tender, familiar, achingly gentle.

Then he leaned in. But not to kiss me.

Just to breathe me in.

His nose slipped into my hair, nuzzling lightly at the crown of my head—an intimate gesture he only used when he was letting his guard down completely. His breath feathered across my ear. His fingers lingered along my jaw, tracing me like I was something precious.

And my body didn't answer.

I felt the steady, comforting presence of a man who trusted me with the pieces of himself he didn't show the world.

But there was no ache.

None of the breathless gravity I felt when Vestro stepped too close or said my name like it mattered.

Just loyalty and friendship wrapped in tenderness.

And that hurt more than anything.

I swallowed hard, the sound tight in my throat, as Andrew's hand drifted to the back of my neck. His thumb stroked the place where my pulse beat fastest. I leaned into him automatically out of habit and duty as the promise I'd made pressed like a weight across my ribs. I had said the words; meant them when I said them.

But now?

My heart didn't lean forward with him.

It stayed behind in the shadowed alcove where Vestro's touch still lingered like a bruise beneath the skin I couldn't rub off.

Andrew didn't seem to notice my hesitation. He was too busy reclaiming himself, straightening his shoulders, grounding his stance. His spine lifted as his king's posture settled over him as his armored mask slid back into place. He took a breath, tested his balance, and nodded once.

"That's enough rest."

He stepped forward toward the small, reflective pool where Corbin and Darren waited on the other side, and I fell into stride beside him.

A flicker tugged at the back of my awareness.

I looked over my shoulder.

Vestro stood near the alcove wall, watching us. His arms hung rigid at his sides, shoulders tight, something unreadable set into his posture.

Damien came up to stop beside us, his expression unreadable as ever. He eyed Andrew, then me, then the silent space behind us.

"Lovely," he said dryly. "Everyone's pretending nothing happened."

Andrew looked at him, confused. A faint crease formed between his brows, like he knew he'd missed something important and didn't know why.

Damien didn't elaborate. He walked ahead, clicked his teeth at the squires, and flicked two fingers toward the cave opening. "Up. Now."

Corbin and Darren exchanged a look—equal parts dread and resignation—before stepping toward the wall. Their boots scraped against the damp stone, and they moved into position beneath the opening as if this were just another miserable task in a long line of them.

The ledge was too high for anyone to reach alone, the stone slick with moisture from the spring.

Vestro crouched beneath the rock face and locked his hands together, bracing one shoulder to the wall. He set his stance, the muscles coiling beneath skin already drawn tight with exhaustion. He looked at Damien and nodded.

Damien stepped into his grip.

Vestro straightened in one smooth, powerful motion. For a heartbeat, it looked effortless. Damien rose fast enough to grunt in surprise as his fingers caught the stone lip. He hauled himself over the ridge and vanished into the pale wash of moonlight above.

A moment later, Damien leaned back over the edge, one arm extended.

"Next."

Darren went first. Still shaken, eyes a little too bright. He stepped into Vestro's hands, boots slipping once on damp stone. Vestro adjusted without a word and drove upward, lifting him in a controlled surge. Damien caught Darren's forearms and dragged him through the opening.

Corbin followed. He hesitated, then stepped in heavier, clumsier. His boots scraped as Vestro reset his grip, fingers flexing once before he lifted again. The movement wasn't as clean this time. Vestro's breath hitched, a low sound in his chest, and his shoulders trembled as he pushed Corbin high enough for Damien to grab him.

Damien hauled Corbin over, boots thudding on stone above.

Vestro stayed where he was, hands still locked, chest rising and falling harder now. A sheen of sweat caught the faint lantern light along his brow despite the cold. He rolled one shoulder, slow, like it burned.

I looked over at Vestro. "You ready to go then?"

Vestro looked at me solemnly, his black eyes steady. He worked his jaw several times before answering me. "Not really. But it's not like I have a choice, do I?"

I smiled at him and shook my head. "Not at this point."

He looked past me, and his face went hard. A little dimple between his eyebrows appeared.

"Ves?" I said. "Ves, what is it?"

Andrew stepped up behind me, his eyes wary. Vestro moved past us to the back of the cave and started digging with his hands at a section of the sand that had been disrupted by the men's footprints. I knelt behind him and leaned over his shoulder. His fingers scooped away handfuls of sand, revealing a thin cylindrical object that looked like it was made of wax, yellowed with age. He grabbed the edge of the object, pulled unsuccessfully, then went back to digging.

"Is that part of a candle?" I asked. "It looks kind of big..."

"Not a candle," he said. His face was studious as he jerked the object free. "And with what's ahead of us I don't think I could find one with a big enough barrel."

I came around the side as he brushed away the pebbles and sand clinging to the surface and attempted to claw away some of the wax. The thing was close to three feet long. It was only a few inches around at one end but sloped to more than double the width at the other end, as if it was molded around something. I reached around his arm and touched the yellow material. Definitely wax.

"So, what is it?" I asked.

"Right now, nothing. But if I can get it work...a weapon."

"A weapon? What kind of weapon?"

Vestro managed to break off a large chunk at the thicker end, revealing a small section of black tube.

I blinked. *A tube like The Holy soldier's weapons.*

What did Damien call it? A gun.

Andrew's hand tightened on my arm.

"It just might," Vestro mumbled. "The cave is cool enough, and the cosmoline is still completely sealed, keeping out the rust..."

"Ves?"

"Don't worry about it," he said. He stood up, hefting the wax chunk, and held out his hand to help me to my feet. "It's been a long time. It probably won't work anyway."

"So...why are you still carrying it?" I asked, crossing my arms.

He chewed on his lip, his eye twitching. "I'd just like to hang on it for a little while," he said. He glanced at Andrew and then away. "Just in case."

"Princess."

I looked up to see Damien watching us from the cave opening.

He nodded at me. "Your turn."

I moved to go next. Both Andrew and Vestro stepped in to help at the same time. For a breath too long, they just stared at each other across the narrow space, shoulders brushing, neither willing to yield.

Then Vestro dropped to one knee, offering his leg as a step. He clasped his hands together, palms up, ready to lift. Andrew steadied my elbow as I climbed onto Vestro's thigh. For that moment I felt them both beneath me—one bracing, one guiding as they lifted—before Damien's hand closed around mine and pulled me up the rest of the way.

I straightened and took a long breath of the mild evening air. I looked down to my right and grimaced where the dead gelding still lay, the horse's coat singed and dry from the hours spent in the brutal sun. A weak sound behind us brought attention around, and I

402

was amazed to see our last horse curled up in the bushes, weak and burned but still alive.

Below, the men lingered. Vestro stayed crouched, hands still clasped, the unspoken offer clear. Andrew stood over him, chest rising, pride taut across his jaw.

The silence stretched. Too long.

Damien's voice drifted down, smooth as silk and sharp as glass. "Well, ladies. Someone's going to have to be on top here. Shall I flip a coin?"

The effect was immediate. Andrew's shoulders stiffened; Vestro winced. Without a word, Andrew planted his boot in Vestro's clasped hands, one hand gingerly braced on his should for balance. Vestro grunted and lifted him up, and Damien caught Andrew's arm to drag him over the lip. Damien leaned back down as Vestro tossed up the wax-covered object.

I drew in a breath and glanced down.

Vestro still stood at the cave floor, alone now, surrounded by nothing but the quiet pool of dim light and the wet drip of the cave.

He rolled his shoulders once, maybe to loosen stiff muscles, maybe to brace himself. His chest lifted on a slow breath. Then he jumped and reached for the ledge.

His hand found the edge, slipped, and he dropped. He caught himself with a hand braced flat against the ground. His other knee hit the sand with a dull thunk.

"Damn," he muttered under his breath.

Andrew heard it. His stance shifted beside me, barely perceptible by just a tightening in the line of his spine. Then he moved toward the edge, dropping to a crouch to watch from a better angle.

Vestro crouched and jumped again, caught the edge, and began to haul himself up. Then his right hand slipped. A raw, unguarded sound left him as his fingers scrabbled for purchase on the sharp stone. He didn't look up. Not once. The exhaustion he'd been hiding since the desert finally broke through.

Damien crouched beside Andrew. "Give him a hand before pride kills him."

"I don't need—" Vestro started, voice low.

Andrew's hand shot down toward him, open and solid.

Vestro didn't take it. He tried again. His teeth clenched and muscles trembling harder now.

"Vestro," I breathed.

His eyes flicked up at the sound of his name—just once, just long enough for me to see how much it cost him to stay upright. He reached for leverage. A sharp rock edge bit across his forearm. His breath hissed.

Andrew's hand stayed extended, steady, unmoving. "Take it," he said, his voice stripped of challenge for the first time. Aware.

Vestro's jaw tightened. He looked at Andrew's hand. Then at me. For a heartbeat, I thought he'd refuse.

Then, reluctantly and painfully, he lifted his hand and gripped Andrew's forearm.

Andrew pulled hard, bracing with his legs, hauling Vestro upward. Damien leaned forward and grabbed the back of Vestro's tunic and pulled, guiding him over the last jut of stone. Vestro collapsed onto the ledge beside us, and his breath shuddered once in his chest. He covered it quickly and rolled to his knees. His shoulders stayed rigid, and eyes fixed on the ground. Blood dripped from the scrape across his arm.

I stepped toward him without thinking.

Vestro didn't look at me, but he shifted a fraction back—so small no one else would've noticed. It struck me like a blow. That tiny retreat hurt more than it should have.

Andrew straightened, dusting rock from his palms. He glanced at the blood on Vestro's hand, then at me. His breath paused, just a fraction, before he looked away. He didn't speak, but something unreadable flickered through his eyes.

Damien rose, brushing dirt off his knees. "Perfect. Now that everyone's pride is properly bruised, can we move on?"

THIRTY-TWO

We didn't speak when we left the cave.

The last of the heat clung low to the sand, rising in shimmering sheets that brushed our boots as we crossed the open flats. The moon hung low in the purple sky above us, the first promise of night finally loosening the desert's grip.

Andrew walked ahead, his shoulders squared and stubborn as ever. But his steps held, and he didn't stumble again. Though I still stayed close enough to catch him if he did. And I knew he pretended not to notice.

Behind us, Vestro matched our pace without ever drawing near. His presence hovered steadily at my back, close enough to feel, but far enough to ache.

We crossed the ridge line just as the air cooled, the dunes giving way to cracked earth and low brush. Ahead, the land shifted again as rows of dark shapes rose in the distance, evenly spaced like old-world plantings left to overgrow. The trees formed long, straight columns stretching into the shadows, their trunks aligned in a way nature never arranged on its own. Like the remnants of a forgotten orchard.

The others slowed as the canopy thickened. Corbin sagged against the nearest trunk. Darren nearly folded where he stood. Damien muttered something under his breath and knelt to check his boots.

Andrew kept walking deeper along one of the ancient rows, past where the others' voices faded, as if the orderly spacing, the rhythm of trunk after trunk after trunk, helped to steady him. He disappeared a few paces in, into the cool dimness of the grid.

I followed without thinking.

The scent shifted as moss and damp leaves replaced the desert's dryness. The neat orchard rows gradually dissolved into wild pines and undergrowth. Cool air threaded through the trees, slipping into my lungs like a long drink of water after days of heat. The canopy thickened with every step, the world dimming to a muted green, and the forest swallowed our sounds one by one: the crunch of sand giving way to soft earth, the rasp of our breath dissolving into needles and loam, even the whisper of our clothing dampened by the heavy air. It felt as if we were being drawn into the lungs of the forest itself, pulled into a hush older than the orchard we'd passed through.

Andrew reached a fallen log beneath a thick cedar and stopped. He sat heavily, bracing his elbows on his knees for a moment as he caught his breath. I stayed beside him, the hush of the forest settling around us.

Then he leaned back and stretched his legs out, boots braced against a thick root and pulled two yellow pears from his satchel. The skins glowed pale gold in the moonlight, each dotted with tiny brown freckles.

My breath caught.

He must've picked them on the way in.

"Where..." I started.

"Found a few trees near the ridge. I saved them for us." He shrugged, casual. "I figured you would be hungry."

Hungry was an understatement. And the simple thoughtfulness hit me harder than it should have.

He took a bite from one, juice slipping down the corner of his mouth, then patted the spot beside him. "Join me?"

I moved before thinking, settling next to him with my knees brushing his thigh. He wasn't subtle about the little smile that earned him.

"Hand it over," I said, reaching.

"My arm does not bend that far, Princess."

I rolled my eyes and leaned closer until my shoulder brushed against. He grinned like he'd planned that. The pear's sweet scent drifted up, green and delicate, soft enough to make my mouth water before I even touched it. I snatched the pear, ignoring the way his gaze warmed as I bit into it.

Gods, it was ripe. Sweet enough to make my vision blur for a moment.

We ate in silence.

The good kind.

Almost.

Because underneath it, something inside my chest felt thin. Fragile. Like I was sitting where I'd always sat with Andrew... but my shape no longer fit there the way it used to.

"Feeling better?" I asked. The words came out soft. Too soft.

He flicked his pear stem with a thumb. "You were right. I drank too much." He gave me a crooked, reluctant smirk. "Do not revel in it."

"I'm not."

"You want to," he said, nudging my knee with his. "You get this righteous look when you are right about something. It is unbearable."

I huffed a laugh and nudged him back. The warmth was there... but only warmth. No pull. No heat. Just care and history, settling quietly between us.

He must have sensed the seriousness because his voice dropped into his familiar teasing drawl. "Though once we are married, I can give you plenty of things to be self-righteous about. Preferably in bed."

I shoved his shoulder. "You're impossible."

"And you like it."

Once, that comment would've sent a flutter through my stomach.

Now, there was only the hollow ache of the space where something used to live.

The pear suddenly felt too sweet in my hand.

My pulse stuttered at the soft crunch of leaves behind us.

Vestro emerged from the trees without care, boots dragging softly through the needles, shoulders sagging with exhaustion. Sweat clung to his throat, the scrape on his arm still raw. He looked up—and went utterly still.

He took in the sight of us on the log—close, easy, fruit in hand— and something shuttered behind his eyes. His head dipped, not quite an apology, and he started to back away.

"Vestro," I said quickly. I swallowed what was in my mouth and lifted my half-eaten pear. "You should eat."

His eyes flicked to mine—brief, sharp, almost startled—then to the pear. His throat worked once, like the offer hurt more than hunger.

"It's fine," he said quietly.

"Ves... it isn't." I stood and pushed my half-eaten pear toward him. "Take it. Please."

For a heartbeat, I thought he'd refuse.

Then his stomach betrayed him with a low, involuntary sound.

He froze, shoulders tight, something sharp flickering across his eyes. Then he stepped forward and took it from my hand. His fingers brushed mine. Careful yet deliberate.

Andrew watched with an unreadable calm and a tightness in his shoulders that hadn't been there a moment ago.

Then, slowly, deliberately, he held out his own pear.

"Here," he said, his tone calm and generous in the way that made my chest ache. "You need it more than I do."

A peace offering. Or a claim. Maybe both.

Vestro hesitated, visible tension rippling down his spine. But he accepted it. His fingers were careful not to touch Andrew's.

"Thank you," he said.

Andrew nodded once, gracious and composed.

Vestro stepped back under the trees, devouring the fruit like he hadn't eaten in days. Because I knew he hadn't.

Andrew leaned back beside me, shoulder brushing mine. "See?" he murmured. "It doesn't have to be a war."

I forced a small smile. *For now.*

Andrew rose from the log, brushing bark from his palms. Then he reached for me, and his hand slid to the back of my neck, warm fingers threading into my hair as he tugged me gently forward.

"Come here," he murmured.

His forehead dipped to mine, and before I could think, his lips pressed softly against my mouth. Warm and familiar.

A kiss meant to steady, not claim. And I let him.

Because he needed it.

Because I had promised.

Andrew's thumb stroked the side of my jaw. He breathed against my lips, relieved, almost tender. Almost the way it had been days ago, before everything shifted.

My heart didn't move.

But something behind Andrew did.

The faint rustle of boots over leaves.

Andrew pulled back, his smile small and hopeful, unaware of the way my world was cracking open inside my ribs.

I glanced past Andrew's shoulder.

Vestro stood between the cedar trunks, half in shadow, the pear in hand. He wasn't eating it. He wasn't even holding it right; just letting it hang from his fingers as if he'd forgotten it existed.

His shoulders were locked, spine too straight, like he was holding himself together by force alone.

His gaze flicked from Andrew's hand in my hair. To my mouth. To my eyes.

Something inside him seemed to break in the space of a breath.

He turned in a quiet pivot of surrender, walking into the shadows without a sound.

"Nadia?" Andrew brushed my cheek, steady, warm. "You okay?"

I swallowed. "I... yes."

But my heart had already lurched in the direction Vestro had gone.

And I stayed rooted exactly where honor demanded I remain.

THIRTY-THREE

The shade of the trees should have been a relief after the burn of mirrored sands, but instead the forest closed over us like a damp shroud of depression. The trunks stood too close together, their bark slick with mold as if we'd stepped into the throat of something alive. No breeze stirred the canopy. No birds sang. The heavy silence pressed down unnaturally, as if even the insects had fled.

The ground was soft with rot, yet it gave no smell of life. Only mildew, iron, and a faint sweetness that made the back of my tongue ache. Each step sank us deeper into gloom where the last scraps of sunlight fractured into patches, sliding across us in bars like the beams through a dungeon grate.

The rest of the day passed quickly as we moved through the mildewed forest, the sun passing overhead and sinking in the west. The dying light filtered through the thick trees in thinning patches, so that each man passed in and out of darkness, disappearing and reappearing in random patterns. No one spoke, other than a few grunts and short orders to change directions or pick up the pace.

Damien led the way, an arrow nocked in his bow, followed closely by a sullen Darren.

I glanced down at Vestro from the stallion's back and felt unease curl low in my gut. His stride was steady, but sweat slicked his throat despite the cool shade, and his skin looked pale beneath the trees.

I closed my eyes and drew a slow breath, searching for something familiar to anchor me. Damp wood. Mud. Pine sap. I listened for birds, for wind in the branches—anything living enough to break the tension coiling through my chest.

The forest was quiet. Too quiet...

I opened my eyes and searched through the growing darkness and the black spaces between the trees. Eyes stared back through the darkness. Red eyes. They grew larger as a scream built in my throat.

"Watch out!"

Something barreled into me, driving me to the ground. The air was knocked out of my lungs as a heavy weight landed on my back. Strong arms wrapped around my waist and rolled me away as a pair of silver claws as long as my forearm smashed into the earth beside me. I twisted my head around. Vestro lay on top of me, his shoulders guarding my face and neck. He gave me a quick nod, then jerked me to my feet. Four crimson lines slashed diagonally across his face, dripping blood onto his collar. He stepped in front of me.

"Stay in the light."

I pulled my sword free from its scabbard with a shaking hand and looked around. Everyone crouched in a circle of light, keeping as far away from the edges as possible. I shared a light patch with Andrew and Vestro. Damien and Darren were each in their own little illuminated spot. I couldn't see Corbin anywhere. I stared into the shadows. Nothing. I whipped around, looking everywhere. Still nothing.

"Vestro, what—"

"Shut up!" he hissed.

Vestro stepped closer to the edge of light, his body tense and rippling. I could almost see the waves of energy rolling from him; it crawled over my skin like a swarm of angry ants. I shivered. Vestro hesitated, then lifted a hand and stretched his fingers toward the darkness. Andrew dismounted and stepped up beside me, his sword held tightly in both hands. I held my breath as Vestro's fingers passed the edge of the light and into the shadow.

A piercing shriek tore through the darkness. I dropped to my knees, hands clamping over my ears as the sound knifed straight through my skull. Cold air ripped across the clearing, sharp and sudden, numbing my fingers and nose.

Vestro jerked as if something invisible had struck him. A searing red line flared through the dark—too straight, too precise—and his hand snapped back with a sharp cry, the smell of scorched flesh wafting through the air.

Andrew swore and hauled me closer, dragging me toward the center of the circle and lifting his sword higher.

Red eyes blinked from the shadows, circling us once before vanishing as quickly as they'd appeared.

I took a shuddering breath and scuttled over to Vestro. He was crouched down with his hand between his knees, his arm trembling. I squatted beside him, rocking on the balls of my feet. His lips were pulled tight in a grimace.

"What happened?" I asked. I frowned when he nodded his head in a stiff jerk. I wasn't impressed. "Can I see?"

Vestro looked at me, his eyes swirling with the milky color of dead flesh. Power seeped out of him like steam from a boiling kettle. It was the energy I always felt right before he shifted. I leaned back on my heels. Vestro opened his mouth, then shook his head and lifted his hand. The tips of two fingers were deep red, the skin shredded until all that was left was a stringy pulp. Blood dripped freely in tune with his heart in fat drops, plunking to the ground with an audible splat.

"Oh, gods!" I grabbed at my cloak, bunched it around his hand, and squeezed to stop the pressure.

Vestro yelled and tried to push me away, but I wrapped my legs around him so that I stuck to his arm like a leech. I knew that he could have easily peeled me away if he'd really wanted to, but not without hurting me.

"Hold still, Vestro," I said. "I need to stop the bleeding."

"Damn it all to hell," Andrew said. "What else can go wrong?"

"What else can go wrong, he asks," Vestro chuckled. All heads turned to him. He shook his head. "First off, night is coming. Second, that's an android out there."

"What's an *an-droid?*" Darren asked from his patch of light. He shifted uneasily, looking out at the shadows.

"What are you saying?" Andrew asked.

Vestro looked over his shoulder. "I'm saying, King, that your mission's been royally fucked."

"You seem to know an awful lot about what's waiting for us," Andrew growled, his voice low. "Yet somehow you never mention any of it until we're already bleeding." His sword lifted toward Vestro's throat. "What exactly are you playing at?"

I froze. The air thickened.

Vestro didn't move. Didn't flinch. He just stared at Andrew with a tired and fed-up expression.

"If you'd been paying a half-fuck's attention instead of pretending to lead and drink yourself stupid," Vestro said slowly. "You'd have seen the signs long before now."

Andrew tightened his jaw. "Do *not* speak to me in such a manner. I am—"

"A *what?*" Vestro snapped. "A *king?* As if any of this feudalistic bullshit is real."

"Enough!" I yelled and stood between the two. I glared at Andrew until he lowered his sword, then turned to a blank-faced Vestro. "So, we're all going to die, is that it? It's one monster, Vestro. We can handle it. We've been through so much worse than this already. Just tell us how to beat it."

"You can't kill it," he said. "I told you, it's an android, not a monster. It's not like the flesh-born creatures we've been fighting off along the way, or even like that hybrid worm. This is much worse. Old, powerful, and smart."

"So, what is it?" I said. "And why do you say we can't beat it?"

"It's a machine." Vestro hesitated and glanced at us. He sucked on his fingers and looked away. "The androids were made to protect Ferrington Pass from intruders. Old-world constructs. They're made of metal and wires, they...you can't just shoot them with arrows."

Andrew scoffed. "Machines don't exist. They're stories told to frighten children into obedience."

Vestro closed his eyes for half a second, like he was deciding whether Andrew was worth the effort. When he opened them, his irritation was sharp and unhidden.

"Andrew," he said flatly, "it's standing ten paces away in the dark. It nearly took my fingers off."

His gaze flicked to the shadows.

"You can debate bad nursery tales later. Right now, we need to not die."

Andrew went still.

His gaze slid to the treeline. The silence. The way nothing moved.

"Like the worm," he said quietly.

He looked back at Vestro, something sharp and focused settling behind his eyes. His hand tightened on his sword.

He nodded once. "How do we stop it?"

"You don't." Vestro's voice stayed steady, but impatience chewed at the edges. "They don't tire. They don't hesitate. They follow their orders until whatever they're hunting hits the ground."

Andrew lifted his chin, bristling. "And you just... know this."

Vestro exhaled through his nose and rubbed his forehead with his good hand. "Because I've seen them do it before."

Silence snapped tight.

Vestro froze, as if he realized what he'd said a second too late. His jaw worked once, like he wanted to pull the words back but couldn't.

Andrew's eyes narrowed, breath coming sharp. "Go on," he said, his temper winding up.

Vestro grimaced and shook his hurt fingers, spattering blood on the front of his tunic. "They were built to be invisible. Slip in, kill the target, vanish. That's it." He wiped his hand on his thigh, frustration leaking through. "They don't hit us in the light because their sensors don't read clean there. Too much interference. In the dark, they can see heat, movement, pulse—everything. They wait because that's when they're accurate."

He stopped abruptly, like he'd realized he'd already said more than he meant to.

Andrew swore and turned away, shoving a hand into his saddle-bag. He pulled out the satchel holding Cipher and swung it over his head, settling the strap across his chest. He bent and picked up a rock, and then hurled it into the growing darkness, screaming out obscenities.

The android in the shadows shrieked, like fingernails scraping against glass. The stallion screamed, and Andrew fought to keep him under control. I looked around in horror at our little haven of dimming light.

One thing was certain; night was coming, and if Vestro was right about the so-called androids, we didn't have much time before our little haven disappeared.

I glanced at Vestro. He'd pulled the strange lump of wax off the saddle and was clawing away at it, shaking his head and mumbling to himself as he tossed away chunks of wax.

"If I could only figure out how to melt the cosmoline, maybe I could get this damn thing to work..."

The patch of sunlight where we stood was not more than ten feet across and steadily shrinking. My throat tightened, as if the android already had its shadowy claws about my neck, squeezing the life out of me. My breath came in short, hurried puffs as I looked back at Vestro. He was shaking his head.

"...then again, I don't even know if it's loaded."

Don't panic, don't panic.

"Vestro!"

The android charged the barrier, and the stallion bolted. The horse jerked the reins from Andrew's hands and passed into the shadows, and the android attacked before the hindquarters had passed out of the light. A red beam of light tore through the horse's throat, decapitating it in a single sweep. The body buckled over and rolled, thumping to the ground in the shadows. Dark blood seeped through the grass toward Damien and Darren, and they gingerly stepped aside from the snaking trail.

Vestro grabbed my shoulders and spun me to face him. His eyes were feral, breath coming too fast, his grip tight enough to hurt. I sucked in a sharp breath and tried to pull back. But he didn't let go. Instead, his gaze cut past me to Andrew.

"When I say go," he said, voice clipped and brutal with urgency, "you run. As fast as you can."

He jerked his chin toward the trees. "We're less than a league from the forest edge.

Cross the barrier into the pass and you'll be out of reach. The android guards the forest; it can't leave its borders."

"Vestro," I said, my voice breaking. "What are you going to do?"

His grip tightened for half a second, pain flashing sharp and unmistakable.

"Do as I say," he said. "Or you're going to die."

I was crying. I didn't remember starting, but suddenly my cheeks burned with hot tears, and I couldn't see as I tore free of his grip and threw my arms around him.

Vestro crushed me to his chest, rubbing his cheek against the crown of my head.

I felt his rapid heartbeat against my neck. And that terrified me because I knew he was scared. Vestro kissed my cheeks and forehead, then he cupped my cheeks with both hands and kissed me. Hard.

His lips trembled against mine before he pulled back, his expression stripped bare and grim. He looked past me at Andrew and nodded once, tight-lipped.

Andrew's eyes cut to us, white and feral in the thinning light. For a heartbeat, the fury on his face was more dangerous than the android waiting in the forest.

I shook my head. "Vestro, what about you?"

Vestro ignored me. "Take her."

Andrew wrapped an arm around my waist and dragged me toward the eastern edge of the light. I dug my heels into the dirt, panic flooding cold through my veins.

"Vestro!" I screamed when he didn't look at me. "What about *you?*"

Vestro glanced over his shoulder at me; there were tears in his eyes. "Run fast, my princess."

"No!"

"Run!"

Andrew seized my wrist and yanked me forward. I screamed as we plunged into shadow, bracing for impact, for pain, for whatever waited beyond the edge of the light.

The creature shrieked.

The sound ripped through my skull, splitting thought from fear. My vision blurred as red eyes flared ahead of us in the dark.

Time slowed.

Something exploded out of the trees and slammed into the metal shape, knocking it violently off course. The ground bucked beneath my feet, dirt leaping as the impact thundered through the clearing.

I stumbled, dragging in a harsh, panicked breath.

Vestro.

Andrew ran along the path through the trees, dragging me along. I tried to look back, tried to twist around as I ran, but Andrew kept a good hold of my wrist, forcing me on. Probably afraid I'd try to turn and go fight. Though I had no urge to come across that nightmare again, I would have gladly slipped from his hand and gone running back for Vestro.

"Don't stop!"

I turned to see Damien and Darren suddenly materialize out of the darkness behind us. They ran full out, stumbling in their haste to reach us. They waved us forward as they neared and didn't stop as they rushed past.

"Look out," Damien yelled, "behind you!"

The trees suddenly parted as the man—no, not a man, *a knight*—came rushing at us in a mad frenzy. I froze as I stared at the all-too-familiar line of the breastplate, the curve of the shoulder plates, the glint of the mirror-like surface beneath the patches of rust and accumulated dirt.

It was my armor.

No, I realized, *it's similar, but not the same.*

There was no engraved horse head on the front, and there was a row of six-inch barbs protruding from each shoulder. The suit was also much larger than mine, standing well over seven-feet tall, with long arms that ended in twisted, claw-tipped hands twice the size of my gauntlets. The head sticking out of the suit was a metal version of a flesh-stripped skull, with remnants of flaked and faded tan paint along one cheek and across the bottom half of its hinged jaw. The red eyes rotated in the makeshift face, clear vines blinking as the mouth opened and closed.

How the hell is this possible? Scrape away the rust and mold, and put a human inside instead of a hellish...what is the word? Android. *A human instead of an android, and that suit of armor is almost the same as the one I'd lost. How did Maurdruik...*

I thought back to before the journey started—a few weeks that felt like years—to Maurdruik's study when I'd first heard of Cipher and this damn quest.

'Machines?" *I had asked, completely lost.* "But those aren't real... You're not talking about the same ones, are you?"

'Demons..." *Maurdruik had answered.* 'Monsters, Nadia. Monsters scarier than anything you've ever encountered.'

My breathing quickened. *He'd known. The armor, the android, the demons, the yellow eyes staring out of the cages in his lab. They are all connected. And Maurdruik knew the whole time—not just known, but created—just like he'd known about Vestro...*

I blinked. The android was almost on top of us. The metal machine moved faster than I would have thought possible and twitched periodically as if they hadn't moved in quite some time, the joints creaking and scraping away flakes of rust. I screamed and leaped to the side as it swiped at me. The men turned and reached for their weapons.

Damien let loose an arrow at the android, but the bolt went wide of the mark. Another arrow followed and lodged in the metal shoulder with a loud crunch, yet the android was unfazed. Damien turned to run, but the monster barreled through him. He fell to the ground; arms wrapped around his ribs.

Darren leaped forward and swung his bow like a club, and managed to smack the android across the head, knocking it backward. Darren darted in and swung his bow again, cracking it against the android's head and knocking the thing sideways.

For a heartbeat, it staggered.

Then the red beam snapped on.

It whipped across Darren's torso so fast the air hardly moved. Darren froze—bow still raised—eyes wide, trying to understand what had just touched him.

A thin line of light pulsed across his middle.

Then he folded.

His upper body slid off his lower half like someone had cut him from the inside out. Both pieces hit the ground at the same time with a dull, sickening thud.

I dropped to my knees, hands hovering uselessly, my breath tearing out of me in short, panicked bursts as I watched Darren's fingers twitching for anything to hold, slipping in his own blood.

A broken, ragged sound tore out of my lungs that scraped my throat raw.

Darren convulsed once and then sagged.

The forest went dead quiet except for the android resetting its aim.

Andrew pushed me to the side as the android came at us again.

He swung his sword and connected with one of the metal arms, searing it off at the hinge in a flare of white and yellow sparks. The red light flashed out again, and we rolled out of the way, but Andrew cried out and clutched his left hand to his chest. I caught his arm and dragged him farther from the spinning wreckage. The outer fingers of his left hand were blistered and blackened, the skin split and burned raw as if seared against a forge. Angry welts rose instantly, swelling beneath my grip. His hand trembled violently, fingers jerking as nerve shock rippled through them. Blood streaked his knuckles where the skin had cracked, slick and hot against my palm.

He tried to close his fist and hissed, the muscles refusing to obey for a heartbeat too long. "I can still fight," he said, even as his hand betrayed him, spasming uselessly in mine.

I let go of his wrist and gripped my sword with both hands, turning to stare at the android. My heart stopped as the whirring sound intensified and the red eyes glowed. I stood steady as the metal claws reached for me.

A deep, concussive boom ripped through the trees, followed by a metallic thunk as the shot punched into the android. The machine jerked sideways, a fist-sized hole blown straight through its ribs. The machine turned to the left, joints whirring, before there was another loud crack and the head jerked back—half of the face missing— hanging limply to the side, held by a single clear vine. The red lights faded, and the android collapsed to the ground. It twitched several times as brightly colored vines and buttons sizzled and hissed from inside the massive holes.

I stood, breathing heavily, as something crept closer through the shadows between the trees. Andrew stood and pushed me behind him, his sword arm shaking as he held his left arm tight to his chest. Damien knelt next to Darren's body with his bow ready, pulling back on the taut string. The shadow moved.

"Don't release, Damien."

"Vestro?" I stepped away from Andrew, but he grabbed my arm and pulled me back.

A hollow black rod hovered horizontally near the tree line, its thick barrel still smoking, a thin line of gray trailing from the mouth. It came forward, followed by Vestro. Little bits of wax clung to the outside of the rod—sealed cartridges, not arrows. He had the other end of the rod propped against his shoulder, his hands gripping the rounded end with one finger on some sort of trigger, one eye closed and the point aimed toward the fallen android. Little bits of wax clung to the outside of the rod. It was the strange weapon he'd found in the cave, and it sounded an awful lot like the smaller versions The Holy had carried back in Roan.

But the way he held it wasn't clumsy discovery.

It was practiced. Memory. He knew.

So why would Vestro know what it was and how to use it?

Vestro took a deep breath and lowered the contraption.

"I thought you said you couldn't kill it," Andrew said.

Vestro stared at us from the corner of his eye. "You can't kill something that was never alive," he said. "It was pure luck that the bubbling springs along the path were hot enough to melt the wax. Who would have thought I'd find an intact and loaded shot..."

Andrew's lip curled. "Convenient, isn't it? You always seem to know how to handle the Holy's toys."

Vestro took a deep breath and shuddered. There was blood covering one side of his face, and his shirt was torn in several places. It wasn't until he turned toward us that I realized he was missing half of his left ear. I gasped and moved toward him just as Corbin appeared from the trees. Vestro ignored me and quickly brought up the weapon again and pointed it straight at Corbin. His eyes swirled to milky white, fury radiating off his skin.

"Where were you?" Vestro said.

"I—" Corbin began.

"Don't fucking lie to me," Vestro snapped. He cocked back a lever on the bar, the sliding *click* loud in the sudden silence. "I've got one more just for you."

No one moved. I stared at Vestro, terror gnawing at my gut. His eyes were wild and deathly pale. His hands trembled with fury as he gripped the gun.

Corbin halfway crouched onto the ground, his hands up. "I-I thought we were all together as we ran, I didn't realize we'd been separated until I heard the fighting." Corbin laced his fingers and put them on top of his head.

Vestro growled. "Your job is to do everything in your power to get them safely to the pass. Not save your own damn skin."

Corbin glanced at Andrew. "I got here as soon as I could."

Andrew shifted, closing the distance with a measured step. His frame angled toward Corbin, shoulders broadening as if to cover him. Corbin straightened under that shadow, not daring to look anywhere but at Vestro's weapon.

I looked from Vestro to Corbin, to Damien's bow leveled on Vestro's chest, and back to Vestro. Vestro's eyes narrowed, and his finger twitched near the small lever. He didn't seem convinced. My heart beat faster. I'd seen the size of the holes the weapon could blow into an armored android—I didn't want to even think about what it could do to a human.

"Vestro," I said. I stepped in front of Andrew and batted his hand away as he reached for me. "Ves, please look at me." I carefully made my way to him, one hand out and one on the sword in my belt.

Vestro jerked his head in my direction, and I almost jumped. I fought to keep my hand steady as I took another step closer toward him. Vestro stared at me, then at my hand on my sword. I took a deep breath and slowly moved my hand away. He narrowed his eyes.

"Are you afraid of me?" he said quietly.

The question surprised me. I swallowed before answering. "At the moment..." I blinked and took a breath. "Yes."

Something in his face changed, and his eyes closed. His shoulders shuddered, and he stepped back and lowered the weapon.

"Ves, please," I said, taking a step closer. "Can I have that?"

He looked down at me, his eyes back to their normal black color.

He sighed and tossed the gun away from us. It landed with a rattling clatter in the short grass. He shook his head and walked past me.

"Let's go," he said. "It's empty anyway."

I stared at Vestro's back as he disappeared in the dark and then looked back at the others. Damien stood up and shook his head, dark wet stains running down the front of his black tunic. His arms were bloody up to his elbows, and he dropped his cloak over Darren's head. Andrew came up behind me and put his good hand on my shoulder, steering me to follow. His touch was gentle, but I felt the tension in his arm. I glanced up at his concerned face, but he was staring past me at Corbin and as the squire trudged on ahead of us, head down, a little too quick to put distance between himself and the rest of us.

"Stay close to me," he whispered in my ear.

Not a comfort. A warning.

I reached up and threaded my fingers through his, squeezing once. Damien fell into step on my other side, portions of his silver hair stiff and dark with drying blood. He already had his bow drawn, an arrow nocked, his eyes tracking Vestro's path into the trees.

For once, I almost agreed with him.

THIRTY-FOUR

I stood along with the men in the waning light for several minutes at the edge of the forest boundary, just staring. The dark covering of trees had opened, and we'd frozen after pushing aside the wet curtain of soggy ferns and vines to stand before a desolate landscape of gray and black. Massive stone, metal and glass buildings stood at attention in a carefully laid-out plan, as if despite the fact the buildings were cracked and half-eroded in places, with dark-brown and green weather lines streaked across their sides, they were waiting patiently for their owners to return. The rows of structures stretched back forever, the edges of the gray scene slowly fading into the shadows of dusk.

I broke away from the group and made my way to the nearest building. I stood at the base and craned my neck back. Though it wasn't two-thirds the height of some of the buildings around it, the structure was the highest thing—save for a mountain—I'd ever seen. I did a quick count of the broken windows and stone overhangs, but with the fading light I lost count after thirty stories.

I stepped back toward the men, my eyes darting to every shadow and broken window. There were no trees, no signs of life. A cluster of dried leaves near our feet twirled around in a lone gust of wind, their brittle skins scraping against the black, rock-hard surface, cracked and pitted and very unlike the multi-colored cobblestones back home.

It's like a giant graveyard, I thought, shuddering. *Everything, the earth, the air, it's all dead. This is an ugly, terrible place. We shouldn't even be here.*

"Who made these?"

"Men," Vestro said, his gaze sweeping the dead stone. "From a time when they thought progress meant permanence."

"This is amazing," Damien breathed beside me. A grin tugged at his mouth."I've heard stories, but..."

"Come on," Andrew shouldered past us. "We don't have time to stand here gawking. We have a job to do."

We walked down the streets, our boots crunching small, loose pebbles against the strange ground painted with long, straight yellow and white lines. Night was falling. The red hues of the dying sun stained the walls of the stone giants that Vestro called 'skyscrapers' and reflected off the few remaining glass windows. It was absolutely hellish, in my opinion. I couldn't believe that anyone had once lived here. As tall as the buildings and as wide as the streets were, it was suffocating the way the metal and glass soared above us, blotting out large sections of stars in the darkening sky.

Things only became stranger the farther into the city we went. Lined along the street edges were strange, metal buggy-like objects twice as long as a wagon. Each one had four black, lopsided wheels. In the giant shells were windows in all directions. I peered into one as I passed, and saw what looked like five padded seats and a strange wheel in front. The ragged remains of a child's doll sat propped against one seat, one arm outstretched toward me as a strange, buckled strap held it firmly against the molded cloth. I shook my head and backed away.

"Where to now?" Andrew asked Vestro, coming up on my right.

I couldn't be sure, but there seemed to be a little bit of sarcasm.

Vestro slowed. Not enough to stop—but enough that I noticed. He glanced at Andrew, then ahead again, as if choosing his words with care.

"Straight on," he said. "If the old layouts still hold."

Andrew stepped around in front of me, his attention narrowing to Vestro alone. He opened his mouth when a sudden whirring noise cut through the silence, sharp and mechanical, and something scuttled across the rocks behind the next building.

Vestro grabbed my shoulder and pulled me forward, motioning to the others. "We need to get inside," he said. "Hurry!"

We ran around a corner of rusted metal beams poking out of a stone wall to a steel-reinforced door set in a wide, white building only a few stories tall. Vestro fought with the handle for a while, then proceeded to ram his shoulder into the door, finally managing to push his way through. The hinges screeched with rust as he shoved the door open as wide as he could, holding it open for everyone before slamming it shut and forcing the rusty bolt into place.

Damien reached into his shoulder bad and pulled out a cut-off pitch-torch and the small metal light I'd see in the cave. He flipped open the top of the metal box with his thumb, flicked at the small wheel, and brought the tiny flame to the torch.

How is it that Damien has so many of the same trinkets I'd seen in Maurdruik's lab?

Then again, how does Vestro know how to use all of them?

The torch flared up and then settled, the thick orange light illuminating the area about us. The room was huge, almost the size of the banquet hall at home. Though after looking around, I wasn't quite sure what this room had been used for. There were several strange-looking tables, with rows of drawers on one side and skinny metal legs. Odd-shaped boxes with glass faces sat on each of the tables, the dusty glass reflecting the table behind it. I tilted my head to the side. Maurdruik had boxes like that in his lab—the ones with the moving images in it.

"Come on," Vestro said, holding open a door in the corner. "We need to get up higher."

Andrew's face became even more twisted as he stared at Vestro, but he nodded as he pulled out his sword and made his way to the wide stairs visible through the door. Damien went first, his torch lighting the way. I followed behind Corbin, with Vestro behind me. Andrew stayed on Vestro's heels, his eyes narrowed.

We climbed several flights of stairs that curled around a metal pole in the center, our footsteps echoing against the smooth walls. I counted five levels before Vestro finally stopped and jogged down the hall, peering into a few of the rooms. I bent my head between my legs, gasping for breath as he searched, my feet killing me. I closed my eyes and listened to the groaning and slamming of doors as he searched. He stopped at the end of the hall and motioned for us to follow.

We filed into the room. Vestro bolted the door and shoved a chair under the handle. The walls were painted a pale blue and seemed to be in quite good condition despite the appearance of the building's exterior. The room appeared oddly dust-free, and the few chairs and tables seemed intact. There were three doors on two sides of the room, each one shut with a little glass window at the top and a tall window on either side. At the far end of the room opposite the main entry door was a large glass window that overlooked the dark ruins below. Vestro ran a hand across his face, fiddling at the wound on his ear.

"Each of the rooms are secure," Vestro said, "and seem usable. At least they will give us a little privacy for the night. I didn't see access to a bathroom though..."

I padded across the room to the farthest door on the left, determined to claim one of them as my own. I twisted the handle, pushed, and the door opened easily on well-greased hinges. I was greeted by an L-shaped wooden desk and chair, and a bookcase full of moth-eaten volumes. On one shelf there was a sheet of glass in a square frame. I let the door close behind me and walked closer. It was a painting of a little girl. She wore a strange animal-like costume—a cow it must have been, with the spots and horns—and held a bright orange bucket full of colorful candy. The painting looked so real, as if she was really inside the frame. My fingers brushed against the glass, smearing away the fine layer of dust.

No, just a painting...

I sat in the chair behind the desk and was amused to find that it spun around in a circle on a single bar. I stopped spinning and stared at the desk as the room tilted and then dove into the drawers. I pulled them open, one by one, pushed through the contents. In the first there were small tablets of paper, the paper yellowed and wrinkled with age, and a small container that held a chewed-on pencil and several of the featherless quills like the one I'd snagged from Maurdruik's lab. Next to them I found a pair of blades with circular handles attached together by a pin in the center that could open and close. I gave them a name—cutters—and put them aside after dicing up half of the tablet into crooked shapes and strips. I also found several stretchy brown bands to use as hair ties, and a fold-out case that had several more paintings of the same little girl on the shelf.

I smiled as I flipped through the small paintings. There was a baby, wrapped in a pink blanket. Next to it the same little girl with blonde pigtails holding a bouquet of flowers and laughing. She was cute. I wondered what had happened to her.

I put the paintings down and went into the bottom drawer of the desk. There were several strange looking books, with metal rings and shiny-coated paper. I pulled one out and thumbed to the middle. There were inked sketches of animals and people, pages of each animal showing different parts of the body in detail, and in different positions with measurements and strange codes written along the sides. There were black and white paintings of bones that matched the animals, too. I shook my head and put the book aside.

I pulled out another book. This one had paintings like those of the little girl, images that looked so real I almost expected them to jump off the page. The paintings were mostly men. It was a close-up of their heads, and then a smaller full body shot. Under each man's picture was a listing of his name, age, and race. I didn't know what they meant by *race*. After thumbing through several pages, I understood the difference between labels such as Caucasian and African American, but I couldn't see the need for clarification. They all looked like men to me.

I shook my head as I read farther down the pages. I noticed that most of the men looked to be about the same age, ranging somewhere between their early and late twenties, but other than that I couldn't see anything that linked them together. Most of the writing I didn't understand, there were lots of numbers and strange words that had to be close to twenty letters long. Though I did recognize a few; griffin, werewolf, kelpie...

Kelpie.

"What the hell?"

I flipped back through the few pages I'd looked at. *Are these records of demons in the city?* I stared down at the man with Kelpie written below his name. He had the same dark complexion and black eyes that Vestro had.

Jugo Martinez. Age 24. Hispanic. Kelpie 94. Failed.

I flipped the page. A heavy-set man with pale skin, blond hair, and the same black eyes.

Brian Jones. Age 26. Caucasian. Kelpie 95. Failed.

I slammed the book shut, stood up, and walked around the desk, not wanting to read anymore. *What did it mean, failed?*

I shook my head and walked out of the room. I closed the door behind me and looked around. Damien was by himself by the back window, staring down at something. Vestro stood several feet back from the Hunter, also looking out. Andrew leaned against the wall, his eyes on Vestro. Corbin was nowhere to be found, but the flickering of a light in one of the closed rooms hailed his existence. Andrew glanced at me as I entered the room and pushed away from the wall to stand near Vestro.

I ignored Andrew and walked toward Damien. He glanced back at me with his arms crossed and jutted his chin toward the window.

"There it is," he said. "Ferrington Pass."

I went up behind him and peered around his shoulder. All I noticed was how high up we were. I stepped back, then took a deep breath and forced myself to the edge.

At first, I didn't see anything, just miles and miles of ruined buildings illuminated by the pale quarter-moon. Damien pointed to the side of the window, and my breath caught in my throat. The tall, craggy cliffs were on each side of the city; the giant mountains dwarfed the stone monsters like a redwood over a seedling. The cliff walls served as a backing for many of the tallest buildings, as if they'd built the structures right into the rock itself. There was a thin tower in the center of the pass, constructed entirely of metal. Its pointed tip rose nearly to the tops of the cliffs. My eyes widened as Maurdruik's words echoed through my brain.

'Once you're there, there's a spire, in the center of the pass. Cipher must be used while standing under the center of the spire.'

"We're in the pass now," I said. "The pass is a city."

"*Was,*" Vestro said. "*Was* a city."

Andrew stepped closer. "You speak as if you've seen it," he said. "As if you know it."

Vestro hesitated. He glanced back at me, drew in a slow breath, then said, "Because I was there."

Silence snapped tight between us. Damien's expression didn't change, but his eyes sharpened, as though he'd been waiting for this answer.

Andrew shook his head once. "These ruins have to be at least three hundred years old."

"Two hundred and seventy-six since the last successful experiment," Vestro said.

Andrew stilled. "What?"

"They weren't ruins then," Vestro said. "But operating factories and laboratories."

Maurdruik had a laboratory at home, but the small room was in no way able to compare to anything here, and I didn't know what he used it for other than to store stuff and breed mice.

"What exactly are laboratories?" I asked.

Vestro shook his head and looked away. His shoulders bunched and quivered, just for a moment. "A place where terrible things are done."

Andrew's hand slid closer to his sword. "You still haven't answered the question."

Vestro turned back to me. He took a breath, held it, then closed his eyes.

"Because of the experiments," he said. "I was one of them."

CHAPTER
THIRTY-FIVE

"I was one of the last successful experiments before the labs were shut down by President Theliem."

Vestro turned, the moonlight cutting across his face as he put his back to the window. The four of us stood in front of him, shadows stretched long on the wall. Andrew's expression must have mirrored mine because I was thoroughly confused. Vestro began to unlace his bloody shirt.

"The labs were used to experiment on living things," Vestro said after a pause. "Mixing of genes—I mean... you know, blood. Combining the blood of creatures to create new ones. At first, they were harmless; the scientists only created new breeds of fish and livestock that grew at a rapid pace to feed the growing urban populations. After a while, they got bored and wanted to test the limits of their abilities."

Vestro undid the last tie and opened his shirt, the star-like scar stark in the hazy glow of Damien's torchlight. I'd seen the scar so many times and was so used to it that I never paid it much attention, but right then it was an eerie thing that made my blood churn. Vestro looked down at his stomach.

"First, they tried to bring back what nature had already killed. Mammoths, saber-tooths, dinosaurs. You'd think the old world would've learned something from its movies about that going horribly wrong. But they didn't because... fucking egos, right?" He gave a humorless laugh. "After the experiments were successful, the Secretary of Defense funded a project to create the ultimate soldier. A superhuman that would be faster, stronger, and more resilient than their enemies. A spy that could change shape, making them impossible to trace."

He exhaled sharply, the sound more like defeat than breath. "Once they had government backing, there was no line left to cross. The problem was that by mixing human and animal DNA, they made something that couldn't stop rewriting itself."

He glanced up with hollow eyes.

"They called it the Retroviral Cascade." He caught our blank looks and grimaced. "Right, that means nothing to you. Think of it like a sickness that rewrites blood—it was meant to fix people, to heal injuries by changing damaged parts into new ones. Only once it got loose, it didn't stop changing."

Andrew frowned. "Rewrite blood?"

Vestro hesitated. His fingers flexed once at his side, as if grasping for something he couldn't quite hold. "Not blood," he said slowly. "Not exactly. There are... instructions inside you. In every part of you. Tiny things that tell your body what to be. How to grow. How to heal."

He paused, brow creasing. "The scientists learned how to change those instructions. Make a man stronger. Faster. Able to see in the dark. Breathe where he shouldn't."

Silence stretched.

"But the change didn't know when to stop," Vestro said, quieter now. "It tried to improve everything at once."

Damien snorted. "Like magic gone wild."

"Exactly," Vestro said. "Except it wasn't magic. It was math that learned how to bleed."

He hesitated, searching their faces. "When the Cascade spread, most humans died. Their bodies couldn't decide what they were anymore." His jaw tightened. "Some survived. Changed. Some became things with too many eyes. Too many teeth."

I swallowed. "Then the demons..." My voice came out small, sharper than I meant it to. "They were people?"

Vestro nodded once. "Some were." A beat. "Others were what the Cascade made after people were gone."

My throat tightened. "Then what about you?"

"What about me?"

"I need to hear you say it," I said. "That you're human."

A shadow crossed his expression. Not anger. Something colder. He blinked once, slow, as if the words had reached him before their meaning had.

"I was," he said quietly. He met my eyes. "I still am. Mostly."

The silence stretched.

"Two months after the outbreak," Vestro went on, his voice distant now, "there was war." His gaze drifted past me, unfocused. "President Theliem believed the world could be purified. That fire would burn the infection out." His mouth tightened. "He was wrong. Cities turned to ash. Other nations followed, and one by one, the world set itself on fire."

He drew a slow breath. "I just was a nobody when everything started," he said. "A mechanic. Long hours. Taking night classes. Trying to build something small and ordinary." His jaw worked. "We'd heard Ferrington had survived," he said. "That it had been spared the worst of the blasts. So I packed up my wife and our infant son and just drove."

Vestro's voice faltered. "We didn't make it." He swallowed hard. "There was an accident on the way. I was thrown through the windshield. I remember the sound more than the pain." His eyes darkened. "They didn't wait for me to die."

His words came flatter now. "They cut me open. Injected the prototype serum. Rewrote my bones. Rebuilt what was left of me."

He touched his scar and shuddered, fingers pressing hard, as if anchoring himself to something solid. His breath stuttered, tight and quiet. "And turned me into this."

I couldn't speak.

Vestro... not a demon? Just a man rebuilt from ruin.

This entire time I thought...

"So, you were once human," Andrew said, his voice brittle. "Then how have you lived this long? Why haven't you aged?"

"Every time I shift," Vestro said. "The virus triggers regeneration. My cells rebuild themselves." He hesitated. "I think it was meant to heal soldiers. Keep them fighting. I don't think they planned on stopping aging altogether."

He looked away. His mouth twitched, not quite a smile. Just something tired and hollow.

"I never thought I'd come back here," he said. "This building used to be the clinic where they sent me for physical therapy."A let out an almost chuckle. "I suppose that means I've come full circle."

Andrew shook his head, clutching his bandaged hand. "It doesn't make sense. How could none of us have known any of this? How could it all be hidden so long—"

"Because The Holy wanted it buried," Damien cut in. He shot me a brief look before turning back to Andrew. "History's easy to erase when the survivors can barely feed themselves. The old world fell, people scattered, built towns from rubble."

Vestro nodded. "Centuries passed. Shelters became towns. Towns became kingdoms."

The myths of magic," Damien added, "are just corrupted memories of science."

Andrew's jaw tightened. "And The Holy?"

"They were the scientists who survived," Damien said flatly. "They passed down what they knew, generation after generation. Their goal has always been the same: rebuild what they lost. Start the experiments again. Create perfection."

Vestro's voice roughened. "But perfection needed something

they never found. Every hybrid broke down eventually. The Cascade always collapsed." He swallowed. "They said they were missing the pure code that could stabilize the virus."

He looked at me for a long moment, something unreadable flickering in his eyes before he turned away.

Damien's brows lifted. A faint, mocking smile touched his mouth. "Funny thing," he said. "Rumor has it that code died out in the first generation."

He turned to Vestro, smile widening into something meaner. "And yet you're still standing at nearly two hundred and ninety years old, give or take." His eyes gleamed. "And it never once crossed your mind to ask why?"

Vestro frowned. "I told you I don't know. Maybe the dose was different.Maybe it was—"

"Luck?" Damien cut in, letting out a short, incredulous laugh. "You've outlived empires, survived the collapse of the world, and your answer is luck?" He tilted his head, voice turning razor-dry. "Gods. You really are a glorified stable hand."

"Watch it," Vestro warned.

"No," Damien said, stepping closer. "I think I'll enjoy this." His gaze raked over Vestro. "Every other original hybrid rotted into dust or madness, and you—sweet miracle boy—never thought to dig into the reason? Didn't think to ask what makes you special? That's not humility, that's stupidity."

Vestro didn't move. When he spoke, his voice came out low and sharp.

"You want to know why I didn't ask?"

He stepped forward. His shoulders coiled, posture tightening like a drawn wire.

"Because for the first three decades after they made me, I was their weapon. Trained. Conditioned. Ordered to slaughter anyone who resisted them." His jaw clenched. "Villages. Survivors. Rebels." A beat. "Men. Women. Children."

The word *children* landed hard.

"They said it was for progress," he went on. "For the greater good. And like a fucking tool, I obeyed. Without question."

Silence pressed in, weighing down on my chest as I watched something behind Vestro's eyes flash. Memories. Nightmares.

"When the labs fell and the generals turned on each other," Vestro said, quieter now. "I was left standing in the ruins. Covered in blood that wasn't mine." He swallowed. "There wasn't a soul left to tell me what I was supposed to be, or even who the fuck I was."

His gaze drifted past us, unfocused. Not grief. Not reflection. Just absence. His lips parted, then closed again, as if the thought had slipped away before it could form.

"They stripped my memories," he said. "Rebuilt me into something else."

His voice glitched—caught mid-syllable like his mind had stuttered. He pressed his fingertips hard to his temple. His breath hitched.

"It took years..."

He blinked—slow and disjointed. Wrong.

"It took years for anything to come back."

Andrew shifted beside me, leather creaking as he angled himself a fraction in front of me. Instinct, not thought.

Damien's smirk faded. His posture sharpened, the torch steady in his grip.

My stomach twisted, and something sharp slid behind my ribs. Not fear of him, but fear *for* him. Not fear of him. Fear *for* him. His eyes didn't look like Vestro's anymore. They looked scraped out. Like someone had reached inside his skull and taken something with them.

Vestro isn't just remembering. He's slipping.

"And when the world started rebuilding..." Vestro dragged a trembling hand down his face. "I wasn't a soldier anymore. I was—"

He stopped.

Blank.

Gone.

438

A harsh sound tore up Vestro's throat. His skin rippled, a flicker of shift breaking loose before he crushed it down, jaw clenching hard enough that a muscle jumped along his cheek.

Andrew's hand snapped to his sword hilt before he forced it still.

"Ves..." I whispered, but it didn't seem to reach him.

Cold crept up the back of my neck. The air felt thin. Wrong. Like if I reached for him, my hand might pass straight through.

"I was the monster they blamed," Vestro forced out, breath shaking. "The thing they chased from their gates. Hunted like a stag."

His pupils blew wide. For a heartbeat, he wasn't in the room at all.

A convulsion ripped down his arm. His fingers spasmed, bones shifting under the skin, the hand clawing at empty air like it had its own will. He wrenched it behind his back, trapping it there, as his breath sawed in and out through his teeth.

"Every time I shifted, something came loose. Snapped out of place. Came back wrong." His voice came out tight. Strained. "Half the time I couldn't tell which memories were mine."

His gaze snapped to Damien. "You ever try asking questions," he said hoarsely, "when your own fucking head won't stay still?"

Damien's grin finally dropped.

"So yeah," Vestro's voice cracked. "I didn't care why. I didn't care what I was. I didn't care what they made me into." He dragged in a breath like his lungs burned. "I just wanted one day—*one fucking day*—where my mind stayed mine."

He shook his head. The movement was small. Uncontrolled. "You call that weakness," he said. "I call it survival."

Damien looked away first.

Andrew exhaled through his nose, sharp and unsteady.

The silence that followed wasn't empty. It pressed in, heavy with things no one wanted to name.

Andrew cleared his throat. "Why now?" he said. "What does the Holy want?"

"I'm saying they never stopped looking," Damien cut in. "And they'll burn through anyone to find it."

Andrew's hands curled at his sides. "Then they put her here," he said, his voice roughening. "They used her."

I blinked. "What?"

"The Holy," he said. "They've hunted this... code for centuries." His gaze flicked between us. "Don't you see it? They planted you. With Nadia." He took a step forward. "Why?"

"When Maurdruik found me," Vestro said quietly, "I'd been living out of caves and burned-out farms. He offered me a bargain; watch over a princess, and no one would ever come hunting again. I agreed before he even finished the sentence." His voice cracked. "For the first time in a very long time I was...useful again." He hesitated. "I didn't ask why."

Silence swallowed the room.

Damien's eyes narrowed. "The Holy doesn't waste resources. They don't save anyone unless there's a reason." He tipped his head. "So if Vestro's their science-fair miracle, and they sent him to babysit our princess..."

"I don't believe you," Andrew said, turning on Vestro, anger cutting cleanly through his confusion. "I think you know more than you're saying. Why Nadia?"

Vestro's jaw tightened, a muscle twitching near his temple. "It's complicated."

The way he said it—careful and deliberate—set my teeth on edge.

He isn't hiding this from Andrew, I realized. *He's hiding it from me.*

Damien leaned back against the wall, torchlight slicing across the sharp edge of his grin. "Complicated means he's not allowed to tell you, Princess," he said. "It means our friend here is working from a script."

It hit me all at once. What they were saying. What they were accusing.

"You think it's me," I said. "That I'm the heir. The code."

My pulse hammered. "That doesn't make sense. Maurdruik didn't want me here. He told me to leave with him at Farmer's Reach. Said I'd be safer staying out of it." I shook my head. "Ves and I ran anyway. He never planned for me to come."

Damien's gaze slid between us. Calculating. "Maybe the plan wasn't to keep you safe. Maybe the plan was to see what would happen when you weren't. To flush someone—or something else out."

Corbin shifted near the doorway. "Or maybe," he said carefully, "we're reaching. The Holy has their claws in half the continent. Not everything leads back to them."

Andrew's head turned, slow and precise. "You've been very quiet, Corbin," he said. "And now you have opinions."

Corbin stiffened. "I'm just saying…"

"Stop," Andrew said, voice flat. "You will speak when I ask you to."

The room went still again. The only sound was the wind through the broken glass and the hiss of Damien's torch.

Heat flared behind my ribs. The conversation was slipping away from me, fracturing into pieces I couldn't grab.

"You knew something," I said quietly. "From the beginning. About me."

Vestro's throat worked, but he didn't speak.

"Vestro," I pressed. "Tell me."

"I can't."

Damien's smirk twisted. "Of course he can't. The Holy's golden boy doesn't improvise without permission."

Vestro shot him a look that could have cut stone, then exhaled. "Maudruik told me nothing," he said, voice rough. "Even if I had tried, you wouldn't have believed me."

A humorless laugh scraped out of him. "I mean, for fuck's sake, look at what we've lived through in just the last few days and you're still struggling accepting it. You were raised on castles and stories. Not labs. Not fallout."

He broke eye contact.

"I didn't think you'd understand," he said. "And I didn't think I could stand what came after."

Something in my chest tightened. The way he wouldn't look at me. The way his voice pulled inward, like he was bracing for a blow.

"You mean pity," I said.

"No." His head snapped up, too fast. His expression slammed shut. "Fear."

"You should have tried."

The words came out flat. Final.

I tipped my head back, staring at the ceiling until the burn behind my eyes eased.

Vestro took a step toward me. I stepped back first. Raised a hand.

"Not right now," I whispered, my throat tight.

"Nadia, I wanted to tell you—"

"Not now, Vestro."

The room held its breath.

I turned and walked for the hall.

Behind me, Andrew broke the silence, his voice rough with something that wasn't pity. "Surprised you didn't end it after the first forty years."

I stopped at the doorway to listen.

"I tried," Vestro said quietly. "Guess I didn't try hard enough."

The sound of his voice hit me like a fist.

Flat. Final.

Not like he was talking about the past.

Like part of him still meant it.

I REACHED my commandeered room and slammed the door hard enough that the wood shuddered. The silence hit so hard it felt physical. My ribs squeezed inward, a slow crushing pressure that stole the air before I could pull it in. Heat crawled up my throat, prickling under my skin, and then everything went cold so fast my fingertips tingled. My breaths snagged halfway, sharp and useless, and the room tilted just enough that I had to grab the edge of the chair to keep myself upright.

I stood in the middle of the room, just holding onto the chair, until my legs remembered how to move. The air tasted stale, dust and old paper hanging thickly. The desk sat where I'd left it, the little stack of books waiting, untouched since before everything fell apart.

I forced myself into the chair. The metal edge dug into the backs of my thighs, grounding me. My hands shook so badly I pressed them flat to the desk until the tremor dulled.

Then I pulled the book toward me.

The pages were thin and dry, whispering as I flipped them. The paper brushed like brittle leaves against my fingertips. I couldn't make my hands steady. I kept catching corners, bending edges, dragging too hard.

I couldn't get Vestro's voice out of my head.

His flinch.

That moment he wasn't there anymore.

Like he didn't recognize the room. Or us. Or himself.

I flipped another page too fast and ripped it right through the rings. My hands shook so much the pages wouldn't stay still. My knuckles went white around the notebook's metal spine just to anchor myself.

I didn't stop. I didn't care.

I just needed something solid. Something real. Something that made sense when he didn't anymore.

I loved Vestro. I'd known it since the night on the riverbank, when I climbed into his arms because I needed someone steady enough to drown in. And I told myself it was allowed because he wasn't a man. Because loving a creature didn't count the same way.

But that glitch—those centuries of pain rising behind his eyes—burned through every excuse I'd ever used.

He wasn't a demon I could want without consequence.

He wasn't just a warmth at my back, or the breath quieting my nightmares.

He wasn't something safe and unreal that I could use.

He was a man.

A man who had a wife. A son. A life that had been destroyed, carved apart and rebuilt.

A man who hurt. Who remembered.

And I had loved him like he belonged to me. Like a thing.

The pages blurred. I blinked hard. My throat burned.

I flipped again, faster, my fingers slipping. My stomach dropped clean to the floor. A cold rush shot through my fingers from where they touched the edge of the crumbling paper.

There.

On the fifth-to-last page:

Vestro.

His hair cropped short against his head. His face leaner and body lighter. No scars. No shadows in his eyes. A smiling stranger wearing a face I should have known.

Elijah Vestrano.

Age 28. Caucasian–Hispanic.

Kelpie 107.

Status: Successful.

My eyes burned. My chin trembled.

Vestro... who were you?

What did they take from you?

What pieces did they leave?

My throat tightened until swallowing hurt. My chest ached, hot and sharp, like my ribs were too tight around my heart.

What pieces of myself had I given away without realizing it?

I slammed the book shut and threw it across the room. It hit the shelf with a crack that echoed. Books toppled. The little girl's painting slipped down with them, smashing against the floor. The glass shattered in a web across her smiling face.

I pushed up from the chair too fast. It toppled behind me with a hollow thud. I didn't know where I was going, but I needed to put distance between me and the book. From the images of hundreds of smiling faces that had been altered by the Holy's gross experiments. My cloak hung crooked across my shoulders, heavy as the guilt clawing at my chest, and my fingers fumbled as I clawed at the clasp until it came loose.

I lowered myself to the cold floor, knees shaking, and spread the cloak out with trembling hands. Smoothing it gave my hands something to do.

Straighten the edge. Press out the crease. Trace the seam. Anything to keep myself from shaking apart.

And then Andrew's face slammed into my mind. His steadiness. His certainty. His hands on bare skin. The fierce way he said my name.

My pulse spiked. Bile rose fast and hot. I clapped a hand over my mouth, swallowing hard as the shame rolled through me so violently I thought I might retch.

Andrew had been safe because he was human. Predictable. Understandable.

Vestro had been safe because he wasn't. Because loving a demon didn't count.

But if Vestro was human—

Then everything I'd done with him was real.

Every touch.

Every breath.

Every moment I let myself want him. The moment I let myself have him.

My hands shook. My lungs wouldn't take a full breath.

I curled onto my side on the cloak, drawing my knees tight to my chest as the cold of the stone bled through the fabric. I pressed the back of my hand to my mouth to trap the sound there.

Because the terrible, quiet truth wasn't that Vestro had changed.

It was that I had never let myself see him clearly.

445

Because if I did, I'd have to see myself. All the wants I shouldn't have had.

Because if I did, I would have to see myself.

All the wants I'd excused.

All the choices I'd pretended I didn't have.

And gods—if I truly had a choice, then I was the one who would have to make it.

I didn't know how.

The silence pressed in from all sides. Heavy. Absolute.

I stared into the dark and sobbed, wishing someone had warned me that the truth wouldn't feel like revelation.

It would feel like grief.

THIRTY-SIX

Early morning thunder rolled low through the floors; rain hissed against the cracked windowpanes. Somewhere down the corridor, a motion-sensor long dead woke for a breath and died again, leaving a ghostly blink of light that never quite reached the corners. The others slept in the main foyer. Breathing rose and fell in the dark, steady and uneven. Somewhere among them, someone shifted once. Beyond that, a single set of boots scraped the floor again and again, pacing.

I lay on my blanket with my eyes open and Vestro's words ringing in my ears.

I couldn't keep still. The quiet here had teeth.

I wrapped myself in my cloak and slipped quietly into the hall, listening. I took two steps before I caught movement ahead and froze, my breath hitching. Shadows shifted down the corridor. A familiar flame flared to life, and a silver-framed face came into view as the small glow caught the edges of an angled profile.

Damien's black eyes met mine. His expression was blank, unreadable. For a heartbeat, I thought he might stop me.

Instead, he tipped his head—just a fraction—toward the hall to my right.

The light vanished, and he brushed past me without a word, disappearing toward the main room where the others slept.

I took the right turn, following the faint glow seeping from a door left ajar at the end of the hall. I turned sideways to slip inside, easing the door shut behind me. A flameless lantern glowed on a metal desk, the gold circle of light pressed back by the room's gray. Through a cracked interior window, the beginnings of dawn threw a paler light from the next room, just enough to paint a thin rosy edge on Vestro's profile.

He looked carved from shadow as he sat on the edge of an empty metal desk. His fingers were laced together in his lap with his head bowed like a man at prayer to a god he'd already outlived.

I stepped quietly into the room, hugging my cloak tighter around my shoulders.

Vestro did not look up at me. "You should rest," he said softly.

My voice frayed. "So should you."

"Machines don't rest." The bitterness in it stung.

"You're not a machine."

He laughed once, the sound breaking before it became anything. "Then what am I?" He looked up then, his face caught between the lantern's gold glow and the pale rising sun, so his face seemed split between two worlds. "You should hate me for lying to you."

My words came too fast, almost a sob. "I hate that you thought you had to hide."

Lightning washed the room in a hard, surgical white, and when the gray returned my hands were shaking. Anger bled into grief and back again so fast I couldn't tell one from the other.

"How could you keep this from me?" I pressed. I leaned forward on the desk, and the rough edge bit my palms. "You let me believe you were some cursed thing, and all the while you were the only thing in this damned world that still worked. The only thing that understood me."

Vestro shook his head slowly. "I can't grow with you, Nadia. You'll age; I won't." His throat worked. "I'll look like this when your hair is gray. When he's gone."

The name didn't need saying. Andrew sat behind every word we never spoke.

I stepped closer. "And you think that makes you less human?"

He hesitated, the line of his mouth tightening. "It makes me wrong by design."

"No," I said, voice shaking. "It makes you mine to choose."

He stared at me as if I'd struck him. "You can't mean that."

"I do." I swallowed, the words burning their way out. "I've loved you for longer than I've had the courage to name it. Since before I knew what you were."

I felt the tears slip, and I let the sob escape my trembling lips. "Maybe that's why it hurt so much when you lied. Because part of me already knew." I took a breath. "And I loved you anyway."

Lightning washed the room in a hard white glare, and when the gray returned, his face looked shaken and stripped bare. Every defense he'd ever built was broken open. I stepped closer and lifted my hand before I could stop it. My fingers brushed the side of his jaw. He flinched, and then he closed his eyes and leaned into my palm.

"You shouldn't say that," he said, so low I wasn't even sure if he'd spoken at all.

"I already did."

He reached for me then, but the gesture faltered halfway, hand hovering in the air. I caught it and pressed it to my chest so he could feel my heart hammering under his palm.

His forehead lowered to mine, his breath warm against my skin, shaky and uneven. "I'm so tired," he said, his voice breaking.

"I know."

He closed his eyes, and the confession tore out of him before he could stop it.

"You were just a child when Maurdruik brought me to the castle to guard you," he said quietly. "And I already knew how to care for one." He paused, his throat working. "I'd already lost my son. Lost the right to watch him grow."

His gaze dropped, unfocused. "So when I was told to watch over you... it wasn't a burden. It was something I looked forward to." He looked back at me. "For years, that was all you were to me. Someone small who needed steadiness. Someone I protected. Someone I would have bled for without hesitation."

Then his shoulders rose and fell in a heavy sigh. "And then you grew up. And you weren't a child anymore." His eyes held mine, unwavering. "You made your own choices. You stepped out from under my shadow. You didn't...need me anymore."

His voice roughened. "And that's when everything I had built broke."

He looked away, shame written into every line of him. His voice fractured; he dragged a breath that sounded like a wound reopening. "I tried not to want you. But every time Andrew touched you, it flayed me. And when you reached for him, I convinced myself it was enough that you were safe."

His hand curled into a fist. "I told myself what I felt had to still be protection. That when you laughed and I wanted to keep the sound in my chest, it was the pride of having kept you safe long enough to be happy."

He pulled away and met my eyes, his black eyes reflecting the dawning light and the thousands of stars he'd stared into over the centuries.

"But it's love," he said, his voice breaking. "And I know it's wrong."

The storm softened to rain. The lantern hummed faintly on the desk between us. His shoulders bowed under the weight of saying it aloud.

"And I've tried to keep my distance," he said. "I've drawn lines. I've crossed some of them—and I hate myself for it every time." He let out a broken laugh that held no joy. "Because if I stop fighting it, I'll take every sin you offer and make it my salvation."

For a moment, he couldn't look at me. "And even now," he said quietly, "standing here, I still don't know if I deserve to want you."

His hand twitched against my chest, a pulse of longing he couldn't contain.

"I'm not sorry," I said. My voice came out thin but steady. "Not for wanting you. Not anymore."

Vestro looked at me then, and the wonder and grief burning in his eyes stole my breath.

"Then let me stop pretending I don't," he said, his voice raw with reverence.

For a moment neither of us moved. Then the last resistance in him broke, his shoulders sagging as if something inside him finally gave way. He bent his head, his mouth finding mine in a kiss that trembled with everything we hadn't said. The room shivered with thunder. The smell of rain seeped through the cracks in the glass, cool and clean against the heat of his mouth.

His thumb brushed my cheek as if he was afraid I'd fade if he didn't hold me steady. I felt him melt into the kiss, not with hunger but with relief, like he'd finally stopped running from himself. My hands slid up his back, over the lines of muscle that trembled under my touch. When he deepened the kiss, it wasn't with heat. It was with an aching need, as if he wanted to memorize each breath I gave him.

His hand cupped the back of my neck, thumb brushing my jaw in a slow, reverent stroke that made my eyelashes burn. "I have walked this earth alone for over two hundred years, waiting for this moment. To be seen by you."

"I don't just see you, Vestro," I whispered, my vision blurred. "I love you."

The wall between us finally broke. He let out a sound that wasn't quite a sob and wasn't quite a laugh, and I leaned in, closing the last inch between us.

When he kissed me again, I tasted salt—mine or his, I couldn't tell. The world around us fell away: the ruins, The Holy, the ghosts of kings and crowns.

At that moment, none of it mattered.

Vestro groaned against me, the sound torn from somewhere deep and feral. His arm wrapped tight around my waist, and then he lifted me and turned to sit me on the desk. The cold metal bit through my leggings, but then he was in front of me, hot, heavy, and shaking with need.

His mouth devoured mine, teeth catching my lip, tongue rough and desperate. His hand slid up my thigh, and then under my tunic, shoving the fabric aside, the calloused drag of his palm searing against my skin. My tunic bunched under his fingers as he pushed higher, then lifting it up and over my head and arms. He hissed through his teeth and merely stared for a long moment.

I let him look. Really look this time; not the glances he'd stolen from the shadows or when he thought I wasn't looking. His mouth curved in a soft, stunned smile.

"You are so beautiful."

I tilted my chin up and met his gaze as his hands cupped my breasts, thumbs carefully circling over my nipples in small circles until they reacted hardened under his touch. Heat rose in my cheeks, and Vestro laid kisses against my warm skin. He sucked gently at my breasts, taking as much as he could into his mouth. I gasped as he gently bit my nipples, rolling them between his teeth.

His body leaned into mine and his breath warmed my cheek, uneven, too close to a sob. I slid my hand up his chest, felt the tremor there, felt it echo in me.

"Look at me," I whispered.

He did. Gods, he did. And the look wrecked me; centuries of hunger, fear, longing, all stripped bare. No mask, no duty, just a man standing on the edge of something he's wanted for too long.

The lantern flickered, catching the sharp line of his jaw and the soft exhaustion in his eyes. His fingers curled into the fabric at my hip, slow at first, then tighter, like he didn't trust the world not to take me from him in the next heartbeat. His forehead brushed mine, a shaky exhale ghosting across my lips.

"Nadia..." he breathed, half-plea, half-warning.

I slid my thumb along his jaw. "Stop thinking."

That broke him. A soft, shattered sound rose from deep in his chest as he kissed me again, harder this time. His hands guided me backward, gentle but sure, until I lay back against the cool desktop. I pulled him with me, fingers twisting in the fabric at his shoulders.

The storm outside cracked, light flaring through the ruined window. For a heartbeat we were lit in white—his mouth on mine, his fingers on my waist, my hands tangled in his hair—two shadows fused into one.

He pulled back, his breath warm and shaking against my lips. "Tell me you want this," he whispered, voice scraped raw.

Something inside me broke wide open; not just fear or lust, but the truth of something I'd been too afraid to touch.

"I want you, Vestro." I choked back a sob. "I always have."

His eyes closed like the words undid something deep inside him. When he looked at me again, there was no fear left. No holding back.

My heart felt as if it would burst with excitement as he slowly pulled my leggings down past my ankles and tossed them aside.

His breathing quickened, and his skin felt fevered where it touched me. He stroked my breasts, hands sliding lower to massage my sides as he lowered himself to his knees. His kisses traced down my belly, then rose from my knees along my inner thighs.

Then Vestro pulled back and stood, licking his lips. The look in his eyes pinned me in place, breathless and unmoving. His gaze held promises. Danger.

Hunger.

He caught the edge of his shirt and pulled it over his head, and the light caught the muscles in his arms and chest. His trousers loosened under his fingers. The sound of fabric sliding down his legs was soft, deliberate. He didn't rush. He wanted me to watch. The lantern glow crawled up his thighs, along the tight flex of his stomach, over the rise of his chest. Sweat—or maybe the heat of the room—made a faint sheen on his skin, catching the dim light and turning it into something that felt dangerously intimate.

I had seen him naked thousands of times. In water. In shifting. In half-lit moments where his body was just another part of the creature he became.

But this?

This was a man undressing for me.

Vestro stood fully bare, his shoulders set and jaw tight. His gaze fixed on me like gravity itself had decided to choose a target.

The air changed. Thicker. Warmer. It pressed against my skin like a warm hand, guiding my knees wider apart in anticipation.

The shadows clung to him greedily, but the lantern caught just enough: the line of his throat as he straightened, the cut of his abdomen, and the heavy length of him hardening as he stepped toward closer.

Every inch of him felt alive, charged, like he was made of the same tension knotting low in my stomach. My breath tangled in my throat as he planted a hand on the desk beside my hip. His knuckles brushed my skin and my whole body went hot as he stepped between my knees.

Heat rolled off him in waves as he slid one arm beneath my thigh and pulled me into him with a certainty that made my pulse break open. The desk dug into my spine as he kissed me, his mouth urgent and starved, every sound he made sinking straight into my bones. His teeth scraped my throat as he kissed and bit his way down my neck, his breath hot and ragged.

A gasp, half-formed in my throat and he swallowed it with his mouth as he kissed me, hungry and starved. His fingers tested my center, and he groaned as his fingers slipped easily inside. I writhed against him as an ache rocked my body and arched my back.

I reached for him. "Ves, please!"

The breath ripped from my lungs and my jaw went slack as

Vestro pressed his length into me. The desk creaked as he thrust, the metal groaning under his strength. His grip tightened under my leg, his other hand bracing at my hip as he moved with a slow, devastating control that turned my breath into broken pieces. He caught a rhythm, steady and measured, so each long thrust jarred my ribs and stole my breath with each deep impact.

My nails dug into his back. My control slipped as ecstasy rolled beneath my skin and lapped at my heart. My fingers tangled in his hair, desperate, trying to hold on to something solid while the world shifted and tilted. He dragged his mouth down my neck, the scrape of his teeth making every muscle in my body tremble until I thought I would simply rattle apart.

Vestro growled, and it vibrated straight through me. My legs circled his waist on instinct. He answered by sliding one arm behind my waist and bracing his legs, and then he drew me up.

The desk fell away from my back as he lifted me, still wrapped around him, still shaking from the feel of him holding me like this— strong and unrestrained.

Vestro kissed me and kept me locked against him as he turned, walked away from the desk, and pinned me against the nearest wall. His forehead pressed into mine, our breaths colliding. His hand tightened under my thigh, lifting me higher to give him room to move. He braced one hand on the wall beside my head, the other gripping the underside of my thigh to hold me up effortlessly. His breath came ragged against my cheek as he began to thrust.

He wasn't careful or soft.

His movements were raw. Honest.

His entire body moved as one, and I felt myself break and restitch every time he ground into me. His mouth trailed down my throat, teeth scraping lightly across my collarbone.

I gasped as his thrusts hit deeper, harder. My entire body jolted and exploded with liquid fire as our bodies collided. I closed my eyes and let my head rest back against the wall as he fucked me like his life depended on it.

"Nadia..." he growled, his voice deep and feral.

I took his face in both hands and kissed him. Hard. He moved with me, against me, the wall anchoring us while his body pressed in, heat flooding every point where he touched me. A sound broke in his chest when I tightened my legs and pulled him closer.

Everything blurred; the wall at my back, his hands gripping my thighs, the way his breath stuttered when I whispered his name. My head fell back as his mouth dropped to the underside of my jaw. One hand tightened around my thigh, lifting me higher to hold me exactly where he wanted me. The other cupped my breast, squeezing hard enough to rip a cry from my throat.

I came alive everywhere.

My body arched into his without thought, chasing his heat, his pressure, and the overwhelming rightness of him.

My voice broke against his shoulder as every nerve lit up, and I shattered around him as something sweet and unbearable tore loose inside me.

Vestro's grip convulsed on my thigh. The sound that tore out of him as he came wasn't a word. It was need. Years of yearning he'd shoved into dark corners. All the stolen glances, all the unspoken what-ifs. Everything ignited at once.

I clung to him, shaking, drowning in the bliss rolling through me. It was dizzying, impossible, more intense than anything I'd ever imagined, and it hit me with a single, devastating truth: this was the man I had dreamed of without ever daring to admit it.

His mouth claimed mine again, softer now but still trembling with the force of the moment. His body pressed close, keeping me tethered as my breathing slowed, as the aftershocks rolled through me in slow, spiraling waves.

The lantern flickered once.

And I melted into him completely.

~

THE STORM's edge had passed when my heartbeat finally settled. Rain ticked softer against the far windows; the motion-sensor down the hall stuttered itself out and stayed dead. Gray light from the adjoining room slipped under the door and cast a rectangle over the floor where we lay, curled up on our cloaks. Vestro's arm curved warm and heavy around my waist. The hum in the walls had softened to a steady, living thrum. For the first time in days, my body felt still.

Vestro stirred. "You still think I'm human?" he asked, voice rough with the kind of sleep he never trusted.

"More than ever," I said.

A slow smile pulled at the corner of his mouth, quiet and sad. "Then maybe there's hope for me."

We began dressing without speaking. Vestro re-buttoned with careful fingers; I smoothed my collar twice and couldn't make it lie right. The air between us was dense with everything that didn't fit into words.

I caught him watching me as I pulled up my leggings, but he didn't shy away and instead gave me a soft, kind smile.

The door creaked. Yellow light from the corridor widened across our feet.

Andrew stood at the far end of the hall, sword belt slung loose over his shoulder. His gaze swept once—my hair mussed, Vestro's cuff half fastened, the shape of us still close—and stopped. Whatever color lived in his face drained away, leaving the stoic calm I had learned to fear.

"Where were you?" he said. The question was simple, but the room heard the verdict inside it.

Andrew's eyes locked on me, then Vestro, then Vestro's hand still gripping my waist. His jaw clenched, his body taut, the silence between us sharper than steel.

Vestro shifted between us like a shield. The softness was gone from his face; his mask snapped back on, but darker, sharper.

Andrew stepped into the room, every line of him rigid. "Nadia."

His dagger flashed free, the blade catching the moonlight as it lifted.

Vestro's arm shot forward, seizing Andrew's tunic in a brutal grip. With one violent yank, he ripped him back through the doorway and into the hall, slamming him into the opposite wall hard enough to crack the plaster.

And then the world exploded.

CHAPTER
THIRTY-SEVEN

The impact rattled the frame. The two men vanished into the hall, voices colliding in curses and shouts.

I stood frozen in the wreck of the room, breath ragged, heart clawing its way out of my chest. Heat flooded my face. My hands fumbled to knot the ties of my boots. My fingers shook so badly it took three tries to thread them, each tug sharp as if it could erase what almost happened.

Thunder rolled, hammering the windows and drowning the sound of the angry voices beyond the door. Their words were indistinct; only rage-filled snarls and shouts. I pressed trembling hands against the desk to steady myself when the world tilted.

Another crash split the hall. A body slamming hard. Their voices rose, sharper now, clearer.

I forced my legs to move, each step pulling me toward the door, toward the fight I already knew I'd find. I burst through the door to the mess in the hallway.

Vestro slammed Andrew back a step, one hand still fisted in his tunic and the other around Andrew's dagger hand.

Andrew's free fist slammed into Vestro's jaw. "You don't get to touch her!"

A low, blood curdling grow rippled from Vestro's chest. His grip tightened, dragging Andrew closer until their faces almost collided. "Stand down, Prince, or I'll tear your throat out."

Andrew's arm jerked loose, and his dagger cut through the air and nicked Vestro's jawline.

Vestro shoved forward, his forearm crushing Andrew's chest against the wall. His muscles twitched with restraint. Vestro sucked in breath through clenched teeth. "Don't make me kill you."

Andrew bared his teeth. "You think you scare me?"

A rush of footsteps skidded to a halt behind me. Corbin stood in the doorway, frozen like he'd stumbled into the wrong nightmare.

The movement distracted Vestro, and his grip slipped. Andrew snarled, jamming the blade forward toward Vestro's side.

Vestro caught the blade with his bare hand, and blood ran down his palm. His arm trembled as he forced the dagger inch by inch above Andrew's head, and then his blood-slicked grip shifted to Andrew's wrist as he pinned it against the wall. Andrew snarled and tried to push harder, but Vestro's hand didn't budge. Andrew's face flushed red, and his hand trembled as Vestro's grip slowly crushed, turning his fingers purple, until the blade slipped free.

Andrew strained against Vestro's arm. "Do it! Prove me right, you fucking demon!"

Vestro's skin rippled, tendons shifting under the surface like something clawed from beneath. He leaned close, his voice guttural. "I should've snapped your neck when you were a child."

Andrew's eyes widened, then narrowed into fire. "There it is. The real you."

Vestro's lip curled. The skin along his jaw rippled as something clawed beneath. His forearm lifted from Andrew's chest and pressed against his throat.

My stomach lurched. I darted forward, grabbing at Vestro's arm. "Stop it! Both of you!"

Neither man looked at me. Andrew drove his knee into Vestro's ribs. Then again. Vestro grunted, then shoved Andrew harder, the decaying plaster raining from the wall as cracks spiderwebbed out.

Vestro leaned closer, his voice low, guttural. "You feel that? That's me holding back."

"She deserves a king in her bed. Not her fucking pet,"Andrew's voice cracked with rage.

Vestro's body went rigid, the kelpie rippling under his skin. His forearm crushed Andrew's throat harder, until Andrew's face turned red, then blotched darker. Andrew free arm clawed at Vestro's arm, gasping for air. His face twisted as his rage bled to something sharper, tighter. Concern. Then the first flicker of desperation.

But still Andrew fought back, his pride burning through the pain.

My stomach turned to stone.

And it wouldn't stop until one of them was dead.

And it wasn't a fair fight.

The thought hit like ice water. My legs snapped free.

"Stop!" My scream ripped out of me. I shoved myself between them, my palms slamming against their blood-slick chests. "Godsdammit, Vestro, you're going to kill him!"

Vestro's eyes slid toward me, milky pale swirling in the obsidian depths. Then his grip slackened just enough for Andrew to drag in a rasping breath. Andrew's chest heaved, eyes blazing with fury.

I stood wedged between them, my heart hammered in my ears.

And that's when I noticed the satchel across Andrew's chest. The small bag that held Cipher; the entire reason we were on this fucking journey in the first place.

And the two idiots were about to destroy it in their fight over me.

"Stop before you break it!" I screamed. "You're going to break Cipher!"

Vestro froze, and his grip loosened just a fraction as he looked down at the satchel for the first time.

Something inside me cracked, and the words tore free before I even knew I had them.

"I can't do this anymore. If this is who you are... if you can't stop until one of you is dead—then I won't be either of yours."

Their eyes snapped to me.

"Fuck! You're both such assholes!" My chest heaved, but I didn't falter. "Right now, this isn't about us. It's not about who gets to keep me or claim me. It's about our kingdoms, and whether we can work together to save them. But if you two tear each other apart fighting over me, there won't be anything left for me worth saving."

The thunder boomed through the broken windows. My words hung in the air, heavier than the smell of blood.

Their faces blurred in front of me.

"I'm sorry, Andrew," I forced out, throat burning, "but I am not your trophy. Not something you get to plant on your arm to prove you've won. I can't marry you."

Andrew's face broke, fury splintering into something rawer. His hand twitched toward me, his lips parting. "Don't..." His voice cracked, with nothing kingly left in it. "Nadia, don't say that. You don't mean it."

I turned away. "And I'm not your safety net, Vestro." My hand pressed against his cheek, blood slick under my palm. "I love you, but I'm not the rope you cling to so you don't drown. I'm not what will keep you human."

Vestro flinched like I'd carved the words into him. His fingers flexed once, like he didn't know whether to reach for me or let me go. He didn't speak, but I felt the words press on my chest: *take it back. Please.*

"I'm not an extension of either of you!" my voice rose, ragged, unstoppable. "I want you—but I don't need you. Because *I am mine.*"

The storm howled through the broken windows. My words felt bigger than me, but they were true. They had always been true.

Andrew flinched like I'd struck him. Something in him buckled, just for a breath—barely visible, but real. His hand twitched toward his temple out of habit, fingers brushing his hair for the crown that wasn't there. Then he cradled the satchel to his chest, hugging it as if he could gain strength from the key he was meant to protect.

Vestro's shoulders sagged, the fight draining out of him. The beast rippled once under his skin, a last surge of rage, before he wrestled it down with visible effort. His gaze finally lifted—not at me, but at Andrew. Not hatred. Not rivalry. Just a hollow recognition that the two of them together had done this.

The silence between them stretched, raw and broken.

A low whistle cut through the hall.

Damien leaned in the doorway, dagger twirling lazily between his fingers and rain dripping from his hair. His sideways grin was sharp as always.

"Well," he drawled, his eyes flicking over the bruises, the blood, and the three of us caught in the wreckage, "that clears things up nicely."

Andrew swallowed hard, jaw grinding as he forced his posture straight. His eyes kept darting to Vestro—sharp and panicked—as if he'd only just realized the scale of what he was losing.

My breath hitched out sharply. "Fuck off, Damien."

Damien winked, the dagger flipping into its sheath. "All this cock-measuring and not a thought between you two alpha males. Fortunately, I've found a map. Your Highness, care to be the first one in this room with a plan?"

A heavy sigh escaped me. "Anything to get me out of here."

I pushed past Corbin, and he shrank back against the wall, eyes dropping fast.

The silence that followed said everything—Andrew and Vestro stiff behind me, Damien giving me a fractional nod as he motioned me forward.

For the first time on this journey, I wasn't moving as Andrew's betrothed or Vestro's shield. I was walking out as myself; clear-eyed, steady, and certain.

This wasn't about us. It never had been. It was about the world we still had left to save.

CHAPTER
THIRTY-EIGHT

The hallway still vibrated behind us as we followed Damien into the foyer.

No one spoke. No one dared.

Andrew stalked a few steps behind me; his breath ragged despite the calm he was desperately slamming back into place. Vestro followed silent and stone-faced, blood drying at the corner of his mouth and eyes fixed on nothing. Corbin trailed last, plaster dust still clinging to his tunic, wide-eyed and ghost-pale.

Damien pause, and then hurried to the far window and looked down. Coiled and alert. He lifted two fingers and pointed.

"Change of plans," he said flatly. "We need to move."

Andrew's jaw snapped tight. "What is it?"

Damien didn't look away from the glass. "We're not alone."

Andrew spun on his heel. "Everybody down the stairs. Now!"

Everything shattered into motion. Vestro moved first to take point, slipping past me with that eerie, controlled speed he used when every emotion had been locked away. Andrew grabbed my arm and shoved me in front of him, sword raised.

"Go," he barked, the word raw.

I didn't hesitate.

Something brushed my palm as we ran—a cold and familiar weight. I glanced down at Andrew's dagger.

"Stay armed," he muttered. "And stay close."

Vestro's jaw ticked once as he looked back, but he said nothing.

I tightened my grip around the hilt, shoved the dagger into my belt behind my lower back, and kept moving.

We hit the stairwell at a dead run. My legs took the steps two at a time, three when panic carried me. The building groaned with every impact of our boots.

Halfway down the last flight, my hand slapped the wall to steady myself and something clicked.

The stairs lurched. The entire structure dropped beneath us with a metallic shriek, dragging the handrail down as the steps folded into themselves and began descending into the black throat of the floor below.

"Vestro!" I yelled, breath tearing out of me.

"Keep going!" he shouted behind me. "Watch your step at the end!"

I ran down the moving staircase and leaped where the last steps melted into the floor. I hit the ground hard and staggered forward into the lobby. Dim glass-fronted boxes on the desks blinked awake as I passed, flickering with dying light. My pulse hammered in my ears as the men landed awkwardly behind me. Corbin slammed into Andrew at the bottom of the stairs, his hands grasping at Andrew's tunic for leverage.

"Sorry," he stammered. "I lost my footing..."

Andrew righted him and pushed him away, and then fixed his tunic and the satchel strap over his chest.

"Well?" he yelled. "What now?

Vestro hesitated. Then pointed. "The tall tower in the center. That's where we need to go."

Andrew nodded and took off at a fast run. Everyone followed close behind. I had to pump my legs double-time to keep up, taking three steps for every two of the men's. I glanced around as we moved. The buildings looked very different in the growing blue light, almost...alive.

Something moved down one of the alleys, a dark shadow that whirred and scuttled against the flat ground, displacing dust and small rocks as metal scraped against the side of one of the buildings. I stopped and turned to stare as I saw a flicker of tiny sparks, but Damien grabbed me by the back of the tunic and shoved me forward.

"Keep going," he said.

"There's something back there," I said, pointing behind me.

Damien caught my tunic and yanked hard. "There's something everywhere. Don't look. Move.

We barreled down a side street, darted past a rubble heap. Red eyes blinked from the shadows. More whirring. Louder now.

My heart pounded in my ears and my breathing was labored as we turned down a side street between a new row of buildings, many with faded, painted signs and wildly handwritten letters and words sprayed across the lower walls, and then turned again to pass a fallen rubble heap. Red eyes blinked from out of the shadows of the crumpled stone piles, and a low whirring noise filled the streets.

More androids?

"We're almost there!" Andrew called from up ahead.

I looked up. The tall metal tower loomed over us, so high that the pointed tip seemed to slice through the gray covering of clouds. I panted and forced my legs to keep moving.

The street widened and we were in a large market square at the foot of the tower. Empty water fountains and withered planters decorated what looked to have been a park on our left. A rusted metal swing set stood crooked in one corner, heavy chains busted at different lengths so that there was only one round, black ring left hanging. A small, hairless doll missing one eye sat propped against one of the swing's supporting poles, the frayed dress so dusty it was hard to notice the small patches of pink underneath.

Yes, definitely a park.

Hooves clattered against the cracked earth as a group of mounted members of The Holy rounded the corner and appeared to our right between two matching brick buildings, their golden cloaks whipping about them as they rode forward toward the tower's entrance, cutting off our path. I counted fifteen men as they lined up in two rows. In the distance, shouts and footsteps meant more reinforcements were coming.

I skidded to a halt, slamming into Corbin's back.

He didn't turn right away. His shoulders were rigid; head tilted just enough toward the line of Holy riders blocking the way to the tower. When he did look back, it was over his shoulder, eyes sweeping past me to the men behind.

Vestro's hand clamped around my arm before I could catch my footing. Not protective. Urgent. His body angled between me and the Holy riders ahead, his breath sawing in and out like every instinct in him had just detonated at once. His eyes tracked their formation.

"Nadia," his voice shook. "That's not a blockade. That's a capture line."

I blinked at him, heart thudding. "What are you—"

"They're here for you," he whispered. "And for Cipher."

Andrew stiffened at that, and his hand tightened on the hilt of his sword as he moved closer.

Vestro pulled me a full step backward, toward the collapsed building on our left. "I can still get us out," he rasped. "I can get you far from here."

"Nadia!" Andrew barked, closing the distance, reaching for me again.

Vestro shifted his body between us, his muscles trembling as if the kelpie strained beneath his skin. "They'll take her," he hissed at Andrew. "They'll take them both."

Then Vestro's eyes dropped to the open flap of the satchel slung across Andrew's shoulder. The blood drained from his face so fast it left him almost gray.

"No," he breathed. "No..."

467

"You—" Andrew started, but the words died in his throat as he checked the pouch and found it empty. His jaw dropped and he looked up in shock. "How?"

Vestro's breath hitched, then broke into something savage as he turned toward Corbin. "You have it."

Every muscle in Vestro's frame flexed like steel under strain. His skin rippled in waves; tiny worms writhing below the surface as his bones creaked before a shift.

The Holy riders saw it. Three of them flinched.

"That's the shifter," one muttered. He raised a long, barreled gun and aimed.

A sharp pop split the air, followed by a hiss.

Vestro jerked. A thin metal dart jutted from his shoulder, the shaft trembling with the force of the hit. His snarl caught mid-breath, breaking into a strangled choke. One knee hit the ground, dust blooming around him.

My stomach dropped. *What the hell...*

Vestro ripped the dart out in a single violent motion. Blood streaked down his wrist. He swallowed. "Nadia..."

Then his muscles seized. A violent jolt made him go rigid and fall to his side as a brutal stutter ran through him as if someone had reached inside and twisted all his nerves at once. His groaned as fingers clawed at the earth. His next inhale shuddered, sharp and wrong.

I reached for him. "Vestro!"

He tried to push up, but his arm buckled as his muscles seized.

Corbin's head snapped around to see Vestro on the ground, his expression annoyed. "Fucking kelpies."

Then his hand shot out and gripped my collar, yanking me off-balance.

"Corbin?" I gasped as he jerked me toward the horsemen. "What are you doing?"

The squire didn't answer. His grip only tightened, knuckles

whitening in the fabric at my throat. I clawed at his wrist, heels digging furrows in the black ground as he dragged me forward.

"Corbin!" I twisted, trying to reach for my sword.

He wrenched me around so hard my neck screamed. For a heartbeat the world went white. When it snapped back into focus, I heard the crack of impact behind me. I twisted around just in time to see Andrew hit the ground face-first, the back of his golden hair streaked red. A Holy soldier stood over him, sword leveled at the back of Andrew's neck. Another had Damien on his knees, blade pressed to his throat, the tip already dimpling skin.

"Corbin stop!" I screamed, the words tearing out of my chest. "Why are you doing this?"

He finally looked at me. Calm. Almost relieved. A small smile tugged at his lips.

"Because it's my job." He winked. "My task was to make sure Cipher made the journey here and then deliver it to our leader."

He jerked me closer to the line of horses. I dug my nails into his forearm, felt flesh give under my fingers.

"Now that we have Cipher," Corbin called, lifting his chin toward the riders, "I'll take credit for you as well, and our leader can deal with the rest of them as he pleases."

I let my knees buckle.

The surprise of my dead weight dragged us both down. I twisted at the last moment and shoved off Corbin's chest, rolling so his momentum carried him past me. We hit the ground hard, his grip jolting loose just enough.

My hand went to my belt, and my fingers closed around Andrew's dagger.

I slashed.

Corbin hissed as the blade carved a line from his elbow to his wrist. Blood spattered hot across my knuckles. His other hand clamped back on my collar, hauling me toward him even as he snarled in pain.

The horses screamed. Hooves clattered and kicked as the Holy line shifted, trying to rein in their mounts.

A gold cloak flashed in my peripheral vision. A hand lunged for my throat and gloved fingers crushed my windpipe.

I gagged and stabbed upward, jabbing the dagger again and again into the man's forearm and bicep. Metal scraped leather, then bit meat. Warm blood sprayed across my face and neck. He screamed and recoiled, grip tearing loose from my throat.

I twisted and drove both heels into Corbin's ribs.

He lost his hold as he flew back.

I scrambled away on all fours, wiping blood from my eyes. The world spun. A man in gold collapsed to his knees, clutching his ruined arm. Corbin rolled onto his back, gasping, clutching the long slice along his forearm.

I stared at the red slick on the dagger. At the mess I'd made.

"Nadia!" someone shouted over the chaos.

I looked up.

Andrew staggered to his feet, swaying, blood matting the back of his hair. He took one look at Corbin, at the line of Holy riders, and charged.

At Corbin.

Corbin saw him coming. He lurched up, grabbed for his fallen sword, missed, and ran anyway.

Behind us, the riders fought their mounts, trying to keep the animals from panicking. They held formation, cloaks snapping, eyes flicking not at us but toward the man at their far left.

"Your orders, sir!" one rider yelled.

The man at the end of the line didn't look up. He hunched over a flat metal device in his hands, the cloudy glass window flickering with a jittering red needle. A single sharp click snapped out of it.

"Sir!" the first rider shouted again. "Sir, your orders!"

Another click. Then two. Then a rapid burst of sharp, escalating pops like hail against steel.

The leader's head jerked up. "Hold!" he barked, throwing an arm out. "Hold, damn it!"

The device crackled again, the needle slamming into the far-right red band. The clicks became a frantic staccato, loud enough that even from where I stood, the hair on my arms lifted.

The man smacked the side of the scanner and stared at the needle vibrating violently against the red. Then his face drained of color.

"Radiation spike," he muttered. "Below us."

They're waiting for something.

Corbin veered, trying to cut around Andrew and sprint back toward the horses. He stumbled once, then again, boots sliding in dust and blood. Andrew caught him with a leaping strike that threw sparks from the stone when his sword clipped the ground.

They circled to my left, in the open center of the square. Corbin's sword lay midway between them, its hilt dusted red. Andrew stalked forward, good hand white-knuckled on his blade. Corbin backed away, bent over his knees, panting.

Corbin feinted left, then dove right. Andrew was faster. Steel flashed. Corbin shrieked as Andrew's blade tore open his palm when he reached for his fallen sword. He spun away, stumbling, chest heaving, legs dragging.

And ran straight toward us.

Damien moved first, hitting Andrew from the side with a shoulder slam that sent them both crashing to the ground. Andrew hit the ground, rolled, and shoved him off.

I spared a glance back at the line of Holy riders.

Why aren't they attacking?

The lead man cursed again, glancing down as the scanner clicked so fast it became a single vibrating rasp, smacked the box against his saddle horn, and turned the knob. The needle shook wildly; the clicking hit a fever pitch.

A red light flashed from the front end of the box, blinking rapidly as a high-pitched whistle sounded across the square and echoed off the buildings.

I caught movement to my left, and I turned as Vestro pushed himself slowly to his knees. His head jerked toward the collapsing center of the square. Something shifted under his skin. His eyes widened, not with fear but with recognition.

"Nadia," he rasped. "You have to move. Now!"

The ground shuddered.

Loose chunks of stone and glass rumbled from the nearby buildings. A wide circle of ground in the center of the park collapsed with a deep, reverberating crunch, and then exploded with a deafening boom into the air. My knees hit the ground as metal speared skyward —several jointed arms ending in wide serrated pinchers, snapping open and shut as they whipped around. A domed body rose beneath them, plates blinking with rings of light as the machine surfaced fully, its arms slamming down and sweeping in a vicious circle. The arms whipped downward, swung around like metal snakes, snapping at anything within their fifteen-yard reach.

The initial explosion threw Corbin and Andrew back and sent them both rolling across the street.

I screamed Andrew's name, but the voice was drowned under the thunder of hooves and the shriek of grinding metal.

Andrew rolled onto his back, eyes wide, staring up at the steel limbs slicing the air above. His gaze darted to Corbin, sprawled face-down a few feet away, then back to the machine. Measuring. His jaw clenched. Something ugly and reckless sparked behind his eyes.

I saw the look of rage on his face.

Oh, you dumbass, don't you do it.

"Andrew! Don't you dare," Damien snarled as he loosed another arrow.

Andrew twisted his body around and swung his blade in a wide arc at Corbin, the sword tip catching the squire's tunic and tearing open a large gash across his chest. Corbin cried out and rolled away, and Andrew dove after him.

He did it.

"Andrew!" I shouted.

"For the love of—Andrew!" Damien barked, fury cracking through his voice as he abandoned his shot and sprinted after them.

The horsemen finally moved.

"Get the girl," the leader called. "Find the key."

The Holy line spurred forward with a roar, swords and bows lifting as they rode around the edge of the machine's reach.

Vestro cursed and lurched to his feet and snatched a fallen soldier's sword near my feet. As the first wave of riders thundered past, he lunged, grabbed me around the waist, and rolled us both out of the path of slashing hooves. I hit the ground hard, breath punching out of me as his body shielded mine.

"Are you all right?" he demanded, pushing up onto his knees, hands framing my face.

I forced a shaking smile and flung my arms around his neck, squeezing tight. "Thanks, Ves."

He held me for a heartbeat, then tore himself away and surged to his feet, bloody sword spinning easily in his hand. He thrust his free hand back without looking.

I grabbed it. He hauled me up and I pulled my own sword free in the same motion.

I looked across the square as Damien yanked Andrew up by the arm, dragging him away from a flailing Corbin. Corbin struggled to his feet and had to drop back to his knees to dodge Andrew's swinging sword.

"Just leave the bastard and help us!" Damien shoved Andrew away with a curse, fitting his bow with an arrow. "We could use you right about now."

Damien spun away and pulled back on his bow, letting loose an arrow. His arrow punched through a rider's eye. The man howled and toppled backward off his horse, hands clutching his face. Another shaft followed, then another; each one finding a target. A gray-bearded axeman's weapon slipped from his hands as Damien's arrow buried in his throat; the man slid sideways out of the saddle and was dragged in the dirt by one boot tangled in the stirrup. Damien stepped aside, calm and efficient, firing into the chaos until the riders were too close for clean shots. He dove out of the way as an enemy arrow flew his way, and he cursed as it grazed his shoulder. He grunted and pulled back on his bowstring.

Vestro crouched over me, watching the scene as he gripped the sword's pommel with both hands. He growled as one of the horsemen jerked its mount's head around and kicked the animal in a run straight toward us. The rider pulled a gun from inside his tunic, the black tip glinting in the sun.

Vestro shoved me back, planted his feet, and raised the sword just as the man barreled down on us.

He snarled and ducked at the last instant, then twisted his whole torso into the swing. The man screamed as the weapon fired off into the sky and his head and shoulders fell backward in a gush of red, toppling to the black turf, his lower half carried away on the bucking horse, his limp feet still locked in the stirrups.

Vestro shook blood from his arm and glared at the Holy soldiers. "You're not supposed to touch her!"

Not supposed to touch me? What–

A high-pitched whistling sound carried over the clanging of metal and clattering of hooves, and I turned, just in time, to see a two-handed broadsword be deflected away from my head. I fell back, landing on my butt. I looked up to see Andrew breathing heavily above me, one side of his face bloody and eyes burning as he gasped for air through clenched teeth. I let out a breath of relief.

"Glad you finally decided to join us," I sneered.

Andrew grinned and offered his elbow. I looped my hands around it and pulled myself to my feet.

Our reunion was cut short when three men rushed at us with swords and axes cocked back. Vestro roared in defiance and leaped high in the air, landing in front of us. One of the men leaped from the saddle at me, his long arms reaching forward, and Andrew spun and kicked him hard in the chest. The man rolled backward, cursing. Andrew pushed me behind him as another man attacked, diving at him.

The second rider came straight for us, his copper helm gleaming and heavy blade raised. I only had time to gasp before my body froze. I didn't move.

But Andrew did.

His shoulder slammed into my ribs, throwing me sideways and out of the way hard enough that my vision blanked.

Only after I hit the ground did I register what he'd actually done.

Andrew hadn't just shoved me clear.

He'd stepped directly into the blade meant for me.

The square dropped into silence, except for my heartbeat.

One slow, heavy thud.

Then another.

Time thickened around me, the edges of everything smearing as if the world itself were holding its breath.

Andrew's scream cracked through the stillness so violently it felt like the air itself recoiled in pain.

A wet sound ripped the air.

I lifted my head, dazed, pushing up on a shaking palm.

The rider's blade completed its arc behind where I'd been standing, and a spray of red followed its path.

For a heartbeat I didn't understand it. I just lay there in the blur, watching the blood float through the air in a long, arcing ribbon that caught the gray light like a torn banner.

Then the ribbon fell.

And so did Andrew. He dropped straight down, as if the ground had vanished beneath him.

"Andrew?" The word scraped out of me, thin and useless.

Andrew hit the ground hard. His sword clattered away. His body twisted unnaturally as he landed, and then—there, at the edge of my sight—something rolled across the ground with a dull, wet slap.

A piece of him.

My stomach lurched. Bile burned my throat.

His right leg was simply...gone. Severed below the knee. Blood gushed in pulsing waves from the ruined limb, splattering the black stone beneath him in sickening, steaming arcs.

His fingers clawed at the ground, slipping in his own blood as he gasped, eyes wide with a pain too massive for any mask to hold.

"N-Nadia..." His hand lifted, shaking. "Don't—"

His arms gave out. His head hit the stone.

My heartbeat slammed back into my skull, fast now, frantic, thunderous.

Hooves thundered on my left. Two riders broke from the smoke, angling straight for Andrew. I called out to him in alarm, but my cries were lost in another earth-shuddering explosion from somewhere behind the line of buildings.

A shadow flickered at the edge of the chaos. I saw Vestro turn sharply at Andrew's cry, sensing the danger but unable to reach us with riders closing in.

Something cold and sharp snapped into place inside me.

If they reached us, Andrew was dead.

And I was the only one still standing.

I ran forward and charged the pair of riders, screaming and waving my arms.

"Nadia!" Damien bellowed, fumbling for another arrow. "Don't be stupid!"

I ran anyway. I sprinted straight into the riders' path, screaming and waving my arms to drag them away from Andrew.

They veered toward me instantly.

Good.

Come on. Chase me you golden fucks.

I ran toward Andrew with my head down, dodging the giant pinchers that smacked down against the ground to smash me, and I pushed him down flat as I passed. The riders ignored Andrew and followed me closer to the disturbed edge of the giant crater the metal arms had emerged from. I glanced over my shoulder. The men leaned forward in their saddles, their arms outstretched to snatch me from the ground.

Please let this work!

The ground trembled again, knocked me off my feet. I rolled along the black ground, scraping my skin as I slid to a stop. Dust clogged my throat and stung my eyes as I struggled to my knees and scooted back.

Drops of hot blood splattered all around me. I looked up, screamed, and quickly backed away. The monstrous metal arms ripped the two bodies of The Holy riders apart. Limp limbs were swung from side to side by the giant machine, like an angry dog with a torn-up slipper, spraying blood and globs of innards out across the black earth, chunks of flesh bouncing and skidding in red, wet piles. I nearly threw up again as an arm landed next to me—still gripping a sword. I covered my mouth with one hand as I scrambled to my feet.

Somewhere behind me, I heard Vestro snarl. He was close but trapped behind the shifting tangle of metal limbs and riders.

A blur of black and silver appeared on my right. I turned my head to find Damien running next to me, his bow gripped in one hand.

My body was already moving; crawling, stumbling, dragging myself across the blood-slick stone toward Andrew.

Andrew's wide eyes met mine as we approached. His breath came in short, broken jerks, chest heaving as he tried and failed to push himself upright. His severed limb pumped out blood in horrifying pulses, splattering against Damien's boots.

"Vestro!" Damien shouted, raw panic shredding his voice. "Get over here!"

Andrew coughed, a wet, choking sound, blood bubbling at the corners of his mouth.

"Dammit," Damien hissed, hauling Andrew up under the shoulders. "Andrew—stay awake!"

Andrew screamed when Damien lifted him, unfiltered and unguarded.

"Andrew, please..." I dropped to my knees beside him, my hands hovering uselessly over the gushing wound. "Please, gods, stay with me."

His eyes rolled toward me, unfocused, glassy. He tried to say something; only a wet cough came out, red froth on his lips. His whole body arched once—a spasm—then went frighteningly still except for a faint tremor running through his fingertips.

Too much blood.

Too fast.

No one could survive this.

"Don't you dare," I choked, pressing my shaking hand against his chest because I didn't know what else to hold on to. "Andrew, please. Stay with me."

He blinked. Slow. Heavy.

Vestro dropped to the ground beside us, his eyes wild, taking in Andrew's mangled stump with a single sharp breath.

"Tourniquet. Now!" he snapped.

Damien was already tearing off his belt.

Vestro's hands were steady as he looped the leather above Andrew's knee and cinched it tight. Andrew convulsed, back arching, a hoarse cry strangled in his throat.

"Hold him," Vestro ordered.

Damien braced Andrew's shoulders. I threw my weight across Andrew's chest, hands slipping on blood, trying to keep him grounded as Vestro twisted the belt tighter, stopping the arterial spray to a sickening trickle.

Andrew gasped. A wheezing, broken sound. His head lolled toward me, eyes glassy, unfocused.

"...Nadia..." he breathed, voice barely a thread.

"I'm here," I whispered, my tears hitting his cheek. "I'm here, Andrew."

His fingers twitched, reaching toward me, then falling short. He sagged sideways, half-conscious, blood soaking the black stone beneath him in a widening pool.

"I can't cover us!" Damien shouted over his shoulder, already grabbing for his last arrows. "Move him!"

"We can't move him," Vestro snarled. "He'll bleed out."

"He's already bleeding out!" Damien barked.

I had to lean close to Andrew's ear to hear him above the clanging arms and shouts of the rushing The Holy.

"Andrew, what—"

"...Three arrows left."

Andrew pressed his left hand against his wound, then he grimaced and grabbed my arm.

"Damien's only got three arrows," he wheezed. His head drooped and he coughed several times, bubbles squeezing out of his side with each jerk. When he looked back up his lips were bloodstained. "Corbin...has Cipher..."

He lifted a shaky hand to my face but faltered just short of my chin. I caught his hand before he let it drop, rubbed it against my wet cheek.

Andrew took a rattling breath. "You need to go. I...lo-lov..." A coughing fit overcame him, sending his body into racking convulsions.

I choked on my tears as I buried my face in his neck, leaning over him so the world couldn't take him from me.

Behind us, someone screamed. Metal arms slammed into stone. Hooves thundered. But it was all muffled, distant, drowned beneath the thudding roar of my own pulse. I pressed my bloody palm to Andrew's cheek. His skin felt wrong. Too cold.

"Nadia!" Damien screamed. "Nadia, get out of here! I'm out of arrows!"

I looked over to Damien, as he hefted his bow with two hands at one end, cocking it back as he got ready to swing at the first of five approaching horsemen. Past them, I could see another band of Holy members clattering around the corner.

Vestro wrenched the belt tighter, his forearms trembling with the force of it. Andrew convulsed, a broken cry tearing from his throat.

"Nadia, stay behind me!" Vestro snapped, his voice raw.

Andrew's hand tightened over mine. "Go..."

I squeezed Andrew's hand and kissed it.

I'm sorry.

I let his hand drop and forced myself to my feet, spinning around just in time to see Corbin sprinting toward the tower entrance.

But I can't just run away.

Vestro's hand shot out blindly, searching for me without lifting pressure from the tourniquet. "Stay with me. Nadia, don't—"

I grabbed Andrew's sword and took off after Corbin. The squire must have felt me following him, because he glanced over his shoulder at me and picked up his pace.

I ignored Vestro's strangled cry that followed me.

CHAPTER
THIRTY-NINE

I reached the front doors of the tower. They slid to the side on their own with a loud whoosh. The room was round and white, from the painted ceiling to the white marble tiles, and empty, save for a single silver pedestal in the center of the room. Directly behind the pedestal I could just make out the square outline of what looked like double doors, but there were no handles or windows, so I couldn't be sure.

I looked closer at the pedestal. It had several knobs and dark buttons that spread out evenly across the surface, and a thin, rectangular box on the front lined with numbers and all the letters of the alphabet. A deep indention sat in the center of the top surface with several short barbs sticking up in a half-circle pattern, as if something fit perfectly...

Like a key.

Cipher.

Something smacked into the side of my face, a white-hot flash that tore the world sideways. I hit the floor hard, skidding across the polished tile. My sword clattered away, spinning across the room like it wanted nothing to do with me.

A bright red droplet hit the floor beside my cheek. Another.

My blood.

A shadow swept over me.

I rolled instinctively as Corbin's blade came down, the metal shrieking across the tile where my skull had just been. The force of it cracked the grout. A shiver ran up my spine.

He swung again. I tucked and rolled, my shoulder protesting, but I kicked out blindly and caught him square in the kneecap. Something popped. Corbin hissed and staggered.

I scrambled up, crouching low. Corbin straightened, weight shifting with a fighter's ease. And of course—he had my sword.

Fuck.

I slipped into Old Red's stance, my shoulder turned and body narrow, ready to spring. Corbin mirrored me, unnervingly natural, like he'd been waiting for this.

Damn, he knows what he's doing.

How does a squire...

I blinked as realization dawned.

Because he's not a real squire.

He probably never was.

"Why?" I asked. My voice sounded raw, feral.

"Why not?" he said. He didn't even try to hide the smirk. "The Holy pays well, and they needed someone to make sure you and Cipher reached Ferrington. My job was to clean up the rest of the mess."

Heat stung my eyes. Trea. Peter. Darren. All gone. Andrew bleeding out behind me. All of it funneling down into the point of Corbin's stolen sword.

Something in me cracked. Something that I knew could never be mended. I'd never wanted to hurt another person before this. That soldier had been mere self-defense, and I'd had no choice. But I didn't want to just hurt Corbin.

I wanted to kill him.

I advanced slowly, cross-stepping over my feet to keep my

stance. I twirled Andrew's dagger in my hand and shifted my grip, fingering the well-worn handle. Corbin rocked back and forth on his long legs, his shoulders tense and ready. He blinked, and his rhythm faltered.

I lunged first.

Corbin reacted fast—too fast. His blade sliced down in a brutal arc. I dove under his arm, feeling the wind of steel on my back, and drove my shoulder into him. He grunted, stumbled. I slashed low with my dagger, aiming for the soft flesh above his boot. He jerked his leg back just in time, and my blade cut a long line down his calf instead. Corbin screamed and fell back, swinging his sword as he spun away, the tip of his blade nicking my shoulder. I gritted through clenched teeth as I stepped back. A warm trickle of blood slid down my arm, staining my sleeve.

Corbin snarled and moved faster than I could clock, grabbed a fistful of my tunic, and hurled me backward. My spine slammed into the glass doors. Pain sparked behind my eyes as the world blinked. My arm twisted as I landed, and I gasped as my wrist crumpled beneath my weight.

"You little bitch," he spat.

Corbin stalked toward me, eyes glinting. I held my wrist to my chest, trying to ease the throbbing. I could move it, so at least it wasn't broken. I grimaced and looked to the right. My dagger was across the room. My sword was in his hand.

Fuck.

I ducked and rolled toward the dagger as he lunged, and his blade hit the glass with a scream of metal. The reverberation shook up the hilt and into his arm. For a fraction of a breath, he winced.

I didn't waste it.

I surged up, jamming the point of Andrew's dagger toward his ribs. But Corbin twisted and caught my wrist. We struggled, shoulder against shoulder, breath mingling in a hot, bloody tangle.

"You fight dirty," he hissed.

"I only wish Andrew was here to watch you die," I spat.

Corbin slammed his forehead into mine. Stars detonated behind my eyes, and I reeled. He swept my legs out, and I hit the tile, my bones buzzing from the impact.

Corbin stalked toward me, sword lowered but deadly.

My wrist throbbed. My head was ringing. I still gripped Andrew's dagger in my hand, and that the weight felt like a curse and a lifeline all at once.

I forced myself up, teeth clenched and charged.

Corbin didn't expect that.

I slammed into him, driving us both sideways. We skidded across the smears of blood on the floor. Corbin's. Mine. Who even knew anymore. He swung wildly, trying to cut me off him, but I ducked under his arm and slashed upward. The dagger caught the inside of his knee.

This time it sank deep.

Corbin screamed. His leg collapsed, and his sword scraped a long, gouging line in the floor. Then his hand shot and he grabbed my throat, lifting me halfway off the ground with raw, ugly strength.

I dangled there, vision dimming, the world narrowing to his sneer and the pressure crushing my windpipe.

"It's unfortunate I can't just kill you," he hissed. "But they need you alive."

My heart lurched. "Why am I so important?"

"You're the only living proof they didn't waste the last three centuries." He tilted his head, pleased with himself. "Didn't you ever think it strange? A bastard living among royalty? That you don't look a damn thing like the rest of them?"

"My mother—"

"Natasha wasn't your mother," he snapped. "She was a surrogate. A carrier. You weren't born; you were designed. Decades of controlled pairings, failures, abortions, stillbirths. Until you."

He gave a soft laugh, almost admiring. "A viable body to restart the Project."

My stomach twisted. "I don't know what you're..."

His chuckle started low and cracked open into a jagged cackle. "You were created for one purpose: to help us rebuild the soldier line. An army no kingdom can stand against. We'll wipe out the old failures—those demonic miscreants—and then crush every kingdom that resists."

He yanked me closer until his lips brushed my ear. The smell of coppery blood and sweat choked me. "You're nothing but a science experiment with a pulse."

His grip on my neck tightened.

But my hand still held Andrew's dagger.

I let my body go slack, made him think he'd won.

His grip eased—just enough.

I drove Andrew's dagger deep into his belly, the blade slicing his flesh with a sickening, beautiful give. He looked down at me in surprise, his lips whitening around the edges. I screamed in his face and used both hands to jerk up on the dagger, slicing up through his stomach until it lodged in his ribcage, where I couldn't pull it any higher. His arms grabbed at me, and his legs collapsed, pulling us both to the ground. My stomach and chest were soaked in liquid warmth as his blood spilled over me.

I twisted around and kicked Corbin off me. He screamed repeatedly, his body trembling violently as blood pooled around his legs and sides, spreading out in a beautiful fan-shape as it caught and ran along the grout lines of the large tiles. I stared down at his twitching body and screamed again, choking on the hot, acidic bile that rose in my throat. Not because he was dead, but because somewhere deep inside the darkest corner of my rapidly beating heart I knew that it was true...

I'd enjoyed killing him.

I hated him for it. I hated him for turning me into this murderous creature that wore my bloodstained clothes and screamed with my hoarse voice. Before this journey I never would have lifted a finger to harm another person if it hadn't been absolutely necessary, because I'd always believed murder was wrong. And killing demons hadn't been murder; I had hunted demons to protect the people around me, to keep the fiends at bay in the dark shadows they lurked in. But Corbin had made me realize that beneath the contrasting casings of skin, there really weren't that many differences between humans and demons.

We were all monsters.

I spat down at his body and tried to squeeze out some of the blood that soaked the front of my shirt. The glass doors swished open, and footsteps came toward me.

CHAPTER
FORTY

I quickly knelt beside Corbin and shoved my hand down the front of his tunic, felt around the wet mess until my fingers met the smooth surface of Cipher. My bloody hands slipped, and I nearly dropped it as I ran toward the pedestal to where my sword lay.

I need to get out of here. I need to take Cipher and run, hide away until I figure out what the hell I'm going to do. I don't...I don't have anyone. I can't trust anything I've been told. None of the stories growing up are true. Everything I've known has been a lie.

A man yelled, and I leaped forward the last few inches. I dove into the pedestal in my haste, and Cipher rolled out of my hand, spinning across the smooth floor. An arm wrapped around my waist and jerked me back just as my fingers brushed the pommel of my sword. I spun, blade half-lifted, but a hand caught my wrist and forced my arm aside.

Vestro!

"Vestro!" I gasped. "What are you—

He was out of breath, as if he'd sprinted clear across the city. The front of his shirt was soaked in sweat and blood. The wound on his ear had reopened, staining his neck in a dark sheet. A cut on his temple trickled down his cheek, and his hair was a sticky mess plastered against his face. My heartbeat raced.

"Where's Andrew?" The question tore out of me before I could stop it. My heartbeat slammed against my ribs. "Is he—did he... Vestro, tell me."

His jaw tightened. His eyes flicked away, just for a breath, and that was all the answer he'd give me. Panic clawed up my throat.

"Vestro," I whispered, "please—"

He cut me off roughly, voice strained. "Give me Cipher."

I slowly looked up as he released his grip on my arm. His expression didn't match the chaos on his body. It was a distant, blank mask. His black eyes stared at me coolly, that unsettling age-old knowledge swirling beneath.

"Why?" I whispered. I stepped back. And again. And again. I lifted my sword tip an inch. "You...you're helping them."

"Don't be stupid!" he snapped. His eyes went wild as he balled his fists and edged closer. "I'm not giving it to those lunatic scientists. I'm going to destroy it."

"You can't," I said. "The pass needs to be secured. The Holy—"

"Fuck The Holy!" he roared. "There is no such thing as demons, Nadia. Haven't you been listening? There is no magic. It's all machines and technology and experiments that should never have existed. And now The Holy wants to bring it all back. Without the key, they can't open the main lab. This is my chance to end it. Just give me Cipher and then we can get the hell out of here."

He knew.

The whole time, he knew The Holy's purpose, their goals. He knew they wanted me, and that they planned on using me, and yet he led us here. He led me here, and I followed. Trusting him, loving him.

I raised my sword higher. "Get away from me."

Vestro's eyes narrowed, cheeks tightening.

"There is a war coming," he growled. "Nothing will stop that.

Destroying the key will level the field. I need that key, Nadia. Then this can all be over."

The muscles in his arms bunched as he hunched his shoulders. He slid one foot across the tile as he inched toward me. I pointed my sword at him with one hand, while I knelt and groped for Cipher with the other. His eyes blinked once. Twice.

He lunged.

I screamed and swung. The tip of my blade caught his flank; he cried out and rolled away.

I slipped on a puddle of Corbin's blood and tumbled. I tried to fall away from the gutted body and smacked my head against the floor. Stars swirled around my vision before Vestro's dark eyes came rushing at me. I rolled to the side and swung again. My blade whistled through the air, just out of reach. I blinked. He wasn't going for me; he was reaching for Cipher.

He was reaching for Cipher.

"Get away from that!" I cried, scrambling toward him. My hands slid on the blood-slick floor.

I dove at him, and my blade sunk deep into the back of his right calf.

He roared and his hand shot out in reflex, backhanding me across the cheek. My head snapped sideways as my body flew across the room toward the pedestal.

I'd known Vestro was strong. I'd felt it in every embrace, every time he carried me across fields. But this... this was the first time he'd used that strength against me. And as I fell, helpless, toward the blood-splattered tile, terror seized my chest. I closed my eyes, bracing for impact.

It never came.

Strong arms caught me, pulling me against a warm body. A hand brushed my cheek. I forced my eyes open. Vestro's face hovered inches from mine, eyes wide with worry.

"Nadia, are you all right?" he breathed. "I didn't mean to—

"I…" My body refused to cooperate. I tried to twist, but my neck wouldn't listen. "My whole body is tingling."

"Oh, God," his voice broke. "I'm so sorry…"

My entire body tingled, as if it had fallen asleep on me. Then suddenly the numbness went away, and a searing pain ripped through my neck and back. A scream tore out of my chest. My back arched, toes curling. The pain suddenly faded to a bearable level, and I stared up at Vestro. There were tears in his eyes, and he opened his mouth to say something, then jerked his head up as the doors opened.

His hands shook as he pulled me tighter to him and kissed my forehead before setting me softly on the ground below the pedestal. Cipher lay on the floor near my head. Forgotten.

Vestro stepped in front of me, blood dripping down his leg.

I struggled to sit up, but I only managed to turn my neck toward the door before the pain seized me again.

At least my neck's not broken.

"Nadia?"

I forced my eyes open past the pain at the familiar voice. Maurdruik stood in his colorful robes next to a middle-aged stranger, trailed by seven The Holy members and a young man in red.

I frowned. The man in white wasn't dressed like anyone I'd ever seen. His white robe was stiff, crisp, almost shiny, cut straight like a butcher's apron but reaching his knees. A loop of thin silver tubing circled his neck, ending in two small metal disks that clicked faintly when he moved. He had strange quills tucked into a square patch of fabric over his heart, but they weren't quills; they were smooth and sharp, like they belonged to some delicate machine.

Something about him tugged at my memory, but nothing fit. No wizard dressed like this. No healer. No soldier.

He looked wrong for this world.

"Good work, Vestro," Maurdruik said. "She made it here under your protection."

490

I tried to speak but my throat produced nothing. My vision blurred. Something wet slid down my cheeks.

Maurdruik stepped forward, his staff ticking on the tile. Vestro's feet scraped against the floor as his stance widened, blocking the wizard's way. Maurdruik frowned, and the weapons behind him rose. He narrowed his eyes at Vestro, and his hands tightened around the wood.

"Partially," the man in white added, craning to look past Vestro. "She looks injured." His face reddened. "You were told to keep her in one piece. We're already late. We must harvest her eggs before the computers finish booting."

Eggs? What the hell are they talking about?

"Who do you think you are to—" Vestro snarled.

"Doctor Reichard," the man in white said, "but I've also been called the Wizard Drahcier of Riverwind."

Wizard...Drahcier? No. That couldn't be right. I had met him before at Andrew's castle—years ago—but he never looked like this.

Reichard nodded toward the royally-dressed man behind him. "And this is Calvin of Krill. Your future emperor."

Old Red's warning echoed:

'...What about Calvin, son of Morgan?' Old Red had asked.

'He is still missing after nine months' Maurdruik said. 'And with no sign or word of his ship we can only assume the worst.'

I swallowed.

It was all part of the coming war. Demons had attacked the royal lines and stolen Cipher to tip the scales, and The Holy had seized the chaos to send the male heirs on a neatly packaged suicide mission— retrieve the key, die trying, and keep their own hands clean.

Now they were gathered in Ferrington, waiting.

Krill stood with The Holy. And the lands would burn.

"Where is Cipher?" Maurdruik demanded.

Vestro growled and shifted closer to me, planting himself between us. "You're not getting anything," he snarled.

Blood dripped from his torn ear and the gash in his calf, pooling dark around his foot. My vision burned as I tried to move. Pain knifed down my spine, stealing my breath and leaving my limbs useless. I clenched my teeth and focused on not blacking out.

Vestro's leg finally buckled. He hit his knees with a sharp grunt. "You just used her," he spat. "All of them."

Maurdruik smiled faintly. "No." His gaze slid over Vestro with open disdain. "You did."

He stepped closer. "A double agent who helped bring her here, then tried to steal both her and the key once you'd learned enough of our plans." His eyes gleamed. "I am no user. I am a scientist." He turned his attention to me. "And she was created for a single purpose."

Vestro went very still.

"How... how did you—" Vestro whispered.

Maurdruik switched the staff to his other hand. "Simple. The tracking device in Nadia's suit transmitted everything said around her for most of the journey. And the transmitter implanted above your right hip made following you trivial once we recovered the discarded armor." His mouth curved. "You were never subtle. And Andrew and Peter were marked for death the moment I proposed the journey," Maurdruik continued calmly. "Unsettled kings complicate empires."

Maurdruik lifted his chin, gaze sliding proudly between me and Vestro. "Creation always begins with two. And for the first time in three centuries, we finally have them."

The pain had subsided. A little. I bit my lip until I tasted blood as I slowly pulled one arm under me. At least I knew my neck wasn't broken. After a shuddering breath that sent thousands of needles dancing across my skin, I managed to move the other one.

Good. No one is paying attention to me.

"Enough of this," Reichard grabbed a sword from the nearest The Holy member, shouldered past Maurdruik, and stalked toward us. "Give me the damn key so I can turn the power on."

I was crying. At least, I thought I was. My cheeks were wet, but after Vestro's backhand it could have been blood soaking into my collar. I closed my eyes and slowly slid one knee closer. Bile rose in my throat, and I held my breath lest they hear me.

"Don't worry," Maurdruik said. "We'll fix her up when we're through."

"I'm not letting you touch her!" Vestro roared.

Time slowed.

I watched The Holy charge Vestro with swords drawn. Reichard reached inside his white cloak with his free hand and pulled out a small, hand-sized guns and pointed the tip at Vestro's chest.

Maurdruik finally looked down at me as I pushed myself unsteadily to my feet, and his face paled as he raised a pointed finger toward me.

Vestro turned at the motion—saw me standing—and relief flickered across his blood-slicked face. He lifted his arm, pointing toward the glass doors. His mouth shaped a single word—*run*—but the world had gone muffled, everything swallowed in a thick, rushing pulse behind my ears. Reichard didn't even look at me. He stepped in, calm as a butcher, and pressed the tip of the weapon to Vestro's chest.

"Don't!" I tried to shout, but the sound scraped uselessly out of my throat.

A crack split the air—too loud, too sharp—slamming into my skull like a hammer.

Vestro's body jolted backward, limbs jerking once before he crumpled. His head hit the tile with a wet thud that punched the air from my lungs.

For a beat, everything froze. All I saw was him on the floor. Vestro. *My* Vestro, with his chest smoking where the weapon had torn into him, blood spreading fast beneath his ribs.

My knees buckled. I caught myself on the pedestal, fingers slipping in something wet. Cipher lay half in my palm, half in the growing pool of red. So much red covered my hands and legs that I couldn't tell whose blood was on me anymore.

I swallowed bile and forced a breath past the shattering in my chest. Gods only knew what I was doing, or what would happen next. There was no thinking. Only moving. Only surviving.

Only doing the one thing left that still mattered.

Cipher was wet as I scooped it up off the blood-slick tiles and turned to the pedestal.

Andrew was right. I needed to think about my kingdom, not about myself.

I was created for a purpose.

And I wasn't about to run away.

I snatched up my sword lying near the bottom of the pedestal, caught myself on the ledge, and pulled myself to my feet. I turned to stare at the men as they rushed me. I roared defiantly at them as I set Cipher on the flat surface, lifted the sword high over my head with both hands, and brought the rounded end of the pommel down again and again against the smooth, silver surface. Gold buttons chipped off, and the round casing slowly dented and then crunched under my attack.

"No!" Maurdruik screamed. "What have you done?"

An arrow sank into my shoulder. Pain radiated across my left side, and I dropped my sword and clawed at the pedestal as I fought to stay upright.

"Do not harm her!" Reichard cried to The Holy members as he rushed toward me. "We need her!"

My shaking fingers felt at the arrow sticking out of my skin and stared at the men as I sank to my knees. My knees slammed into the tile hard enough to rattle my bones, but I barely felt it.

Warmth soaked through the knees of my pants.

Vestro's blood.

He lay only a breath away, half-turned toward me like he'd been trying to reach me even as he fell. His chest hitched in shallow, uneven pulls. His mouth parted like he was searching for air. Or me. Maybe both.

I shuddered. "Vestro…"

His eyes found mine instantly. Even now, bleeding out on a cold floor, he looked at me as though I were the last thing tethering him to this world. Relief flickered there—raw, heartbreakingly pure—and it tore something open in me so violently I thought my ribs had split apart.

I dragged myself through the slick warmth until I could touch him. My trembling fingers brushed his cheek, and he leaned into them with the faintest instinctive pressure, like even in agony he was trying to steady me. His lashes trembled, his breath catching as though he were trying to hold on just for me. Blood trailed from the corner of his mouth. I wiped it away with shaking fingers, smearing it more than clearing it.

"Don't..." his voice faltered, rough. "Don't let them...take you."

A sound tore out of me—half-sob, half-breath—as my vision blurred. The world around us warped, depth bending wrong, like water disturbed by a stone thrown too hard. The tile, the walls, and the shouting behind us wavered out of focus, rippling around the center of him.

I pressed my forehead to his, desperate to anchor him, to anchor myself.

"Vestro, please..." My voice cracked open.

He drew in a trembling breath, fighting for it. His eyes fluttered, then opened again—just barely. Enough for one more look. Enough to drown me.

"I love you, Nadia," he breathed. "I'm-I'm sorry."

His exhale brushed my cheek—soft and warm, like the last sigh of a wave pulling back from the shore. My body clenched around the loss even before it came. My fingers curled into the fabric of his shoulder, trying to hold him here, keep him from slipping under.

But you can't hold water.

Not when it's leaving.

His chest lifted once, then again, slower and shallower.

"Vestro..." I whispered, the word unraveling.

His body went still in my hands.

For a heartbeat I couldn't breathe. It felt like the world had gone airless, like my lungs were trying to draw water where none remained. A hollow surged through me, sharp and aching, the sensation of falling into a drained pool with no depths left to catch me.

"No..." The word slipped out before I even knew I'd said it.

I pressed my palm to his cheek, trying to memorize the warmth before it bled away into the cold tile below us. My fingers curled, helpless, as if holding him tighter might coax the tide back into his chest.

Tears slipped down my face, hot and relentless, and for a moment I couldn't tell whether they were mine or the world itself was flooding beneath me, rising to fill the depth he'd left behind.

Tears slipped down my face, and for a moment I didn't know whether they were mine or the world was flooding beneath me.

A shadow rose over us. Maurdruik. He lifted his staff and called The Holy forward.

I didn't look at him. I couldn't.

My hand found Andrew's dagger on the tile. The same blade that had saved me, killed Corbin, and protected us more times than I could count. The handle was still warm from my grip, and slick with Vestro's blood.

Maurdruik shouted something behind me, but I didn't hear him.

I couldn't hear anything.

My eyes stayed on Vestro.

His body lay still, chest unmoving, the last warmth of him fading into the floor. I traced the line of his jaw with my gaze. My throat tightened, my pulse hammering against the inside of my skin like it wanted out.

Only Vestro remained sharp; the only stillness in the chaos, the only depth left in a world that suddenly felt too shallow to breathe in.

"You won't take me," I whispered, the words catching on a trembling breath. "Your empire will never come to light."

I leaned toward him, toward the last warmth fading from his

skin, toward the dark, quiet pool I had always found myself pulled back to. My vision tunneled until there was only his face, serene and impossibly still; the surface of a water I had never feared.

"I'm right behind you, Ves," I breathed.

I pressed the edge of dagger against my throat.

"Wait," someone barked. "Stop her!"

No.

They don't get to drag me away from him.

The room blurred at the edges, warping like heat over boiling water.

Men shouted. Boots pounded closer. All of it washed away.

I never looked away from Vestro.

And then I pulled.

There was no pain. Just a warm, swallowing numbness, like slipping beneath the calm surface of a warm bath and letting it close over me. I smiled as I imagined Vestro's hands sliding across my skin, gently pressing in all the right places as he worked out the kinks and the pain until I floated peacefully in his arms. The world dimmed, and colors bled into black as hands grabbed at me, close voices rising in panic.

"Get me a rebreather—tube her—IV now!"

"We need the damn lab doors open!"

I felt pressure at my neck and frantic hands scrambling. Yet all of it was distant and muffled, nothing but noise above the waterline I'd already crossed.

I held my breath and smiled as the darkness drew me deeper, into a quiet that felt almost like sinking into him.

They were too late.

EPILOGUE

Beep...Beep...Beep...

I woke up.

Not a gradual waking where sleep slowly releases its hold and lets you drift calmly back into reality, but simply a heartbeat between sleep and full awareness. It was so sudden I wasn't even sure that I'd been asleep. Though somehow, I knew. Maybe it was the fact I was lying on my back, staring at an unfamiliar ceiling, the bright white circles of light boring down on me and burning my eyes.

What am I doing awake?

I blinked my eyes and turned my head. The simple movement sent waves of nausea rushing over me, and I froze, swallowing down bile. After the dizziness passed I tried again, slower this time. There was a machine next to me with blinking lights. The lights blinked in tune to the annoying beeping sound coming from somewhere above my head.

I slowly tore my eyes away from the flashing buttons and lay back against the not-so-comfortable pillow, squirming against the rough material. It itched. I reached down to pull up the blanket, and it took much more effort than I liked. I frowned when I couldn't find it. I sighed and let my hand brush against my stomach. My eyes widened. I was naked.

Where the hell are my clothes?

The steel door in the corner swung open, and two men in white coats entered. I didn't give them much notice. My attention focused past them, out the door. An android stood guard—like the one we'd fought back in the forest but clean and polished—its beeping lights and buttons mocking me. A cold prickle crawled up my spine. For one horrible second, I swore the thing recognized me. My heartbeat sped up a notch, and the beeping came faster, catching the men's attention.

Three more men came into the room wheeling a new machine and a glass-faced box. My eyes locked onto the men, each wearing a yellow suit with matching gloves, boots, and some type of odd glass-faced helmet, so that not an inch of skin was left uncovered. The men breathed funny, the air swishing to and from their masks and out of a large clear rope behind their backs. Each breath they took fogged the glass of their helmets, and for a heartbeat I thought I saw their eyes widen; not at me, but at whatever their monitors were showing.

A wave of tingling brushed over my skin, as if it would peel off and walk away on its own. I closed my eyes and again swallowed, ignoring the sharp pinpoints of pain as new needles were added to my neck and legs. Somehow the pain felt good, it helped take my mind off my crawling skin. An old man in a white, starched coat stepped closer and bent over me, smiling. My eyes widened.

"Good morning," the castle wizard said. "We were beginning to wonder if you would wake at all."

I dragged my gaze across the room, the shapes of men blurring together, before it snagged on Maurdruik. His white beard had been trimmed straight beneath his chin, the neatness of it drawing attention to the deep lines carved around his mouth and eyes. My lips moved before any sound came out.

"Where am I?" My voice was thin, scraped raw. I swallowed and tried again. "Where's Vestro? Where is he? Is he—"

Maurdruik's expression shifted with something carefully measured.

"You are safe," he said gently. "And you are where you need to be."

That wasn't an answer.

My heart kicked hard against my ribs. "Please, tell me he's OK," I whispered.

Maurdruik exhaled, slow and deliberate, as if choosing each word. "What happened at the end was complicated. Some outcomes stop fitting into words like living or dying." He held my gaze for a long moment. Then he looked away. "You should rest. You've been through more than you know."

He turned away and exchanged glances with one of the men. Several harsh words were shot back and forth as they flipped through pads of paper. I grunted and pushed myself upright, the room tilting immediately. I covered my breasts with one arm, the other bracing against the mattress as black crept in at the edges of my vision.

A sudden wave of dizziness nearly sent me tumbling off the bed.

No, not a bed. Some type of table made of...made of... I swallowed and closed my eyes. I couldn't form the words over the building pain in my head.

The spasm of pain passed, and I glanced down, and my blood froze.

My skin was tanned, darker than it should have been, and covered in a thin layer of clear slime.

The scent hit me; wild, metallic, familiar in a way that stabbed straight into memory. My breath hitched.

My vision blurred and my skin danced in front of his eyes. I blinked and shook my head, and my breath caught in my throat. The slime was coming out of me. It slid from my pores in slow, rippling sheets, like my body was shedding itself.

"No..." I whispered.

No!

The dizziness came again, and I screamed as my skin felt like it would burst.

Maurdruik was immediately at my side, screaming at the men for help. The gray machines beeped faster around me, doing their best to catch up to my racing heart.

One of the men swore under his breath.

"Help me!" I screamed. "Help me!"

"Nadia, you need to relax," Maurdruik cooed. "It's all right, we have everything under control—"

I jerked away from Maurdruik and ripped at the wires connecting me to the machines. Blood sprayed in wispy trails as the needles came loose, staining the magician's scruffy bead. Several hands grabbed my arms and threw me backward against the table. I fought against them, and I was surprised at how easy it was to send two of the men flying across the room. Their bodies hit the wall with a force that shocked even me. Something powerful was waking under my skin, stretching, testing itself.

Thick metal bands extended from slits in the table and tightened across my arms, legs, and chest, binding me down tightly.

The men stepped back as I writhed beneath the restraints. My body burned like they'd lit my feet on fire, the warmth spreading from my toes and racing toward my heart. The heat pulsed upward in waves, each one sharper, hungrier, as if something was clawing its way toward the surface.

I glanced down at my slime-covered body and screamed as gray hair sprouted up through my skin across my body. More of the clear slime oozed out as the hairs spread, until I lay in a pool of sludge. My ribs cracked like splitting wood, pushing outward, reshaping me with every brutal snap, stretching my breasts and tearing my skin.

"What have you done to me?" I screamed. "*What have you done?*"

"Stop her before she changes completely!" someone yelled.

Maurdruik stumbled back, his face draining of color as he reached for a control on the wall with shaking fingers.

The ceiling above the bed opened, like a giant blinking eye, and several metal arms whizzed down from the opening, snapping at my face. Oil dripped from their joints and hit my cheeks like hot rain as they descended. I howled as one arm drilled itself deep into my stomach, another slipping down my open mouth and into my throat. The metal twisted and burned as it moved, scorching everything it touched.

I had only one thought before I blacked out: someone was going to pay for this, because I knew I wasn't going to die on this fucking table.

No. This is only the beginning.

The restraints groaned, metal straining against the thing I was becoming.

And I'm going to kill every last fucking one of them.

About the Author

Danielle Kaheaku is a USA Today bestselling author and award-winning screenwriter. With more than twenty years in storytelling, she has helped shape dozens of novels across genres and continues to write the kinds of books she's always wanted to read.

A devoted teacher, Danielle shares her passion for writing at two universities and her local community college, where she encourages new voices and helps writers discover their creative strength.

When she's not writing or teaching, Danielle can usually be found outdoors—camping under the stars, wandering new trails, or curled up beside a campfire with a good book. She believes the best stories grow where ambition and adventure meet, and she brings that same energy to every project she creates.

She lives in the Pacific Northwest with her two children and a blue heeler.

instagram.com/daniellekaheaku
facebook.com/daniellekaheaku
tiktok.com/@daniellekaheaku

ALSO BY DANIELLE KAHEAKU

The Sa Tskir Brothers Chronicles

The Scouting

The Abduction

The Keeping

The Remaining

The Recruit (coming 2026)

The Daemon Progeny Trilogy

Artificial Selection

Cells of Time (coming 2026)

Standalone Novels

He Rode a Dark Horse

Anthologies

In Love with an Alien

California Screamin'

Abaculus

Abaculus II

Abaculus III